THE DARK STIRS

BOOK ONE OF THE DARK MATTER SERIES

JOHN P. WALLMAN

ISBN (Paperback): 978-1-7322198-6-1

ISBN (eBook): 978-1-7322198-9-2

Library of Congress Control Number: TXu 2-178-879

Cover Artist: Clementine Kornder & Lexi Mohney

Book Designer: Lexi Mohney

Editor: Cheyenne Sampson

This is a work of fiction. Unless otherwise indicated, all the names, characters, businesses, places, events and incidents in this book are either the product of the author's imagination or used in a fictitious manner. Any resemblance to actual persons, living or dead, or actual events is purely coincidental.

Courage Publishing, LLC

Ann Arbor, MI, USA

First Printing Edition 2022

❋ Created with Vellum

For Debra—*she got me started.*

For Deborah—*she kept me going.*

INTRODUCTION

All the world's a stage,
> And all the men and women merely players:
> They have their exits and their entrances.
> - William Shakespeare, *As You Like It*

A stage? The world has moved way beyond Will's dramatic "wooden O." We are in an ostentatious opera. Look at the big players of the world stage. All the posturing, the histrionics—the *extremes*. If a proverbial pendulum swung over this opera, the only time it would be in the middle would be on its way to the other limit. Equilibrium is irrelevant in an opera. Some of the players on the stage push the pendulum to its emotional terminus on one side, then let it fall only to have others push it to the other side.

This pendular motion of extremes has taken the place of logic and common sense—some would even say decency. We shouldn't be surprised by this. As a species, I believe, we humans like to push boundaries. All boundaries. Old boundaries become boring. We can't go back. We have to keep pushing. At some point in the late-20th Century—I'll allow you to determine when—humanity crossed a boundary between the mundane dramatic stage to the opulent operatic stage.

Is this a natural condition of evolution?

I'm not qualified to answer this question. I can only observe and opine.

Back to the operatic pendulum. I think we can all agree there would be no right stage without a left stage. The pendulum goes one way then the other. Most of our living happens between the sides. Us and them... society and individualism... religion and secularism... peace and war... right and wrong. What side of the stage will we take? Decisions.

These binaries are a function of each other. They need each other. When you think about it, humanity has always been like this —exploring the sides of all these binaries that rule our existence. Before we had crossed that boundary from drama to opera, there had been a third consideration: moderation. There had been a middle. Think about it. If the pendulum doesn't swing too far one way or the other, the middle becomes an important part of the motion.

But the evolution of humanity's need to push boundaries, to keep pushing further than before, to push the pendulum to extremes, has made the middle moderation—irrelevant. This extremism has evolved the civilized drama into a vulgar opera.

Here's the rub, so to speak. Neither side today wants a middle. How can a side of the pendulum eliminate the other side? By pushing so hard the pendulum goes all the way around. There is no left if the pendulum eternally swings right. No them if there is only us. No peace if there is only war.

No light if there is only darkness.

No good if there is only evil.

When the pendulum circles around once, it only takes a moderate push to keep it going. Around. One direction.

The book you are about to begin, and the ones that follow, explore my fear that there might be other forces behind the extremism of this opera in which we now live.

The Dark stirs, for now is its time.

PART ONE
THE NIGHT

This is the night
That either makes me or fordoes me quite.
- William Shakespeare, *Othello*

A full moon
Locks the shadows of the night
A dark moon
Liberates them from the light
- William Loote, "Night Light"

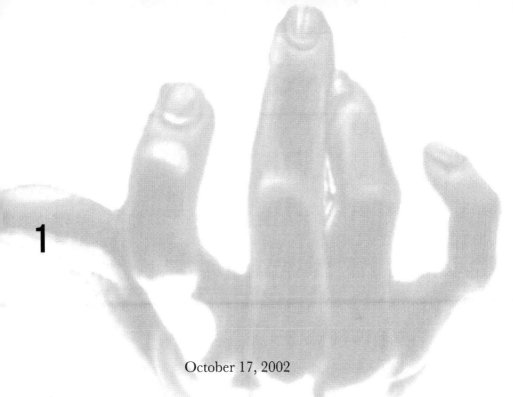

1

October 17, 2002

Angelique Carlson found a pen in a drawer and signed her name to a birthday card. She slipped it into its envelope that matched the green foil wrapping of the gift. She never licked envelopes closed, and she didn't sign the recipient's name on the front.

Angelique pulled the covering off the adhesive part of an iridescent bow and placed it on the wrapped gift.

Perfect.

She couldn't wait to see the faces of The Gang when they saw its contents.

"The Gang" had met last year as a part of a study group preparing for a midterm political science exam. The class's professor was known at Johns Hopkins for ass-kicking exams, and after the disastrous first one, students self-organized into groups. Angelique found herself in a good one. They all ended up with great scores and decided to continue to hang after the class completed.

Even her shadows didn't seem to mind The Gang.

Ever since she was a child, Angelique had shadows that followed her from dusk to dawn. At first, there were only movements on the periphery of her vision, and they scared little Angelique. Sometimes

3

they touched her—a soft, furry-yet-cold caress if her arm or leg were outside her covers. Sometimes a shadow moved over her foot when she watched T.V. Shivers ran like cold mice across her skin.

As she grew older, her shadows grew bolder, became more physical. And they didn't like to share Angelique with others. When a friend came over to play or to stay overnight, the caresses became pokes and pulls, and Angelique would scream out and scare those friends. Eventually, young Angelique had few friends.

Except her shadows.

So, when they accepted The Gang, Angelique was relieved.

They would follow Angelique to gatherings and parties and mingle with her human friends. And these friends would catch her smiling at them, misinterpreting it as affection.

Her shadows' antics always amused her. All it would take was a shadowy tickle on a girl's neck, and she would shiver and jump. A black blotch would appear on a boy's crotch then move down his leg, looking like he'd peed himself.

Her friends thought she was happy; she was only amused.

Angelique patted the gift and smiled.

This birthday party is gonna be fun.

The October evening demanded a leather jacket, and she slipped on her black one. She grabbed her black clutch. Save for her red blouse, she was all in black tonight. Her black jeans were oh-so-tight, and the black pumps she held in her hand would make her legs even longer and sleeker. She wasn't one for much jewelry. Tonight, she wore the diamond studs her father had given her on her first decade birthday.

It was the last birthday gift she would receive from him.

She immediately regretted thinking about *that*.

Dear ol' Daddy always talked about the decade birthdays, how special they were, and how they would be particularly special with him.

At ten A.M. on her tenth birthday, Daddy picked her up from school and took her to the mall to buy her a proper dress for a proper lady. Then, they went to a spa to have her hair done however she wished, and Dear ol' Daddy even allowed her to have some makeup applied. They ended their excursion at a fancy restaurant.

4

"This is your first decade present," he said and handed her a small, wrapped gift. She had thought the dress and spa and getting out of school was the gift.

She remembered pulling the paper off and opening the jewelry box.

"Diamonds are a girl's best friend," he chuckled.

The studs sparkled. Young Angelique said, "You're my best—"

Angelique pushed that memory down—*deep*—with all the others.

She felt the stud on her right ear. *Just had to go and die on me, didn't you?*

And that memory dug its way up. Not even a year later, just before her eleventh birthday—

Down!

Angelique scooped up the gift with her empty hand, stuffed her clutch under her right arm, and opened the apartment door. Pulling it shut behind her, the sound travelled down the hall and stairwell. She lingered a moment.

A door off to the right in the hallway squeaked.

She loved that sound.

She was the closest the dorks in this apartment building got to a beautiful woman. They all thought they were clever in the way they oiled their doorknobs and hinges, but these old doors always betrayed them. They couldn't help but try to catch a glimpse of her.

Angelique relished their worship.

She waited a few moments more and went to the stairwell railing.

Another door creaked.

She smiled.

She looked up the stairwell at the bright upper floors. The western windows allowed the setting sun to shoot bright yellow-red light along the hall and across the stairs. Motes of dust floated in the stuffy air. The trees that surrounded the western and southern sides of the building hid the sun from the lower floors. She looked from the light above down the stairwell to the darker floors below.

This time of the evening, the shadow time just between day and night, made her anxious. She never knew how'd they'd behave—her shadows: sometimes aggressive, sometimes gentle, and sometimes they'd hover on the periphery.

Angelique looked at her watch. She was going to be late, but that was okay. She liked to make entrances. And she liked big exits even more.

A fluid movement of blackness caught her eye near the bottom. She knew if she looked longer, she'd see more. Her mouth was dry, and she found she was holding her breath.

She hated living up here. She needed to be on the ground floor. She wouldn't have to run these steps in bare feet.

"Fuck it," she whispered. With the gift in her left hand, her clutch secured under her right armpit, and her pumps in her right hand, she started down the cold steps.

The shadows moved up the stairwell to greet her.

Angelique's legs and feet moved quickly, and as she rounded the first landing and started down the next flight to the second floor, she felt something tug at her shoes. She almost dropped her purse.

"Shit." *Keep going.*

At the second floor, she saw the shadows become thicker.

The door to the closest apartment on the left was already cracked open. She could easily call out, and perhaps he'd come out to accompany her down the steps, chasing the shadows away. But her pride wouldn't allow it.

A cold hand pushed her left shoulder.

She ran and rushed down the next flight, concentrating lest she trip.

Bare feet slapped across the next landing. Angelique turned to go down to the first floor.

Something pulled her ponytail, and she yelped, stumbling down a few steps. She almost let go of her pumps. She stopped for a moment to get her balance.

That was a mistake.

A shadowy hand grabbed her left breast as if to pull at her heart, its cold penetrating her jacket. She swiveled her body, but the things she was holding made evasion difficult.

"Stop it!" she hissed. *Fucking shadows.*

She made it to the first floor and pushed through the thickness

6

of them. The shadows now had hands all over her body, squeezing and probing.

They pushed, guiding her down the last flights to the ground floor. She couldn't see. They kept her on her feet, stumbling but moving.

Miraculously, she hadn't dropped anything.

The front exit door was just there, the light of its outline dimmed in the curdling dark.

Two. More. Steps.

The hand with the pumps fumbled with the button to release the door. She pushed with her right shoulder to keep the purse secure. The door swung out and thumped against something.

Light flooded in.

"Shit!" a voice called out.

Angelique's eyes adjusted quickly as the shadows pulled away from the cool twilight outside, flowing back into the dark hall.

An arm flailed in the air in front of her, and she hooked her hand with the gift around it and pulled, relieved another human being was there. She steadied the person and saw it was John Paul Wilkins, the student who lived just below her. His backpack slipped off his left shoulder and fell. Blindly—and impressively—he caught it as his body bumped against the porch rail.

His mouth popped open.

"Sorry," Angelique said quickly, recognizing that moon-eyed gaze all these geeks in the building gave her, like a starving waif with no courage to ask for a bite to eat.

Just not hungry enough, she thought.

Not that she'd have anything to do with any of them. They studied, watched T.V., studied some more, played video games, and read their geeky fantasy and sci-fi shit. That was their concept of having fun. And God forbid they ever talk to a girl.

Wilkins was the worst of them. He deferred to her, almost bowing to her like a servant. Eunuchs didn't impress her.

She smiled, sickly sweet. "Hey, good catch." Four words in a week: more than he deserved. She balanced on him and slipped her pumps onto her feet, now standing a couple inches taller than Wilkins.

"What?" he stammered, his blue eyes looking nowhere but at her dark ones. He ran a hand through the messy brown hair that matched the messy clothes. He was an all-around mess.

Angelique knew he wanted to look her over, and he struggled to keep her gaze. She nodded at the pack in his left hand. "Good catch." Two more words.

A little devil in her put her free hand on his arm and squeezed almost affectionately. "Later, J.P." She hopped down the few steps, walking swiftly to get away from him and the shadows within the building.

She turned right onto the sidewalk, knowing he was lusting after her, and she put a little extra swivel in her hips. In a matter of minutes, he would be in his room whacking off.

All these little boy geeks were the same.

But a small voice in the back of her mind wondered why her shadows had been more physical with her than they had in a long time.

2

John Paul Wilkins took the bus every weekday to the Community College of Baltimore County Essex Campus. He took the bus straight home from classes. He rarely made any detours in this routine. Typically, he'd have an hour to change clothes and grab something quick to eat before he'd head back out the door and down the steps to the parking lot of the building and to his 1995 brown sedan he affectionately called "The Turd." He'd drive this reliable eyesore to his job then back home after work. He'd grab a snack and study a little. John Paul repeated this procedure every day.

Except on the occasion he worked the late shift. Like tonight. He didn't have to be at work till eleven. Being the assistant manager really meant being the manager's assistant. But that was what responsibility was: filling in the holes the less responsible made. And that meant working late when all he wanted to do was to chill and study a little.

He grabbed a Mountain Dew from the fridge, the half bag of Funyuns from the counter, and he plopped onto the sofa to watch two hours of *Star Trek: The Next Generation.*

But literally bumping into Angelique had rattled him. He knew he was a coward. There was another part of him caged *way down*

9

there that had howled at him to say something witty— or, at the very least, ask her where she was going in such a rush.

That other him, the Wild One, sat down on the couch next to him.

Data and Geordi were investigating something in the episode, but John Paul couldn't concentrate with the Wild One there.

It was a dangerous, feral part of John Paul that had appeared a few months ago, after the building tenants had a little Fourth of July party.

Angelique and her friends had come with their sidewinders (one of his mom's euphemisms for smartass comments) and boulders (another one for rolling eyes because they rolled like boulders), drinking the beer and eating the food, before leaving not even an hour after they had arrived.

John Paul remembered the Wild One appearing at his side as he stood there watching the goddesses leave. It whispered, "What the hell are you doing? Why don't you go, too? Ask them if you can come with them... *with her*. John Paul remembered a physical reaction like one of those shivers he got while taking a piss.

That Wild One had appeared a total of five times since, and it always started with the same question:

"What the hell are you doing?"

John Paul continued to look at the T.V. Captain Picard was giving orders on the bridge.

The Wild One followed with another question, "What happens to a dream deferred?"

It laughed. It was a mocking, snarling sound that made John Paul's stomach sour.

A dream deferred...

That old Langston Hughes poem had a way of showing up over the years—twice in high school and twice in college—where it had become more poignant.

He realized he really had no dreams of his own to *dry up like a raisin in the sun*. Why was he doing a double major in hospitality management and marketing?

His parents.

John Paul Wilkins had no aspirations. He allowed himself to be guided by his parents' fantasy of the American Dream: to pass along a family legacy. They had worked hard over the years to build their bed and breakfast brand into something that practically ran itself.

The Wild One chuckled. "But you gotta prove to them you deserve to be a part of their dream." It leaned close, smelling of old leaves and wet fur. "*Their* dream."

A dream deferred...

But John Paul had no dreams.

"And there's the old man."

Mr. Jarrez... Tio. He owned the bodega Corazon where John Paul needed to be in a few hours. Tio was a good man, and he had hired John Paul as a favor to his nephew.

"He's holding you back, too."

John Paul ignored the Wild One. He liked Tio and working at Corazon. Besides, the Enterprise was under attack. This was a good episode, but the Wild One enjoyed distracting him.

The Wild One leaned close and growled, "There's no dream when you don't have the freedom to find it."

School and work. Idle hands...

The Wild One grinned. "Fun is not idle."

"Disciplina," Tio would reply. "El exito proviene de la disciplina." Tio would also add, "Y la perseverancia."

John Paul—or as Tio called him, Juan Pablo—had come to love the old man.

One of Tio's endearing qualities was his easy slippage into Spanish. In the months he'd been working at Corazon, John Paul had picked up some Spanish, but Tio rattled it off like a machine gun. Then he'd see the young man's face, smile and blush, and start over in his broken English.

Recently, Tio's focus had been on John Paul's love life—

The Wild One growled, "Or lack of it."

But John Paul smiled at the memory of Tio taking the young man's hand, patting it, and nodding his head. "Listen to me, Juan Pablo." The store was empty at the moment. Tio waved a hand to encompass it. "Este es mi Corazon. Cuando me amor—"

He caught himself and said, "When my love died, this is all I had left of her. Esta bodega. My wife and I made it our heart. Si? You are young, Juan Pablo. You find your love, and there, you find your heart."

John Paul laughed at the irony of that moment. He had no love, no heart. But he understood what the old man was saying.

Or, he thought he did.

A few days later, two nights ago, Tio came to him again. His brown eyes sparkled as brightly as his white hair. John Paul could still feel those rough brown hands holding and patting his. And those white, false teeth emphasized a knowing grin. "Un buen hombre es en la demanda—" Tio caught himself. "You are in demand, Juan Pablo. Los hombrecitos that... bob around the barrio, they are like the produce we throw away. Foul y podrido. You are... un pepino fresco, Juan Pablo."

John Paul couldn't help but smile at being called a fresh cucumber, Tio's favorite thing to eat. The old man often had a plate of sliced cukes behind the counter.

He tried to be serious and said, "You aren't being fair."

"No, no, I see them come in here. They are rotten because their hearts are rotten." He poked John Paul's chest, at his heart. "Pero your heart es fuerte. A beautiful woman desires a good, strong heart." He reached into his pants pocket and put a piece of paper in John Paul's hand. "No hang your heart on a woman like a coat on a peg."

How the old man knew about Angelique in the apartment above him, John Paul still didn't know.

"It's because you have a pathetic, cowardly look on your face all the time." The Wild One was relentless.

But Tio's voice pushed the beast aside. He tapped the folded piece of paper and said, "One of these may want to *wear* it."

John Paul unfolded the paper. It listed seven names and phone numbers of young ladies.

Tio grinned and added, "One for each day of the week."

Defeated, the Wild One threw one last punch right into John Paul's balls. "What're you going to do next May when you graduate?"

The beast disappeared but left that big question in John Paul's lap like a steaming pile of shit that demanded to be cleaned up.

Reluctantly, John Paul deferred the question and focused on the T.V.

The Enterprise crew watched a new alien race depart for its home world as new friends of the Federation. The crew had the courage *to boldly go* into the unknown, to seek adventure and knowledge and experience—to make themselves better today than they were yesterday. But they had writers and directors and great actors to make their lives interesting.

John Paul had himself. He didn't have the courage to go out and make time for something interesting or exciting.

And there was the Wild One. He had to admit he was scared of that part of himself.

He thought of the list Tio had made him put into his wallet.

With a Funyun halfway to his mouth, John Paul Wilkins realized the Wild One was right—soon this life was going to change. He crunched down on the snack and followed it with a swig of Mountain Dew.

3

Not even an hour here, and Angelique was bored.

The party was boring. Her friends were boring.

She didn't get the reaction from her gift she had wanted, as if they all had expected it to be over the top, and it was. Same old Angelique. Have to one up everyone.

Even the bar was boring. Alternatives was known to be a meat market on Thursday nights. It was packed as usual but with the same old people, rubbing the same elbows, chatting about the same mundane crap.

The Gang sat around a table, but Angelique barely noticed them. The birthday girl said her thank-yous. Someone made a toast. They mumbled responses as if they, too, were bored, occasionally sipping their drinks.

The music became louder, thumping through the chairs. Strobe and moving lights whorled about. Dancing had begun, and some of the friends stood to move out to the floor.

Angelique waved them off, pointing to the toilets.

A tall glass of dark beer appeared in her face.

When she took it, the waitress disappeared before she could ask about it.

Angelique went immediately to the bar.

Bartender Steve slid over to her smiling. He aspired to be a model but had settled on being a bartender—a pretty good one, too. A lot of the girls hovered at his end, trying to catch his eye, but Angelique had already looked into those deep blues and found them shallow. He'd let his brown hair grow out a little on top and had it slicked back, like he'd just gotten out of the shower.

Their relationship had lasted two weekends. He was like one of those old-style rollercoaster rides, the ones made of wood and steel: short and intense but nothing special. The second ride was enough.

She cocked her head to the side, held up the beer, and gave him a *You?* look.

Steve pointed at himself with mocked surprise. "Ange, you know me better than that." True. The ladies usually bought *him* the drinks. He leaned closer and replied, "Dark and lonely at the end of the bar," nodding to a stranger sitting literally alone near the waitress station. No one was within five feet of him, which was odd considering the bar was filled shoulder to shoulder. "He specifically requested you be covered for the night."

Dark and Lonely brooded over a drink, swirling it around and watching the ice move in circles. Oddly, he wore black gloves, the expensive thin leather ones that fit like a second skin. Long blond hair pulled back in a ponytail, his face was down, shadowed from the light directly above him. He wore a black leather jacket and a black and yellow plaid scarf at his neck, obscuring his shirt. From what Angelique could see, he was handsome enough.

More importantly, he was intriguing.

Steve smiled and said, "I know that look." He grabbed a few empty glasses and placed them into a tub under the bar to be cleaned later.

Angelique rolled her eyes, continuing to look at the stranger and said, "*Used* to know that look."

Still smiling, he shook his head and said, "Ouch." He had been beaten with her sarcasm stick enough to walk away while he still had some dignity. Before he did, he added, "He said to tell you his name is Anders."

Anders. An odd name. It sounded Germanic or Scandinavian, which fit given the somewhat European, metrosexual look he had.

He probably wore the gloves to protect his manicure. He had that look of wealthy sophistication. Probably well-traveled, too.

She could imagine a trip to Paris or Athens in her near future. She smiled.

"I know that look," came another familiar voice behind her. Jarrod Jambotti was one of The Gang and one of her conquests. It had been a shorter ride than Steve's—one of those classic hot, torrid encounters with the regrets the following morning and the "let's just be friends" agreement, though she did occasionally catch him looking at her. And her calling him her "Italian Thoroughbred" under her breath didn't help. No one else knew of that night, so she kept her retort in her mouth.

Still holding the beer, she raised an eyebrow at Jarrod and made her way through the crowd to the other side of the bar where Anders sat.

He continued to gaze at his drink as if he were trying to read something.

"I have you to thank for this?" Angelique took a sip of the beer.

She saw him smile, but he continued to look down.

"You are Angelique," he said, a soft voice of erudite sophistication with a slight foreign lilt. The lights softened, and Journey's "Lights," a favorite in the bar, began. Anders looked up at her. "And I am Anders Saffenssen."

He held out a gloved hand, but all she could see were his eyes.

Gray whirlpools, glowing despite the faint light of the bar. The strangest eyes in the world. Angelique immediately thought, *Rabbit holes*, and wondered if she looked a moment longer, would she fall into them? Something gripped her, and the bar shifted vertiginously to the left. Blood rushed in her ears. She leaned into something cold and hard.

Brick. A building.

Cold. *Shadows*.

Angelique looked about. She could feel the beat of music through the wall, hear it wafting from around the corner. She stood in the alley between Alternatives and some other building. She looked down. Puke stained the wall and asphalt.

How did she get out here?

She looked at her watch: 10:17 P.M. She had been at the bar way longer than she planned.

"Shit," she hissed.

A prickling feeling moved up her spine to the back of her head. Were her shadows here?

A silhouette emerged from the darkness further into the alley.

Accompanied with a growl.

A large dog jumped at her, its hackles standing straight, baring its teeth. It barked, crouching.

Angelique saw Rottweiler in it, blacks and browns and a white bobtail. Growling, it lunged at her again.

She screamed and jumped back, tripping and falling onto the sidewalk. Her back hit something soft and yielding.

She heard a thump from the direction of the dog. A quick yelp.

A piece of brick lay where the dog had been.

Anders crouched down beside her. "Are you all right, Angelique?" He offered a gloved hand for help. "You ran out suddenly."

She put her hand in his. The leather felt odd, soft but strong. He stood and gently pulled her up. She looked down the alley.

"The cur is long gone by now." Anders picked something from her hair and from her shoulder. He looked her up and down. "None the worse for wear, though your jeans will need a proper cleaning."

She noticed a little puke on her left leg. "Damn."

He produced a napkin.

She smiled, a little embarrassed, and took it. Trying to wipe the mess away, she said, "I don't know what happened. I had asked you about the beer, and..."

He helped her to keep balance.

He smiled. "That was nearly two hours and four drinks ago."

Angelique gritted her teeth. That was a total of six for the night —dangerously close to her limit when she could lose control.

The streetlight nearby illuminated Anders' face. His expression hinted of an on-going joke to which only he was privy. His red lips curved up. They were darker than any she'd ever seen, with a delicate sheen indicative of lipstick. His nose was long and thin, and there were those strange gray eyes.

Is he wearing makeup? She could swear he was wearing foundation.

"I hope that is the first of many."

"Many of what?" She resisted the urge of batting her eyes. It might have worked on American boys, but she knew Anders would see right through it.

He motioned towards the street. "The first of many smiles, of course." She stumbled, and he frowned. "I must insist on walking you to the bus stop."

She looked about, anxious. "My purse!"

He produced it. "You left it at the bar. I am only happy that I found you before that beast could hurt you."

Angelique smiled and took it. "I need to walk this off." She slipped an arm around his. "Could you walk with me for a while?"

"I will walk with you for however long you wish."

Anders said, "I have thoroughly enjoyed our walk, but I must depart."

They had stopped, and he had taken her free hand in his. The leather felt soft and cool.

She looked about. They were on the sidewalk in front of her apartment building.

"What? How did we get here?" She didn't understand. It was a forty-minute walk, and she couldn't remember a single second of it.

He frowned. "You're worrying me, Angelique. You may be dehydrated. Please drink a glass of water before you retire." He let go and said, "Good night."

"Wait!"

"We'll see each other again, soon, I believe." He gave her a slight nod of his blond head and turned, leisurely walking away from her.

"What the hell is going on?" she muttered. That was twice tonight she had lost track of time. She didn't feel sick or drugged or even that drunk. It was as if her memory of her time with Anders had been wiped away, like pages ripped out of a journal.

She needed to get to bed if this was how things were going. She had classes tomorrow.

4

W *here the hell is that wallet?*
 John Paul had been searching for nearly ten minutes. He looked at his watch: 10:58. He should be at the bodega, ready to start work. Tio was old-school punctual.

He hated to disappoint the old man.

He pulled the cushions off the sofa and felt into the crevasses. An old piece of Funyun. Nothing. He put the cushions back.

John Paul went to his hands and knees and looked again under the sofa.

He started to growl, frustrated.

When he stood up, it was in plain sight right on the coffee table. "Whatever," he mumbled, and grabbed it.

John Paul stuffed the wallet into his back pocket, patted his jacket pocket for his keys, went to the door, and pulled it shut. He locked it and checked it. He all but leapt down the two flights of stairs, turning at the bottom to go to the back door and The Turd parked in the lot beyond it.

5

"**F**ucking door," Angelique growled.

It was the second time this week the front door had done this to her; others in the building had complained, too. She walked down the front steps and proceeded around the building to the back entrance.

Her mind drifted to Anders. He had been the perfect gentleman, but she had a suspicion he was more. She smiled at that thought. His parting comment that they'd see each other again was promising.

Halfway along the side, she saw the backlight go out. *Fucking light, too,* she thought and considered calling the management tonight.

She emerged from the shadowed side of the building and stopped at the steps, using the moonlight to search her purse for her keys. She held them up to find the one for the back door.

Something grabbed under her arms and lifted her sharply, compressing her ribs. She let out a strangled, "Oh." Her keys and purse fell to the ground, and the back of the building moved quickly away. Her hands and arms pointed out, and her head moved forward, hair flowing into her face.

"Think happy thoughts, Tinkerbell, so you can fly!"

Anders!

Angelique flew across the parking lot, the few cars there passing in a blur. No sound but a rushing of air. No steps or labored breathing. It was as if Anders himself flew and carried her. In a matter of seconds, she was in darkness again, between two garages. He slammed her against a wall, knocking out her breath, her vision swimming with blotches of white.

Her eyes could see nothing, but she felt his cold breath on her cheek and left ear. "Parting was such sweet sorrow," he whispered, "that I could not wait upon the morrow."

She blinked. Why was there only darkness?

She gasped. *The shadows!*

"Yes, little Tinkerbell. Life is only a shadow of death." She felt him smile. The darkness evaporated, and he stood against her, his arms pinning hers against her body.

He was strong. Cold, living steel. She shut her eyes, unable to look into his mad, smiling face. His lower body pressed hard against her, and his left hand moved slowly up her right arm to her head. He took a handful of hair and pulled roughly, exposing her neck. She gasped and saw he wasn't smiling. He grimaced as if fighting back something.

His body flattened against her. Her chest and pelvis screamed in pain, but nothing came out of her mouth.

The other gloved hand came up to her face and glided along her jaw to her neck. He squeezed her neck, choking her. Her vision darkened and faded. He let go, and all she could see was his perfect white nose an inch from hers. "There it is," he purred. He smelled her neck.

Anders leaned back and looked to the apartment building then smiled and faced her. "*When night darkens the streets, then wander forth the sons of Belial.*" He shook his head as if to a child. "Naughty Tinkerbell. Didn't your daddy teach you never meet a stranger at night, for he may be a demon?"

The gloved hand around her throat moved to his mouth. The dark lips opened to reveal two rows of white glassy teeth—and two long *fangs*!

Her mind screamed. This wasn't real. It wasn't happening.

He bit the leather tip of the middle finger and pulled the glove off. He put it into his jacket pocket. "I've come for you, my dear, on *this October night, this lonesome October night of this most immemorial year.*" He chuckled, and his hand waved in the air near her face, the white fingers moving and flexing. The other hand pulled her hair more severely, exposing her neck even more.

"You will want to scream as you die, but you will be a helpless little Tinkerbell. Know that I thoroughly enjoyed your company."

The white hand touched her neck, and a sharp coldness moved into her jaw and spread down her body. It traveled through her veins and arteries, shocking her nerves like striking a funny bone. The faint sound that issued from her mouth came from somewhere deep inside—even deeper still—as if every cell in her body had coalesced in her compressed belly, rushed up her throat, and out into the night like a soft vomit.

Before she passed out, she saw the look of feral delight on Anders' face as he opened his mouth wide for a bite.

6

The end of the hall was dark. It should have been partially lit from the bright back porch light. "Fucking light," John Paul growled as he turned the knob and opened the door to the cold, dark October night.

The bright moon lit the steps enough for him to take them quickly. He darted across the gravel lot to The Turd.

He dug out his keys from his jacket and unlocked the door, noticing a paper flyer under his wiper. As he reached for it, movement across the alley street between two garages caught his eye.

He opened his door and turned on the headlights.

They illuminated a couple necking in the dark. But... the woman's feet dangled in the air. She looked limp as if unconscious.

A buzzing began in the back of his head.

John Paul stepped around the door. Part of him said to leave them be, that if he were to cause a fuss, he'd most certainly be embarrassed. A larger part of him screamed something was wrong. The Wild One howled!

The man had his hand on the woman's neck. His pelvis pinned hers against the wall. He moved the hand down to her jacket and unzipped it. He reached up to her blouse collar and ripped it down. The sound of it was huge in the night.

John Paul yelled, "Hey! What's going on?"

Did he hear a growl?

The man faced John. His eyes were white and— Was he smiling?

The victim's head moved, and John Paul recognized her. "Angelique!"

Still looking at John Paul, the attacker let her fall to the ground. His smile distorted into a lupine bearing of his teeth. And there was something else. A trick of the light?

The man vanished.

John Paul ran to Angelique. She had crumpled to the ground on her knees with her body bent forward, her head to the ground. Her dark hair was disheveled and splayed out. John Paul knelt beside her and gently moved her to lay her on her back. Her face was a grimace of pain and horror. When he touched her cheek, she took a deep and sudden breath as if she had been holding it a long time then let out a gargled choke.

Her body began to tremble. John Paul pulled her to him, trying to comfort her. He looked back at the apartment building.

Two men, both silhouettes but still distinguishable in the night, stood at opposite sides of the structure.

"Hey!" he called out. "I need help!"

They turned to each other in the darkness as if they had just noticed the other's presence. The man on the right disappeared, and the other moved to face John Paul and Angelique. He stood there for a few moments before he turned slowly and walked away.

John Paul stood. "Hey, you! I said I need help, you asshole!"

Pissed off and disappointed, he grabbed Angelique under her shoulders and dragged her to his car. Her feet trailed behind them, bumping on the rough road. One of her shoes fell off.

In the headlights, John Paul looked her over. She was in some kind of shock. Only her eyes moved, and they pleaded with him. A tear fattened and trailed down across her temple.

"You're safe," he whispered. He moved her ripped shirt across her chest.

He stood and looked at the apartment building. The light shone from the window of Tom Schuller, the apartment's resident med student. He looked down at Angelique, knowing he would struggle to get her up the steps and to the apartment's door. But he couldn't leave her. He squatted and lifted her, awkwardly cradling her. She didn't feel too heavy, but he managed only small steps across the gravel lot.

His arms burned as he neared the back porch. He huffed up the steps, his arms and back screaming at him to drop her. Luckily, the back door hadn't shut, and he used his foot to open it. His legs shook. He shuffled down the now seemingly narrow hall to Tom's before he laid Angelique down and thumped on the door. "Tom!" he yelled, thumping the door again. "Tom! Open up!"

Locks rattled and clicked, and light streamed out into the hall. Tom looked out, not seeing John Paul and Angelique on the floor.

John Paul tried to make her comfortable. He looked up. "Shit, Tom, down here! Call 9-1-1. Call now!"

The police arrived in minutes; the ambulance followed soon after.

As the paramedics examined Angelique, one of the officers asked John Paul about the incident. He couldn't think. All he could do was look at the woman on Tom's living room floor.

"Sir..." the officer said, touching his arm.

John Paul looked at the man. *What's happening?* was all he could think.

The paramedics lifted Angelique to place her on a stretcher.

A wail rose from her, and the two paramedics leaned back from her, surprised.

John Paul grabbed her hand and leaned close. "It's okay, Angelique."

She wouldn't let go, and he walked with the stretcher to the ambulance. As the paramedics prepared to load it, Angelique squeezed John Paul's hand and pulled him close.

She swallowed before she let out a hoarse whisper.

"Teeth."

Something gripped his balls, and his head buzzed. Panic thickened in his throat.

What his brain couldn't comprehend until Angelique's revelation—the attacker's savage face in the headlights—had been long, sharp teeth.

Her hand slipped from his when the paramedics pushed the stretcher into the ambulance.

Angelique's face contorted, and she let loose another wail ending with "Joohhnnn!"

One of the paramedics put a hand on John Paul's shoulder. "Can ya come with? I have a feelin' she'll be a tad uncooperative if not."

"I was going to insist."

"Thank ya."

The short drive to the hospital was uneventful. Angelique kept her eyes closed, but she allowed the paramedic to do what he needed. She never let go of John Paul's hand.

He held her hand through the hospital entrance, through more doors and turns, and into a private room. A doctor and two nurses wearing gloves awaited them. No one challenged him to leave. Angelique moaned when he had to let go to allow the paramedics and nurse to move her from the stretcher to the bed.

"John!" she yelled and looked around.

One of the nurses removed her ripped top and put it into a plastic bag.

John Paul looked away. "I'm here."

Bra, jeans, and panties were bagged. The nurses put her into a hospital gown.

"John!"

He moved to her side. Hand to hand, she became at ease again.

A nurse found a chair for John Paul, and once he was seated and kind of out of the way, she whispered, "The doctor is going to use a rape kit to—"

"She wasn't raped," he whispered back.

The doctor stood at the end of the bed. She looked at John Paul and the nurse. She said nothing and proceeded with the examination.

The police officers arrived, accompanied with two in plain clothes. They stayed outside the room while the doctor worked.

Down the hall, they heard a commanding woman yell, "Where is my Angel? Oh, God, where is she?"

Like Moses parting the Red Sea, a short woman ordered, "Out

of my way!" She didn't rush as the audience in the hall made a gauntlet for her. A nurse stood at the door and said, "Mrs. Carlson, we've—"

John Paul looked up. Mrs. Carlson? Angelique's mother?

The short woman threw her fur coat and sparling black purse at the nurse and stormed into the room. Adorned in a black cocktail dress, she had obviously been at some ritzy function. She looked like a dressed-up doll next to Angelique's bed.

"Little Angel," she whispered repeatedly, stroking her daughter's hair.

The doctor watched this for a moment, secured all the evidence she had collected, and stepped back to the wall.

The other nurse hovered behind Mrs. Carlson, checking a monitor.

A female detective took the rape kit and handed it to one of the uniformed officers. She moved to the end of the bed.

Mrs. Carlson tried to take her daughter's hand and noticed the I.V. in it. She saw the strange young man holding her daughter's other one. She frowned.

John Paul locked eyes with her. He tried to convey his helplessness, but she calmly asked, "Who are you?" It was more a question of *What makes you important enough to be holding my daughter's hand at a time like this?* There was no anger in the question, just a kind of reserved curiosity, the kind that hinted at experiences with a daughter who unfailingly slung surprises at her parents—mostly of the bad sort.

The nurse looked down at the anguished mother, bent to her ear and said, "He's been with her the whole time. Your daughter won't let him leave." She smiled at John Paul and added, "He saved her."

The doctor said, "We felt it prudent to let him stay to keep her calm so that we wouldn't have to sedate her."

John Paul felt compelled to say something. A strange mix of irritation, compassion, pride, and now embarrassment swirled within him. As he opened his mouth to respond, all within the room froze a moment. The detective at the end of the bed stepped closer. The group whispering at the door stopped and turned, waiting.

John Paul said in the only way he could: "I, uh, live with

Angelique, ah, but not *with* her." He was as surprised with his awkwardness as all of them.

Mrs. Carlson continued to look from his face to the embraced hands. "Well, you must have a name, young man." It was clear Angelique's antics over the years had tempered this woman's concern over the people in her daughter's life—what few she may have met. She wanted to know in case he would be around longer than her daughter's two-week play period.

John Paul, still shocked at his inept response, only blushed.

The detective stepped closer. She flashed a badge and said, "Detective Florent, Mrs. Carlson. This is Detective Hamplin." She motioned to her partner near the door. "We're investigating."

John Paul looked around. He realized all in the room knew Mrs. Carlson. She was someone of importance, more than the mother of the victim and patient on the bed.

Detective Florent stuffed the badge back into her jacket pocket. She nodded at John Paul. "This is John Wilkins, a student who lives in your daughter's apartment building. He witnessed the attack and scared off the perp."

Angelique continued to lay still, her eyes closed, but not asleep. She squeezed his hand.

When John Paul smiled, the room waited to see if he would say something more. He became hot and uncomfortable.

Another nurse entered the room and saved him from further embarrassment.

"Diane Carlson?" When the woman turned, the nurse continued, "A man in the lobby would like to know if you want him to stay."

Mrs. Carlson slumped, making her even shorter. "Bill," she uttered. She looked at her daughter. She bent close and whispered, "You didn't need to do this to stop me." She locked eyes with John Paul, again, knowing he had heard her. Her look asked for discretion. As she straightened to address the nurse, John Paul got an idea.

"Mrs. Carlson?" The room stilled again. All looked at him. "Can you come around here?" He motioned to her to come next to him.

He bent to Angelique's ear. "Angelique," he whispered, "I have to talk with the police." He looked around the room. "And I need to use the bathroom." She breathed deeply.

Mrs. Carlson was only a head taller than John Paul sitting down.

He pried Angelique's hand from his. A moan moved through her body. As Mrs. Carlson reached for her daughter's hand, John Paul took it. It was cold, and he placed it between both his warm hands. At first, the mother's eyes darkened, but she realized what he was doing. He squeezed the hand reassuringly and put it into Angelique's.

He whispered again, "I'll be just out in the hall."

"Not..." breathed Angelique.

John Paul smiled. "Far."

Angelique's face softened.

John Paul moved so that Mrs. Carlson could sit. She looked at the young man. Her lip quivered as she mouthed, "Thank you."

John Paul smiled, rubbing the circulation back into his hand. "No, thank you, Mrs. Carlson."

"Diane, please." She looked at her daughter. "I, I don't know..."

John Paul put a hand on her shoulder. "I was lucky I was there to help." As he turned to the door, he added, "I'll find your friend and tell him."

They both looked at Angelique.

She was asleep.

7

B ill hung his head, dejected, but he didn't look too surprised. He must have been hit by the "Angelique stick" a few times in the past. It seemed like everyone who knew her had this resigned look as if this tragedy had happened before. A number of times.

The man shook his head as he left the emergency room.

A familiar voice said, "We need to talk, Mr. Wilkins."

The hyenas come a-callin'. John Paul wished he could say such things aloud and not care what people thought. He turned and saw the detective, noticing her for the first time as a pretty woman in her thirties, brown hair to her shoulders, one side pulled behind her ear. Brownish-red lipstick complemented the browns and blues accenting her dark brown eyes. Her tan jacket covered her blue blouse, which was filled rather nicely. John Paul didn't want to look any further down, fearing he would look like a letch. She stood eye-to-eye with him, just a little shorter than Angelique.

This detective did something that shocked John Paul: She smiled... and she looked away as if embarrassed—*as if she* were the one caught being a letch.

"Can we, um, sit for a couple minutes?"

Is she going to buy me a coffee and ask for my number? That was how he felt at the moment. It was the strangest vibe he got from her. And he never got vibes from women. The pretty ones, like this one, always walked the other way. Then, he connected this vibe with Angelique's room, how every time he opened his mouth, everyone stopped and listened.

She put a hand on his arm and directed him to the elevators. "Let's head down to the cafeteria and find a quiet table, maybe get a coffee."

His imagination was churning.

A short time later and with a couple coffees in front of them, John Paul finished his story.

"And that's all?"

It sounded like a leading question, but to where he didn't know. There was no way the detective could know about... No. Even now he couldn't complete the thought. He looked about as if searching his memory, which probably didn't convince the detective of anything. "Nope," he confirmed. "That's all I can tell you."

Detective Florent looked at her little notebook then took a sip of coffee. She searched back a couple of pages, just like detectives did on T.V. She shrugged as if that was it, but John Paul knew it wasn't. "I guess that leaves what Miss Carlson said to you in the ambulance."

There it was, and he knew this detective probably already knew the answer. The paramedic must have overheard. He tried to be coy. "She didn't say anything to me in the ambulance."

Her face said she knew otherwise.

Here we go. "As we were getting *into* the ambulance, she said..." John Paul hesitated—not to be dramatic but to reaffirm in his own mind and memory just what Angelique did say. Then he saw again the horrible image in the light of his headlights, illuminating in an alley a white man with white eyes and white hair and white—

"She said, 'Teeth.'"

A phone beeped. *Saved by the bell.*

Detective Florent paused for a moment looking at him. "Excuse me," she said reluctantly and brought out her cell phone. The text message raised her brows. She clicked it off and said, "It looks like Miss Carlson is awake and asking for you."

John Paul took another sip of coffee and stood.

Detective Florent flipped open her notebook to a blank page

and pushed it to him. She held out her pen. "Could you write down your phone number? I may need to contact you." She added quickly, "For follow-up questions."

It didn't happen exactly as he had imagined, but there it was: coffee and a phone number. He smiled as he wrote it down. He pushed the pen and pad back across the table.

Detective Florent took the pen. "If you think of," she reached into her jacket pocket and brought out a business card, "anything else, please call me." She wrote something on the back. "That's my cell."

She had written her first name as well. "Emily," John Paul read. "Thanks, I will."

Emily had that smile and look on her face again. *Hand in the cookie jar.*

They went silently back to the room.

8

*S*omething cold on her lips.
She opened her eyes to darkness and shadows.
Someone was beside her.
He was kissing her before he was going to kill her!

Angelique flailed her arms and tried to sit up. "No!" she screamed.

A crash. A movement.

"Get away!"

A little of the room materialized in her vision. A hospital.

She was alone.

A shadow moved on her right. It said, "Angel..."

She remembered John Wilkins. He had chased away the shadow —Anders. Vampire! "Where is he?" The shadow tried to push her down. "Fuck! What is that?"

Another shadow appeared. Hands gripped her and tried to hold her down. A third shadow. He was going to kill her!

"The lights!" she yelled. "John!"

Angelique twisted her body to get away from the shadows, but they were so strong. A cold shadow pushed her head down on the bed. Shadows grabbed her ankles.

She let out a scream from the depths of her belly.

The shadows hesitated.

Angelique tore away her arm and pushed at something soft.

The lights flickered on.

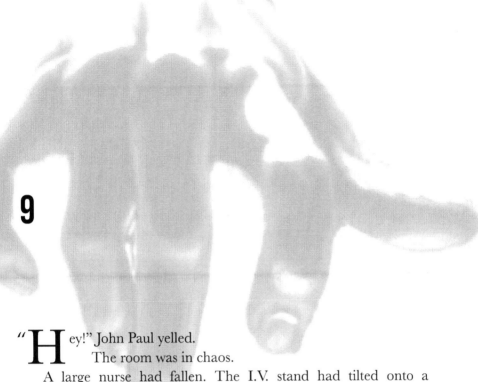

9

"Hey!" John Paul yelled.

The room was in chaos.

A large nurse had fallen. The I.V. stand had tilted onto a machine. Another nurse was trying to grab a kicking ankle. Bright blood had covered Angelique's arm and hand where the I.V. needle had been pulled out. She was pushing her mother away, nearly slipping over the edge of the bed. She was finishing her scream when John Paul had turned on the room light.

The room froze.

Another nurse pushed past John Paul and Emily. She fumbled with the hypo and plunged it into Angelique's thigh.

Upon seeing him, Angelique yelled, "They were here! The light! You said you'd be here!"

Within moments, the medication took hold of her, and she calmed. She let out a short cry; her arms reached for him.

It was another Angelique on that bed, calling for him, reaching to him.

He moved to her, the nurses stepping back. Diane sat in the chair. He took Angelique's slick, sticky hand gently, but she pulled him into a hug.

"Thank you, thank you... you keep them away," she whispered.

When she didn't release him, he slowly, tentatively moved his arms around her.

He fell into her embrace, and something audible inside him popped. He didn't know what it was, but he moved his face into her neck, felt the soft tickle of her hair on his nose and forehead. His shoulders released as if he had just shrugged off a cold, wet, heavy coat. They stayed like that a few moments until she moved her hands to his face, cradling his cheeks. Angelique beamed, honest relief and happiness in her smile and eyes.

"They go away when you come," she said.

The universe shifted back when a nurse gently put a hand on his shoulder. The IV needle had to be put back in, and the monitors had to be reattached. John Paul moved back, and Angelique's face twisted into panic until he slid around the bed to the other side, taking her free hand.

Diane moved to the window as John Paul moved to her side of the bed. "I don't know what happened. She was waking, and I put an ice cube on her lips like the doctor told me to. She started screaming. I'm sorry."

John Paul looked around the room. "Angelique," he said, "this is Detective Emily Florent. She needs to talk to you about what happened."

Face softening, Angelique sat up a bit, but her eyelids looked heavy. "Yes," she said, "the police."

The detective came forward, notebook and pen at the ready. "Miss Carlson, can you tell us anything about the man who attacked you?"

Angelique shook and looked at John Paul then back to the detective. "I know exactly who did this," she declared, "and he wasn't a man." She looked back at John Paul. "You had to have seen."

The detective looked at John Paul. Her left brow rose. She asked Angelique. "What do you mean?"

The buzzing started again in the back of John Paul's head. Something was trying to get out. An image, a memory. He knew exactly what Angelique was going to say, and he wanted to stop her. She was going to sound insane.

The room darkened.

Part of him was certain it must have been a trick of the light. A deeper part of him grew cold.

Angelique closed her eyes and shuddered. She squeezed John Paul's hand. "I—I was frozen." She shook her head slowly, staring blankly at the white hospital sheet covering her. When she looked up at the detective, her eyes brimmed, and her mouth contorted. "I mean, he touched me," the hand with the I.V. moved to her neck, "and I was frozen."

The detective nodded and wrote something on her pad. Her partner stepped up beside her.

"No!" Angelique shook her head. "It wasn't fear." She rubbed at her neck. "He just touched me, and this *cold* spread through my body." She seemed in pain, and she gasped.

"He—" she swallowed. "His teeth—he had *fangs!*" She spat the last word, and all but John Paul physically moved back.

The detectives looked at each other.

Angelique gritted her teeth and squeezed her eyes shut. "His name is Anders Saffenssen," she announced, "and he is a vampire."

Time froze. All within the room must have been playing back what Angelique had said, just as John Paul was. Even though he knew what she was going to say, hearing it was impossible to process.

Diane stood, hand to mouth. She resumed the clock. "Of course, Angel, he was a monster." She stepped behind John Paul and stroked her daughter's hair.

That movement seemed to animate the room. Detective Hamplin took out his cell phone and went into the hall. Nurses moved into routines. Emily was about to ask another question.

"Tired," whispered Angelique.

The atmosphere of that little hospital room seemed normal, but John Paul felt the world tilt. He pulled within himself to find the gyroscope that had suddenly malfunctioned. He was going to be sick.

A nurse touched his arm. "Excuse me."

His awareness expanded back into the room. He looked at the

nurse, a plump woman with short black hair. He was afraid to open his mouth. That strange pre-vomit saliva had oozed in.

She smiled. "Your face," she gestured. "You have blood on it."

He looked at Angelique. He was afraid that was the least of his worries.

PART TWO
WHAT'S PAST IS PROLOGUE

And by what destiny to perform and act
    Whereof what's past is prologue; what to come,
    In yours and my discharge.
    - William Shakespeare, *The Tempest*

A saint cries in life,
    Laughs at the end of Fate.
    A sinner is all smiles—
    Cries at the Pearly Gates.
    - John Trubadir, "Dipole Duo"

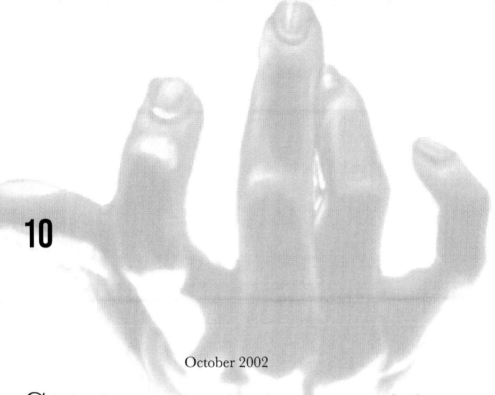

10

October 2002

S he bought two extra lamps for each room—even one for the bathroom. She put one-hundred-watt bulbs in the old and new lights. Next on her list were Christmas lights. She put sets under all the furniture, the bed, in the closets. Everywhere.

For now, the dozen extra flashlights would suffice.

Soon, there'd be nowhere a shadow could hide.

Angelique sat on the sofa, knees to her chest. A cup of Earl Grey tea and a half-eaten box of Lindt Chocolates sat on the coffee table. There were empty boxes of chocolates in the trash, and she looked at that trash can in the kitchen.

Her gaze fell to the chocolates on the table.

She hadn't eaten this much chocolate since Bryce Stapleton, but she couldn't think about that. It brought up the *shadows*, and that was the last thing she wanted to think about.

Angelique found the remote and turned up the T.V. She'd been watching a lot of Comedy Central lately. Anything to get her to smile, maybe to laugh.

Laughing kept the shadows away, too.

Three sharp raps on her door made her jump.

She looked at her watch. It had been only thirty-seven minutes since John Paul had checked on her. He promised to come every hour. Besides, he didn't have to knock. Angelique had given him a key so that he could just come in and check on her.

At the top of the hour, there'd be a quiet slipping of the key into the locks, a faint scraping of the bolts as they opened. And he'd enter with his smile.

It was too early for him.

A stranger stood outside her door.

Strangers were good. The shadows didn't like to play when strangers were around. And the two security guards hired by her mother watching both entrances kept the shadows away, too. But what worked the most was John Paul Wilkins.

She hadn't seen one shadow since The Night.

She went to the door and looked out the peephole. Detective Hamplin. He was probably in his mid-thirties but had the graying hair of a fifty-year-old; he reminded Angelique of slushy winter roads, dirty and messy with cinders. He was chewing gum and looking down at something. Perhaps he was trying to quit smoking.

Odd, that he was here and not Detective Florent.

Angelique disengaged the locks and opened the door.

"Miss Carlson." He looked like a doctor about to deliver bad news.

"You haven't found him."

Hamplin shut his little notebook. "May I come in?"

Angelique waved him in and shut the door. "Do I need to sit for the bad news?"

Hamplin passed through the short hall and stopped at the living room. "Nice place." He chomped on his gum. "Lots of light."

Angelique followed him and moved around into the room. "Too bright?" She smiled, knowing the answer he wouldn't give.

"Very clean," he replied.

She said, "I've surprised myself with becoming anal about cleanliness lately. I wonder if it's some kind of shock reaction from the attack?"

Hamplin stopped chomping on his gum.

Angelique sat on the sofa. She motioned to the matching seat.

"You look like you need a seat." She used the remote to turn off the T.V.

Hamplin looked at the chair, and Angelique could see some kind of debate behind his eyes. He didn't want to get comfortable. He had bad news to deliver. Angelique flirted with the notion of offering the detective a drink just to see if he'd take it. The guy probably gave the "bad news duty" to his partner.

Speaking of which, where was she?

Hamplin sat and opened his notebook. He said nothing.

Angelique became bored... and a little pissed. "What? No leads? Can't find my little vampire?" She liked the way the detectives— even John Paul for that matter—winced when she said that word.

Hamplin looked up, took a breath and spewed it out: "Miss Carlson, there was a murder. It happened two nights ago. We found the body this morning."

Angelique knew there was more, and she knew she didn't want to hear it. As the detective opened his mouth to continue, she grabbed the arm of the sofa.

Hamplin took another breath and paused when he saw the terror in her face. "The victim was your age, same height and build, same hair color. She was arranged into a fetal position on the ground behind a dumpster near the Old Town Mall building. They have their annual haunted house."

Angelique pushed back into the sofa. He continued, "There was a note—"

"To me." It was a whisper. Angelique's vocal cords refused to work. She looked at the blank T.V. screen. She couldn't look at the detective.

She felt something in her gut and knew the vampire's perfect white hand—the hand that had sent the freezing cold into her nerves and bones—it was going to claw its way up her esophagus and burn her throat as it crawled out of her mouth to encircle her neck.

"Perhaps we should call your mother—"

Angelique stood. Only a small part of her was aware of it—that little logical part that could stand outside of one's self like a spectator.

As the freezing cold hand scratched up to her throat, she knew what she had to do.

Hamplin stood. "Miss Carlson?"

Every part of Angelique's awareness focused on that hand in her throat, but she felt her legs move. She went to the door and opened it. She swallowed hard to keep it down. She wanted to step across the threshold to the stairs…down them to the next floor…to the first door, his door.

Nothing moved but the hand, the fingers wiggling at the back of her tongue. She gagged. She couldn't breathe. She couldn't move.

But he appeared. Angelique had summoned the one person who could make this go away.

John Paul Wilkins embraced her.

She felt his warmth, his strength. It melted the cold. The hand retreated down her throat to her belly. Everything was brighter, brighter than all the lights. He was like the midday sun had walked through her door.

Angelique opened her eyes. Detective Florent just made it to the top of the stairs.

Angelique let him guide her to the sofa. Florent shut the door.

Angelique felt John Paul's weight on the cushions next to her. She squeezed his hand, and he gently squeezed it back.

Florent made a hesitant scan of the room, and Angelique could see the word *paranoia* in Florent's eyes. *Dread* was still all over Hamplin's face.

It was difficult for her to think beyond John Paul's hand right now. She was glad he had come.

John Paul looked from one detective to the other. "What? What can be worse than that message?"

Angelique squeezed his hand. She didn't want to talk, didn't want to open her mouth. She was afraid of what might come out.

John Paul looked at Angelique. He looked at them. "You haven't told her?"

Detective Florent looked at her partner. He said, "I hadn't had the chance to finish—"

"Angelique," Florent said, "we haven't finished processing the scene, but we came here as soon as we could. It will be on the news

44

this evening." She sat on the arm of the chair. "The media won't be able to connect you to it," she caught herself then added, "yet. But when we saw it, we knew."

Angelique felt split in half. The half that held John Paul's hand was scared, afraid to open her mouth because a scream waited in her throat where that hand had been. The other half felt like laughing at how they all thought she would crumple up and cry. *What the fuck? Say it!*

Florent leaned forward. "There were two lines written on a piece of cardboard, written in the victim's blood, like it was a script or a play. The first line said 'A' colon 'What big teeth you have?' The second: 'A' colon 'The better to eat you with, my dear.' And the girl, the victim. She was exsanguinated, but not at the place we found her."

Hamplin had a look of relief.

Florent waited a moment to let Angelique process the information.

Angelique looked at John Paul. She found her voice. It was about to say the only word she could say.

Florent interrupted, "This Anders Saffenssen must *think* he's some kind of…" she didn't want to say it, but she knew Angelique would, "…vampire. But I assure you, Angelique, he's a man, and we'll get him. With the information and description you've given us, and what we could get from the bar, the Baltimore P.D. will put its full resources into getting him. Especially now that your attack is possibly linked to a murder."

Standing next to his partner, Hamplin added, "And we'll add some officers to the security your mother has hired."

Florent turned to Angelique and asked, "Why don't you stay with her?"

"She and her mother don't get along well," John Paul answered. "I've been checking in on her every hour when I can."

Detective Florent looked around at the lights in the living room. "Try to get some rest, Angelique." She looked at John Paul and smiled. "You, too."

Both detectives gave them business cards. Florent stood, and Angelique and John Paul rose as well.

Hamplin shut his notebook, and Angelique realized he had never really looked at it nor written anything in it. It was a crutch for stressful situations like this. He did, however, look her in the eye and say, "If we discover anything more, we'll let you know." He nodded towards Florent and added, "Like she said, you've had a tough week. You two really need to try to rest. This building's covered. There's nothing that can get in without someone seeing it."

Hamplin almost sounded patronizing. Angelique said, "Unless he flies up here like a bat."

That got the wince she wanted.

But John Paul squeezed her hand, so she said no more.

"We'll be okay, detectives," John Paul said.

Detective Florent hesitated a moment, looking at John Paul, like she wanted to shake his hand, but she gave a half-smile, nodded at the two of them, and left with her partner.

Angelique wanted to say, *What the fuck? See? A vampire!* She knew, however, John Paul thought like the detectives: *This Anders is a lunatic with fake teeth who is trying to terrorize the city—especially Angelique.*

They stood silently for a moment, and he turned to her and said, "I don't know what to think." He hugged her briefly—as if he didn't want to tell her what he really felt—and added, "I'll be back in a little bit to check on you. You okay?"

She shrugged indifferently, but it was a lie. She was scared. Anders the vampire was sending her a message. She needed to think about this. Alone.

He hugged her again, looked around, then quietly left.

But she couldn't think about it. Her brain felt like a train with everything rushing by fast. She couldn't focus. It was only when John Paul came to check on her that her brain seemed to slow down.

Later, Angelique watched the news report of the naked girl found murdered near the Old Town Mall haunted house. The reporter mentioned a bloody handprint on the wall near the girl. The detectives failed to mention that little detail. But there was no mention of the note and no connection made between the murder and an assault on a Johns Hopkins University co-ed last week.

Then she woke up on the sofa.

The light in the room seemed dimmer. Angelique looked around and found the bulb in the lamp on the kitchen table had gone out. As she replaced it, one of the flashlights pointed under the sofa went out.

She halted. If one more light went out, she'd scream.

"Fuck it," she whispered.

She slipped on her sneakers, not even bothering to tie them, grabbed her purse and coat, and left. She locked the door.

She hesitated a moment at the top of the stairs and looked down into the shadows. Nothing moved. But that didn't mean anything.

All she needed to do was rush down one floor and take three steps to John Paul's door.

Thoughts of shadows and bats and wolves and mists—and teeth—froze her at the steps. She couldn't move.

But she had to.

Go!

Like tap dancing, holding out her purse in one hand and the coat in the other for balance, she scurried down the steps, holding her breath. A few long moments later, she stood in front of John Paul's door.

She looked around.

She knocked.

Nothing. She looked around again.

She knocked again.

Did he leave? Did he go to work? *What the fuck?*

She heard something. The bolt of his lock scraped open, and the faint light from within hit her like warm water. And there he was.

"Ange? You okay?" John Paul looked like he'd been sleeping. He rubbed an eye.

She couldn't say she was scared, that the lights in her room were going out, that she couldn't stay there knowing a light could go out at any moment.

He saw this, and his face melted into a shared pain. "C'mon."

She moved into his warm, safe, bright arms.

No shadows—and she wanted to believe no Anders—could suffer the warm light of this man.

He shut the door behind her, but they hadn't even made it to his sofa when a double knock sounded from it.

John Paul went to the door and opened it to find his neighbor, Jimmy. "Hey, what's up?"

Jimmy held up a door mat. "How'd ya get this?"

"What?"

"My mat, dude. It was layin' right here in front of your door."

Angelique came up behind John Paul and saw Jimmy's pimply face get red. She didn't care about what he saw and what he thought.

"That wasn't there just now," she declared.

John Paul scratched his head. "No idea, man. But sorry." He shrugged.

Jimmy looked from Angelique to John. He wanted to say more but only muttered, "Whatever," and turned and left.

They heard his door shut.

John Paul didn't seem to think anything of it.

Angelique, however, felt her entire body go cold. She looked about for shadows.

What John Paul didn't consider was the building rule about no welcome mats in the hall.

Jimmy's mat had been *inside* his apartment.

11

The note on the inside of the building's front door, as well as another on the back door, asked a question everyone in the building had been asking:

Whoever is messing with the mats,
PLEASE STOP!
JPW

Angelique said she knew who it was but fell short of saying "*the vampire.*" Yet John Paul knew how she felt about it.

Three days ago, he had said, "I think there's a sick asshole in this building who's getting all of us ready for Trick or Treat, with a focus on the trick." That morning, every mat in the building—nine mats of various sizes and colors—had been found at John Wilkins' door, and that morning, like the other mornings, he laid them out in the hall so that their owners could claim them.

Their detectives, Emily and Emmerich (they were on a first name basis now), couldn't figure it out after having spoken with all the mat owners. The building manager had even paid him a visit, promising there was no one else who could have a master key.

Today, John Paul had invited Angelique down for some home-made pizza and beer. He wanted to take her mind off of Halloween and all the *other things* the night suggested. As he molded the dough onto a cookie sheet, a knock sounded at the door to their apartment—

Their apartment. Angelique had been staying every night for a week now, and John Paul had easily slipped into the notion that they lived together. But he never mentioned it to Angelique; he didn't want to jinx it. He was happy enough with the feelings that swirled within him.

At dusk, even after he'd given her a key to his apartment, she'd come knocking with her pillow in hand, and they'd watch T.V. or rent a movie and have a little dinner. Or, when he came home from late classes or a late shift at Corazon, she'd be sitting there watching T.V. or reading a book.

Even though it was platonic, it felt right to John Paul.

Angelique answered the knock at the door.

"Tom Schuller," she said, "if I didn't know better, I'd have to say you're checking on me."

John Paul stepped back from the kitchen to see the tall, thin man in med scrubs, his brown hair pulled back in a ponytail. Today, he looked even more unkempt than usual. His beard looked like it had growth spurts in spots. He must have had some seriously long rotations at the hospital.

"'Sup, Angelique?"

"C'mon in," John Paul said. "Wanna beer?"

His teeth seemed brighter surrounded by the dark beard. "Only if I can have three."

He came in and got right to business. "Listen, I had a patient today." John Paul handed him a beer. "Thanks." He took a sip. "So this patient knows about cameras and computers and can maybe set up something in the hall out there."

Before John Paul or Angelique could say anything, Tom added, "It'll be short term, and it'll be free. The guy is trying to get into the security business." He took another swig.

Angelique and John Paul looked at each other.

"Listen," Tom said, "I know you think this is some kind of prank, but really, which of these guys would do such a thing?" He looked at Angelique. "To you?"

Tom knew about the murder last week. Everyone did; it had been all over the news, but no one knew of its connection to Angelique. With Halloween tonight, and the city's preparation for all the festivities this week leading up to it, that murder had disappeared into the stew of all the other murders and news. And this prankster with the door mats? Tom was right. No one in the building would be as callous and malicious as to frighten Angelique after what she had endured.

Neither John Paul nor Angelique liked where Tom was leading them.

A familiar three raps sounded loudly from the door.

"Sounds like Em and Em are here." Angelique's disdain was belied by her eagerness to answer the door.

Tom and John Paul watched as she opened the door to two long faces.

Tom downed his beer and said to John Paul, "Think about it. He can come by tomorrow and talk you through it."

John Paul watched the two detectives come in. They might as well have held neon signs that read "bad news."

Tom put the empty bottle on the counter and left. "Detectives," he said in passing. He'd had a few chats with them and didn't seem concerned they were here.

They didn't even look at him. They watched Angelique as if trying to measure her emotions.

John Paul took a drink of beer to wash away the desert that had just formed in his mouth.

He noticed Detective Hamplin—Emmerich—held a manila envelope.

For some reason John Paul looked at his watch: 4:33. He was supposed to be at work in an hour. He felt he would need to call Tio soon. He hoped Orlando would cover him tonight.

The detectives came into the living room. They stood next to the chair; John Paul and Angelique sat on the sofa. Everything was as it had been a week ago, except now in John Paul's apartment.

Not exactly. Angelique seemed prepared for this. "My little vampire has been up to some more antics."

Both detectives' faces hardened. Emily replied, "There have been two more murders now attributed to Anders Saffenssen."

Emmerich opened the envelope and removed some photos. He laid one on the coffee table. It showed a large piece of cardboard leaning against a brick wall. The note from last week—in blood, the words composed neatly. But there was something different.

"You said 'eat' last week," Angelique said. "This says 'bite.'"

A: The better to bite you with, my dear.

Emily sat in the chair. "That's my fault. We should've written it down, but we came to you as quickly as we could. We knew it was addressed to you."

Emmerich added, "That old story sticks with you." He placed another photo on the table: a bloody handprint on a wall. "This info we gave to the media."

John Paul remembered.

Emmerich hesitated with the next photo. "We, uh, need—"

Emily broke in. "Listen, if there had been any doubts—and there weren't any with us—they were gone when we saw the body and the note in blood, even the bloody hand, we knew it was connected to what had happened to you. Homicide, however, needs more convincing. We deal with *special* victims—rape, domestic violence, trafficking—but when there is a strange homicide..." She halted and looked at the photos on the table, but her eyes were somewhere else. "We had used *vampire* as a keyword in our report. We were called to that scene." She pointed at the photos.

Angelique looked at John Paul then back to Emily. "Exsanguinated." She pointed at the bloody hand. "All of them?"

Emmerich saved Emily and placed the next photo on top of the previous. It showed another piece of cardboard:

Therefore, fair A, question your desires.
Know of your youth. Examine well your blood—
The jaws of darkness do devour it up.
So quick bright things come to confusion.

Again, neat letters, written with a finger with what looked like paint, but they knew it was blood.

"The two naked bodies were placed together, spooning like lovers," Emily said. "They were a young man and a young woman in their mid-twenties. The male was killed two or three days ago. The female last night. They were placed in another alley sometime before dawn today."

"Their identities are being withheld pending notification of their families," said Emmerich. He placed the last photo on top of the others. It was of a wall with a set of four bloody hands arranged around a strange symbol like a featureless head with an odd hat.

Emily pulled out the handprint from last week and placed it next to the new one. "The same hand made all of these."

Emmerich assembled the pictures and put them into the envelope. "You both know nothing about these pictures or the crime scenes."

John Paul and Angelique had sat through the presentation like statues.

Emily said, "The second note is lines from Shakespeare's *A Midsummer Night's Dream*."

Angelique took a haggard breath. "Romeo and Juliet! He said lines from Romeo and Juliet—but they were different." She shut her eyes and tried to remember. "Adapted, like those. *Parting was such sweet sorrow that I could not wait upon the morrow*." She concentrated harder. "There were others, but I can't remember."

Emily's face brightened. "That's good, that's more. Any details you can remember will help."

"He likes Shakespeare," John Paul said. "Maybe he's into drama or acting."

Emily smiled at him and replied, "It's worth looking into."

Emmerich said, "The media will report on this tonight before the kiddies go out for Trick or Treating. And we have to warn you. They're calling him the Vampire Killer."

Angelique looked at the detective and smiled sarcastically. "Tell me, Emmerich, just how did these *exsanguinations* happen?"

He and Emily looked at each other. "We're not at liberty to tell you that."

Now John Paul was perturbed. "But you can show us pictures you're not supposed to."

The tension in the room rose a couple notches. John Paul watched Emily's jaw clench then relax.

The detective stood. "We need to get back. Angelique, I suggest you stay with your mother or a friend while all this is going on."

Angelique stood and faced her. She placed a hand on John Paul's head and said, "I've been staying here since the first victim."

John Paul felt the blood rise in his face. He stood and felt like he needed to say something. "The sofa is surprisingly comfortable."

The detectives looked at them.

Was that disappointment in Emily's eyes?

Emmerich nodded. "Good." He stepped back to let his partner by. "We'll notify your security."

"Speaking of security," John Paul said, trying his best to sound normal, "we're looking into some cameras for the hall in front of the door, what with the prankster and the door mats."

Emily turned and said, "Perhaps that's another reason to stay somewhere else? Get out of this place," she looked around, "and away from the memories?"

Angelique slipped an arm around him. "I feel safe when I'm here. I sleep much better."

Was that a grin twisting on Emmerich's lips?

What was going on here?

Emmerich opened the door. "You have our contact info if you think of anything that might help."

Emily said to Angelique, "Or if any more memories come back to you."

"And feel free to stop by if you find out anything more about my little vampire."

Emily forced a smile. "We'll be in touch."

"Have a nice day, detectives," Angelique said as the door shut.

She turned to John Paul. "Melts with the mouth and a slap of the hand."

"What the hell just happened?"

Angelique laughed. "You didn't see how...?" She let out an exasperated breath, and her eyes threw boulders at him.

He did understand one thing. "You implied we're living together."

Angelique shrugged. "What Em and Em don't know won't melt them." She added, "They would have insisted I have someone be with me all the time."

Both she and John Paul knew he had school and work, and that she liked her independence.

They looked at each other for a moment.

John Paul glanced at his watch: 5:17. "Shit." He looked at Angelique, at the uncooked pizza, then back at Angelique. "I'm gonna call Tio—"

"No," she smiled, "you go ahead. I'll finish this, and it'll be waiting when you get home. I'll be fine." She had already brought her bag and pillow. "Besides, I'm certain Diane will be calling soon. I don't want her appealing to you to force me to stay with her."

Diane. It made him cringe inwardly when she called her mother by her name. He knew there was history there, and she intimated as much, but he knew it wasn't any of his business. And he had no right to ask.

John Paul almost asked her if she was okay. They had just heard their little *psycho* had killed again, targeting the killings at her. How does one process that?

"What?" Angelique asked, seeing him intently looking at her. Her face softened. "Listen, I meant it. What I said about feeling safe here... how *you* make me feel safe." She put a hand on his shoulder. "But seriously, I'll be fine. The pizza will be waiting for you when you get back."

The top of his head still tingled from her touch—now his shoulder. God, she was beautiful.

Before he could say more, she added, "And I will stay right here. No wandering about."

When he returned from work that night near midnight, the pizza was done, and she was asleep on his bed. Her back was to him so that the light from the kitchen wouldn't bother her. He watched the movement of her breathing, how her dark hair splayed across the white pillow.

For him, it was enough.

The Wild One, however, howled at him to get into the bed with her, spoon with her...

He pushed it down and went to the kitchen. He halved a slice of pizza and stood at the kitchen sink with his beer, eyeing the sofa and the folded blankets and pillow at the far end of it.

He finished his beer and washed his hands. He tiptoed into the bathroom across the little hall from the bedroom, shut the door, turned on the light, and did his brief ablutions. He'd take a shower tomorrow when she went back to her room.

A few moments later, he spread one of the blankets across the sofa. He fluffed up the pillow—

"I can't sleep."

John Paul jumped. "Jesus!" His heart leapt into his throat.

Angelique stood at the dark opening of the bedroom. She wore a pair of loose gray shorts and a tight white top. No bra. John Paul had never seen her in her pajamas; she usually put on a robe.

"Sorry."

The Wild One told him to go hug her.

But he said to her, "I have no idea how you could. I'm not very tired myself, given what we heard today." He put his pillow down. "Wanna watch some T.V.?"

"No." She took a breath and said, "Can you come lay with me?"

I feel safe when I'm here. I sleep much better.

How you make me feel safe.

He gave into the Wild One. John Paul moved to her, and she moved to him. She let him put his arms around her, her scent filling him, their heat mixing.

The Wild One warned: "Don't fuck this up."

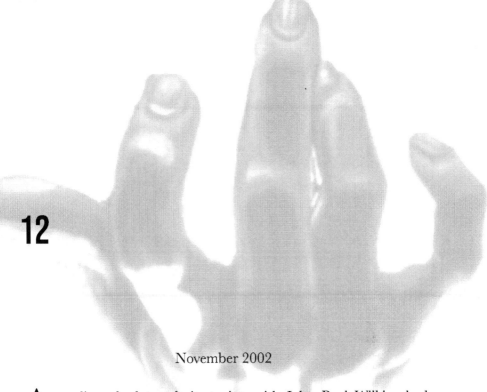

12

November 2002

Angelique had to admit staying with John Paul Wilkins had made enduring all the drama around her attack and the subsequent murders, at the very least, a little bearable.

She had not seen her shadows since.

The Vampire Killer was all over the news, but there still hadn't been a connection to her. Thank God. The police had been careful not to give the *special messages* to the press.

Her local trickster hadn't played with the door mats since the last murders, either.

Angelique had made that connection: Only a shadow could steal into someone's locked apartment and take the doormat without a sound—let alone nine of them in one night. Her local trickster, her shadow, her vampire.

And it'd been one week since the last set of murders. No shadows, no lurking vampire, no new murders.

However, her friend Ashley, the birthday girl for whom she had gone to Alternatives that fateful night, had come by two days ago to bring hellos from The Gang and to apologize. The poor girl had assumed responsibility for what had happened: Angelique wouldn't have been there had it not been for her, would not have endured...

what she had endured. But Ashley was quick to say, once she discovered Angelique was living with her savior, that her friend seemed more relaxed. Calmer. She smiled a lot at John Paul, and Angelique knew that look of envy. It was the same look Emily the detective gave him.

Angelique loved playing it up with John Paul, making him squirm and making Ashley and Emily virtually froth at the mouth.

Angelique stood at the sink with a cup of Earl Grey tea in hand, the steady sound of the running water aiding her reverie, and now wondered about this enigma named John Paul Wilkins.

Any other man would have had his hands all over her. The guy laid in bed with her, spooned with her (she had to admit the heat from his body was comforting), and he didn't even get a hard-on. He kept his hands in neutral places. Even when she occasionally tried to move to get a reaction, and even when she fell asleep, she'd wake later to find him turned the other way.

The guy was either a virgin or a monk. Perhaps both.

She wiped the cup with a soapy dish rag and rinsed it before she placed it on a folded towel to dry and turned off the water.

Was this what *unrequited* was like?

Did she *want* John Paul to make a move on her?

Would she let him?

Why was she thinking about this?

A month ago—a different Angelique, she had to admit—the thought of John Paul Wilkins would have brought feelings of contempt, like a vomit burp. And that contempt had manifested into her little nickname for him: J.P. She had known he didn't like it and had gotten half the building to use it. But since The Night, he had earned a new-found respect from everyone. Even her. She hadn't called him J.P. since.

Angelique had to think about that.

The Night.

The Night had changed everything, had changed John Paul totally, but he couldn't see it.

He was still a dork, but now he had a little swagger, a little confidence. He was brighter.

And he kept the shadows away—kept Anders away.

Perhaps that was why the vampire had started his killing spree. He couldn't get to Angelique because of John Paul Wilkins.

The thought of a *reward* crossed her mind. No. That was petty even for her. He was a good man, and he deserved better.

And there were the looks Emily and Ashley gave him. She knew that look. Angelique wondered if he got other looks on campus and around town, in the bodega, from all the Latinas who came in.

Angelique laughed aloud. She dried her hands.

Was she jealous?

The notion of taking a bus to Corazon to surprise John Paul crossed her mind when the landline rang.

She let it ring away and went to the bathroom to brush her teeth.

Perhaps she would indeed head over to Corazon. She was too curious now.

As she began to brush, the phone stopped, but a few moments later, it started again.

She spat and washed out her mouth and went to the phone.

She wanted to answer *What?* to throw off the caller, but this was John Paul's phone. It could be his parents.

As sweetly as she could she answered, "Hello?"

There was a hesitation at the other end. The caller had expected to hear John Paul. "Would this happen to be Angelique Carlson?" The woman's voice had a strong, deep quality, like an actor or a—

Angelique replied, "Why, yes, it is. With whom—"

"This is Miranda Kelly from WMOR-TV. Do you have a couple minutes?"

"Baltimore's number one news source," Angelique said mockingly.

Another hesitation. "Yes, it is. And I am the Morning Show's local special interest reporter. I have a special interest in a story I heard about how a young man saved a young woman from a sexual predator, and how they fell in love."

Angelique felt her blood boil in her face and neck. There was only one big mouth who could have done this.

"And how do you know Ashley Wetzel? May I call you Miranda?"

Either this reporter measured her words very carefully, or Angelique was batting a thousand at unbalancing her.

Miranda said, "Miranda's fine. Ashley is my cousin."

Angelique almost said, *Of course, she is,* but instead she asked, "What can I do for you, Miranda?"

"I would like to feature you and John Wilkins in a local special interest story. You know, like how a dangerous situation brought two people together?"

Angelique got even more pissed. "You mean how the damsel in distress is saved by the hero, and they fall in love and live happily ever after?" Now that it had been brought up, that is exactly how it looked.

But something clicked in the back of her head. Her little vampire Anders had killed people because of her, like little acts of love to let her know how he wanted her. She hadn't been connected to the murders, not yet, and that must grate at him. Perhaps a little media exposé on how unrequited love became true love through an act of courage might aggravate him and make him make a mistake.

There was that word again: *unrequited.* Was she in some kind of ironic mirror?

Her mobile phone buzzed. John Paul. Then, there were three raps at her door. Em and Em were here.

When it rains, it pours.

"Hello? Angelique?"

"Yes, we'll do it. I'll need to talk to the hero. Call back on Monday."

She answered the mobile, "Hey, there," as she stepped to the door.

"Ange, a reporter was here a little while ago..."

Angelique opened the door. Her mother stood there, the detectives behind her.

A huge chill ran down her back.

"Angelique?" came from the phone.

Diane Carlson was as white as a ghost. The detectives wore their bad news faces.

"John Paul... you need to get here A.S.A.P. Em and Em are here with Diane."

"Shit. Okay. I'll get there as quick as I can."

Angelique heard the phone beep. The call ended, but something else was about to begin.

Diane jumped into her daughter's arms. "My Angel."

"What's going on?" She moved her arms around her mother, but she didn't hug her.

Emily asked, "May we come in?" She was formal. This was business.

Angelique guided Diane into John Paul's living room.

Emmerich pulled out the two chairs at the small table in the kitchen. Diane sat in the seat next to the sofa. And once again, Angelique sat on the sofa to receive bad news.

Without John Paul.

"Where is John?" Diane looked a mess, as if she hadn't gotten any sleep in a week. She didn't even bother putting on makeup— that's how upset she was.

"He's at work, but he's on his way here." Angelique looked at the detectives. "What's happened?"

They looked at Diane, but she wasn't in any condition to say much. Emily began, "There were two more murders. Not much evidence like with the others. Same scene as before: a dirty alley, a male and a female, spooning like a sleeping couple. There were no bloody hands on the wall this time, but there was this." She motioned to Emmerich who pulled out a photograph from inside his coat.

He laid it on the coffee table. A dirty brick wall with an oval mouth and two triangular fangs drawn in blood. Anders had put a lot of blood on the fangs so that they dripped.

Diane gasped. "What is this? The murderer has been drawing with blood?"

Angelique ignored her mother. "No hands," she said. "There have been five total hands, and now five bodies."

Emily leaned forward. "We can only hope at what that implies."

Diane looked at them. "What are you all saying? She doesn't know? I told you last week!" She put her head in her hands. "And today..."

Now it was Angelique's turn to be shocked. "Tell me what?"

Emily put a hand on Diane's shoulder. "Your mother contacted us last week after the names of victims two and three were released to the media."

"Your father and I knew them!" Tears streamed down her face. "They were children of our friends! You went to school with them!"

"School?" Angelique didn't understand. Ashley had said The Gang was doing okay. *Children of our friends!* "High school?"

She only had two close friends in high school, and one of them moved away her sophomore year. She hadn't seen any of her acquaintances since graduation.

Emily continued, "Your mother told us the first three victims were children of members of an old Bible study group. When the new victims were found early this morning, we went to her with pictures of their faces. She confirmed the identities. We brought her here to tell you." The detective enumerated the names slowly.

But Angelique didn't want to know. She didn't want to be any more personally connected to the murders. If Anders' attack on her had been an opportunity, that was one thing. How could he know of these old "acquaintances" if he hadn't been stalking her?

Angelique realized she didn't want Anders to have anything to do with her shadows. Because that would mean...

Where was John Paul? She needed his strength and steadfastness right now.

And on cue, he burst into the apartment panting. "What's going on?"

Angelique jumped up and into his arms. It felt better now. She could feel him breathe, and as he mastered his own breathing, she mastered hers.

Emily stood. "There have been two more murders."

Angelique said into his ear, "They're connected to my family."

He pulled her back to look into her eyes.

"All of them," she confirmed.

Angelique turned to see Diane watching her open-mouthed. Then the woman slowly looked about the apartment. Angelique watched her mother solve an additional equation: being in John Paul's apartment in the middle of the day plus hugging John Paul plus some of Angel's décor about the apartment plus some of Angel's clothes equals…

"Is this where you're staying, Angel? You said a friend was staying with *you*."

Angelique opened her mouth to shoot a barb at her mother, but Emmerich stood, his bulk between them.

"Miss Carlson," he began, converting to formalities in front of her mother, "when was the last time you had any contact with the victims?"

John Paul guided her to the sofa and sat beside her.

A small animal had appeared in her chest, scratching to get out.

She couldn't remember their names. She couldn't think of anything but...

The teeth—odd, glassy teeth and two long fangs.

That animal pushed hard beneath her sternum. She squeezed John Paul's hand hard.

And he squeezed back.

The animal abated.

Angelique looked at her mother. The woman's eyes darted over the both of them. She was hurt and angry.

That made the little animal disappear.

Angelique took a breath and said to Diane, "I am safe here."

The detectives exchanged a glance and sat back down. Diane did, too.

To Emmerich, Angelique said, "I haven't seen or heard from anyone from high school for years." She looked hard at her mother. "They weren't really friends." She wanted to add they were typical two-faced high-school brats: holier than thou when around adults and fucked-up crazy everywhere else.

She looked at Emmerich and almost said it, but they were dead. Possibly because of her.

That animal stirred again, but John Paul squeezed her hand, and it went away.

She asked Em and Em, "Was there another note?" She wondered how much Diane knew.

"Note?" the woman asked. That answered that question.

Emily turned to Diane and answered, "What we are about to

tell you is confidential. It has not been shared with the public." She put a hand on Diane's arm. "We want to keep your daughter out of the investigation as much as possible. We believe the perpetrator thinks he has a personal relationship with your daughter. He doesn't care about the public, nor is he doing any of this for notoriety. He's left notes at each scene specifically addressed to her."

"Mostly bastardized quotations from Shakespeare," added Emmerich. He placed a photo on the coffee table: another large piece of cardboard leaning against a brick wall, words written in blood:

I'll follow thee and make heaven a hell.
To feast upon the hand I love so well.

"That's *A Midsummer Night's Dream*," Diane said. "And, yes, it's not correct."

Em and Em looked at each other. Emmerich pulled out a number of other photos and found one he was looking for. "This?" he asked, placing it on top of the other. It was from the second crime scene.

Diane looked from the photos to Angelique to the detectives. "Oh my God. Yes."

Emily looked intently at the woman. "How do you know these are from that play?"

"Because I saw it at the Chesapeake last month. And I love Shakespeare."

Emmerich wrote something in his little black notebook.

Angelique barely heard any of this. Her eyes saw the word *feast*, but her mind saw teeth.

Anders' vampire teeth.

64

13

Yesterday, Angelique told him she was going to take a break from school. She had already contacted her instructors to inform them of her taking some weeks off after the attack, and they were sympathetic. But she told John Paul she didn't feel like going back for some time. She needed a break from the expectations of life, she had said.

After all that was happening with the Vampire Killer and his obsession with Angelique, John Paul couldn't blame her. In fact, he wanted to bring up professional help, but something told him that would be a powder keg.

Then, she said something that surprised him. She and her mother—she said the word *mother*—had a private appointment with the Dean of Arts and Sciences at Johns Hopkins to discuss Angelique's future there.

Diane was a faithful donor to both the university and the hospital foundations. The meeting was a formality, but the women wanted to ensure that whenever Angelique wanted to return to school, there would be no impediments.

John Paul looked at his watch: 12:07. They were probably having that lunch meeting right now at some swanky club.

He folded a pair of her panties—just like the way she wanted—and set them atop the others he had already done. He hadn't been one for folding underwear and socks, so he didn't have a particular method when he did. But when Angelique "unofficially" moved in with him, and she discovered he didn't mind washing clothes—especially down in the basement of the building where she was now afraid to go— she instructed him on how she liked things folded.

And he wasn't oblivious to how she had especially handled her bras and panties and the occasional thong when she had demonstrated her method.

The Wild One had howled at how cowardly he had been lately. How he couldn't, even after her little demonstration, try to kiss her, hold her hand outside times of distress, or put an arm around her.

Fuck you for being a gentleman, it sneered. *Call it what it is. You're a coward, man! How many signals are you going to ignore? Thongs! Why would she wear a thong in your apartment? She probably wears no underwear at all!*

"Fuck off," he said to it.

He remembered how Angelique had felt, or not felt, about him before The Night. No, there had been something there before. Something like contempt. He knew she had started the "J.P." nickname, and knew she had considered him a geek and a nerd, but he was what he was.

But you haven't been such a nerd lately, have you? the Wild One countered.

When had he last watched *Star Trek* or went to Aaron's place to play Dungeons and Dragons? Now that he thought of it, he hadn't seen any of his old friends since The Night.

Tom Schuller came up to see them at least once a week. And that friend of Angelique's, Ashley. She had come over once.

B ut that was it.
Emily and Emmerich came by more than anyone else, and that was to deliver bad news most of the time.

John Paul and Angelique really had no one but themselves.

The Wild One was relentless. *All the more reason to get close to her.*

John Paul had no illusions about his relationship with Angelique. He had saved her, and she felt safe around him (though he didn't really understand that).

Like Tio had told him: you save a life, you have a responsibility to it.

That was all John Paul was willing to invest in this situation.

Coward.

Practical.

So, she says no. So what? That's nothing less than what you already have.

It would make things uncomfortable. She'd leave. Then he would definitely have less than what he already had.

John Paul Wilkins could live like this forever. He could look at her in her loose top and sweatpants washing the dishes, or he could look at her with that long thick pink robe sitting on the sofa watching T.V. He could look at her whenever doing whatever—or doing nothing at all.

She was an angel living with a human, a divine presence who had deigned to stay with a mortal man.

You're gonna make me sick.

"Fuck off."

There was a small part of him—that wasn't the Wild One—that did have a little nauseous turn of the stomach. But that part knew this arrangement wouldn't last forever. She would leave. She would move on. She would eventually forget him. Everyone would forget how a geeky young man saved a beautiful goddess, how he took care of her for a time. How he did the right thing.

Unless...

He left the bedroom and went to his coat on a hook near the door. He rummaged in the internal pockets and found a business card: "WMOR-TV, Miranda Kelly, Special Interest Reporter." She had written her mobile number on the back.

With all the excitement on Thursday and dealing with the shock of it yesterday, John Paul hadn't had a chance to talk about this.

Miranda Kelly wanted to do an exposé on them, how his saving her from a sexual assault, and possibly death, had led to a relationship and romance. He didn't disabuse the reporter from her fantasy —one for which John Paul secretly hoped—because he knew that was the "special interest" angle of it all. He had a feeling Angelique would play along. She would see it as a little joke on the media and on everyone they knew.

Now that he thought of it, even his parents knew about Angelique staying with him. They had been proud, if not a little concerned, that he had stepped into a dangerous situation. If they only knew the whole truth. They even met Angelique a couple days after The Night.

If he and Angelique did this interview, and it played on "Baltimore's number one news source," the whole city, his parents, his classmates, Tio—everyone—would know about The Night and the hero.

John Paul dialed the number from his landline.

"This is Miranda Kelly, and you are John Wilkins."

He smiled. She had been expecting his call. "Yes, I am."

"Your girlfriend seemed a little out of sorts Thursday when I called. I'm glad you warned me to call her and not show up. Thanks."

John Paul almost corrected her, but instead said, "You can imagine she's still a little strung out about the whole thing."

"Yes. She told me to call her on Monday."

He got the distinct feeling she was working him. "I haven't had the chance to really talk to her about it, but I know she is game."

Three light knocks at the door.

He started toward it and said, "Listen, I have Monday off, so why don't you..." he looked out the peephole and saw Emily Florent, "...come by around eleven that morning, and we can have that interview."

"It will be more like a chat with a camera in your face." He could tell she meant it as a joke, but it came off a little abrasive. "Perhaps you two can show me what happened, since it occurred there behind your building."

"Gotta go, Miss Kelly."

There was an awkward silence. "Sure. You have my number if you need to contact me." She had definitely started the interview on the phone just now. "And please call me Mira. My friends all do."

"Goodbye, Mira." He hung up.

John Paul unlocked the door, and only half of Em and Em stood there. Smiling.

"Hello, John Paul." She continued to smile. "Mira... Kelly?"

He waved her in.

When he didn't say anything, she stepped through and added, "Mira and I went to high school together. Both of us were on the soccer team." John Paul took her coat. "She's very competitive—and very intelligent. She can get the Devil to give up the security code to the gates of Hell."

Given there was a psycho running around Baltimore who thought he was a vampire, John Paul didn't think that was funny.

Perhaps Emily didn't mean it to be.

As she walked into the living room, she said, "I don't believe you've ever taken my coat."

"This doesn't seem to be an official visit."

She sat on the far end of the sofa, almost asking him to sit next to her.

John Paul got that weird vibe again, like the one he had when she questioned him on The Night.

He did his best to be nonchalant and sat on the sofa.

Her face grew concerned. "Unfortunately, this is an official visit."

Unfortunately? John Paul found that interesting.

"Emmerich is at home sick." She dug into her purse and pulled out an envelope.

"Will this end?"

Emily looked at him. John Paul got the distinct impression she was going to say, *I hope not.* Not that she wanted innocents to be brutally murdered, or that she had a weird obsession with chasing psychos. He saw it in her eyes; she wanted to be here alone with him, face to face.

That weird vibe.

She replied, "Perhaps."

The weird vibe lifted with that one word, like emerging from a bumpy, scraping ride in a dark forest onto a sunlit paved road.

"You guys and your envelopes."

Emily smiled as she opened it. John Paul remembered that smile, a relaxed smile. The last time he had seen it was in the hospital cafeteria on The Night just before she got the text that Angelique had awakened.

"Yeah, well, some pics need protection."

John Paul responded, "Seems like we're the ones you've been protecting from *them.*"

Emily looked up from the photos she had removed from the envelope. "We have been working hard to find this freak." She added, "I can only bend the rules so far."

John Paul held up a hand and said, "No criticism from me, sorry. I was pointing out that you've kept a lot from the public to save us from the circus."

Her face softened a little. "If you talk to Mira, you're inviting the circus in."

"We'll be careful," John Paul said. "What did the wacko say this time?"

Emily placed a photo on the coffee table. "This is a much different scene than the others." It was of a woman in the back seat of a city bus. She had long brown hair like Angelique and appeared to be naked, lying across three seats. She had a long, black coat thrown over her, covering her face down to mid-thigh. "The bus driver didn't remember her boarding, and he had no riders at the last three stops on his run before pulling into the bus depot at one A.M. The cleanup crew found her around 2:30."

"Exsanguinated like the others?"

"Yes, and, like the others, somewhere else rather than where she was placed."

John Paul felt Emily was leaving out something important, but he didn't press her. "And the note?"

Emily shuffled through the photos and placed one on top of the other. It was of a note on a yellow sheet of legal paper, eight and a half by fourteen. The lettering was the same as the others but written with a stylus. John Paul could envision Anders dipping the pen into the bloody neck and writing…

My dearest A, I am heartily sorry for having offended thee. I detest all agony and misery I inflicted upon thy delicious soul because I dread the loss of Hell and the pains of Heaven. I firmly resolve to sin no more against thee, and I pledge to dedicate all future occasions of sin in thy name.

"A bastardizing bastard," John Paul reflected. "A warped Act of Contrition." He looked at Emily. "I hope it means what I think it means."

"This victim has no connection to Angelique's family or her church that we can find. The note is different, found in the breast pocket of the coat. This one is off from his schedule." Emily paused again, as if editing herself. "If this victim's random, and this is a show of contrition..." She let that hang.

"But if he disappears, won't that make it difficult for you to catch him?"

"We're hoping the Chesapeake Theatre lead from Diane Carlson gives us something. We have officers still going through security footage and purchase orders from the performances last month."

"Could be a wild goose chase."

Emily collected the photos and returned them to the envelope. She sat back and uncoiled. "I hope you're wrong." She seemed nervous about something. "Listen, Emmerich and I are not an official part of the homicide investigation. We're working Angelique's case as a potential rape, but homicide now wants to bring her into it. If her attacker is the Vampire Killer, and if the notes at the scenes are addressed to her—and they still have doubts—then you two will be brought into the circus, and you won't be able to avoid the press and public scrutiny."

She leaned forward and placed a warm hand on John Paul's arm. "And it sounds to me like Mira might have had a sniff of Angelique's connection to the murders. She's a bitch about pursuing a story, believe me. She says she's special interest, but that really means Mira's interest."

John Paul smiled. "She'll have her hands full with Ange."

Emily stood. "I'll have to return later to give all this to Angelique."

John Paul stood, too. "I'll get to see you twice in one day."

The blood drained from Emily's face like she'd been caught at something, and he again got the weird vibe from her.

She went to her coat.

They heard keys fumbling at the lock. John Paul opened the door, and there was Angelique.

"Hey, look who's here," he said and moved aside to let her through.

Emily had her coat on, and she gave a little half-smile to Angelique as John Paul took hers and hung it.

"Hello, Angelique. I was just telling John Paul that I'd have to come back to give this report."

Angelique looked at John Paul and back at Emily. She looked around for the other Em.

John Paul joined her at the sofa. "Emmerich is sick." He looked at Emily. "May I take your coat?"

Emily went through the report again. John Paul kept silent and let Angelique ask the questions as he usually did. When Emily brought up the investigation and the homicide detectives potentially connecting Angelique's attack to it, and the media circus that would erupt around them, John Paul used that as a segue into his call to Miranda Kelly.

Angelique said, "I'm glad you called her. If Anders is going to disappear, maybe a little media coverage around us and The Night might keep him interested a little while longer. Maybe he'll slip or make a mistake."

Emily nodded. "It's a long shot, but you need to be careful about what you know about the murders. That reporter is crafty and charming. If she believes you are connected to the Vampire Killer, she'll dog you until you make a mistake." She stood to leave. "That is a major reason why Emmerich and I have been the only investigators to come to you. If she has you under surveillance somehow, she'd know the difference between us and homicide."

"Or maybe," John countered, "she's just interested in, how did she put it, how love evolved out of danger and heroism."

Emily said her goodbyes and left. John Paul locked the door and turned to find Angelique right there.

"If she wasn't frothing at the mouth, then I've never seen a rabid dog."

John Paul laughed. "Have you?" He went past her to the fridge to get a beer. The weird vibe memory returned, and a little doubt about the nature of the visit blossomed.

"As a matter of fact, I have. My uncle had a dog go rabid, and it had to be put down." Angelique followed him to the kitchen.

As John Paul opened two beers, the Wild One came up to have his say, but he put that beast down with a big gulp. He handed the other beer to Angelique.

"Did you see her face when you mentioned love evolving from danger and heroism?"

He shrugged. "That was how that reporter put it to me. She even said as much when I talked to her earlier."

Angelique took a sip and added, "She implied I was a damsel in distress, and you were my hero."

"I didn't feel very heroic that night." John Paul remembered the two dark figures beside the building, how he wanted them to help and take the responsibility from him.

Angelique's face softened. "But you were. You are." She sipped the beer again. "I may have been his first victim were it not for you."

The Wild One appeared. *Do something! Say something! This is your chance!*

The humble gentleman in him struggled with what to say. "I was in the right place at the right time." He shrugged. "I did what anyone would do."

You're not an opportunist! the Wild One screamed. *You're a coward!*

John Paul took huge gulps from the rest of the beer and swallowed down the beast. *And stay down!* he added.

They ordered a pizza later and watched some reruns. During commercial breaks, they discussed her lunch with the Dean and her mother.

No surprises there. Whatever Diane Carlson wanted Diane Carlson received. Whenever Angelique wanted to return to school, she needed only to let the Dean know. An hour of eating and talking and it was taken care of.

Around eight o'clock, Angelique declared she was tired and went to the bathroom.

John Paul felt the Wild One come up, and he put it down—deep down.

He watched the bathroom door shut, and the hall became dark. Watching the bright line of light at the bottom of that door, he saw shadows move across it before the door opened and light flooded into the hall. He listened to her brush her teeth, the soft twang of the dental floss, and heard the brush glide through her hair. The sink handles squeaked again, and the water ran; he knew she was washing her beautiful face. She was using those strange pads to remove what little makeup she wore. He heard the palmfuls of water hit the basin as she rinsed. The handles squeaked, the water stopped, and the light turned off.

He looked at a commercial as a faint goddess passed by in his peripheral vision.

The bedroom door softly shut as a new episode started.

John Paul needed to watch some *Star Trek*. That would get his mind away from her. Something with action and battle. "Yesterday's Enterprise"—that's a good one. He searched through his cabinet to find *The Next Generation* season three.

"You know..."

John Paul jumped.

Angelique suppressed a giggle. She stood at the threshold of the bedroom in her robe. "I was thinking we need to be convincing to Miranda Kelly when she comes to see us on Monday."

The Wild One leapt into his mouth. "You mean that crazy little thing called love?"

Now she smiled, one of the biggest grins he'd ever seen on that dazzling face. "What's love got to do with it?"

Angelique undid the tie on the robe. The fold opened barely enough to see she was naked underneath. She moved into the dark of the bedroom.

John Paul didn't turn off the T.V. or the lights.

But he did shut the bedroom door behind him.

14

S unday turned out to be the calmest day she'd had in what
seemed an eternity—or at least since The Night.

They had gotten little sleep last night.

And she had to admit that being the "director" in bed had been
kind of fun. He was a fast learner. He definitely wasn't a virgin, but
he was indeed inexperienced—an eager pupil whose focus was on
her. That was interesting. He was intent on her pleasure, and she
told him exactly how to do it.

Angelique hadn't realized how selfish most of the men in her life
had been.

With J.P., however, he seemed to hunger more for her pleasure
rather than his own.

She smiled as she remembered when she had restarted the nickname. She could feel as his first orgasm tensed, and he fought to
control it like an animal in a cage. Then she said it: "Give it to me,
J.P." She knew he hated the nickname, and he let her know it. There
was a rage in his eyes, and she grabbed his face and met that rage,
eye to eye, and he let that animal out. And when she laughed and
told him not to stop, he let that animal continue to ravage her until
she finished.

Still holding his face, his sweat dripping between her fingers and down the backs of her hands, she pulled his mouth to hers and breathed the words, "Now, you are *my* J.P."

And he kissed her and growled. He *growled*. She knew right then there was something more to this man, something deep inside. She would have fun teasing it out.

Angelique laid in bed and smiled at that.

The phone in the living room rang.

Who's calling this early?

Angelique looked at the clock on John Paul's dresser. 10:12 A.M. It was later than she thought. Fuck it. The caller could leave a message if it was that important.

His voice activated: "Hello, if you're attempting to communicate with John Paul Wilkins, he is away on a mission. Please leave your name, number, and a brief transmission, and he'll return your communication as soon as possible. Make it so." *Beep.*

He was such a nerd.

"Hello, John, this is Mira. Just wanted to remind you and your friend that I'll be at your place with a camera crew tomorrow at eleven sharp like we discussed. See you then."

Friend? "What the fuck," she said aloud.

She sat up, and her exposed skin cooled, tingling. She shivered.

Like this is about him!

A wave of hot anger moved through her.

Angelique swept out of the sheets. Her feet hit the cold floor. She was surrounded by cold.

How long had he been gone? She wished she had looked at the clock when he had gotten out of bed to announce he was going to get some good coffee and bagels. The bakery was three blocks away. Busy time was over an hour ago; everyone wanted their bagels and muffins before going to church or whatever. He was probably on his way back, rushing—probably running—to get back before everything got cold.

She jumped up, grabbed her robe, went to the bathroom, and started the water for a hot shower.

The steam beckoned her to step in, but she was still hot from that call. She'd get in there soon enough.

If she played this right, she'd tease that animal even more.

What did Diane call it? *Poke the bear.*

She stood at the threshold to the bathroom and waited a few minutes.

The apartment door shut, and she stepped back into the bathroom out of sight. She heard the bag rustle. The microwave opened and closed but didn't start.

She heard a *beep.* Here it comes.

"Hello, John, this is—"

Beep-beep. Deleted.

Angelique leaned into the shower, grabbed her shampoo and conditioner, and placed them on the sink. She slipped into the hot waterfall, the heat making her anger hotter. She put her face into the spray and moved her hands through her hair to get it soaked.

She took a deep breath to steady herself. "John?" she called out. That'd get his attention. "Is that you?" She saw his shadow through the opaque glass.

"Hey, I'm back. Got the—"

"Be a sweetie and hand me my shampoo and conditioner. I don't know why I put them there." She slid open the door at the end away from the water and held out her hand. She didn't want him to hand them over the top of the glass wall.

He moved to the sink then to her hand.

As his hand with the two bottles appeared, she grabbed his arm and pulled him into the opening. His gray sweatshirt turned dark where she touched it. The bottles slipped out of his hand, clanking on the tub surface, tumbling behind her.

Shocked, he started to pull back from her, but she grabbed him with both hands and pulled harder. He nearly tumbled into the shower.

"You're on a first-name basis with *Mira?*" She shook his arm with each word.

He almost started to laugh until he saw the rage in her face.

"Listen—"

"No, *you* listen. You either step in here right now, or I'm dust in the wind."

He didn't hesitate, stepping over the tub and into the shower. His black sweatpants became darker.

"Does she know *your* nickname?" Angelique poked him twice in the chest as she answered her question. "J.P."

His face hardened.

There you are, she thought, grinning. "Now, take your shoes off before I take off your clothes." As she said that, she looked down.

His feet were bare.

"I'm not stupid," he growled and pushed her up against the cold wall, kissing her hard, his tongue seeking out hers.

Her body recoiled from the cold shock, and she pushed him away. "What the—"

His hands grabbed her head, pulling her mouth to his. Then his hands were all over her. She gasped, "My J.P."

He stopped. "Now take off my clothes."

She grinned as she untied his sweatpants.

15

When they watched it, John Paul could feel Angelique seething.

"Hometown Heroes" was a Friday segment on WMOR Action News at Six, featuring people giving back to the community, saving an animal, or helping an elderly neighbor in need.

John Paul had rarely paid attention to it. He only watched the news for the weather, which came on before Hometown Heroes. Once the weather was over, he was either getting ready to eat, getting ready to go to work, or getting ready to watch one of his shows, usually one of the incarnations of *Star Trek*.

Until Angelique began staying with him.

They watched the news every night looking for anything on the Vampire Killer they didn't know—which was little to nothing. They also watched for Angelique's name to be associated with the murders. They were relieved each night. And they ignored the Hometown Hero segment.

Except this week.

On Monday, John Paul tried his best to ensure the news team went to Alternatives. He led them to the alley where the feral dog had growled at Angelique, walked them along the road leading to their building, and let them examine the place where the attack had occurred. John Paul had even parked his car in the exact spot as that night.

Despite his best attempts, Miranda Kelly told the story of a nerdy young man with an unrequited infatuation for the girl upstairs, how he had saved her from a sexual predator, and how his courage that night sparked a love affair. It made Angelique look like a helpless child—which was what John Paul had wanted to avoid.

She had spoken with some of the others in the building and even with Tio who had mentioned again how when someone saves another's life, the savior is responsible for that person. The only person that was spared her scrutinizing gaze was Tom, for some reason.

Ms. Kelly—there was no more "Mira" after the exposé. She must have thought it was cute.

But he was pissed off.

Angelique was like a matchstick, however, flaring briefly before burning low and finally extinguishing. Her reaction was nothing like he had expected.

John Paul turned off the T.V.

They sat on the sofa.

"Do you think the vampire saw this?"

He wanted to correct her: *Vampire Killer*.

"We haven't heard from Em and Em this week. Maybe that—whatever it was—that note with the last victim was the end of it. I'm just glad we avoided the circus."

"And the danger."

John Paul looked for relief in her face. He saw disappointment. "You want him to keep killing?"

Her nostrils flared, her lips thinned, and her cheeks blushed. "I want them to catch it! They have to catch it! I have to see it."

John Paul realized she had doubts, too. She wanted to believe what she saw. She wanted to believe in vampires. She had named it, and she didn't want to be wrong. She wanted the world to be wrong. The alternative, for her, was unthinkable.

Her next words proved him wrong.

Angelique reached to his hand—something she had never done before. She needed him. To be present and to listen.

It scared him.

He squeezed Angelique's hand like he had done on The Night, when she was on the stretcher about to be loaded into the ambulance. This time, a little part of him, an antithesis of the Wild One, whispered he didn't want to hear this. He was still on calm waters despite all that had been happening, but she was about to take him into rapids, maybe worse.

She looked into his eyes, and she hesitated.

This was a revelation, an opening of her heart.

John Paul squeezed her hand again.

Angelique must have seen what she needed to see in his eyes, for she took a hitched breath and began.

"That Night, when we bumped into each other—" she stopped and shook her head. "No, nearly all my life." She closed her eyes. This was something painful for her to say.

John Paul's heart opened. He wrapped his left hand around hers, his warm hands cradling her cool one. He tried to have his hands say what he wanted to say aloud, fearing any sound from him would break this delicate moment.

I'm here. Always.

She took another breath and said, "There are shadows in my life. Real, physical things—to me. At first, when I was a child, they were on the periphery, in a corner, under the bed. Then they started to touch me." She shuddered. "Like a soft caress, like cold feathers." She looked down. "My parents thought something was wrong with me. They sent me to specialists. Shrinks."

She continued to look at John Paul's hands. He maintained the message, *I'm here.*

Angelique's eyes returned to him. As she squeezed his hand, she smiled.

The Wild One came up, pushing down that weakness, and whispered, *This is it, Johnny Boy. Fear is the food of courage. Let's dine.* Where had he heard that before?

He couldn't waste another thought on that. He needed to stay *here.*

So, he didn't smile back. He was ready to accept her fear, these next moments, her past, her present. Everything. He leaned forward, just an inch. His entire body said, *Share it all with me, beloved.*

And she did. All of it. Like a confession, as if he were the first person ever to listen to her, to hear her. Perhaps he was the only soul to hear her soul.

She told him about toys disappearing from her bedroom then reappearing in the living room.

She told him how they pulled her hair, how their fuzzy cold poured into her mouth, how they pinched her when she went to junior high dances, forcing her to go home early from any social event or gathering.

She told him how they chose her friends in high school, only leaving her alone when she hung out with the bad boys and slutty girls.

John Paul felt she avoided saying, *And I became bad and slutty.*

She ended with their encounter on The Night.

"They hadn't really bothered me much when I came to Johns Hops. But when I moved into this building, they started showing themselves more, as if to tell me they weren't too happy with being here." She looked at their embraced hands again. "That evening as I was coming down the stairs, they assaulted me—like the one time..." She faded into a memory. She squeezed her eyes to push out something she didn't want to share. "It was like I couldn't get out of the building fast enough. Then you were there." She looked into his eyes again, searching. "They wouldn't have come outside into the twilight. But you," she looked over his face, "I now know they fled when the door opened to you."

John Paul squeezed a little harder. He wanted to say something, but it still felt delicate. He was afraid he'd say something stupid. The Wild One agreed.

"And in that alley outside of Alternatives. I felt something for a moment. Then the dog... and he—*it*—was there. And later—" Angelique took a heavy breath, her free hand moving to her neck.

John Paul held to the other: *I'm here.*

She looked back to his eyes. "I was inside the shadow with it for a moment. That vampire *is* my shadows."

She watched his face when she said *vampire.*

He stayed in the moment. *Still here.*

She seemed relieved. "It saw *you*. It wasn't the light from your car. It was you." She pulled him to her, and their lips touched. She finished, "It fled *you*, and it hasn't been back since."

She kissed him deeply. She moved into his arms.

He felt like he needed to say something, but no words would come. Was this the cowardice of which the Wild One always accused him? The beast was silent.

Angelique whispered into his ear, "You're the only one." He felt her breath against his neck. "Yes," she confirmed, "my parents, my doctors, my friends—no one knows but you, John Paul Wilkins." She moved to look him in the eye and grinned. "My, J.P." She kissed him again before he could respond.

She stood, her hand lingering on his cheek. "I'm going to the bathroom. There's still some wine left."

He wanted more than wine.

When the door to the bathroom clicked shut, he got up and found the bottle of sweet red wine on the counter and grabbed two wine glasses. As he poured some into one of the glasses, the dark red rose like—

Blood.

—Angelique's words rose with it: *It hasn't been back since.*

It—her vampire, her shadow—whatever it was, it hadn't haunted her since The Night, but the Vampire Killer had been tormenting the city.

And the implication of that hit John Paul like a big fist in his chest.

If it fled him, if, somehow, he'd kept it away from her, then could these murders have happened because of him?

Did he believe any of this?

Angelique did. And she'd unburdened herself on him, expecting him to take off running—probably like some had in her past.

Still here.

He emptied the bottle into the second glass. The first had a little more, so he took a sip to even them out.

"Not fair," she said from behind him. Her arms encircled him;

her chin weighed on his left shoulder. She released him so he could turn to face her.

She was naked.

He smiled. "*That's* not fair."

"Really..." She opened her mouth, and he put one of the glasses to it and gently poured a little wine.

"Even."

She swallowed. "Not even close."

She turned, and like the regal goddess she was, she flowed to the bedroom.

Whatever John Paul had been thinking turned to smoke. He moved through it with two glasses of wine and became her adoring worshiper.

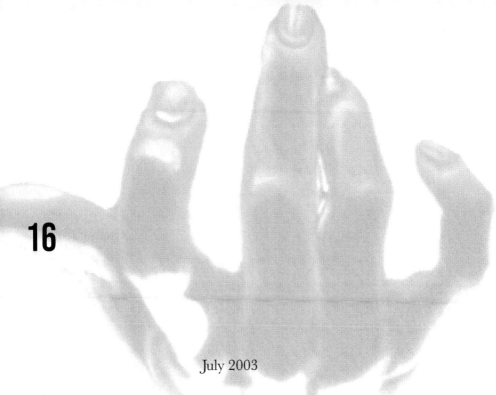

16

July 2003

Angelique had been in this pathetic apartment with John Paul Wilkins for nine months. She still paid for her own apartment upstairs, but she wanted a new place. Their place. If she was going to live with him, they had to get a bigger place. Besides, the landlord had been dropping hints about raising rents. She had been wasting money on her apartment for far too long.

It was time to get out, get away from this building, get away from the dorks who lived here. Get away from the memories.

She needed new memories to bury the old ones.

Everything around her played on her mind, like a little whisper, like a shadow on the periphery of her life.

When Tom downstairs had said casually a few weeks back the bulb at the back porch had burned out again, she heard *Hello, Tinkerbell.*

One of the few times she had decided to walk to the store three blocks away, she had stood at the top of the stairwell and looked down. She felt the cold, fuzzy touch of the shadows.

She couldn't even walk out back to John Paul's car. She'd see the narrow, shadowed alley, the hard wall. She'd feel that cold touch...

see those long fangs. She'd have J.P. bring the car around to the front and come up the stairs to meet her at the landing.

Everyone in the building looked at her with pity.

It made her sick.

She was tired of living here.

So, Angelique began devising a war plan. She knew it would be a war with J.P. He was a creature of habit. He put things in the same place, and he knew the timing of every move to and from the few places he needed to go. He got perturbed when someone parked in his spot in the back lot. He told her he put an emergency cone in his parking spot at work when he left. And he expected to see her smiling face when he came home from work.

What was it one of her professors had said? A quote by Henry Brooks Adams: "Chaos breeds life when order breeds habit."

Since his graduation and the start of his management job at the Highlight Hotel, J.P.'s life had become too ordered—and Angelique had allowed it. For a time after The Night, order had been necessary.

But another word for order is *boring*.

Time for some chaos.

Time to move.

She thought she would be clever talking about their emancipation from this place on Independence Day—to throw off their old way of life and start anew, to find a nice place and move in together.

There was dinner. Angelique paid special attention to how they moved about in the kitchen. It was like a dance: J.P. putting cheese on the garlic bread and sliding the cookie sheet into the oven; Angelique draining the pasta, putting it back into the pot, and pouring the sauce over it; they switched places so that the pasta could be warmed on the stove, and J.P. could start to cut cukes and peppers for the salad. She watched him closely to ensure it all moved smoothly.

She didn't normally care about such things, but she wanted a subconscious rhythm in J.P. when a new home was brought up later.

When they finished eating, they watched a movie, Angelique drinking her red wine, J.P. his beer. They curled up together on the sofa, his warm arms around her. They weren't even thirty minutes into the movie when fireworks across the city started popping and booming away. She told him she wanted to make their own fireworks.

And they did. And she was very explosive.

As they lay in bed, wet and warm and floating in the atmosphere of the room, she laid out her arguments. Memories and shadows and a darkness that reminded her daily of how close she had come to dying. How could she move past The Night if she was unceasingly reminded of it? She lived in a constant state of fear, especially of the dusk. The shadow time. He was the only thing in all of this that was right, one bright, colorful piece in a kaleidoscope of blacks and grays.

Angelique had been especially proud of that image.

Silence. He was thinking. That was good.

She snuggled into his arms, sweat tingling as it evaporated, making the room humid. She knew he had to feel it, too. It felt almost magical, as if their sex had cast a spell around them.

She breathed into his ear, "We spend all this money on two places, my J.P. Two crappy places. Why be together but apart in our accommodations? I don't want to be roommates anymore."

He took a breath. Here it comes. "I think we can conclude from our situation that we aren't just roommates." She was still. He took another breath.

"What you propose is more than—"

More than you realize.

Angelique put a finger on his lips to stop what she knew he was going to say.

She kissed his cheek, and his arm pulled her closer. She said, "We don't need to make any decisions right now. Just think about it."

Angelique knew exactly what she was asking—and what he was saying.

He had been in love with her from the first moment he saw her. The day she moved into this building. They *all* fell in love with her. They couldn't help it. They didn't know what to do about her. She had thrown off their pathetic geeky rhythm. She had become their chaos. They all fumbled and stumbled their hellos and watched her with pathetic eyes. And J.P.? He had been the worst of them.

He just now confirmed to her what she knew already: He was afraid of her, afraid she'd consume his love and chew up his heart.

Angelique knew she needed to guide him to make the leap.

A week later was the night of Jarrod Jambotti's party, celebrating his becoming co-owner of Alternatives. Among the guests were all of The Gang including Lauren, who had made a fool of herself a couple months ago after making a pass at J.P.

Angelique had crushed her and sent the girl running. The bitch had to go ruining the one time she had gone out—which played into Angelique getting her hooks into J.P. even more.

Tonight, however, it was Bartender Steve who had engaged the field of battle.

Why did her so-called friends have to make things difficult?

Steve had made Angelique a dirty martini, and he was in the middle of J.P.'s 7 and 7. He gave her a knowing look, like he and she were in on a little secret.

J.P. watched Angelique take a small sip. He looked incredulous and grinned. "Really? You pass on olives all the time." He looked at Steve and said, "Olives, dill pickles, pepperoncinis..."

She took another sip and smiled. "I just like saying I'm drinking something dirty." She leaned to J.P.'s ear and whispered, "Besides, I do like pickles—if they're sweet and big."

He blushed.

Then Steve asked, "So when're you two gonna finally get out of that tiny place and move in together?" He had that knowing grin on his face again like he already knew the answer to the question.

For a moment, Angelique's mind blanked when she saw the look J.P. gave her: anger and even betrayal. He believed she had set this up, to get an old lover to manipulate him. But she was more subtle —and physical—than stooping to something like this. He had to know that, too. Then it came to her...

Angelique slipped an arm around J.P.'s and sweetly replied, "Oh, it's come up, but we're taking things slow and steady." She put her head on his shoulder for emphasis.

Steve handed J.P. his drink and shook his head confused. "Wow," he said, "the new and improved Angelique. Gotta hand it to you, John. You've tamed what we had all thought was untamable."

She remembered playing horseshoes with her uncle—long ago and far away—and getting her first ringer. J.P.'s look of dumbfounded admiration felt like that.

She downed the dirty martini. *Winner.*

A week later, she had lunch with her mother, and it started pleasant enough—the usual barrage of small-talk.

"How are you feeling? Are you eating enough? You look thinner. How is John? How is his new job? Is he taking care of you?"

Then the little volcano bubble started to form.

"I see you're still paying for your apartment."

When the waiter brought their meals, both had ordered grilled salmon and salad, Angelique ordered a double margarita over ice, no salt.

"It's been a few months now, Angel," Diane said as sweetly as she could.

The new and improved Angelique kept a lid on the eruption. She let the volcano bubble build. "Actually, *Mother,* J.P. and I have been talking about our relationship lately." She let that melt over the bubble as she took a sip of her drink.

And she got the reaction she wanted from Diane.

First, Diane didn't like the nickname, and she wasn't used to her daughter using the word *relationship.* That was like being led into an unlit room. In this, mother and daughter were alike. They both needed to see the terrain of the battlefield. Diane didn't like being blind.

She looked up and stopped chewing her mouthful of salmon.

"That's right, *Mother,*" Angelique said, looking Diane straight in the eyes, "J.P. and I have been together for quite a few months." She looked to the side, feigning consideration. "You know, *Mother,* this is the longest relationship I've ever had—outside of you and daddy." She took a sip of her margarita.

Daddy had been one of those explosive words. Even thinking about him at this moment picked at the scab of his wound on her heart. But she was the new and improved Angelique. This wasn't a time for explosions.

Their pleasant lunch, as usual, had become hot and acrid.

Angelique let the volcano bubble percolate, lava oozing over them.

Smiling and relishing her mother's bewilderment, she said, "We're thinking about moving in together."

Diane swallowed her bite. She forced a smile. "That's nice to hear, Angel."

The lava burned through the food, the drinks, the table —everything.

Angelique could see Diane wanted to say more—a lot more— but the woman was afraid of her daughter at the moment.

Diane picked at her plate. Silent.

"How is everything?" the waiter interrupted. "Is there anything you two need?"

Angelique smiled and replied, "Yes, I need to leave. Can you box this up, please?"

Later that evening, as she watched J.P. eat half of the salmon with tortilla chips and salsa while she had the other half and the salad, she wondered briefly if she should have told him the truth of the lunch encounter with Diane. She gave him the usual platitudes when it came to talking about her, and he was respectful enough to let it be. But when he asked why Angelique had left without eating the meal, she had the brilliant idea of diverting an issue she knew had been playing in quite a few people's minds.

"Diane," she answered J.P. as he scooped up a large glob of salsa with a chip, "as usual, said something that pissed me off." He followed the bite with a swig of beer, eyes intent on her. "She asked if I have considered seeing a shrink."

J.P. froze.

There. He's been thinking it, too.

This little lie would last her a while with him.

That night she had her first nightmare that wasn't about The Night.

Angelique jumped out of bed, bile rising in her throat.

She barely made it to the bathroom before vomiting on the floor and across the closed toilet lid. She slipped and fell to her knees, catching herself on the sink. She puked on the toilet again before she could get it open. She heaved violently, as if her body were trying to force out the nightmarish images from somewhere deep in her belly.

When all that was left was her body trembling, she felt John Paul's warm hand rubbing her back. She felt empty, physically and emotionally. Intellectually, she was fully aware of how he helped her up and out of her nightie, how he guided her into the shower. With his own pajamas still on, he bathed her with hot water and her cucumber melon body wash.

She closed her eyes as he dried her and half-carried her to the bed. She didn't want to see the pity in his face. He gently tucked her in.

Yet, she couldn't sleep. She could feel the nightmare there, just behind her.

Like a shadow.

And she didn't know what part of the dream terrified her more: that she had mutilated her mother and lathered blood all over herself—or that she had loved every second of it.

17

John Paul looked out the peephole and considered not answering the door.

Detective Emily Florent stood out there, and she was alone again.

It wasn't that he was afraid of her or what she had to say.

Angelique would be back soon. And Angelique had all of—he turned back to the living room—*that* all over the place.

That was an array of nighties, lingerie, panties, and bras laying across the seat and back of the sofa, bikinis laying across the coffee table, thongs and such covering the chair. Other clothes lay on the kitchen table and chairs.

Three more knocks startled him.

Now that he thought about it, he might be a little afraid of Angelique finding Emily alone with him in the apartment.

She had taken to calling the detective a little shit-fly. Just between him and her, of course. To Emily's face, Angelique was cordial and considerate. But Angelique had lately become sensitive to the detective visiting to give progress reports about the investigations. Not that there had been much to report for over a month now. John Paul had wondered why Emily or Emmerich couldn't just call.

He even said as much aloud to Angelique. That was when she

explained about how shit-flies couldn't help but to be attracted to piles of shit.

Angelique went into a calm but edged discussion about how women swirled around him because of that "Godforsaken news story" on WMOR: Hometown Hero. As she continued, her voice became sharper, more sarcastic, describing how girls and women shook his hand for saving her.

"Fucking flies fucking hovering every-fucking-where."

"So, you're calling me a pile of shit?" he had asked defensively.

But she kissed him and replied, "You're *my* pile of shit."

"That makes you a fly."

She laughed. "Oh, no. I'm a pile of shit, too."

John Paul had to admit that he hadn't really noticed women "hovering" until Angelique had pointed it out.

And the worst of all the shit flies, Angelique had declared, was the Em-shit-fly. She came a-calling every week, which was bad enough, but when she appeared last May with the other Em at John Paul's graduation, and two days later at his party at Corazon's, Angelique growled into his ear that she needed a flyswatter.

And that night in bed, as she reminded him that he was her pile of shit, she warned him that no flies were allowed to *land* on her pile of shit.

There had been a lot of talk about shit and flies back in May.

Angelique was a stack of enigmas. The first was the "why" of her appearing in this den of geeks, this apartment building. He remembered hearing a few of the guys make theories, but there was no clear answer. Even Angelique herself didn't know why she chose this place. It was the first available place when she looked, she had told him a while back.

The next was The Night and her belief in this vampire fellow—and his connection to her through the murders. And, on top of that, the weird way the homicide detectives refused to make a clear connection between Angelique's attack, the Vampire Killer, and the notes he left.

John Paul was a fantasist of sorts, but only as a literary enthusiast. He liked a good supernatural horror story, but he didn't *believe* in creatures of the night. Even if one didn't believe in vampires, one had to see the links between Angelique and Anders. It wasn't that big of a leap. It was a huge enigma in the back of John Paul's mind.

Then there was her staying with him. Really, he believed she would have been gone after a week or two. She had her own security; some of them were outside now. Yet, she had told him—told everyone—that John Paul Wilkins kept her safe, like he was some kind of talisman that kept the "shadows" away.

Angelique Carlson was the most beautiful woman he had ever seen. She could have any man she wanted (and perhaps had done so in some respects), but she chose to stay with him, chose to be with him, chose to allow him to worship her. He smiled at the idea of carnal knowledge, but she had yielded more than her body. She had told him secrets, given him *Angelique knowledge*.

And he looked at some of that knowledge spread across the living room and kitchen.

John Paul turned to the door. As he reached to the knob to open it, he heard—

"It's Detective Florent." Angelique had that edge to her voice. "What a surprise." She went over the edge and into sarcasm, which said to John Paul: *Has the Em-fly come to hover over my shit again?*

John Paul looked through the peephole and saw the side of Emily's head. She half-smiled and said, "Miss Carlson."

The use of formalities told him they knew where each other stood. This could get ugly. He opened the door. They looked at him.

"Ah, J.P., look who's come to see us."

Emily's impassive face looked at Angelique. "I've come to speak to you."

The faint sarcastic humor that had lit Angelique's face darkened.

Something was going on here, and John Paul had no idea where it was going. So, he stammered, "No Emmerich?" As soon as he said it, he saw the "Told ya" look in Angelique's eyes.

Emily smiled at him and replied, "Just me, I'm afraid."

"Don't be an ass, J.P. Let us in. The detective obviously has something to tell us."

He didn't want to. He didn't want to let the detective in and let her see what was going on, but both Emily and Angelique pushed by. He shut the door and decided right then to keep his mouth shut.

Emily stopped when she got to the living room.

Angelique had had one of the security guards take her to the mall to get a couple things. She set her shopping bag next to the coffee table. "We're going to the beach for a much-needed vacation." She suppressed a grin, but she shot John Paul a look that said, *My pile of shit.*

Emily stood at the corner of the entry hall and the living room, surveying the arsenal of seduction.

John Paul went past her and into the kitchen. "Anyone want a drink?" He tried to sound normal, like this display was out like this all the time. No big deal.

Emily said, "No thanks. I can't stay long." She looked at Angelique. "I'm glad you two are getting away. You both need it."

Angelique moved around the coffee table and pointed to the bras, lingerie, and nighties on the seat of the sofa. "I can clear this off—"

"No really. Don't bother. I—"

"We're heading to Sandbridge Beach in a couple days." When Emily didn't say anything, she continued, "Lazy days in the sun and crazy nights." Angelique's arm swept over the arsenal to emphasize *nights.*

Emily fidgeted with the button of her right sleeve cuff. She looked up and said, "Listen, Angelique, we have come to a wall in both investigations. Homicide," Emily shook her head, "won't embrace a connection between your assault and the murders. They are still pursuing the killer, but resources for your sexual assault case are being redirected. It's like this man showed up for a couple months in Baltimore then disappeared."

"You mean vampire," Angelique corrected. She looked at Emily, challenging the detective to contradict her.

Emily looked down. "Whatever or whoever this Anders Saffenssen is, there's been no trace or leads for months." She looked from John Paul to Angelique. "We have to put your case on the back burner until new evidence comes up." She looked miserable. "I'm sorry."

Angelique looked from Emily to John Paul then back. "I see. So, you just give up?"

John Paul and Emily heard that question differently. John Paul heard it as Angelique claiming victory. Emily heard it as a challenge to her profession.

Emily winced. She wasn't used to these kinds of conversations. "If something comes up in either case, you'll be the first I call." She stepped back into the entry hall. "I'm sorry about this."

Defeated, Emily left. The door clicked shut.

Angelique shook her head. "Sorry you won't have a legit reason to come flying around."

"C'mon, Ange—"

"C'mon what? She couldn't look at you. You're as much a part of the investigation as I am."

"It happened to *you*."

She pointed to the direction of the back lot. "Right back *there!*"

John Paul moved to her and hugged her tightly. Perhaps she was right. Perhaps this place had too many bad memories, too many shadows.

He remembered her nightmare a few nights ago. This whole thing was gnawing at her.

The beach would be the perfect escape for them.

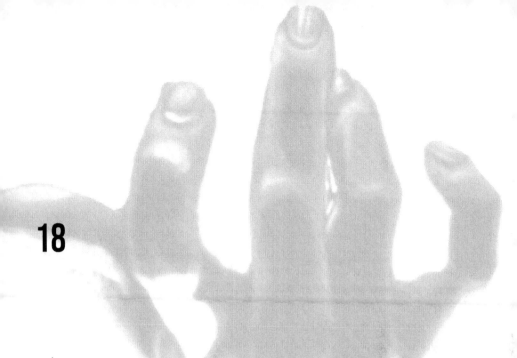

18

A ngelique likes these games. Part of it is the chase—and the screaming at the end. She imagines she can feel the sound of that scream enter her ears and travel through her body to her belly. An appetizer before the main meal. A larger part of it is the rush of blood down her throat, mixing with that scream. What a delight!

But there's the annoying little bit of her that is appalled at the outcome. It doesn't want to see the inside of another body, doesn't want to see her hands dig into the sternum and rip it open, doesn't want to feel the patter of bright blood on her dead skin, doesn't want to feel the slavering darkness within her rise up—and it certainly doesn't want her to put her face into the gaping chest filling with blood.

Angelique pushes that annoying little bit of her down into hole, an oubliette of the mind.

The quarry makes a quick turn down an alley, her feet making clacking sounds echoing off the brick walls.

Angelique *flies*, a great wind swirling around her, lifting her. She feels the darkness within her push out like invisible wings, touching the walls, the pavement, throwing trash and debris up and over her.

The quarry is…just there…just out of reach…blond hair…

Lauren?

Angelique forced herself to wake.

Still sitting up in the bed, she felt a scream rise like vomit, and she slapped a hand over her mouth. She swallowed it, but she felt the pressure of it in her belly, clawing to come up.

She looked beside her. John Paul was gone.

Hand still over her mouth, she looked to the bedroom door. It was open. The faint light from under the closed bathroom door across the hall lit the floor.

Angelique felt the air cool the sweat over her naked body. She thought she had gone to bed with pajamas on. When did she take them off? Did she have sex? Angelique couldn't remember anything before the dream…the hunger…the blond hair.

She shivered.

The commode flushed.

Angelique, hand still over her mouth, lay back and pulled the sheet up. She turned on her side, facing away from J.P.'s side of the bed.

The light went off, and it became darker. A little panic tried to move up her throat. She heard the bathroom door open. A shadow entered the room, but floorboards creaked, moving around the bed. She felt John Paul's weight ease onto the bed. He tried his best to be gentle, getting comfortable under the sheets.

His naked body spooned against hers. Heat radiated from him as his arm encircled her. His hand cupped her breast. She felt her body absorb his heat, and it calmed her. The clawing in her stomach faded.

The fucking birds woke her that morning, a cacophony of chirps and whistles and flapping wings, a morning performance just outside the window to welcome her to a new day. Bright light outlined the drapes. She remembered today was Saturday.

They were leaving for the beach on Monday.

Angelique lay loosely in J.P.'s embrace, his soft snore contrasting with his stiff cock that poked her ass. But he was like that often, and she liked that she could push him quickly to his back and sit upon him and ride as he woke. By the time he matched her rhythm, she was coming. Sometimes she'd get lucky and he'd stay hard after his explosion and she'd come again.

She did exactly that, both of them smiling a "good morning" when they finished.

She chuckled when he pushed her away to run to the bathroom to piss. Men and their morning piss. They could piss twice throughout the night and still have to run to the bathroom when they woke.

Angelique followed him into the bathroom to brush her teeth, and she smiled as he eyed her naked body. She knew what she had, and she knew how to use it. She continued to smile as her breasts grazed against his back as she moved to the shower. She bent provocatively to turn on the water, nice and hot. She could feel his eyes on her and suppressed a smile.

She noticed the nearly empty bottle of shampoo. "Be a dahling," she said, affecting a rich bitch tone, "and fetch me a new bottle of shampoo."

She felt him bow when he replied, "As you command."

Angelique stepped into the shower and let the heat soak into her face and down her chest—like J.P.'s body—filling her like an empty glass.

That heat expanded on her head when soapy hands massaged her scalp, moving down through her long hair and massaged her shoulders.

She let out a hitched sigh, like a knot becoming untangled.

Her back and ass warmed when J.P.'s body pressed against her.

How could he be hotter than this water?

Something told her he wasn't finished with his good morning.

And because of this good morning, she let down her guard.

John Paul was in the bathroom getting ready for work. Since he was a new employee and hadn't accrued enough time for vacation, he had struck a deal with Andrew, the hotel owner, to work this weekend and Labor Day weekend to get the time for the beach trip.

Angelique would have played the trauma card and not sacrificed any weekends, but she knew that kind of manipulation wasn't possible with J.P. So, while he was flossing his teeth, she looked through the hall closet and found his little luggage case.

She chuckled. He hadn't been anywhere outside of the Baltimore area, probably even Maryland. She could see him washing all his clothes before going home and filling this little thing with a couple sets to wear for a weekend.

Now that she thought of it, J.P. didn't go home much at all. The two of them had only gone to his home once in all the time she had been with him. Angelique had felt the tension between all of them. She knew there was an old conflict about the family business, that it was water under the bridge with J.P. it had been and was still raw with the elder Wilkins.

She loved how the tension turned to shock when he introduced her as his girlfriend. She had met them a few days after The Night and remembered being relieved when they had agreed their son should take care of her. It was obvious that they didn't expect a relationship to develop. But to be introduced as his girlfriend? Their faces. At that moment, Angelique had wanted to correct him and say *lover*, but she held her tongue.

Angelique looked at that little luggage case. Not good enough.

She had two up in her room that would be perfect.

When he came out of the bathroom to get a bite to eat before leaving, she had his case on a kitchen chair.

"This just won't do for two. I have one a little larger," Angelique told him. "Since we don't need to take much," she held up a bikini bottom, "it should suffice."

He crunched on a piece of buttered toast. He had already picked out his clothes and left them in a neat pile on the bed. All basic guy stuff. But as he looked at the arsenal throughout the room, she smiled.

"You didn't think I was going to take *all* of this?" She grabbed his hand with the toast, guided it to her mouth, and slowly crunched a small piece. "You don't need much to wear at the beach or in bed." She took another small bite. "Trust me."

John Paul took a swig of orange juice. His smile said more than any words could. He gave her a kiss then left.

She spent the next hour or so choosing the precise weapons she needed from her arsenal. She placed them next to his pile before she put the other clothes away.

Now to get her luggage. She also wanted to check her messages.

Angelique hadn't been up to her room for a while, and like she imagined, it was dusty and dank and dark. She stood in the open doorway and listened. She looked into the shadows. She wished she had opened the drapes of the window in the living room the last time she had been here. Sunlight would have been pouring into the apartment right now.

A little fear turned in her belly. It had been a long time since she had seen...

"Just get it over with," she whispered.

She hurried into the apartment and went straight to her bedroom, found the luggage case she wanted, and brought it out to the still-open door. It usually closed on its own. It probably needed some lube or something. At this point, she didn't care. She was glad it was open. Placing the luggage between the door and the threshold, she went to her answering machine and checked the indicator. No messages. A little part of her was disappointed. She had lost everyone since The Night.

She shivered. Angelique thought of calling Diane when the phone rang. She jumped.

She picked up the phone but didn't say anything.

After a moment: "Hello? Angel?"

Diane.

And with that voice, an image of her bloody hands inside the chest of her mother overwhelmed her.

She gasped.

Shit!

"Angel, is that you?"

Shadows!

Why hadn't she opened the windows? But as soon as she thought that, she realized it didn't matter.

Her hands were dark and sticky.

A pungent smell of blood filled her nostrils.

Her nightmare was a shadow—and it was inside her! Was she becoming a shadow?

Angelique thumbed the off button and dropped the phone.

She swallowed down the bile burning her throat.

Something moved in her hair. On her leg.

She shivered again.

He was here! Her shadow! *Anders!*

"Oh, God!" she choked and tripped toward the door, an end table kept her up.

She looked to her leg where he'd touched her. A bloody mark, like three fingers, went across her thigh just above her knee.

She looked around for his shadow.

A bloody handprint appeared on her upper arm.

Her own hands dripped with blood!

Was she touching herself or was it *him?*

A hand grabbed her hair again, pulling.

Angelique twisted around the corner and into the little hall to the door.

It was closed.

A scream clawed up from her belly.

The slick blood on her hands made the doorknob slippery. She had to get out!

She pulled the door open, tripping over the luggage. She landed on it.

The door slammed shut.

Angelique flipped over, her back to the floor.

Her hands were clean. No bloody marks.

She heard a door click shut down the hall.

She wanted to scream, *Fuck you!* but she was afraid to open her mouth. That other scream was just there, behind her teeth—and hot vomit beyond that.

The shadow within roiled about in her belly. It compressed her heart.

The nightmare was still with her—inside her.

She breathed deeply through her nose. Out through her nose. She did that two more times.

Her heart felt better.

She looked herself over again.

Clean.

What the fuck?

She stood, grabbed the luggage case, and sprinted down the steps to J.P.'s room.

Stupid! Stupid! Stupid!

Her eyes burned. Her vision swam.

Stupid! Stupid!

She reached for the doorknob—the door swung open and *he* was there!

She screamed!

Warm arms embraced her. "Sorry, babe," he whispered. "Sorry."

She dropped the case and embraced him.

His brightness and heat dissipated the shadows. He held her face between his hot hands. God, they felt good. He looked into her eyes and said, "If you had told—"

Angelique pulled him to her again, her lips on his hot neck. How could he be this hot and not feel it? "I'm just—" the words choked in her throat.

"Hey, I have good news." He guided her into their apartment.

"Why?" she asked, stopping. "Why are you here?" She couldn't let go of his hand.

He smiled as he peeled her hand from his. He reached out to the hall and retrieved the luggage case. "That's the good news. Drew let me have the weekend." He shut the door behind him. "Let's pack and get out of here."

He went to the bedroom.

Yes, she thought, *permanently*.

19

October 2003

John Paul had thought moving into this small house would solve the problems he saw growing in Angelique: the jealousy about flies hovering over shit (let alone referring to him as a pile of shit), the violent dreams (she *had* to tell him about them), the increase in alcohol (he liked a beer or two most evenings, but she had started drinking tequila)—

And the sex. That was the most ironic thing of all. For a guy who had stumbled through one sexual encounter before Angelique, lately he had begun to think there was the possibility of having too much sex.

She'd find him hard in the mornings and purr, "You're soooo predictable," and have at it, like he was crack and she was—

John Paul liked a good fuck, too, but *every morning?* And *every night?* It was like she had to have an orgasm or two to start the day and at least one at night before sleep.

He felt guilty thinking this, but there just wasn't any *love* in it anymore.

She was like all his dreams had come true. This beautiful goddess came into his life, he saved her, they fell in love.

She had told him she loved him at the beach. When he showed

her this place, she jumped into his arms, hugged him tightly, and whispered in his ear, "I love you so much." They told each other "I love you" all the time. They held hands like a couple. She wasn't embarrassed to kiss him in public. They cuddled.

And he loved her. God, he loved her. He could look at her and think: *If I died right now, I'd be happy with that last vision.* Sometimes she'd catch him just looking at her.

"What?"

"You."

"Me what?"

"You and me and this place."

And before he could say more, she'd say grinning, "And our bed."

But that wasn't what he was going to say. He'd open his mouth to say, "I'm so blessed," and she'd cut him off: "I'm the one who's lucky."

It was a routine. They did some variation of this at least once a week.

Yes, he loved her.

But there were little problems.

John Paul likened them to cramps in his leg. The little ones where he could rub deeply and get it out. They'd go away, but he knew they would come back.

Yet, there was no denying he loved her.

And, just maybe, he was addicted to her, too.

John Paul had hoped—prayed—that moving into this little house would be the answer to the problems.

Andrew Peterson, the owner of the Highlight Hotel and his boss, had the awesome news when he returned to work after the vacation. His grandmother had died nearly a year ago, and he had reservations about letting just anyone stay in the house. Andrew hadn't even considered the couple until John Paul had mentioned Angelique wanting to move into a larger place—a more private place.

Andrew had shown it to him that very day. John Paul had loved it, but it would be up to Angelique.

She had jumped into John Paul's arms.

However, Andrew wasn't finished. He asked Angelique right there in the empty house if she wanted to work part time at the hotel.

She had looked at John Paul like he had set this up, but he was as surprised as she.

Angelique fixed her beautiful eyes on Andrew and replied, "Only if you have your grandmother's furniture to put in here."

John Paul thought Andrew was going to cry.

August became the best month. A new place, a new job for Angelique, and she was even talking about going back to school part-time. They were saving money.

He had rubbed hard at the problems, and they did go away—for a time.

Angelique hadn't had a nightmare since before the beach. The tequila disappeared. She didn't talk about shadows or the "shadow time," the gloam of the day. The word "vampire" hadn't come out of her mouth for quite a while. She even showed off to the flies that occasionally hovered about. And there was less urgency about their sex. They enjoyed each other.

Angelique became busy in September with the three classes she took and learning the procedures and processes at the Highlight Hotel. She didn't flirt with John Paul on the job, but she did catch him looking her way. Everyone seemed to marvel over their story and their love.

John Paul would sometimes see Angelique talking with a patron and discover later she was telling their story. They were minor celebrities in a sense, and if that brought a little more business to the Highlight Hotel, then everyone won.

A tequila bottle appeared the first week of October.

Angelique started to look a little haggard, a little tired.

She didn't complain about nightmares or sleeping problems, and there were no screams or puking, but John Paul could see it in the lines on her forehead and the sunken look of her eyes, the hard, straight line of her lips.

He knew the first anniversary of The Night approached.

She began to avoid the "shadow time."

She glared at the flies.

John Paul realized the problems had become worse than little cramps. It was like he carried her idiosyncrasies in a bulky bag on his shoulders.

He had danced around the topic of *therapy* only twice in all the time they had been together, but as the anniversary approached, perhaps it was time to revisit it.

She had exploded.

She got drunk.

Oh, how she fucked him that night, scaring him with her voracity, the near-violence of it.

That bag of idiosyncrasies got heavier. He kept carrying it because she refused to acknowledge it. Perhaps she had lived with them for long enough now that she couldn't see them. That was what John Paul told himself.

There was another part of him that felt she knew exactly what was happening to her, and she embraced it all. Why wouldn't she see a therapist? Did she like the nightmares? Before, she *had* to tell him about them; now she kept them to herself.

When midnight the morning of the seventeenth passed by, John Paul had put a very drunk Angelique to bed. He stayed awake as long as he could into the anniversary, but the dark quiet of the room and his own couple of shots put him into La-La Land.

But it wasn't the same place Angelique had gone.

"Fuuuuuucckk!" she screamed, clutching her heart.

She jumped out of bed, scrambled to the bedroom light, flicked it on, then proceeded to turn on every light in the apartment. She ended in the bathroom just in time to puke into the commode.

Like most of the other nightmares, John Paul helped her out of her clothes and stood with her in the hot shower, gently rubbing her down to relax her. He dried her and placed her under the covers. After she settled in, he turned out all the lights. He spooned her, holding her shivering body. When he felt her calm, he relaxed.

John Paul felt something strike his shoulder. He felt a commotion in his bed. He sat up and heard a thump on the floor.

"No-no-no-no..." A shadow stood near the door. The light went on.

Angelique stood at the door. "Fuck!" she screamed, again

holding her chest as if she tried to keep her heart inside her. She ran about, flicking on the lights again, and ending in the bathroom. She heaved but there was nothing left. "Why is this happening to me?" she moaned.

All John Paul could do was to rub her back. He had an answer she didn't want to hear, and he struggled to keep silent. He noticed the time: 3:03 A.M.

When she finished, she swished some water in her mouth then brushed her teeth. She took a small drink, trembles running through her body.

They got back into bed.

Neither of them could sleep.

Angelique pulled John Paul close. She whispered, "I'd be in a straitjacket right now, if it weren't for you."

John hugged her, but he wanted to say, *I'll be in a straitjacket if this continues.*

Two nightmares hours apart.

And there was more night to come.

Late that morning, working on his fifth cup of coffee, John Paul helped Angelique shuffle out of the bed and onto the sofa. He turned on some talk show talking about healthy alternatives for Halloween candy.

He brought her a cup of Earl Grey tea with a little honey.

That must have been the moment Angelique officially woke up. She smiled when he handed the warm cup to her. She said, "You're soooo predictable."

Because of the tea? He often got her tea in the morning.

She saw his brows knit. "You already took the day off." She took a sip, blew on it, and took another.

John Paul wanted to say, *It's my anniversary, too.* He wanted to follow that with, *What the fuck happened last night?* He recognized the Wild One and told it to go away.

Instead, he leaned down and kissed her forehead, then he went to the kitchen, topped off his coffee, and joined her on the sofa, her legs overtop his.

They relaxed for the rest of the day.

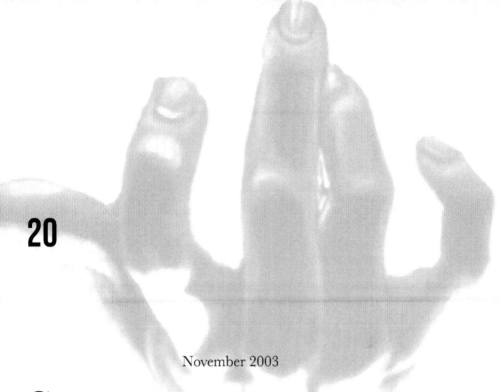

20

November 2003

S ince the anniversary of The Night, Angelique couldn't relax.
Part of it was J.P. She could feel his eyes sneaking looks at her. It was almost like she could *feel* the big question aching to come out.

What happened that night?

That was the other reason she couldn't relax. She couldn't remember what had happened, couldn't remember if she had a dream or if she had some kind of fit. She didn't even remember turning on the lights.

All she could recall was a kind of cold suffocation, like something icy had taken away her ability to breathe. It reminded her of Anders, but it was something else. It was in her, but also behind her, outside of her. And there was a vertiginous falling backward, and she knew she couldn't let herself go too far.

Then she was in the bathroom puking or heaving.

It wasn't a dream, and it was fleeting like smoke. The more she tried to grasp it the quicker it dissipated.

Now she could barely remember it.

And J.P.'s eyes begged the question she couldn't answer.

She hated the question, and she hated her only response because "I can't remember" sounded too lame.

She could feel the question in his body when they laid in bed. He held her a little tighter as if his strength could keep it—whatever it was—away from her. He hadn't made any romantic moves at her besides the occasional kiss, and she hadn't really felt like it, which, she had to admit, was a bit strange for her.

It would all pass soon, she knew, because it was dissipating more by the day.

They were watching *Star Trek: Another Humdinger* (or whatever it was called) tonight. She saw the images on the screen, but she had no idea what it was about. Normally, she studied during his two-hour T.V. time (it was easy to ignore), but tonight she didn't feel like using her brain. They laid on the sofa, heads at opposite ends, her legs between his.

During the commercials, however, his eyes tried to sneak peeks at her.

Just ask the question already!

"Ask what?"

Did she say that aloud?

Fuck it. Angelique sat up. "You've been treating me like some expensive, delicate ornament," she stated, irritated. "You've wanted to ask me a question since..." She hesitated. She wanted to say "The Night," but it wasn't The Night. It was the anniversary of The Night. And that sounded awkward. This entire situation was awkward.

Now J.P. sat up. He muted the television.

She saw it in his eyes. It wasn't her behavior that night he wanted to ask about.

"Stop!" she commanded. "Don't even go there."

His face shifted. It turned a lighter shade than the red of his shirt. His mouth opened, but the words he wanted to say were stuck in his throat.

Angelique was glad he was a coward at that moment. She didn't want to get more pissed off than she was. She understood why he couldn't ask the question all this time. It was about doctors and shrinks and "talking." And that was something she didn't want to talk about. It was easier for her to say she didn't know what had happened the other night. That was what, nearly three weeks ago? It already felt to her like a year. She didn't have to lie. She couldn't remember. There was nothing *to* remember.

But doctors and shrinks?

No fucking way.

She put all of that into her eyes—like a dare.

And he backed away.

He was soooo predictable.

After a moment, he put the sound back on the T.V. If he had tried harder to be indignant, he would have looked comical. If he had started sulking, she would have puked—this time on purpose.

She knew how to get him away from the thoughts moving about in his head. She could see them in his clenched jaw and his shallow breathing. And his eyes. They didn't see the screen and his show. They were looking at how bad Angelique could get if she exploded.

She couldn't let this go on. She didn't feel like fighting.

Angelique pulled back her legs from his. He looked to see if she was pissed off, but she looked as calm and uncaring as she could. She stood, went to the kitchen, opened the fridge, and grabbed the chilled vodka on the bottom shelf of the door. Orange flavored. Not her favorite, but she knew someone in this house liked it. Pulling open a cabinet, she found two shot glasses and placed them on the counter. She knew he was listening. She pulled off her shorts and shirt and let them lay on the kitchen floor. She grabbed the vodka and shot glasses.

She emerged into the living room, and J.P. looked straight at her. His eyes moved to the objects in her hands and back to her face. She didn't look at him and went to the dark hall and stopped, her back to him.

She clicked the glasses to the bottle. "Care to join me?" She went back to their room.

Angelique moved quickly to her side of the bed and put the bottle and glasses on the nightstand. Knowing she had only seconds, she pulled off her bra and panties, poured two shots of vodka, and jumped on the bed. She grabbed the two shots and waited.

For only a few more seconds.

Angelique downed one of the shots as John Paul appeared in the doorway.

"I just couldn't wait," she said. She lay seductively on the bed. "Are you here for this shot?" He just stood there. She poured half of it from her breasts to her belly button and placed the half-empty shot glass there. "Oops." She felt the vodka drip over her skin to the bedspread. She didn't care. And from the look on John Paul's face, he didn't either.

John Paul was soooo predictable that Angelique wasn't surprised a few days later when Diane appeared to take her to lunch. It wasn't out of missing her daughter and the desire to spend time together.

No.

Mommy Dearest would have been aware of the anniversary. J.P. wouldn't have had the courage to contact Diane, but he definitely would have told her about the fits and the lights and the puking. He may have even told Diane about the previous dreams—not the details, of course. She could see him painting a picture of a troubled woman they both loved who needed their help.

Mother and daughter sat across from each other in the restaurant, like they did every so often, making their superficial small talk. This time, Angelique had ordered a medium-rare steak, something she *rarely* ate (she smiled internally at her pun), new potatoes, and green beans. Angelique waited for Diane to make a move for her purse.

"If you have a particular business card in there to give to me, don't waste our time."

Angelique had a pink piece of steak on her fork and put it into her mouth when Diane looked up at her.

"Angel, please."

Angelique chewed and swallowed. "Don't worry, Mother. We're in public." She cut off another small piece of meat, forked it, then moved it around in the bloody juices on the plate. If only Diane knew the irony of this. A vision of her murderous dream threatened to make her lunch come up to join them.

Diane's face hardened, but she put her purse down. "Angel, I—"

"I would prefer you stop calling me that. We both know I am no angel."

"But your father—"

"Don't." The calm command struck Diane to silence. Angelique put her utensils on her plate. "Never bring up either of those topics *ever* again, Mother." She removed her napkin from her lap and placed it on the table beside her plate. She caught the waiter's eye. "I can forgive J.P. and his honest concern for me, but you and I shouldn't pretend."

This may have been the first time Angelique had been able to bring Diane close to tears—that she knew of. There had been many of Angelique's actions in their past that may have done the deed, but the woman never had shown more than her stony, disapproving, disappointed face to her daughter. Not that the woman was incapable of feelings for Angelique—The Night had proved that—but Diane Carlson purposefully wore her stony face as a show of strength and authority. It worked on everyone but her daughter.

The waiter appeared, and Angelique said to him, "Box only the meat, please, and make certain the juices are poured over it." The waiter acknowledged her, took the plate, and left the women facing each other.

Angelique leaned toward Diane. "I will make it clear to my lover that I do not need his help, your help, or even God's help. This will be the last time we will speak of this." She remembered something said by Ralph Waldo Emerson. "'Act, if you like, *at your own peril.*'"

Diane's stony face returned. The left corner of her mouth turned up. "Will you be a victim or a slave?"

Angelique downed her margarita. "Master," she replied and set the glass down as the waiter appeared with her boxed food. She stood. "Thank you, Diane, for this lovely lunch. Can't wait to do this again."

Angelique looked at her watch as she walked out. Under an hour. It was as long as she could stomach.

21

December 2003

"You are soooo predictable."

Angelique had dipped the accusation in contempt and had sprinkled a little anger on it like an ice cream cone of shit. She handed it to John Paul. He didn't know what to do with it. He knew she interpreted his silence as weakness, but he honestly had no idea of what to say.

Plus, it was her birthday, and they were in Sulatra, one of Baltimore's most expensive restaurants. He didn't want to fight.

Her indifference to the night had begun when he had come home from the hotel and asked her to put on her best cocktail dress. They both knew it was her little provocative purple one, but she went with the standard black, which still made her look ravishing. He put on a suit. The drive into the city was quiet, and he found it difficult to converse. The last few blocks became a tense silence.

Last year, Angelique's birthday had been spent in her mother's home, a quiet gathering with The Gang and John Paul. The party had ended not even two hours later. There were a few gifts, the standard cards. Not many smiles. It had been too soon after The Night and the Vampire Killer. As far as everyone knew, that psycho had still been running amok in Baltimore. Only John Paul, Angelique, and the police knew the truth. The last murder and note had signaled the end... and it had.

John Paul wanted this birthday to be grand and exciting. He had been planning and saving for it since he started at the hotel. Plus, a lot had happened since the last birthday—their declaration of love, their moving in together, Angelique's partial return to school, and her taking a part-time job at the hotel. He didn't want to think about the idiosyncrasies that kept getting larger in the bag he carried for Angelique. He wanted this to be a positive night, a lovely night. He wanted to make her happy.

But she was bored and irritated.

When the hostess walked away, he asked, "Did you think we'd be coming to Sulatra?" He pulled out her seat. As he went to his, the waiter approached.

"I'll have a martini," Angelique announced before the waiter could ask anything. She looked at John Paul and added, "Dry."

He had seen this scene in a movie or T.V. show. The sarcasm and irony were meant as a slap. Angelique was gathering a huge ball of shit to throw into the fan pointed at John Paul.

What the hell was happening?

"7 and 7," he said to the waiter. John Paul didn't want to sit, but he slowly pulled out his chair and slowly put his ass into it. He looked about then back at this beautiful, dark woman. He only now noticed she had worn darks as her makeup, like three steps in the direction of goth. At least, he knew being in a packed restaurant afforded him a safety net now that he had found he was high-wiring across a deep canyon.

Angelique eyed him a moment and said it: "You are soooo predictable."

She might as well have stabbed him in the heart. He wanted to say, *Why don't I just put my cock and balls on the little plate here and let you cut them off?* But he said nothing.

Angelique opened her clutch and removed three folded pieces of paper. "I'll tell you how predictable you are, J.P. I wrote down three parts of your little birthday surprise on these three sheets of paper."

She laid the three papers on the table between them.

He was stuck. He indeed felt emasculated. A toilet bowl had suddenly formed in the center of his body, and Angelique had flushed it. He felt himself swirling around, the hole getting bigger, consuming what little courage he had.

When he made no move, she took the paper on his left. She slowly opened it and showed it to him: RESTAURANT.

Okay, he thought, *a lot of people do restaurants on their birthdays.*

She crumpled it up, now a ball of nothing on the table—just like he was starting to feel. She took the middle paper and opened it: PEARLS.

Shit.

A box with a pearl necklace sat in his jacket pocket. He had thought it was a clever double entendre. She made it seem salacious.

The third paper opened: SHOW.

Fuck. Me.

What the hell was wrong with her that she had to destroy this? He wanted to scream *Fuck you!* and storm out, but he realized that his safety net was hers, too. Was she trying to tell him something? *What the fuck is happening?*

He looked absently at the three balls of paper on the table. He wanted to become a fourth and let her put each into the frosted cup with the candle in it to burn away into nothing.

Thank God she wasn't smirking. He would have puked.

The waiter arrived with their drinks.

"He'll take another immediately." Angelique's face was grave, serious, and a little disappointed. She was a mind reader, too. She lifted her martini, saluted John Paul, and took a small sip.

John Paul shakily took the cold, wet glass and drank half in two gulps. His impotence wiped away his presence of mind. He felt like a marionette, and he looked at the master across the table. He had been told to drink this yellow-brown liquid, and he did. It tasted like cold smoke and rotten lemons. He forced the rest of it down, and his eyes followed the glass to the table. He couldn't look at her.

"My guess," her words were loud, like a whip cracking in his ears, but the logical part of him knew she whispered, "is that there are rose petals leading to the dozen on the bed. It's why you had to go back in for your wallet just before we left."

Somewhere back there, the Wild One came up to say, *Tell her to fuck off and find her own way home—preferably to her mother!* John Paul swallowed that down, and it choked him like a half-chewed piece of meat.

Thankfully, the waiter brought his second drink—Angelique had predicted correctly he'd need it—and he took a large sip. That washed down the Wild One but left him empty again and with nothing to say.

His right hand, however, had a mind of its own, and it reached into his breast pocket to remove an envelope. He tossed it across the table, and it landed neatly on the bread plate in front of Angelique. Her brows raised. He felt filled with something, like he had been a glove and a strong hand had slipped into it.

The waiter was about to ask if there was anything else.

That strength filled John Paul's lips and tongue; his jaw moved and air pushed up and out of his mouth. "We'll go ahead and order, please. I'll have the filet mignon—*rare*—and she'll have the mako."

Angelique almost laughed, caught off guard by the drama of it all.

The waiter smiled and replied, "Excellent choice, sir."

Whatever had entered John Paul, *it* looked directly into Angelique's surprised eyes, picked up the glass, and took a small sip of his 7 and 7. When the food arrived, *it* slowly ate his meal, causing Angelique to wait for him to finish. *It* paid for the meal and left a handsome tip for the waiter. *It* stood and removed a box from his right jacket pocket, opened it, then came around and put the pearl necklace around her exquisite neck. *It* reached for the envelope and put it back into the breast pocket. *It* ignored Angelique's seat and walked calmly to the coat room.

Surprised, and a little irritated, Angelique got up and followed.

It didn't help her with her coat.

It tipped the valet nicely, too.

It waited for Angelique to get into the car, nodding a thank you to the valet when the young man shut Angelique's door.

It said nothing during the drive, ignoring Angelique's stare, ignoring her completely when they arrived at the theater. She hurried to keep up.

The show was an internationally known Queen cover band called Gary Mullen and the Works. This thing inside John Paul rocked with everyone else, dancing at his seat and clapping and singing with Gary, who must have been channeling Freddie Mercury; the man looked and sounded like the deceased legendary rocker.

Angelique watched him.

And John Paul watched *it* ignore her. He was the one back there, detached from it all like he was viewing a movie starring himself. The Wild One had traded places, and John Paul was a little envious he couldn't be more like this: not really caring whether or not Angelique cared.

Later, after they had come home, John Paul—*it*—had gone straight to the bathroom to take a piss; *it* washed his hands; *it* proceeded to brush his teeth.

Angelique stood in the bathroom's doorway, like she was going to block him from leaving, and she commanded, "What in the fuck was all that about?"

It spat, brushed a little more, spat again, and *it* rinsed the toothbrush.

"Well?" she demanded.

It swished some water around in his mouth and spat. *It* splashed water on the inside of the sink to ensure all the spittle had gone down the drain. *It* dried off his mouth.

All she could do was widen her eyes when *its* hand shot out to grab her wrist.

"Owww! What—"

It pulled her down the hall and into their room.

It threw her on the bed. *It* had its way with her.

And when *it* was finished, *it* growled, "How's *that* for predictable?"

It went to the bathroom for a shower.

John Paul awoke the next morning to the curtains wide open to a rising sun.

The ripped panties on the floor a few feet away told him last night wasn't some nightmare.

He slowly sat up. Had all that happened *with* the drapes open?

Angelique still slept—though he couldn't understand how she could sleep with the sun streaming in. She was naked under the covers, rose petals in her hair. They were like little spots of blood all about the room. Her ripped dress lay across the end of the bed. The room looked like—no, it *was* a crime scene.

Guilt and shame gripped him, hot and heavy in his gut. He looked at her peaceful face, and he wanted to pray his apologies to her.

He felt the *thing* he had let out, the Wild One, stir inside him. *It* wasn't gone, just dormant, asleep. He knew if *it* awoke, *it* would tear at his guilt, a savage beast, a Wolf (with a capital "W"); *it* would gnaw at his humanity, ripping and shredding and howling.

Last night, as Angelique devastated his love and honor for her, as he felt the pain and helplessness of her savagery upon him, that Wolf slipped into him—and John Paul wanted it to retaliate because he really was too much of a coward to do it himself. But that wasn't true. The Wolf was a part of him he had kept suppressed, crouching in the dark of his soul, chained by his sense of what was good and right. Last night, John Paul had let it out, and he knew it was dangerous. And that meant a part of John Paul Wilkins was dangerous.

What scared him even more was that he had seen a part of Angelique that enjoyed that hunger and danger.

John Paul squinted at the sunlight, and he managed his weight and balance to get out of bed. As he pulled the drapes shut, he saw he was naked, too. He took a couple steps, stopped a moment to watch Angelique, and grabbed her robe on the doorknob as he left the room.

He went down to the kitchen. What he really wanted was another shower. The Wolf made him feel dirty. He settled for a glass of water. He took a sip and watched the water fall from the faucet, swirl around, and go down the drain. He wanted to stand under that cold water and scrub himself until he bled.

"Did you see this?"

The four words shocked him. "Shit!" he yelled, turning around quickly from the sink.

She stood naked at the entrance to the kitchen. Her hair was disheveled, a single rose petal on top. She held her ripped cocktail dress.

The Wolf, now awake, chuckled but said nothing.

A little grin moved in the corner of Angelique's mouth, and she tossed the dress in the trash can. She moved against John Paul at the sink and turned off the water. She looked him up and down, and her left brow rose. "That's a little small on you, isn't it?" She undid the tie and yanked the robe off him, letting it drop to the floor.

She turned and kicked out a chair and pushed him into it. "We're not finished," she declared. She pulled her hair into a ponytail and tied it with a band. She looked down, grinned, and added, "I see you agree."

The Wolf smiled.

It was a wild animal that had been let out of its cage, and John Paul knew he could never put it back in—could never put himself back to what he had been before. He had to admit that this fevered animal that growled when it devoured Angelique was exhilarating... the freedom that came with allowing it to prey, electrifying.

It took John Paul months to get ahold of its leash, to control it, to embrace it as a part of him, for without that control, he would hunt everywhere he could. When nearly any woman walked by and smiled, he could feel it pull on the leash and bare its teeth, its mouth filling with hot saliva, its low growl forming deep down within him then rumbling up into his throat. He often caught that growl and pushed it down. He wondered how he appeared to the prey, if he looked dangerous. They only smiled, which encouraged the Wolf even more.

As long as Angelique played with the Wolf, John Paul could keep it in check. The urges of the beast gnawed at him, however, thickening the guilt that gripped his heart, and to ease that conflict, John Paul had to give the Wolf much slack on the leash and let it prey upon the woman he loved. Her pleasure eased his pain. Yet, there was no passion in their sex, no love anymore. It was hunger for hunger, and it demanded to be fed, approaching the line of brutality until John Paul yanked the leash, reminding the Wolf he was in charge.

Angelique loved the Wolf.

John Paul hated her for it.

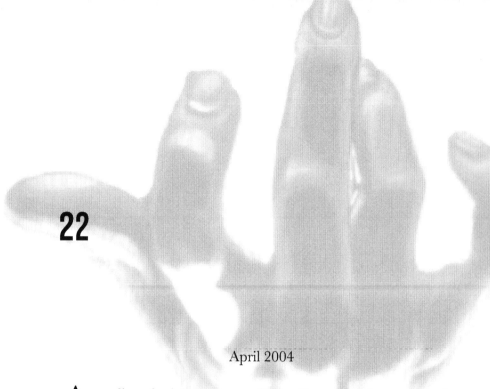

22

April 2004

Angelique hadn't seen any of The Gang in quite a while, then Jarrod Jambotti came strolling into the lobby of the Highlight Hotel. He went straight to J.P., and together they went to his office. The tall Italian didn't look at her. He had eyes for John Paul. He was a man on a mission.

A short time later, they came out shaking hands and smiling. She wished she had told J.P. to go ahead and go home rather than to stay and wait for her shift to be over. Then Jarrod would have had to deal with her.

"Miss?" The man and his family stood at the main desk, waiting for their room keycard.

Angelique gave him a bright smile. "I'm sorry," she replied. She put the keycard into a little envelope and handed it to the man. "Room 217. Enjoy your stay." She gave him a little wink and made certain the wife saw it. She smiled when she saw the woman grab her husband's arm.

"I saw that."

J.P. had that stony look, the new one she had difficulty reading. His mouth and jaw were relaxed, but his eyes had a slight hardness of disapproval. It was a look that excited her, for it usually meant he might "punish" her later—or it could mean he would ignore her. If he ignored her, she would work hard to get his attention, then he would punish her anyway.

J.P. had let his hair grow a little longer, and he parted it on the side. He quit wearing a tie, but he wore a sports jacket with his open-collared shirt. He sometimes wore the shirt untucked, as he did today. Often, he wore a lot of blues that made his blue eyes pop. Which is what he wore today: tan Dockers, blue jacket, white shirt with blue pinstripes. Even his Argyle socks were blue and white.

There was nothing exceptional about him—not like Jarrod who had just left—but this cavalier attitude excited her. Especially when other women jumped when he entered the lobby. He treated them all fairly: about a minute of attention and a smile.

And they couldn't stand it.

"Excuse me, John." A woman even now hovered to try to strike.

His eyes became a little harder toward Angelique—*We'll talk about this later, naughty girl*—before he turned to the woman. "Yes, Mrs. Causill?" he asked, smiling. He took her elbow to guide her away from the desk.

The woman was probably creaming herself, Angelique noted. Angelique wondered what these women would do if they had any idea what he was like in the privacy of a candlelit room—as she was going to find out later.

Angelique smiled and looked at her watch.

Seventeen minutes would be too long.

Once home, Angelique sloughed off her coat and went straight to the fridge. She took out two beers and cracked them open.

J.P. had set the Monday night wings on the table and was reaching for two plates when he said, "I'm having lunch with Jarrod Jambotti tomorrow."

She stopped the fridge door with her foot, handed one of the beers to J.P., and reached into the fridge to pull out a veggie tray. "I thought I had seen him. Wasn't sure."

"Uh-huh," he replied sarcastically. "That's why you were naughty with Mr. Dincher. His wife caught me as I was leaving. She complained that you were rude."

Maybe you'll have to punish me, she wanted to say, but she knew this dog wouldn't bite if she did. She had learned quickly that if she expected anything, he would refuse her. It was a little game they played, she and this new John Paul. He thought he was in control, but she played him to get what she wanted.

Since her birthday back in December, this new, angrier, darker J.P. had become exciting and a little dangerous. Oh, she knew he wouldn't really hurt her, but the extremity of his physicality and his near-aloof attitude made him interesting.

She had finally found a man who was just like her.

Angelique smiled to herself. She had *made* a man who was just like her. "Dog" was a perfect way to describe him. He sniffed and he took and he dared her to refuse or he punished her. If she got out of line, he punished her. He acted like he didn't care, but she managed him in a way that she got what she wanted.

It was a game she loved to play, and her closet was filled with clothes and shoes and purses and, of course, lingerie at which she knew the old John Paul would have balked.

This little life of theirs was good, but Jarrod's appearance had shaken things. Angelique had to know what was going on.

"I knew you were watching me," she said.

He looked bored and went to the living room to watch T.V.

Angelique smiled.

John Paul had seen every episode of *Star Trek: The Next Generation* at least five times, but he watched the two hours of *TNG*, as he called it, every Monday night without fail—unless his beloved Baltimore Ravens were on *Monday Night Football.*

He always bought Buffalo wings at Choosers on the way home from work, and he sat and watched and ate and drank for his precious two hours. Angelique might sit with him for a little bit, eat a few wings and drink a few beers, then go to the bedroom to study. He'd be in his world, she in hers.

That was before the Dog.

The Dog liked games. Oh, it growled and snapped when she tried to get his attention, and at first, she was unsuccessful. Her mother gave her a $200 Visa card for her birthday, and she knew exactly what to do with it.

She already had the knee-high black boots and a black thong.

The red TNG captain's shirt she had gotten a size too small so that it wrapped around her like a skin. The first time she used it, she came out in the middle of the second show and asked, "Will there be anything else... Captain?"

The low growl and the flash of a smile had been his answer.

But Angelique didn't play *TNG* every Monday night. No. She kept him guessing, and she paid attention to which episodes were the good ones. She loved to watch the conflict in his face as he looked from her to the T.V. If there was no growl, all she had to do was to turn and flash her thonged ass. He had ripped up three of them over the past few months.

Tonight, however, she remembered she needed to finish an English paper, which was due for peer editing groups tomorrow, so despite the possibility of punishment, she really needed to get to the room and get some work done.

As Angelique picked up her school backpack, she looked at John Paul glued to the T.V. then headed upstairs to the bedroom. She tossed the backpack on the bed then went to the small desk next to a tall chest of drawers (she liked to use the side of it for sticky notes), and woke up her computer. The draft appeared on the screen: "A Comparative Analysis of Female Characters in Shakespeare's *King Lear* and *Hamlet*." She had enjoyed reading *Lear*, but the females in *Hamlet* were boring. She saw her notes on the desk below the screen and realized she had more to do than she thought.

Angelique turned to the bed—

John Paul startled her in the doorway.

"Shit!" She put a hand over her heart. "How'd you get up here without me hearing?" Realizing his show was still on, she asked, "Everything okay?"

"No," he replied, stepping to the bed and tossing the backpack onto the floor. "Time for your punishment."

The most exciting games came when least expected.

And she didn't expect to be as nervous about J.P.'s meeting with Jarrod, but she could hardly concentrate during her Psych class. She was better during her English Lit class and the editing group. There was no way she could fake it with those guys. But forget the Stats class. It was over at four, and that would give her little time to get ready for J.P. She had to have everything just right for the discussion, the right number of distractions so that she got the most out of him.

Angelique took a bus to their favorite store and bought all the necessary groceries for dinner.

She got home an hour before he was due home. There had been no calls from him about working late. No messages. She prepped the fish the way he liked it and got it into the oven. She jumped into the shower. Her hair wrapped in a towel to keep it wet, she hurried down to the kitchen to start the water for the mac and cheese. She assembled all the rest of the food on the table to have it ready to prep.

Back upstairs in the bedroom, Angelique found a pink top she knew J.P. liked, no bra, and she pulled on a pair of tight gray yoga pants, no panties. She kept the towel on her hair.

As she checked the haddock, she felt her nervousness rise, and she wasn't certain why. She finished her third beer and opened a fourth.

Why did J.P. talking with Jarrod make her feel like this? She wasn't just nervous, she was defensive... and a little self-conscious. What could they have to talk about other than her? Why would Jarrod *want* to talk to J.P. about her?

What could Jarrod tell J.P. that he didn't already know?

Why did she care?

She shut the oven door and checked the time. The fish would be done in a few minutes. J.P. would be home in around twenty. Perfect.

When he pulled into the driveway, everything was set.

She rushed upstairs to act like she was working on her hair.

She tossed the towel on the bathroom floor and grabbed a brush. Then she decided to turn on the shower. She pulled off her clothes, put them on the back of the toilet, and stepped in. The hot water felt good on her face and scalp.

A large shadow stood outside the opaque shower curtain.

Angelique screamed.

"Shit, Angelique!" John Paul yelled.

"Me? Don't fuckin' sneak up like that!" She swallowed down her heart. "You know how I am."

The shadow moved and stood for a moment. "I'm sorry," it said. There was something familiar in his voice. "I'll wait for you."

Sorry? *No, no, no... * Wait? *Oh, fuck no!*

The Dog was gone. John Paul the mouse was back.

She toweled off quickly and pulled on her clothes, her hair wet and stringy.

John Paul wasn't in the room. His work clothes lay on the bed.

He had retreated to the kitchen.

This wasn't good. Not one bit.

Sitting at the kitchen table, John Paul looked plain and average. He had pulled on a Ravens sweatshirt and faded jeans. He held a bottle of beer in his hand, but he hadn't taken a sip. The Dog would have only removed his sports jacket and had half of the beer gone. It never would have allowed him to look so mundane.

The mouse was a different man than the Dog—the two had different faces, different postures in a chair, different gaits. Angelique wondered if all people had these different sides to them.

She recalled herself as a little girl, a tween, and she saw that she had pushed aside that child for the Bitch she was now. She smiled: Bitch with a capital "B." Her smile fell when J.P. looked up at her.

Shit! A cold anger expanded in her belly. What did that asshole Jarrod say to him?

"We need to talk." John Paul looked sad, as if he was about to deliver bad news.

Angelique scrambled to recall those weeks she had spent with Jarrod. She had been a little wild, but she hadn't been crazy over-the-top. It was hazy, like trying to look at distant mountains on a humid day.

J.P. took a sip of beer. "I have to apologize to you."

Apologize? For what?

Angelique sat in the other chair at the table. All this food was getting cold. All this work she did to get this ready for him—he didn't even see it. She wanted to shake him, slap him, make him growl in anger.

This can't be happening.

J.P. eyed the beer in his hand. He couldn't even look at her. He took a deep breath. "I've been a terrible man these last few months."

How to deal with this? She wanted the Dog back, not this mouse. Angelique's stomach began to turn. She needed a beer, but she didn't want to disturb this delicate moment. He looked like he'd take off running if she did or said the wrong thing.

He took another breath to continue.

"Stop." She imitated a calm, soothing voice. God, how she wanted to scream. Angelique reached out to take his hand and said, "I have never complained about anything." She was afraid to be too specific, that it would scare this little mouse into a hole somewhere, and he would never come out.

John Paul looked fragile, close to tears. *Don't fucking start crying, or I'll kick you in the balls.*

"What happened that made you so upset?" She sounded like a mother talking to a child, and it made that pre-vomit saliva gush in her mouth. She swallowed that down. *Fucking Jarrod fucking Jambotti.*

"I know about the clubs."

Angelique's brain had been revving like a machine, turning over memories, searching for actions and decisions she had made with that fucking Jarrod, scrambling for anything that asshole could have told J.P. to cause him to be upset. It was like a factory of machines turning, flipping, slapping memories on conveyor belts, grabbing the next memory, hundreds of machines looking for something—

... know...

Present tense.

"What?" Her factory stopped, the silence unbearable. She shook her head to get the machines going again. "What are you talking about?"

"I know it's because of how I've been treating you." It sounded rehearsed, like J.P. had been scripting this whole thing on the way home from work.

What the fuck are you talking about? she wanted to scream, but she knew that whatever it was, he was very upset over it. She had to be careful. Her brain factory kept churning away. *Clubs... about the clubs... clubs...*

Then—

128

Barcode-Oh. It was a techno bar she and her study group had gone to after a huge exam a while back. They all had kicked ass and wanted to celebrate. She remembered thinking she had seen Jarrod there, but she knew he hated techno music, so she wrote it off as someone who had looked like the prick. She had had a few drinks—none of which she had bought—and perhaps danced a little provocatively.

Then—

There was the goth bar Velvet Freaks. The groups had gone there after a research presentation. She had let Lainey do her makeup, and she had worn leather and lace. She had smoked a little pot that night, and drank a lot, too. And there was the dancing. Had Jarrod been there?

Had he been following her?

Angelique saw J.P. was looking at her, waiting for her to say something.

But he had known she had gone to those bars. He called them "clubs."

Fucking Jarrod fucking Jambotti.

The brain factory found an old argument she had had with Jarrod—over her going to a couple clubs with other people. It had been so petty that it had become one of a handful of reasons she broke up with him. "What did Jarrod tell you?"

J.P. looked confused. "This isn't about him."

"Really? You go to lunch with Jarrod, and you suddenly become all apologetic over nothing?" Angelique felt the cold anger expand into her shoulders. She wanted a shot of tequila, and she wanted it now. She stood. "I told you I was going to those bars."

His eyes hardened a moment, his nostrils flared. *That's right*, she thought, *let the Dog come out and play.*

He retorted, "All dressed up and dancing all crazy?"

Fucking Jarrod fucking Jambotti. J.P. had obviously not noticed her when she had come home from Velvet's.

Then it hit her. Jarrod had *warned* J.P. of her behavior. She could see the prick telling John Paul that he liked him, that he didn't want to see him get hurt. She could cut the asshole's balls off.

"Listen," John Paul said, "I've been torn up about how I've been behaving lately. That hasn't been me. I don't blame you..."

Angelique had done nothing wrong. Was J.P. *forgiving* her?

Fucking Jarrod fucking Jambotti. Ruined fucking everything!

John Paul the mouse was back. The Dog was gone.

Angelique felt hot, like she had been in the oven with the fish, heat rolling off her. She needed a drink. Bad. And she knew where she needed to go.

She said nothing as she stood and walked calmly upstairs, grabbed her purse, slipped her feet into her sneakers, and came down the stairs. As she put on a jean jacket hanging on a hook near the front door, she didn't have to look back to know John Paul still sat at the kitchen table covered with cold food. She pulled the front door shut and got into the car.

Angelique went to her old haunt Alternatives.

Some of the regulars were there, asking how she was doing, where she'd been. The story of "the great bet" circulated around the bar, and when some of the newer regulars asked, "That was you?" she became a little celebrity again. Three shots of tequila and a couple drinks later, she was dancing.

Around 10:30, she saw him: Fucking Jarrod fucking Jambotti.

He was leading some coed to the dance floor, when Angelique grabbed his arm and dragged him to the men's room.

Outside the door, he shook her off and yelled, "What the hell, Angelique!"

"You want to do this out here?" A few people had gathered for a spectacle.

Only music played for a few moments, and they looked at each other. He opened his mouth, but she cut him off. "You had no reason to say *anything* to J.P.!"

"What the hell are you talking about? We had a business meeting. Steve and I want to open a bar in his hotel."

"Bartender Steve? He was with you?" That's fucking great. Two exes—double barrel. When Jarrod didn't say anything, she asked, "You said nothing about Barcode-Oh and Velvet Freaks? I know I saw you at both places."

Now he laughed. Jarrod was a big man, six-four, broad shoulders, lean and strong. When he laughed, it was loud, and he laughed right in her face. "You know, it's not all about you, you crazy drunk bitch."

He stomped off into the bar.

She awoke a couple hours later, parked in the dark end of a convenience store lot. At least she had that much presence of mind.

The brain factory slowly got started, but it churned out a fuzzy version of what had happened. Fucking Jarrod fucking Jambotti all but said that he hadn't said anything to J.P. That left the possibility of Steve, but she didn't think he really cared much to bother about anything besides himself. A business meeting.

So, what the hell was J.P. talking about?

And she meant to ask him that when she got home.

But when she saw the pathetic look on his face—old John Paul the mouse—she went straight to bed.

As she slipped between the sheets alone, wondering if the mouse (she couldn't capitalize it) was afraid to come to her bed, she heard the muted base of his voice downstairs. He was on the phone— probably speaking with Diane.

She's okay. She's home. She's drunk.

Angelique could see him calling her immediately after she had left. She knew he told Diane only generalities: the agitation, the increased alcohol. But not the sex. He wouldn't tell Diane about the Dog and the Bitch. No. He wouldn't say anything that would cast himself in a dark light. He wanted to be a good man. He wanted to be supportive, to provide for her happiness. He loved Angelique, she could hear him tell Diane, and he was concerned about her mental health. She needed to see—Angelique couldn't even *think* the word. But she knew he had said it to Diane.

No. He wouldn't talk about the Dog—and how he knew she wanted the Dog.

And that he had caged it.

Angelique hated John Paul for that.

23

T he lies came within an hour of each other.

John Paul hated lying to Angelique, but lately he had felt the Toilet Bowl of Life opening its yawning lid, beckoning all the shit of his world to jump in and have a good time. Of course, that meant he had to go in with it all. He was afraid if he looked in, he would find Angelique in a skimpy string bikini laying out on a raft with a shot glass in one hand and a bottle of tequila in the other.

"If you love me, you'll join me."

The problem was that he didn't feel like shit. Yet, he took on Angelique's every time she harangued him... or woke up screaming in the middle of the night or ran about turning on the lights.

That had started again, but only occasionally, usually on nights when she managed only a few beers, a "soft buzz" as she called it. He knew she drank to keep those nightmares in check. And he knew the nightmares and the drinking were eroding her away.

John Paul's biggest fear was he felt Angelique saw him as a massive turd that deserved to frolic with her and all the other crap in the Toilet Bowl of Life. He had to do something, or the Toilet Bowl of Life would flush her down—and probably him along with her.

"If you love me, you'll join me."

That had been what she said last night as she had "dessert" after dinner: a couple shots of ta-kill-ya.

Angelique had more or less traded beer for tequila. Immediately after dinner, she would say, "Now for dessert," and down a few shots. It was the night after a nightmare when she'd have four to six to "chase 'em away." Sometimes he joined her, sometimes he passed.

But last night there was something different in her...

"If you love me, you'll join me."

... something in her eyes—something predatory, challenging.

John Paul had smiled and joined her and got fairly lit up.

When they went to bed, she fuck-punished him, slapping and hitting and scratching and abusing. It was like she was getting back at him for something, and this was the only way she could do it: force him to get drunk and sexually punish him.

He couldn't remember the last time they had made love. It was all fucking and screaming now. John Paul could feel the Wolf in him howl to come out to play, but he only allowed it to come within sniffing distance. That seemed to piss her off even more.

"If you love me, you'll join me."

Last night, she seemed to cross a threshold. Rather, she had jumped into the Toilet Bowl of Life. She beckoned him to join her. John Paul felt like she was testing him to see how far he'd go. When he tried to be tender, she screamed at him to "be a man."

"Better yet," she had said and slapped him hard, "let the Dog come out and play."

The sting on his face was nothing compared to her anger when he pulled away from her. She scared him—not from her anger, but from her request, her use of "Dog" as if it were a term of endearment. She had no idea what the Wolf was really about.

John Paul was not certain himself, for that matter. That, too, scared him. What he understood in that moment—had he not turned from her—was that the Wolf would have retaliated, and neither of them would like it. Even now, the Wolf told him she was no longer worthy—and there was no way *it* would allow him to jump into the Toilet Bowl even if he wanted.

John Paul, however, couldn't give up so easily. He had to try to get her to come out on her own. He knew what he needed to do.

So, he told two lies.

He rationalized it was for a greater good, but they were lies, nonetheless.

The first came when Angelique had come out of the bathroom a little sooner than anticipated. John Paul had called his boss to tell him he had to take a personal day, but that he wanted to keep it quiet. John Paul was fortunate that Andrew was also his friend, and as a friend, Andrew knew of some of Angelique's issues—not the dark and eerie ones, naturally—and knew that John Paul was a little torn up about the woman's problems. They both knew it had something to do with The Night, but John Paul had made it clear Angelique would not entertain counseling of any kind.

Andrew even suggested John Paul should get counseling.

John Paul had been standing in his closet looking at his suits while speaking to Andrew when he turned to find a naked Angelique toweling her hair. She looked tired and haggard. Purple shadows hung beneath her eyes. However, he knew she would work her makeup magic and look dazzling for summer-school classes later. She held out her hand for his cell phone.

He handed it to her without hesitation.

"Why, hello, Andrew," she said into the phone. To the untutored ear, she sounded sweet and sincere; John Paul heard festering sarcasm. "Whatever are you having my lover do that would require him to look at his suits?" Angelique eyed her lover as she listened to Andrew. Her face became a little harder. "I will have to give him a kiss for success in this endeavor." Angelique clenched her teeth and gave the phone back to John Paul.

He quickly said bye and hung up.

They looked at each other for a moment. She asked, "Does this have anything to do with Jarrod fucking Jambotti?"

John Paul knew exactly what Andrew had told her. He sent his friend a silent thank you. "Yes," he replied, "Drew wants financial options for renovations to the lobby."

Angelique had already turned to her dresser. "Wear the blue suit." Her naked body made the Wolf stir.

John Paul yanked on the chain to keep the beast down. He grabbed the blue suit.

Andrew must have had this already worked out. All the employees knew he had been canvassing the area banks the last few days for financing. It was no secret he wanted to expand the lobby with a bar, and Jarrod had been the first to approach the Highlight Hotel with a plan. Why not send his manager to, say, Philadelphia, to check out a few options? John Paul had told Andrew that was where he was going, and his friend used it as a means to make the ruse seem true. He owed his friend big time.

The second lie came on the heels of the first.

Down in the kitchen, the miracle beauty that was Angelique waited on the coffee maker to finish. She wore a tight jean skirt and a black spaghetti strap top. Hair pulled back in a ponytail, she had transformed into the goddess John Paul was certain most of the boys in her classes secretly worshiped.

It gave him a small sense of pride to know other men coveted Angelique.

But lately, this drunk, angry Angelique scared him. This recent version was some doppelgänger or changeling—no, a possessed Angelique that needed to be exorcized.

When she heard him enter the kitchen, she turned to ask, "Would you like for me to do your sugar?" It was the sweet Angelique, the one that sometimes accompanied the drinking Angelique. *Had she started already?* There was an edge in her voice that made his ears prick up a little.

These last few months, John Paul had become attuned to Angelique's voice, for it often signaled her mood—managed by how much booze she'd had. She'd have to push all her negativity down during the day, be the sweet, pretty woman to the outside world, especially when she had to deal with a professor or work a shift at the hotel. That negativity would bubble up on the drive home, and on the evenings she prepared dinner, her voice screeched, raking like a board of rusty nails starting from his mid-back up to the top of his scalp. A verbal diarrhea of negatives and expletives spewed out of her as she cooked.

At first, she spewed about everyone at work or her college

instructors or stupid students, then she would turn on him. Her favorite was how she had three jobs: work, school, and *him*.

Angelique would start by ticking off one on her index finger. "I have to work in that rinky-dink hotel with the trailer-trash you and Andrew have employed." She'd tick off two on her ring finger. "I have to go to these stupid classes with little kids who moan about how much work they have to do." Then the middle finger would come up just for him. "And there's taking care of you. You get to sit there all night and watch your *Star Trek* or read—do fucking nothing —while I have to get dinner ready then study…" The middle finger would turn and point at him. "…*and* give you what you want to keep you happy."

He had made the mistake of pointing out the flaws of her diatribe the first time she had heaved it, and that had been the last time. Since then, he heard some variety of it at least twice a week, and he'd sit there silently and take it, confirming her argument.

After the meal, some beer, and a few shots of tequila, she'd shift into her sweet voice, and she'd apologize for her "harsh words" and snuggle against him on the couch. Only once in these past few months had she mentioned the shadows; she had thanked him for keeping away the shadows.

She hadn't spoken of them for a long time. They'd watch the news, and she'd sweetly comment on the reports. Sweet buzzing Angelique.

John Paul quit letting his heart unwind from the knots she caused because he knew a short time later—especially if she didn't have another shot or two (or three)—he'd meet the sexual animal that taunted the Dog to come out to play.

The many faces of Angelique Carlson, he often thought.

So, when she asked John Paul about the sugar in that sweet voice, John Paul struggled not to look for the tequila. He returned her smile and replied, "Yes, please."

She poured the hot brown liquid into a cup, dipped a spoon into a sugar bowl, put the white crystals into the coffee, and stirred it. As she placed the cup near him on the table, she asked, "Would you like for me to get you a bowl of cereal?"

Okay, this wasn't the sweet, buzzed Angelique. It was the

sarcastic Angelique, another of the many faces. She knew something was going on this morning. There was no way she could know what he was going to do, but she certainly sensed it. The cereal question sounded like a match being lit, now held close to a fuse leading to a bomb inside her mouth.

Normal. He had to act normal. But what was normal to a rubber band twisted to the point of breaking? He needed to get away as quickly as possible. "Oh, no worries," he said. "I'll get something on the road to Philly." He hoped it was enough to assuage her.

"But I do worry, J.P."

Oh, shit, here we go.

Angelique opened a cabinet and grabbed a box of Fruit Loops.

Where the hell did that come from?

She broke the seal on the top and brought up the plastic bag within, pulled it open, then placed the box so that he could clearly see the front. She turned to the cabinets, and from a different one, she removed a bowl and placed it on the table next to the Fruit Loops. She poured a heaping pile of the loops into the bowl; not one dared to fall off. She got the milk from the fridge and poured it into the bowl, stopping when a green loop fell off. She picked it up and put it gently on the mound.

It was all a show.

"You know what they say about breakfast," she said, feigning sweetness and caring.

The Wolf pulled on the leash, growling to be let loose. John Paul didn't want to deal with her, so he kept the leash taut. He let *it* smile at her, stood, and took the one loop she had put on top. The Wolf looked at her and placed it in his mouth and said, "Yummy."

It dared her to explode.

Astonished, Angelique looked down at the Fruit Loops then back to him with a face that said, *What am I supposed to do about this?*

The Wolf didn't take his eyes from her. *It* said, "I'll be home around four." *It* took one more loop for good measure.

John Paul and the Wolf both knew he would be home later than that.

He collected his things and left.

The Wolf wouldn't let him kiss her or say bye.

A few days ago, when John Paul felt his rubber band of stress had double and triple knotted, so twisted up by Angelique that he had a constant tone in the back of his head, he called the only person he knew who might be able to understand.

Dr. Tom Schuller.

The big question was just how much John Paul was willing to tell him.

After a long wait on hold, finally: "This is Doctor Tom."

That voice. It always made John Paul smile. It was like a cool, hip Mr. Rogers. It was a voice that said, *Hey, I'm here for you. Whatever's wrong, we'll figure it out.* John Paul's heart lightened a little as he said, "Tom Schuller, how the hell are you?"

There was a pause. "Wilkins?"

"Yep."

"Shit, man, how the hell are *you?*"

"Faaaan-tastic." John Paul tried his best to sound happy and positive. Tom's voice brought up all kinds of emotions, crowding up in John Paul's throat, each wanting Tom's undivided attention. "Listen," he said, "I'm going to be up in Philly on Thursday. Got time for lunch? Catch up and shit?" It was like they were back in college, back in that old apartment building. That was Tom. He made it easy to let down the guard and take off the mask. That probably served him well with his patients.

More silence. It became uncomfortable.

"Yo, Tom?"

"Yeah. Sorry. I'm texting my receptionist right now. Clearing out that afternoon."

"No, man, you don't have to do that. Just a little lunch—"

"Seriously, dude? You call me out of the blue on a couple days' notice?" More silence. "Make it one o'clock, and I'm all yours."

What could John Paul say but, "Cool. See you then. What's your address?"

Driving now to the Highlight Hotel, John Paul knew he had that little sheet of paper with the address folded in his wallet between credit cards. He couldn't take any chances with Angelique, the way she'd been lately.

He parked in the valet zone and went straight to his office. He turned on his computer and printer.

What did the world do before MapQuest?

He printed out directions to the two banks Andrew wanted him to visit (so that it wasn't a total lie), and from one of the banks to the parking garage Tom wanted him to use. Not surprisingly, Tom didn't want him to park near his office. He implied a strange car in the neighborhood where he practiced might attract the wrong attention.

John Paul had to be at the bus stop at the garage by 12:30. He had plenty of time to see the loan officers at the banks. Without these directions, he would've wasted tons of time driving around Philly.

Thank God for MapQuest.

He rushed through the banks. Hello... Here's the plan... What are your options... My boss will review... Thank you... Goodbye.

The bus was right on time, and at 12:57, John Paul was stepping off to find Tom Schuller waiting for him.

They almost hugged. Tom held back, opting for a firm handshake. They stood there at the bus stop a moment, eyeing each other, as if Tom were looking into John Paul's eyes to see into his soul.

Finally, Tom said, "C'mon, I ordered a nice lunch."

Three years ago, Tom Schuller was a skinny man who sported a scruffy beard to match his messy, wrinkled look. He never ironed his clothes, probably donning them straight out of a laundry basket—and that was when he wasn't wearing scrubs. His dark hair had been on the longish side, parted down the middle and pushed behind his ears. Most of the time he had it in a small ponytail with a surgery cap.

He thought it was cool. It never got him any chicks, though. He had been as pathetic as the rest of the nerds in the old apartment building.

And he had been just as smitten with Angelique as all the other guys.

A few days before Tom had left for his job in Philadelphia, he had confessed to John Paul he was jealous, that he was happy for his friend, but he couldn't fathom why Angelique chose to stay with him.

"I guess an attack like that changes a person," John Paul had replied. He often wondered the same thing.

Tom said that it would change John Paul, too. And he wasn't wrong.

The Tom who walked beside him along South Philly streets had put on a few pounds and had filled out a little. And with his now-short lightly-colored hair sporting that mussed, spiked look that was so popular these days, he looked mature and confident.

He had been gangly and skittish in college, but now he looked like he could hold his own in a game of pick-up basketball. His smile was the same: genuine and happy. Dr. Tom loved what he did, and it showed on his face.

They approached an old building that may have been a small department store in the past. "Med Clinic" in large blue letters hung above the door; they probably lit up at night. A large window revealed a few people in the waiting area.

Tom opened the door, and they were promptly met by two nurses. The one behind the reception counter was on the phone, but she flashed a huge smile. She was a little heavy, but she was cute with her short red hair. She hung up, stood, and wasn't much taller than she was sitting down. The second stood at an open door to the left of reception. She must have just called a name, for a little girl with dark skin and dark corn rows contrasting with a bright-yellow dress approached her.

This taller nurse, nearly as tall as Tom, had milk-chocolate skin and black shoulder-length hair. She saw John Paul and Tom enter, but leaned down to the child and said, "You can go into room one," she pointed back behind the door. "I'll be there in a couple minutes." She had an athletic build and a very exotic appeal. As she straightened to face the men, the other nurse joined her. Both smiled broadly.

The little redhead mocked a perturbed look. "Is this the one who is causing all this trouble?" She didn't mask her flirting.

Tom stopped a moment and shook his head. "Yes, well, these two are vixens," he said to John Paul, and they beamed proudly.

"Sabby here may be short, but she could kick the ass off any WWF wrestler. Her talons are sharp, so watch out. And I had better get between you and Candace. Her teeth are sharper than Sabby's claws."

"Candace?" the taller nurse admonished Tom. She put out her hand and flashed an even brighter smile at John Paul. "I'm Candy."

John Paul chuckled and replied, "I'm sure." He shook her hand and also Sabby's. "Candy for Candace. Sabby?"

The redhead stepped closer. "Sabrina."

Tom stepped between them and said quietly, "I believe little Kalisa is waiting."

Sabby exaggerated a disappointed look, curtsied, and went back to her reception desk.

Tom looked at Candy, and she, more reluctantly than Sabby, went to examination room one.

They followed her through the door back beyond the examination rooms to an office. Tom opened the door as he said, "I have to apologize for all that." He smiled and waved his friend into the room. "I had no idea you were such a ladies' man."

Tom's comment barely registered as John Paul eyeballed the food on the desk in the office. Philly cheesesteaks, nachos, and a six pack of beer looked like a treasure at the end of a rainbow. The smell wrapped around John Paul and his mouth watered.

The office seemed larger than the clinic, more suited for a professor of literature than a medical doctor. Bookshelves covered two walls with texts ranging from Homer to Cicero to Jung to *Grey's Anatomy*. Tom must have kept every science fiction novel he had ever read: Wells and Dick and Asimov and Bradbury and Verne and Clarke and Herbert and on and on. Michael Crichton's *Prey* lay at the end of the desk.

On the wall behind the desk, ten framed medical licenses, three doctors and seven nurses, hung neatly in two rows, but surrounding them, like a disorganized cloud, hung dozens of small pictures of people, all smiling: babies, old gents, teen girls, burly men, pubescent boys, strong mothers. They were happy and healthy.

"Don't get any bright ideas. This isn't my office," Tom said. He stood next to John Paul, both of them looking at the wall of photos.

"That's our Wall of Fame. This office is our general consulting room where we bring in people to discuss good news or uncomfortable issues."

Tom moved behind the desk. "You still a bottle man?" He removed a beer from the cardboard holder and handed it to John Paul. An opener lay beside the pile of nachos, and he used it to remove the cap. He tossed it to Tom, and, in a moment, they were toasting old times.

John Paul sat across from Tom who motioned to the food.

"Nachos are getting cold, my friend," Tom said, reaching instead for his Philly.

John Paul took a paper plate and used tongs to grab a bunch of chips and cheese, ensuring he got a few jalapenos. "You said 'apologize?'"

"Damn that's good." Tom took another bite and said with a mouthful, "Geno's is the best." He swallowed it down with some beer. "Yes, that little drama out front. I told them you'd saved a woman's life then fell in love with her. They spent the morning on the Internet reading that article in the Baltimore News and watching that Hometown Hero video from The Morning Show."

John Paul stopped chewing.

Tom chuckled. "I suppose you didn't know that little video on their website has over twenty thousand comments. It's probably got more on YouTube."

John Paul had hoped it had been a one and done thing, lost among all the other Hometown Hero stories.

"That's thirty, forty people a day viewing it." Tom was amused at John Paul's embarrassment. "Probably all of them are hopeless romantics like the two hellcats out there, wishing they had a hero to sweep them off their feet." He sat forward. "Speaking of which, you don't seem to have any problems talking to women anymore."

John Paul shrugged and took a sip of beer. "Angelique calls it the dog in me. I guess dating her has released some kind of animal instinct or something." The Wolf within stirred.

Tom saw a change in his friend's face. Time to get to the reason for this visit. "So, you have a problem."

They locked eyes. John Paul took a bite of his Philly and chewed.

Tom put his sandwich down. "Angelique? She has difficulty sleeping?"

John Paul swallowed and took another bite.

"Dreams? Nightmares?" When John Paul said nothing, Tom continued, "Moody. Manic-depressive. Sexually aggressive. A poet but didn't know it?" Tom didn't take his eyes from his friend's. "Me, not her."

John Paul had stopped eating. His mouth turned up in a slight smile, but there was no mirth in his eyes. He had spent some time on his way to Philadelphia thinking about what he would and wouldn't tell Tom, yet his old friend had just labeled every idiosyncrasy he held in the bag of burdens he carried for Angelique.

Tom took a sip of beer. "And there are even darker things you won't tell me."

What the hell? "I suppose you're a mind reader, too." The comment croaked out of John Paul's dry mouth, and he reached for his beer. Empty.

Tom opened another and gave it to his friend. "Look, there's no big mystery here. It's been, what, nearly two years since that night? I'm surprised Angelique hasn't already imploded. She was a high-strung drama queen back then—throw a scary attack on top of it? And those murders?" He leaned closer. "Most of us in that building had connected the arrival of the detectives to the reporting of the murders."

"No one..."

Tom shrugged. "We all talked about it. A lot. Some of the guys were scared the killer was nearby, playing with the welcome mats."

John Paul smiled. "Angelique did, too." Then he shook his head. "The computer guy with the security cameras?"

"That was us, but it was a dude I knew who had the equipment and knowledge. Tom sat back and chuckled. "Everyone pitched in to pay for it."

And it stopped immediately, he thought. But the murders didn't.

Watching the thoughts and memories play across John Paul's face, Tom said, "She is suffering, and she needs help." He produced a couple books he must have had ready for this discussion. "Post-traumatic stress disorder. It happens a lot with people who go through these kinds of things."

John Paul looked from the books to Tom. "Right. PTSD." He took a sip of beer. "Like I haven't tried to talk to her about it."

"My guess is that it'll get worse."

John Paul couldn't imagine how much worse it could get. "Are you speaking as a friend or a doctor?"

Tom picked up his Philly and replied, "Both." He took a bite and followed it with a drink of beer. "PTSD can evolve into serious mental and physical health issues."

The irony of the situation struck John Paul like an ice-cold glass of water. Here they were discussing the grim health issues of the woman he loved, and they were doing it over Philly subs and beer. He looked at the half-empty bottle of beer in his hand.

"Is she drinking?"

Tom's question was like another punch in a heavyweight fight where John Paul's hands were tied. It was like one of those comedies where the weakling runs around in the ring to avoid the real fighter, John Paul replied, "No."

"She probably will. And she'll start going AWOL, maybe for days at a time." Tom finished his Philly like they were talking about the cons of the latest *Star Trek* flick. He downed the last of the beer in his hand. "Listen, my friend, if she is having the symptoms you confirmed, and you throw on top of those drinking, maybe drugs, and disappearances. She's in danger—and so are you."

"What are you suggesting? Commitment?"

"We can start with an intervention."

John Paul laughed. The look on Tom's face made him swallow hard.

"I'll help. I know the perfect mediator." He pulled off a couple chips with thick hardening cheese. "And we'll have to get her mother involved."

That would certainly make things interesting.

They spent the next couple hours speaking via a conference telephone with the "perfect mediator" Tom had spoken about, a sometimes-girlfriend whom he said was so smooth and sweet she could get the Devil to confess and ask forgiveness.

Christina Kaffreid did dozens of interventions a year in between treating patients for various addictions and mental health problems. She agreed that she would do the intervention in Baltimore, but only after John Paul agreed to see a counselor himself. They felt mid-August would be best, between summer school and the beginning of the fall semester. This would give John Paul time to iron out his own life and his relationship with Angelique. PTSD, Dr. Kaffreid told him, affected loved ones as much as sufferers.

Once the call was completed, Tom put a warm hand on John Paul's shoulder. "I know this is tearing you up inside and affecting how you feel about Angelique."

John Paul had thought he had been smooth and circumspect in his responses and non-responses.

Tom looked him in the eyes. "You don't call her 'Ange' anymore."

John Paul hadn't realized it, but it was true. He hadn't used the diminutive for a while. That endearment had faded away. A little cold cube of fear appeared in his heart. What did that mean?

At least he had a plan to try to melt this fear, to try to get Angelique some help, try to get her out of the Toilet Bowl of Life before it decided it was time to flush.

John Paul left Tom's clinic at four o'clock and pulled into his driveway near 6:30. His lie was complete.

Angelique wasn't home from classes, and it was the shadow time. Not a good sign.

John Paul was relieved when she called from the library on the Johns Hopkins campus. She asked if he could come to pick her up.

That was promising.

24

August 2004

The whispers started during finals week of summer school.

At first, she hardly noticed them, like the sparse susurrations in a theater.

Yesterday, however, during a Stats review, the whispers became boorish. For a while, she had thought it had been students behind her chatting and murmuring up in the back of the auditorium, but every time she'd turn around to shush them, she saw them watching the professor intently. It irritated her. She pushed through it.

But in today's German studies class, it got worse. There were only twenty-seven students in the hall, but they were all focused and attentive to the lecture. It had started with a high-pitched whine in the back of Angelique's head, just behind the ears, a stress tone she attributed to the beginning of a new semester. Then another sound joined it, a strange rhythm like how she had, as a child, played her father's LPs at seventy-eight RPM speed on an old turntable. She'd giggle at the high voices, not knowing what was being sung.

This whine in the back of her head reminded her of that squeaky voice. And like when she was a child, she'd switch the speed to forty-five RPM, and the squeaky voice inexplicably slowed into an indiscernible whisper.

146

Swirling like wind in her head, the odd words—not any language she'd heard before—had the cadence of sentences. And it was a woman's voice. She was inside her skull, just behind her ears, whispering with passion and conviction, reciting something, an actress on a stage, a stage of her mind, and the only audience was Angelique.

Was she speaking to herself? Was there another Angelique back there?

The voice sounded familiar.

... tick... tick... tick...

And there was something else: like at the end of a record, a bump or a click, a pulse...

The whispers—what did the woman say? Angelique felt she should know.

... tick... tick... tick... tick...

Something grabbed Angelique's left hand. A warm, soft hand squeezed hers. The brightness of the lecture hall made her eyes water. The other hand belonged to a girl sitting beside her. Connie. Yes, she knew Connie. She had hung out with Connie a few times.

Connie made the whispers go way back in her head.

The girl let go, but something tapped a button inside Angelique's left arm that made her hand move on its own.

... tick... tick... tick... tick... tick...

Angelique's fingernails kept rhythm with the thing in her arm.

She dropped the pen in her right hand and grabbed the left to stop the tapping.

"You okay?" Connie whispered.

The whisper released the other whispers, volume on ten, a throbbing static in her head.

Angelique grabbed her backpack and purse and scooted across the row to the aisle and ran up the stairs and out into the cool morning.

25

Stop by my office first thing.
-A

Andrew signed all his notes with an "A." This one had been folded and taped shut so that Marcia at the main desk couldn't see it. He knew John Paul always checked his messages and mail upon arrival every morning.

Something whispered for John Paul to go straight to Andrew's office—don't pass go and don't collect two-hundred dollars.

The last time he had seen Andrew's office this messy was just after he'd been hired. An elderly woman had sued the hotel over a wet chair in her room. She claimed the daily maid had pissed on it, hoping she would sit in it. And it was urine, for certain, but analysis had determined it was the woman's and more investigation revealed that she was beginning to suffer from dementia. For the three weeks of the ordeal, however, Andrew's office went from anally-organized to tornado-touched.

Rarely did John Paul go to Andrew's office, and it'd been a few weeks since he'd been in it. For it to be as bad as this again, something serious had to be gnawing at his friend.

"Summer cleaning, I hope?" John Paul tried to sound humorous, but it only made Andrew's face twist in agony.

148

The owner of Highlight Hotel was standing, and he pointed at the chair across the desk from him. The papers and folders that had been in it had been put into a pile on the floor. "Have a seat."

"Hell, Drew, if you needed some help, all you needed to do is ask." John Paul felt uncomfortable under his friend's gaze as he watched him settle into the chair.

Andrew sat, too. "How are you doing? I mean, *really* doing?"

Oh shit, thought John Paul, this was the inquisition voice Andrew used when he was getting ready to unload on an employee for fucking up. His mind churned over the past few weeks: no complaints that he knew of, happy departures of patrons, a few thanks from area restaurant managers for the recommendations—the usual. He decided to throw it back at Andrew. "I'm doing great, but you're not doing so hot." He looked about the room to emphasize the situation. "What's going on?"

"How's Angelique?"

Did John Paul just hear the handle of the Toilet Bowl of Life jiggle a little?

He felt his life, his *worth*, was being weighed like a butcher with a hunk of meat. Slap it on the scale. If it was the right size, it was a keeper. The problem was that this particular piece of meat being examined at the moment belonged to Angelique—but it was attached to John Paul. If it was too big (John Paul thought of all the idiosyncrasies), if it was too expensive, it would have to be carved smaller.

He didn't know what to say, but he knew what he wanted to say:

Gee, Drew, how's the love of my life doing lately? Well, let's see. She's a fucking nightmare rollercoaster of emotions, my friend. She drinks more than a fish, gills within gills, you know what I mean? She screams and thrashes about in the middle of the night, scaring and waking me. Oh, and that's after she's fuck-punished me for being me. Other than that, I guess you can say she's doing pretty good.

John Paul's hesitation must have confirmed something, for Andrew nodded and began: "Look, I don't know how to say this, so I'm just going to say it." He shook his head slightly at the awkwardness of his comment. "There are some serious allegations that have come to me recently."

When Andrew used words like allegations, he became *An*drew the owner, and business trumped friendship. "I'm going to give you the names of the accusers because I believe you two deserve to know who's pointing the finger." Andrew paused and continued, "David Tripp approached me a week ago saying he smelled alcohol on Angelique's breath, and Sharon Arribe reported she found her sleeping at her desk. She thought Angelique was drunk."

There—it was said, replete with last names and words like *approached* and *reported*. This was a grand jury inquest. John Paul heard it again: Fate jiggling the handle on the Toilet Bowl of Life. A buzzing started in the back of his head, and the Wolf howled at him to hit Andrew right between those two eyes that challenged him. It didn't matter if any of it was true. No one challenged the Alpha! John Paul somehow remained calm, but he was unsure of what to say.

Andrew became impatient. "Does she have a drinking problem?"

John Paul had that feeling of being filled again, and he knew the Wolf had come into him. He didn't fight it, but he didn't yield. What came out of his mouth flowed easily, like an actor on a stage. "You know Angelique. She likes her cups, as my grandfather liked to say. We have a beer or two in the evening." He nodded at Andrew. "I know you like your evening Scotch." The notion they all liked to drink softened his boss's eyes. "A week ago? That could have been the day after our neighbor's dinner party. Hell, I was still a little buzzed the next day. But this sleeping thing? I'll have to look into that." The explanation was perfect: no outright denials and no confirmations.

Should have been a politician, John Paul thought. The Wolf had surprised him with a clear mind and a steady confidence.

It surprised Andrew, too, and for a moment, John Paul thought his friend was going to say, *Bullshit*, but his face melted into relief— as if John Paul's speech had indeed denied all the accusations. Andrew's eyes said, *Of course, this is all some kind of misunderstanding.* He let out an audible sigh, and the Wolf told John Paul that Andrew had been more worried about losing his friend and manager than some cute employee. John Paul knew at that moment if Angelique had been sitting here, she would have been fired.

Worse than the games we play with others were the games we play with ourselves.

The Wolf told John Paul this was no game. It was a hunt. He had to find David and Sharon.

26

The door opened and bright sunlight, like a lighthouse in a dark night, pierced the heavy air of the bar briefly then disappeared. Two men entered and went straight to the bar.

The younger of the two noticed Angelique at the dark end of the bar and smiled.

She ignored him. She flirted with the idea of giving him the finger but guessed he might take it as an invitation. *Fucking barflies.*

She smiled at herself. She was one, too, but she was disappointed the other flies had arrived. She wanted to be alone, and she had even told the bartender as much.

"Three shots of tequila and don't talk to me. And turn off the T.V. while you're at it." She had considered asking him to shut off the neon signage behind the bar, but it probably would have earned her a "fuck off outta here."

He provided the shots, shut off the T.V., and had disappeared through a threshold to a backroom behind the bar.

When the new barflies entered, the bartender reappeared, poured them both a beer, and disappeared.

Angelique ached all over, particularly in her shoulders and lower back. It interfered with her introspection about what had happened in the lecture hall. Those whispers. They haunted her. And this tick in her left arm. She couldn't think. She needed the tequila to help her focus.

Angelique downed the third shot and looked at her watch: 11:03 A.M. and she didn't care. Twenty minutes and three shots had stopped the tick and the shaking.

"Yo, Terry!" the older barfly called out. His voice sounded like a bullhorn next to Angelique's ear.

She winced.

Terry the bartender came out, looked at Angelique, and bent his head to the two barflies.

A silence followed.

When Angelique opened her eyes, she saw the three men looking at her. Terry had a remote in his hand.

She almost laughed. They were asking her permission to turn it on.

"Whatever," she said, and pointed at the empty shot glasses.

Terry pointed the remote at the T.V. "First and ten from the thirty-seven," blared from it, then trailed down to whisper level. "The Eagles with twenty-two seconds..."

Fucking ESPN. Big fucking surprise.

She felt them looking at her again. They were watching her. Had she said that aloud?

Terry came over, filled her shot glasses, and disappeared.

She downed one immediately with a quick, easy motion.

The pain was still there, but she was beginning to care less about it. She felt a little better. That was all that mattered.

Angelique looked at the other barflies. They were intent on their Sports Center. She looked at the neon signs of various beers and liquors. The glorious rows of colored and clear bottles glowed from the faint light of the frosted windows and the bright square one in the door.

A large fluorescent sign over a mirror read Patches.

It occurred to Angelique she had never been here before.

Everything about sitting at the bar irritated her.

She knew there was a booth behind her, one of those circular ones with the soft seats. No lights. She grabbed her remaining two shots and turned on the stool to view it.

Something to the right caught her eye, a movement. She thought maybe it had been the bartender slipping down the dark hallway to the bathrooms.

She heard a "Yes!" from one of the barflies, and she looked to see them—and the bartender—watching something on the T.V.

Angelique turned to the hall. Something inky and wet oozed out of the shadows onto the floor... and moved directly towards her.

She downed the shot in her left hand.

This couldn't be! It was daytime! A public place!

And like a dream, the whispering returned.

"Fuck you!" she screamed and threw the other shot at the approaching shadow.

27

Little Sharon Arribe looked scared.

She was almost two feet shorter than John Paul. She had wavy brown hair with highlights, wore too much makeup for John Paul's taste, and paraded about in a tight buttoned white blouse that exposed cleavage that everyone knew was expensive. The little woman obviously felt she should have something that wasn't small.

Her daddy was in real estate and gave his little daughter anything she wanted, which also included a hot little Lexus in the employee section of the parking garage. Too bad everyone looked at her big ears instead of her big tits.

John Paul yanked the chain on the Wolf.

He almost wanted to kneel down before her, like an adult to a cowering child. Instead, he took a step back, and Sharon seemed to ease a little. She even smiled.

They stood in a small office behind the main desk where Angelique and others typically processed paperwork. John Paul had acted like he was busy with the lobby checklist, but he watched the little woman until she went into the office. He followed her and shut the door behind him. They had done a little dance, the Wolf smiling as she tried to get past him.

He stepped at her and said, "I had a talk with Mr. Peterson. He said you saw Angelique sleeping on the job," and Sharon had cowered back. Her big ears turned red.

The Wolf smiled as his prey explained what she had told Andrew.

"I always bring the checkout list to her around 1:30. She was in that chair," Sharon nodded at the desk, "but her head was down and to the side." She hesitated a moment and added, "She was drooling. I didn't tell Mr. Peterson that." She looked up at the Wolf and smiled back. "I tried to wake her, but she wouldn't. I almost went to get Anne who was at the front desk that day, but Angelique woke up."

"Did she say anything?"

Sharon shrugged a little. Her ears faded to pink. "Yes. She slurred her words. She said sorry and thanks."

They stood silently for a moment, smiling at each other—each for different reasons. Finally, he said, "Mr. Peterson said you thought she was drunk. Did you smell anything on her?"

"Well, no. But she looked it."

"Disoriented... slurring her speech, as you said... tired."

Sharon was silent. She saw where he was going, and the look on her face said as much, for it was as red as her ears.

The Wolf continued to smile. "Now, I'm going to ask you a question, Sharon. I need for you to be very honest, even if you think it'll hurt my feelings."

Concern moved across the woman's face, but she continued to look into his eyes.

He asked, "Before this little episode happened, had you perhaps spoken to Dave Tripp?"

Sharon's face went white, making her ears crimson.

"That's what I thought."

He turned and reached for the door.

"She doesn't deserve you, you know?"

He stopped. He yanked hard on the Wolf's chain, but he didn't put the animal away. He turned to Sharon, still smiling, but the Wolf was howling. "Really? And why is that?"

She stepped back, startled. "Uh... she, ah, she says things about you, behind your back."

"I'm certain you heard these things yourself." He almost laughed.

Sharon's face went from white to red. "Fuck you."

John Paul felt the Wolf settle into his body, that movement, again, of a hand into a glove, flexing to ensure a good fit. There was no longer a need for a chain, and in that moment, in that curse from little Sharon Arribe, John Paul felt like he had dived into a warm pool—or had put on clothes that had just come out of the dryer. It was a physical thing that felt right. There was no struggle for his soul or fight for control of his consciousness.

The animal *thing* that had been *back there*, deep in the abyss of John Paul Wilkins, the *thing* he called the Wolf, entered his heart, filled it, became a part of him he now realized he had been missing. He had feared it and treated it as a separate thing, an alter-ego, an antithesis. But it had been a necessary part of him all this time.

Treated with fear and kept locked away, it had behaved like an animal when it had been allowed out of its cage, forced to wear chains. Now, John Paul embraced it, let it enter the home and become an intimate part of his nature.

John Paul Wilkins looked with pity at the little young woman standing before him. "I'm sorry, Sharon," he said with mock sincerity, "but you're not my type."

Sharon took another step back.

John Paul turned and left, still chuckling.

28

It smelled like a hospital.

The air was clean, as if it had been scrubbed. She took a deep breath and became light-headed. No clotting shadow choked off her lungs.

"Angel?"

Mom?

Angelique couldn't move. Part of her thought the shadow that had climbed up her leg and thigh, pulling her down to the bar floor, pushing into her mouth and nose, had created this dream of her in this hospital room, her mother somewhere nearby. She expected Anders or *something* to ooze from the darkness to envelop and rip up her mother.

She was home in bed. She had to be.

The screaming and teeth and blood were moments away. She didn't want to open her eyes.

She couldn't. Their slightest movements beneath her lids created a flicker of aches that promised nauseating pain if she opened them.

Something cool touched Angelique's face. Agony! Her body came alive—a thumping of pains like a hundred little hammers pounding every square inch of her face.

Her wrists and ankles exploded when she tried to reach up to her face.

Mother! she wanted to scream, but her mouth and throat were sandpaper.

She had the distinct impression she was on an altar to be sacrificed to some blood god.

Now she did open her eyes—to a new agony.

Shadows moved in her periphery.

A gargling, gravelly noise rose about Angelique, barking each time she writhed her body. She realized the sound was her own dry voice.

She felt her will pulled down, like the glitter in a snow globe when it stopped shaking. The noise, her voice, eased, and her throat relaxed.

Angelique felt vertigo, and her vision shifted on a strange axis.

"Angel? Angel, dear, they had to give you another sedative. You'll be all right."

Her last fuzzy thought was that she had never been all right...

29

As John Paul pulled into the driveway, he expected his stomach to constrict, that shrinking feeling he sometimes got when he knew he had to face someone important, the feeling he always got whenever he argued with his father, or, lately, in those first few minutes when he came home on Angelique's school nights. He just didn't know what to expect from her, and it often generated this feeling of dread in his belly.

But that was yesterday: the old John Paul, the one who had been on the back side of the threshold he had crossed. The John Paul Wilkins who sat in this car at this moment wasn't the one who had been possessed months ago by "the Dog" as Angelique had called it. This John Paul Wilkins felt complete, full. Before, he had felt like a half full glass of beer, he reflected.

He smiled.

A half-filled glass of beer looked incomplete. There was something wrong with it. It begged to be topped off. That was how he felt. Topped off, filled to the brim.

Complete.

There was something about a complete glass of beer that made one look at it before taking a sip. There was a beauty to it. One needed to appreciate it—the thin white foam at the top, the clear amber color, the singular bubbles floating to the top—before partaking of it. John Paul needed to do this, appreciate the new fullness of himself.

But he needed to deal with Angelique.

And there was no fear in him as he exited the car.

The house was dark. It was almost eight o'clock, well past the shadow time. He knew there were no messages on his phone. She should have been home.

She'll start going AWOL. Dr. Tom's words echoed.

Perhaps she was napping. She had just started summer school finals. Long nights studying and the stress of the tests would wear out anyone. She came home and went to bed.

She'll start going AWOL.

John Paul marched up the steps to the door.

Once inside, he called out to Angelique.

Nothing.

He turned on the lights and went upstairs to the bedroom.

Empty.

She'll start going AWOL.

He called her cell. Voice mail. "Hi, babe. I'm home. Call me and let me know what's going on. Miss you." He tried to sound pleasant and nonthreatening.

... mental and physical health issues...

"Shit." This felt wrong.

He considered calling Angelique's mother, but he decided to wait a while.

Absent without leave.

Since when did Angelique ever ask for his leave to do anything?

30

A ngelique came fully awake.

She knew she was in a hospital room. She saw her mother sitting in a chair reading a magazine. The short thin woman sat absolutely still. Bifocals straddled the end of her nose, dark eyes intent upon the article she read. Her short black bob of hair squared her face. Then a hand moved a page. Her mother could be as still as stone, as silent, too—and as obstinate.

Diane Carlson had been the real ruler of the Carlson household. Angelique had heard her father joking one time that Diane didn't have a spine—she had a solid steel beam that was inflexible. Her mother rarely raised her voice. She would turn those dark eyes upon whoever happened to cross her, and she would become cold steel. Her victim (often Angelique) would just do whatever the woman wanted.

Cobras did that, too, Angelique mused, some kind of mesmerizing stare before they struck. Diane Carlson was a cold steel cobra.

But when Diane smiled, it was like a sunny day on the beach.

Their eyes met. The room became brighter.

Angelique tried to smile, her lips cracking a little. She rolled her thick dry tongue in her mouth and tried to generate some spit. She was so thirsty.

Her mother was at her side with a cup of water. Diane guided the straw to her daughter's mouth. Angelique took a tiny sip, moved the cool water around her mouth, then took another longer one. The water magically awakened her body, even though it felt like someone had taken advantage of it with a baseball bat. Even her pinky toes were sore.

Her face must have revealed her pain, for her mother said, "The doctors are not certain what's wrong with you. They have more tests, but they were waiting for you to wake up."

Wake? How long have I been asleep?

"It's a little after eight, dear." Diane wanted to put a hand on her daughter's face but knew the slightest touch could send her daughter into painful spasms. "An ambulance brought you here from a bar. The owner said you had a few shots and fell to the ground screaming and shaking. One of the nurses in the ER recognized you and called me. You have awoken twice screaming in pain. The doctor has given you something strong which seems to be working." She held the straw to Angelique's mouth again. As her daughter took another sip, she added, "I told them about your attack. And your lack of sleep."

Angelique looked sharply at her mother, and even that small movement sent a painful throb through her eye sockets and forehead. Her wrists and ankles were still bound. An I.V. poked into her left hand.

The whole thing brought up the last time she had been in a hospital. She quivered and let out a gasp. A tear oozed from her right eye.

"Oh, my little Angel..."

A short doctor in a long white jacket entered the room. His jet-black hair, dark skin, and aquiline nose hooking over his mustache gave him a Mediterranean look, Sicilian or Greek maybe.

He went to the left side of her bed and took a file from somewhere on the wall behind her. He shuffled through a few pages and said, "Miss Carlson, I am Doctor Toskas."

A taller, blond nurse with a puffy face and red nose came in behind him and checked her I.V.

The doctor looked up from the file and asked, "Do you

remember Doctor Richards? He received you and ordered your CAT and MRI."

When Angelique didn't respond, he continued, "You were in what seemed to be some kind of seizure. You were very violent in the ambulance, and we have had to restrain you and sedate you." He paused. "Doctor Richards took some blood, but that analysis will not be completed for a while. The scans show nothing about your condition. He wants to do an EKG on your heart and an EEG on your brain, but you have to be awake for those."

Angelique still said nothing.

"So far, Miss Carlson, we've found no physical reason for your fits and pain."

Now Angelique did ask a question. "What kind of doctor are you?"

Dr. Toskas smiled and replied, "A psychiatrist." He put the folder back from where he had taken it. "I understand you were attacked nearly two years ago." Angelique became silent again. "I'm certain you know about post-traumatic stress disorder. Have you also heard of fibromyalgia?"

31

John Paul awoke on the couch, his neck sore and stiff.

He had decided to wait in the living room to be near the door when Angelique came home. He would make her sit and talk about this—all of this—and together, they would map out a plan to deal with it, and that included therapy. He didn't care if she exploded in rage: deal with it or deal out of it.

John Paul looked at his watch: 12:27. Nothing on his cell. Nothing from her. He guessed he had been asleep for a couple hours. He considered calling her again. He even considered calling her mother. Neither option was appealing.

He decided to do nothing. Wait.

He didn't like that either.

32

D r. Toskas' implications were finally voiced when the last of the results came in—except for the blood work—and she knew the least they would find was a lot of alcohol. Even that would fit with what Toskas just told her:

"If our collective diagnosis is correct—and it will take some time to confirm it—then you need to understand there are not many therapies for fibromyalgia. Pregabalin is promising, but it is in clinical trials. I might be able to get you into it, but you will have to go to rehab. Alcohol inhibits Pregabalin. And you will have to begin serious counseling for your obvious PTSD. It is causing the pain, your sleep issues, and your need for alcohol. From what your mother has told me, much of what you are experiencing, I believe, goes back to that incident, and perhaps even further back."

You only know a fourth of it.

Angelique wanted to ask if she could stay on the Vicodin, but she knew the answer. It was so much better than tequila. And she could have neither.

Rehab. Like some addict or alcoholic.

PTSD? *Please.*

Dr. Toskas left her to think about her situation.

But this pain was a constant, like the feeling of the extreme heat of a griddle through a kitchen hot glove. The Vicodin covered her so well. This was no broken bone that would soon mend with everything going back to normal. The pain in her back, her ass, her knees, her elbows—it wasn't going to go away with a cast and some physical therapy. This was a break in her psyche that would take a long time to heal.

And Angelique knew there were things in her life that no shrink, not even Freud or Jung themselves, could bring to light.

Shadows and vampires.

No one understood, not even John Paul, who might empathize but could never comprehend—

Shit.

She and her mother were alone in the room. Diane—her mother; she hadn't called her *mother* and meant it for a long time—was back in her chair, a statue reading another magazine. "Mom? What time is it?"

Diane looked at her watch. "3:47."

Angelique tried to sit up. Pain throbbed through her body. "Fuck, this hurts." She took some deep breaths. "You need to make a call."

33

A little while turned into three hours.
    John Paul had received a call from Angelique's mother at 3:51 A.M.

Three fucking fifty-one in the fucking morning

"It's Diane. Angelique has been in the hospital since yesterday morning. We'll be home in a little while. I know you have a lot of questions, John Paul. We'll answer them when we get there. Please be patient."

All of fifteen seconds. Diane hung up before he could utter a sound. He had tried to call back several times. Nothing. He knew this was Angelique's doing—the call and the not answering.

John Paul considered getting a shower. He felt half-dirty, the half of him that was pissed off that there had been no call since yesterday morning. The other half heard *hospital* and was concerned about what had happened. The dirty half wanted to see their faces as they walked through the door, wanted to hear the spider web they had been weaving. The other half thought about calling Tom Schuller and starting the intervention, but it was too early in the morning.

Fortunately, just before one A.M. John Paul had called Andrew to let him know a little of what was happening, but mostly to tell him neither he nor Angelique would be at work later this morning. Things had reached a climax, he told his friend. He didn't say it would be a showdown.

Now it was dawn. The bottoms of clouds in the distant east glowed orange-red like embers. John Paul glowed hot inside. God knew he was fucking pissed.

And he was scared. He had to admit it, standing in the shadows of his living room, looking out the front window. Waiting.

Why was he waiting?

That dirty half—he might as well call it what it was: the Wolf—itched for a fight. It wanted a confrontation... the showdown. Duel at dawn.

But the Wolf loved Angelique, too. It loved how she snapped back at him. Alpha to Alpha. But John Paul had kept the Wolf on a leash. Hell, he had kept it in a cage. The Angelique Alpha had been given free rein without challenge for too long.

And even now, as John Paul felt the Wolf mixing more with the human, he felt the savage intensity of it lessen.

Salad dressing. He smiled at the thought. Wolf-Man balsamic. Yes, this felt like a salad dressing. The vinegar and the oil and the herbs were there. What better place to keep them properly mixed than in the heart? Wolf-Man balsamic. John Paul chuckled.

That chuckle pushed away the fear.

What was he waiting for?

As the sun rose to a new day, John Paul realized he had been waiting for Angelique. She was afraid of the dawn and of the dusk —the shadow times she called them. Shadows. Moving shadows... *living* shadows, she had called them. They beckoned her to join them, pulled at her to embrace them.

Angelique was doing the same to him.

She had become the thing she feared. She became a shadow to John Paul. She couldn't see it, for she lived a twilight existence, stuck between moving forward into the future and The Night of her past.

Loving her had made John Paul stuck, too.

The morning became brighter.

John Paul decided he would no longer be stuck. He knew, as

certain as Tom Schuller and Christina Kaffreid had explained to him, Angelique could never move past The Night, could never enjoy the living, until she confronted what had happened to her.

Tom's voice emerged in the back of his mind: ...*evolve into serious mental and physical health issues...*

The evolution was over. Angelique had been in the hospital with her mother.

Neither had thought to call him.

Tom had said something about Angelique going AWOL, but John Paul didn't think this was what his friend had meant. Angelique must have had some kind of episode, perhaps a breakdown.

Perhaps this was what she needed to avoid the Toilet Bowl of Life from flushing.

Headlights shone into the living room. Diane Carlson's BMW pulled into the driveway. John Paul moved back from the window into the dark, the shadows, of the living room. He smiled at that.

Shadows... monsters... vampires.

The Night. This all came down to The Night.

John Paul saw Diane get out of her car and go around to the front passenger side. He watched her carefully help her daughter to shift in the seat and stand. Angelique was slow to move, stepping aside to let Diane push—not shut—the door, as if to avoid the sound of it.

He fought with himself to go out and help. It was clear Angelique was in pain.

They slowly shuffled to the walkway.

The anger melted away.

He pulled open the door and hurried down the steps to the other side of Angelique. She looked up—

The last time he had seen this fear in her face was...

He asked, "Can I carry you into the house?"

She nodded.

John Paul ignored Diane. He swept Angelique up, and she grimaced and stifled a moan as he carried her into the house.

"The sofa," she whispered, and John Paul gently placed her on it.

The last twelve hours boiled up in him, and he forced himself to remain calm. He would at least hear what they had to say before he tore into them.

34

Angelique saw an uncharacteristic anger harden J.P.'s face. She wondered if that was the Dog. She had no patience now to explore that.

The dull ache in her shoulders, neck, and pelvis made her grimace, and she tried to shift her weight. That only made other parts of her ache. The Vicodin was wearing off.

J.P.'s anger wasn't. Her discomfort didn't faze him.

Angelique was glad the lights of the room were off. Yet, she could see the morning sun would peek over the roof of the house across the street in a matter of minutes. "Could you please shut the drapes?"

John Paul was stone, a monolith in the living room.

Diane saw this, and she gave him a withering look. She went to the line at the right of the window and pulled it down. Both sides of the curtains skipped a couple feet to the center. "Before you go getting all indignant," Diane said and pulled the line again, "let me say—"

"You know," John Paul cut her off, but his eyes stayed on Angelique, "I don't know what hurts more: You not calling me or you not calling me."

Diane turned. "What?" she spat. "How dare you? She's been in—"

"Mother," Angelique interrupted her, looking directly at John Paul. "I think you should leave and let us talk."

Neither John Paul nor Angelique saw Diane's mouth open and shut like a fish out of water.

Finally, Diane said, "I don't think—"

"Please, Mother."

Diane loitered a few moments more.

Angelique and John Paul had eyes only for each other, yet they were aware of Diane backing away. They heard the front door shut.

The Angelique of two days ago would have said: *Not call you? Kinda had important, distressing things happening to me. Oh, yeah, kinda passed out, too. Sorry I couldn't think of you through the pain.*

Saying that many words would probably hurt.

Besides, as she thought it, she realized she hadn't wanted him there fawning over her, a face of compassion and concern. Her stony mother had been the perfect thing for her in that hospital room. She wanted to say all this, but the Angelique of now wanted to ask for the prescription in her purse.

She forced her eyes to stay on him.

Then the sun appeared, a bright white vertical line down the middle of the room shining through the gap in the drapes, cutting the sofa in half, cutting her off from J.P.

The silence became heavy. Angelique realized he was waiting for her. She said nothing.

He must have seen her pained look from the light, for he stood and pulled the line making the drapes move closer together, the line fainter and thinner... but still there.

He was too good for her. He deserved something different than her. And she wanted something different than him, than this life. Schools and jobs... family and kids. They all seemed tertiary to her own needs.

She wanted to know what The Night was all about.

But she needed first to get through this, to push this aside—push *him* aside.

She looked into his blue eyes, now less stony than a minute ago. She took a breath and said, "I'm going away."

35

What Angelique told him was no big surprise.

She laid out a plan much like what Dr. Tom and Dr. Christina said she needed to do: rehab and therapy. It was just going to be without him.

John Paul sat through her narrative as the morning sun rose, the line of light emphasizing the divide between them. The split between them. Both sides of himself were divided, a mix of sorrow and relief.

When dreams dissolved, they eroded a part of the positivity in life. He had dreamed of Angelique for nearly a year, and when that dream became reality, he believed his life would be—he didn't know what his life would be, but it was going to be better than this. He should have known that a dream built on a trauma, born from The Night, would become a nightmare swirling in the maelstrom that was the Toilet Bowl of Life.

It all came back to The Night.

As he thought about it, it was more than The Night. It had brought them together, but there were things about Angelique that were dark and twisted.

Sitting on the sofa, the room was dark but for the vertical slit of light and the glow around the curtains, the air became thick like just before a storm, expectant. John Paul figured a storm of sorts had touched Angelique and was about to engulf her; he equally understood he had somehow avoided it.

She talked about her drinking and the tick in her arm that had become a fusillade of hammers on her body, how she needed to sober up before being admitted to a drug study for... whatever this malady was. She talked about PTSD and therapy.

She talked about everything she needed to do.

Except she mentioned nothing of the shadows and nightmares —and Anders and the Vampire Killer. Those were the things that had been shredding her humanity.

John Paul wondered about her childhood, if there was some other horrible event that had manifested in these shadows she claimed had haunted her all these years.

Watching her in this gloom, he realized there wasn't much he knew about her. She hadn't spoken much about her youth, other than to say she was a little wild in high school. All he really knew about her was that in these couple years, he'd loved her.

Angelique Carlson had been a puzzle he had wanted to take the time to solve. He had wanted to invest himself into finding the pieces and putting them into place. However, the gaps in the picture were wide and *dark*—and the largest gap, The Night, was an abyss that perhaps had no pieces he could find on his own.

John Paul understood in this dark moment that Angelique was taking the puzzle away from him.

Dr. Tom had told him: "You can't fix her. Try, and it will drag you down into that Toilet Bowl you mentioned. She has to fix herself."

Dr. Christina had said the old cliché was true... about the horse and water.

John Paul heard nothing. Angelique had become silent.

They were staring at each other's hands in their laps.

He felt her move. She grimaced, trying to sit up a little. "You haven't said much."

John Paul discovered he had been barely breathing. He inhaled the warm, heavy air, and the anger that had been covering him cracked like dead skin. He wanted that shower more than ever. He needed to scrub all this away.

He replied, "What's there to say? I'm happy you've made a decision to get help."

"I kind of thought you'd be angrier."

Angelique seemed more like the helpless Angelique she had been after the attack. There was a little glimmer of his past feelings for her, but it was overwhelmed with the fact that she was going away. Their relationship was over.

John Paul shifted his body to face her, leaning closer to the line of light separating them. "Given what you've told me, and my concern for you—" he paused, considering his words. "Listen, yeah, I was pissed. I was fuming. But you know me. My anger is like a match." He wanted to reach her, but crossing that line felt wrong, and he felt she'd flinch; he didn't want to see that. "You coming home like this—it blew the match before it could go out by itself."

He couldn't bring himself to say what he really felt: *I can no longer take this.*

Seeing her in pain right now... remembering the pain she caused him... hearing the handle jiggle on the Toilet Bowl of Life...

If you love me, you'll join me.

He couldn't. He wouldn't.

After a few moments, Angelique said, "I can tell you're not happy."

He couldn't respond.

"I'm not either." Angelique shifted and let out a slow breath. "I'll move out. I'll talk to Andrew and give him my notice."

Like you're giving me my notice? "Nothing has to be done immediately," John Paul said. "You can stay here as long as you wish, until you make your arrangements."

Angelique smiled, and John Paul noticed the morning was at its peak.

She said, "Diane is already on that." She looked intently at her purse and tried to lean forward.

With all that had been said, the line of light didn't seem to be so important. John Paul reached over and grabbed Angelique's purse.

"You'll find my 'scrip' in there. I need it."

The pills were Vicodin, and he wondered—but he put that thought out of his mind. She was clearly in pain. He twisted off the child-proof top and shook out a pill. She motioned for a second. He placed them in her hand, and she popped them into her mouth. She never used water to wash down pills.

She smiled, opened her eyes, and said, "You're in dire need of a shower. Help me to the bed, I need to rest." With an ornery smile, she added, "Maybe you'll get lucky later and help me take one."

Later that day, after a second dose of Vicodin had kicked in, John Paul helped her bathe. Then she wanted him. It had been the first time they had made love in a long time.

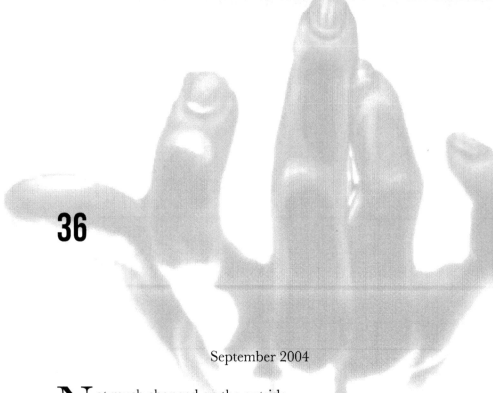

36

September 2004

Not much changed on the outside.

Angelique still lived with John Paul. They ate dinner together. They talked. Some. They still had sex, though not as frequently, and because of her condition, it was tame and normal. At least he still made her come.

The two things that did change were school and work. She withdrew from college, and she resigned from the hotel. The Dean seemed genuinely concerned about her and wished her well; her place would be waiting for her when she wanted to come back. This he said with a smile at Diane.

Andrew Peterson at the Highlight Hotel wasn't surprised. In fact, it seemed like he was somewhat relieved, and he gave her a perfunctory "Thanks for your contributions at the hotel." The prick was glad she was leaving. She wondered at how much he knew about the circumstances.

Diane (funny how quickly the woman had gone from Mother to Diane again) came over daily to discuss rehabs. Angelique guessed it was mostly to check on her.

Angelique only drank her tequila after Diane left, and she quit an hour or so before J.P. was due home.

The shadows—Anders—still appeared in her periphery, little reminders that they hadn't forgotten her. They stayed outside of the house, as if its walls were a barrier they couldn't cross. Whenever she stepped out to go shopping or to have lunch, these days in the full sun, she'd catch a shift of movement behind the boxes of pasta or beneath a tablecloth. It was like the good ol' days, and like those days, the only thing to betray Angelique's nervousness was her shifting eyes.

That was the outside of Angelique's life.

Inside, however, she was all calculations and machinations. She kept J.P. happy so that she could stay at his place (Andrew's place, she reminded herself) while she readied herself for her rehab farce. There was no way she could stay with Diane. So, she kept the drinking to a minimum in front of him.

She had no illusions that if she went on a binge, he'd call Diane with no hesitations. This proved to be taxing, but she managed it. As long as she fucked him, he seemed to be okay with the status quo. For all she knew, he was fucking her to keep her steady. That would be like him—soooo predictable.

She kept Diane and J.P. busy and happy for one reason: She needed time to do what she really wanted to do.

She had asked Diane (she had become *Mother* that day, but she knew Diane wasn't buying it) for a new laptop to research the list of rehab centers and her various maladies. She told Diane she didn't want to use J.P.'s, and didn't want him to be reminded of her "situation" when he might happen to look at his search history.

Diane more than obliged. She expected daily briefings on what Angelique liked and disliked about the rehab choices Diane proffered. And Angelique made her silly reports.

When she wasn't under scrutiny, she was online purchasing books. She still had her father's inheritance and some of the money she had earned from working at the hotel. She used a good portion of it on her library of everything occult—particularly anything about vampires. They arrived one or two a day, and she hid them away in boxes as she packed to leave.

They would be safe in storage while she was on "hiatus."

37

The old John Paul may have been predictable, but the new one wasn't fooled by this disciplined Angelique.

There was no doubt he liked this calmer and steadier Angelique, especially when she took her Vicodin and perhaps had a shot or two of tequila. When he had asked her if that was wise, she had shrugged and said she was going on "hiatus" to get cleaned out, inside and out, and that these few weeks were her last hurrah.

He didn't want to argue, so he gave her a pass. But he saw how she looked at the cabinet where the bottle stayed, and he could feel that old Angelique under the façade. He didn't doubt she'd really go to rehab, and he knew she knew she needed to get the alcohol demon under control. But that was the "outside" part of her. "Inside" she had her shadows, and he knew she wouldn't let them go away.

She had pulled herself out of the Toilet Bowl of Life, and he was happy for her. As the days went by, he became happier that this part of his life was coming to a close.

But he had this nagging feeling, like someone softly poking his back, that she was up to something. It had started with the word "hiatus"—like going to rehab was a break or a vacation. The word had pricked up the ears of the Wolf. John Paul gave it permission to hunt.

A couple times a week, she would zonk out after Vicodin sex, allowing him to sniff around. He carefully searched her drawers and dressers, all the closets, all the cabinets, within and under everything. He found nothing. But the Wolf in him was relentless. It wanted to exhaust everywhere in the main house before the basement. And on this night, it was time to go down.

The stack of boxes that was the sum of Angelique's time with John Paul seemed small. Not that two years was a long time. They hadn't traveled or vacationed much. They had spent most of that time in Baltimore.

A little part of John Paul felt bad for that. Perhaps if they had done more together, things would—

The Wolf growled. It reminded him of her darkness.

He grabbed a towel from the pile of dirty clothes on the dryer and went back up the steps to the door that opened into the kitchen. He listened. Only silence. He folded the end of the towel and stuffed it under the door before he turned on the lights.

He came back to the pile of Angelique's life. John Paul knew there was something in these boxes that would confirm his needling suspicion.

He looked at it closely, memorizing how the boxes were stacked before he removed two smaller boxes on top and grabbed a larger one from the middle. He brought it to the steps to a worktable where Andrew's father probably had had dozens of tools arranged on the wall and lying about. Now, there was a small toolbox, a power drill that could also operate as a screwdriver, and a couple hammers and wrenches. He opened the box and found a knife and some glue, then he grabbed a hand towel from the dirty clothes.

He sat on the third step, the box between his legs, his tools on the step beside him.

As a boy, John Paul loved to open sealed boxes; he had become quite good at it. All it took was a sharp knife, some glue, a towel, and patience. Time, too. To do it right, opening and resealing a box took time. He knew it was a little after midnight. He could get a couple boxes done by three o'clock.

He looked at the "SUMMER CLOTHES" box before him and at the boxes in the pile. All were sealed with a single strip of tan packing tape along the flaps and a couple inches down the sides. This was going to be easy.

Using the knife, he carefully slipped the tip under the corner of the packing tape and gently pulled the corner up. Then he used the tip and sharp edge to cut the fibers where the tape met the box. Thin fibers gave way easily, and he worked the tape until it came up to the box flaps. The adhesive of the tape had left a discernible discoloration, and had Angelique used clear packing tape, this would have been problematic. But tan tape, when using a thin layer of glue, went back on as if it had never been removed. He removed the tape on the other side of the box.

John Paul looked along the length of the tape on the top flaps and found a pucker. He worked the tip of the knife in and got to work on just one of the box flaps, ensuring the tape on the other side stayed in place.

This was where patience mattered. He had to be careful cutting the fibers, for if he went too fast or cut too hard, the tape could rip and become a tell-tale for anyone looking that this box had been opened. He felt sweat on his brow, and he used the towel to wipe it. He had to bend close to where he operated, watching where tape met cardboard, so that he could let the knife edge glide over the fibers, loosening the tape from the flap. He certainly didn't want any sweat to drip on the cardboard. That could leave a pucker mark. He wanted no evidence that could say this box had been opened.

He finished freeing the tape and relaxed for a moment. He held his breath and listened, looking up at the basement ceiling. Silence. He guessed it was around one o'clock. He took a slow deep breath and looked at his handiwork.

Both box tops were free, with the tan tape still attached to the left side, a two-to-three-inch tongue sticking out at both ends. He smiled. He still had it.

He wished he had brought down a glass of water. He couldn't risk going up to the kitchen. With this invasion of privacy opened like a cadaver in an autopsy, he couldn't risk any sound that might wake Angelique.

John Paul opened the box and smiled again. Fortune was on his side. Bikini tops and bottoms had been loosely tossed in. That would make it easy to replace. He removed them and placed them in a pile on the step behind him. He stood and reached in, removing a number of t-shirts—

"Gotcha," he hissed.

He placed the tees next to the bikinis on the step.

Inside the box, he saw two hardback books, both written by Montague Summers. *The Vampire in Lore and Legend* had a red cover with a drawing of a strange bat or gargoyle creature in a family crest. The dark cover of *Vampires and Vampirism* had some old painting of a beastly creature sitting on the belly of a sleeping woman.

John Paul looked at the other boxes in the pile on the basement floor and knew each had a book or two like these hidden within.

Angelique was going to pursue her shadows and nightmares.

She wasn't going to try to work towards healing and living. She was going to get herself *physically* healthy, but anything that might change her path into darkness she'd bluff her way through. She'd get out and start hunting for answers.

Angelique Carlson wasn't stuck between The Night and the future. She had never left that alley and that man—Anders.

And unbidden into his mind's eye, John Paul saw the long teeth. He saw the photos of the victims, holes in their necks.

Exsanguinated.

He shuddered and looked about into the basement's dark corners and beneath the stairs.

He quickly put the clothes back the way they had come out.

This is fucked up.

He used the glue and rubbed a thin layer on the fuzzy part of the tan tape. He fit the tops together then sealed the top, the sides. Perfect.

Fucking crazy bitch.

He placed the boxes exactly as they had been.

As he put the knife and glue back, he heard something behind the stack of boxes. He froze, listening. Now he was getting all paranoid. All he could hear was his own heart thumping in his ears.

He looked around, wiping his brow and the glue off his finger with the hand towel.

After a moment, he grabbed the towel under the door and put both into the middle of the dirty clothes.

Upstairs, John Paul walked carefully into the living room and sat on the sofa. It was raining outside, blowing at the window, making faint tapping sounds on the glass.

He needed to calm down.

An old analog clock hung on the wall between pictures of a beach much like the one they had gone to last summer and one of a beautiful night scene of Baltimore on the river. The clock read 1:54. He hadn't been down in the basement as long as he'd thought.

He looked back out into the night, listening to the rain hitting the window.

The Wolf told him he'd know when to use this information.

A short time later, he climbed into bed next to Angelique. He closed his eyes, but he couldn't sleep.

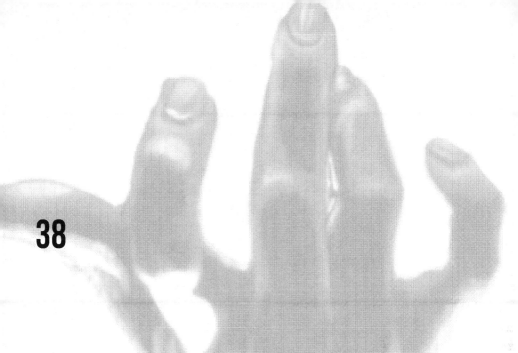

38

Andrew Peterson was a great friend to J.P. It irked Angelique that he seemed a little aloof to her, as if he held back a smoldering anger.

Perhaps he was jealous of his friend; perhaps he lusted after Angelique. Most men did. Lust and desire made men behave strangely.

Regardless, Andrew had given J.P. three days off to see to Angelique's departure. She was a little paranoid on the first of those days, for she had a package arriving.

Fortunately, J.P. had been out to the grocery store when it arrived. Angelique opened the fat envelope, removed the book within—*Vampires: The Occult Truth*—and placed it in the bottom of a box of school books. She closed the box, taped it shut, and took it down to the basement where she had stacked all her items for moving out. Angelique walked back upstairs, found a pair of scissors, and cut up the envelope. She shoved the pieces deep into the garbage.

As she washed her hands, she felt much better.

Actually, she had been feeling better physically as well. The body pains came and went, but they were manageable. She only took Vicodin once a day, mostly at night, and she had begun to cut back a little on the tequila, though that proved to be a little more difficult.

Her imminent departure left her feeling excited—which in turn disturbed her.

Intellectually, she knew she should be feeling sad about what was happening. Emotionally, she felt she was being released from prison. She had thought about this dichotomy a lot over the past few days.

Her conclusion: J.P. was a constant reminder of The Night. She attributed all of her condition to this revelation. And it seemed that once she determined this, she had started to feel better.

Diane had rented a truck and a self-storage bay, and J.P. had asked a couple of new guys from the hotel to come over and help him load. There were a few pieces of furniture and the boxes from the basement. It took them all of an hour to load it all into the truck. J.P. sent them away with two twenties each and told them to have fun. He, Angelique, and Diane stood awkwardly at the open end of the truck.

Angelique looked at John Paul and wondered briefly if he felt as relieved as she. Forcing down a smile, she continued to look at him and opened her mouth.

He beat her to it. "Diane, would you mind giving us a couple minutes?"

Diane put a hand on her daughter's shoulder and said, "I'll be in the car." She had hired a man from the rental company to drive the truck to the storage site. Since he hadn't been paid to help with the loading, he had sat in the cab listening to the radio. He would unload the truck into the bay, however, and take the truck back.

Diane would drive Angelique to the rehab center.

When they were alone, Angelique smiled. *Should I shake his hand?*

J.P. made no move.

She leaned close to kiss him on the cheek. It felt like the right thing to do.

But he turned his head and met her lips with his, and it turned into a lingering kiss that said to her, *I'm going to miss you.*

A goodbye kiss.

There was nothing left between them.

His hands moved to her shoulders, and he held her—not an embrace, but a steadying grasp to keep her still. He moved his mouth to her right ear and whispered, "Enjoy the vampire books."

Was that the Dog? Had J.P. allowed it to come up to sniff and snoop and find her stash?

Angelique saw his disappointment. No Dog. She had hoped to see a little turn of victory on his mouth or in his eyes. Just mundane disappointment.

He moved to shut the truck, and the resounding slam startled her. He secured the door then pounded it twice again. She jumped again.

No more words. He turned and went back to the house.

It was over.

She hadn't been as clever as she'd thought.

"Fuck him," Angelique said aloud, watching him go into the house. "But I already have."

She walked to the car, got in, and allowed Diane to take her to her hiatus.

PART THREE
WORKIN' THEM ANGELS

"Quiet, child,"
　　She said.
　　She pointed at his arm,
　　Bent in the wrong place.
　　She said,
　　"What'd you expect,
　　Workin' them angels like that?"
　　- Edgar Tappestry, "Grandmother," *Oracles*

Oftentimes, to win us to our harm
　　The instruments of darkness tell us truths,
　　Win us with honest trifles, to betray 's
　　In deepest consequence.
　　- William Shakespeare, *Macbeth*

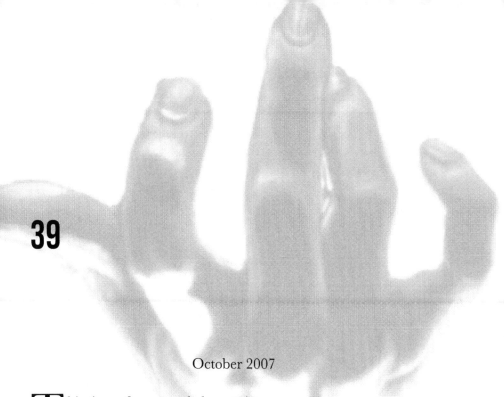

39

October 2007

T his time of year made her squirmy.
    She found herself waking multiple times in the middle of the night catching her breath, listening to the dark—realizing she was still days away from the nightmares she knew would slam her mind, squeeze her heart, and churn her belly into a volcano.

Angelique Carlson was coming up to the Anniversary—with a capital fucking "A."

Okay, she felt more than squirmy. She could already feel the nightmares churning within her, just under the skin, like a dog scratching at a door to be let out.

Within the nightmares was the shadow.

She used to believe there had been more than one shadow. They had been a part of her life since she was a child.

But there was only one.

A white hand... long thin fingers...

She tried not to think of that hand, but it always dug its way up into her, like that hand on *The Addams Family*—or that stupid movie about an even creepier, deadly hand. But those were disembodied hands.

Angelique's special hand, so white and elegant, was attached to something: a vampire named Anders Saffenssen. It had killed people close to her family. It had terrorized the city of Baltimore and had led the Baltimore Police Department around by the nose. And it had touched her. It had removed a glove from its white elegant hand and put its freezing fingers around her neck. Just before the ice of that touch consumed the heat of her body, she saw its fangs.

Anders' hand was somehow deep inside her, and it clawed to get out on the Anniversary of The Night.

Tinkerbell.

Long blond hair.

Soon.

The teeth.

Happy thoughts.

Deathly white hand.

Want to scream.

The teeth.

As you die.

The *teeth.*

Hot salty metallic blood filling her mouth.

And then she would scream and jump out of the bed and turn on all the lights and run about until she puked.

The Anniversary. It was nightmares of blood and violence—most of them she didn't remember—didn't want to remember.

Until she had gone to rehab.

She had promised her mother twenty-four months to detox and get serious therapy. She entered the facility a month before the Anniversary. She shook and sweat and took her pills and laid in bed until she could walk. Then she ran. She worked out. She had been in the process of pushing out every molecule of alcohol in her body. She had started AA meetings. She told truths and half-truths and lies.

She played the little game of cat and mouse with her therapist.

Angelique had believed she had been the cat and that little bald man the mouse.

But fucking Dr. Kellim mentioned it in a session: *You know, the anniversary of your attack is in a few days. How does that make you feel?*

Fucking asshole. Fucking ruined everything.

The shadows came up, and for three nights she woke screaming and thrashing about, even puking on a nurse. She had to be sedated. And Kellim, that bald mousy fuck, made her talk about it.

He brought up the shadows. And he agreed: they were some kind of fear. She allowed him to drag out of her how a cold Mommy offered no comfort after Daddy turned away from her and died.

Then there was the vampire.

She allowed Kellim to drag out of her what he wanted to hear: *There are no such things as vampires. The attack on The Night was only connected to the Vampire Killer in her own mind. The police didn't find a connection because there was no connection.*

She said the words and acted the part.

But the dreams on that Anniversary and the following year had only reminded her of what she had to do: find the vampire. And to find the vampire, she had to do as much research on these creatures of the night as she could.

And that meant getting out of the mental health facility as quickly as possible.

She worked harder, played all the parts she needed to play. Took all the meds she was told to take. Got into the best physical condition of her life.

Even her mother had been impressed.

All agreed Angelique could leave three months early, with the recommendation she stay with her mother during that time. A "provisional release," they called it.

On June 14th of 2006, Angelique said goodbye to her friends, acquaintances, nurses, and doctors, collected her materials and belongings, and walked out the doors whispering, "Good riddance."

However, she wasn't free.

For three months she had to please her mother and attend more therapy sessions with Dr. Kellim.

She enrolled half-time to resume her anthropology degree at Johns Hopkins.

All had been pleased at her progress.

Finally, on September 13th, Diane Carlson and Dr. Kellim signed off on Angelique Carlson's recovery.

She was free.

That was a Wednesday, and by Friday, Angelique had rented a cheap apartment and had moved all her materials there. She dug out all her books on the occult and vampires. She bought used bookcases and assembled her private little library.

She added to it extensively. She researched everything she could about the Baltimore Vampire Murders and what little was known about the Vampire Killer.

She still lived with her mother. She spent most of her days in the classrooms. In the evenings, she "worked at the library."

But that October, the first Anniversary outside of the rehab, saw the nightmares return, this time with a screaming fit at her mother's. Angelique had run through the house and had turned on every light. She ended up on her knees in the kitchen in a puddle of puke.

Diane Carlson had not been phased. She had expected as much, she told her daughter. Dr. Kellim had warned her something like this might happen near the Anniversary. And for two more nights Mother Carlson endured the screams and lights and the racing through the house. Both those nights Angelique ended up in bed with her, like the little Angel of long ago.

Now she was coming up to her second post-rehab Anniversary. Three nights of hell on the horizon. Angelique felt it, the shadow, clamoring to come up to play. Soon it would be crawling under her skin and infecting her dreams.

And Anders the Vampire Killer—Anders, creature of the night —would be within the nightmares.

She sat up and got out of bed. She needed a drink of water.

A sharp intake of breath, and she heard from the bed, "Hey, babe..."

"Go back to sleep. I'm just getting some water."

"'Kay," he mumbled and turned toward her. He was back to sleep in three seconds. *Lucky bastard.*

In the dark of night, at the threshold between the room and the hall, Angelique stood and looked at her boyfriend. How was he going to react? Would he demand to know about the nightmares? What would she tell him? She had to give careful thought to this. It would be a turning point in their relationship, she was certain.

She needed him. He was critical in her plans.

She went to the kitchen for that water.

40

C hange was a strange thing. Most of the time it crept up and hugged like a lover. After such a warm embrace, change was endurable, expected—welcomed.

Sometimes, change was a storm on the horizon, edging slowly nearer, the wind picking up, cold rain stinging the face. Then came the hail and the rumbling approach of the tornado. This change was endurable, expected—fleeting. Time was spent cleaning up the mess and rebuilding. Though things were never exactly the same as before, the cleanup allowed the good parts of the past to remain. And the world moved on.

Then there was the flash of change, like a sudden explosion. One moment life was one way and the next it was different. And it was unexpected. Permanent.

This last change, John Wilkins reflected, was his life after The Night.

He'd been going to work like any other night. He'd saved Angelique Carlson's life, and he'd become a hero. He didn't want to be a hero, but there it was: in the newspapers, on the T.V., on the radio. For a time, he had to endure it—and Angelique. But he'd discovered his heroism had become a permanent story on the Internet. He said a silent thank you to the universe for not making Angelique a permanent part of his life, though.

He stood at the bus stop, earphones in his ears but no music playing from his MP3 player. He was coming out of a familiar reverie, thinking about her and his old life. That was five years ago. Nearly. In a few days it would be the Anniversary, the explosive flash of change that had altered his life inside and out.

For all her talk of shadows and (he could barely say the word) vampires, there had indeed been something happening those weeks after The Night. That flash of change had been like a massive earthquake followed by weeks of aftershocks. John had saved Angelique from Anders Saffenssen, but he couldn't save her from herself. Angelique broke down and eventually ended up in rehab.

Good for her. He truly hoped she had found the help she needed.

For the most part, John had forgotten about Angelique. His life had moved on. But with the Anniversary of The Night looming, he couldn't help but to think about what had been, and that all the chaos she had brought into his life was now behind him.

John knew from the magnitude of that change how explosive it had been, that he could never go back to what had been his life before Angelique Carlson. It had indelibly changed him.

And not all for the worse.

Women liked him now. And John knew it had something to do with the Wolf.

Before The Night and its explosion of change, John could barely muster a few words to a pretty young lady. Here, as he navigated this post-change world, he felt as comfortable talking to a strange woman as he did with his friends.

John was afraid the Wolf lurked close to the surface of his consciousness, and this was what made him attractive. As much as he tried to control it, it managed to stay in the conscious part of his mind. He and the Wolf were now inseparable. And he accepted that.

But it also scared him.

A truck's brakes squealed as it stopped in front of him at the stoplight. The logo on the side read "Caster's Catering." It popped him from his reverie, and he took a sudden breath as if he had forgotten to breathe while he was in the past. The truck revved up and took a right turn.

As he was about to start some music on his player—

Just below the glowing "don't walk" sign across the street, a strangely familiar face looked straight at him. The man wore a blue suit and white shirt; he held a newspaper. Their eyes connected: John's with confusion, the stranger's with recognition. The man smiled broadly, a grin of happiness. John couldn't help but to smile back.

Another truck passed by, and the Blue Man was gone.

John Wilkins wasn't a paranoid man, but this was the second time this week he had seen that man and his look of joyous recognition.

No fear passed through John. Just curiosity.

His bus arrived. He pushed play on his player, and the heavy bass of Aerosmith's "Sweet Emotion" blasted into his ears, pushing the Blue Man from his mind.

That smile, however, lingered.

He sat with his eyes closed, the music filling his mind, the bus rocking seemingly with the song.

In the few seconds between songs, John remembered the first time he had encountered the Blue Man. Three days ago. He had waited in line to get his usual latte at Perry Perc. The Blue Man had been sitting at one of the two small tables reading his newspaper, waiting for his drink.

"Here ya go, sir," the barista had called out.

The Blue Man had gotten up, gave John that wide grin of extreme happiness and recognition, leaned close and murmured, "Nice to see you again." He had laid a ten-dollar bill on the counter, took the cup, and walked out.

The barista recognized John and said, "Wow, this's gonna be two in a row."

Still looking back at the door, John had responded, "Huh?"

"Two specialty drinks in a row," she had replied. "That guy got a caramel-cinnamon latte like yours. Rarely happens." She then opened the cash register and made change, stuffing it into her pocket. "Good tipper, too."

Those few seconds between songs seemed an eternity. Something tickled in the back of his mind about the Blue Man, where he might have seen or met him, but he just couldn't scratch it. Obviously, that man had encountered John.

The smile said it all.

It was one of those stupid smiles of recognition followed by the realization of a mistaken identity.

A happy, chance encounter—then oops wrong person. Sorry for the mistake.

Except that the Blue Man knew he had made no mistake.

"Living on the Edge" started in John's ears.

The bus rumbled down the street.

A few blocks from work, John jumped in his seat.

The older woman sitting beside him shot him a look.

He was between songs again and that smile appeared in his mind.

He turned the player off.

In his mind's eye, he saw that stupid grin again. He stepped back from it, and he saw a middle-aged African-American woman. He had also seen her twice these last few weeks. Both times she had been dressed in green, and both times with that wide happy grin of recognition—

Like the Blue Man.

The Blue Man and the Green Woman.

Somehow the color seemed important.

Am I being followed? Am I being investigated?

41

G lass of water in hand, standing in the dark, Angelique could barely see Everett on the bed. She took a sip and recalled the night she met him.

It was at a university party—for whom and for what, she had forgotten. Angelique simply knew that important people would probably be there: medical doctors, biologists, researchers. She didn't even have a formal invitation. A little black cocktail dress cut down her chest a tad too far and perhaps a tad too high up her legs. Red pumps that matched the red ruby that hung at the top of her cleavage. Red studs on her earlobes. She had worked on her tan for a week—not a bit of white on her body. Someone was going to get lucky... if he said the right word.

Two hours and two trips to the bathroom (cranberry juice went right through her), and she finally heard it.

Blood.

"C'mon, Everett," an older man was saying to a cute younger one. "You're the best I've had in a decade."

"I'm not interested in blood, Peter." The cute younger man sipped a glass of dark beer. His dark hair was cut short on the sides with that planned, mussed up look on top. The dark, thick brows accentuated his green eyes. He had a Mediterranean look about him, Greek or Italian. His natural skin was as dark as Angelique's tan, which contrasted nicely with the white shirt and khakis he wore.

He licked his lips and said to this Peter person, "And I'm the best you've *ever* had." He smiled as he made his boast. Peter touched his glass to Everett's in agreement, and they both took a sip.

Peter shrugged. "It's one of the largest grants Hops has ever received. The World Health Organization has pledged to eradicate malaria by 2020. You could become a part of medical history." Peter smiled. "You'll become bored after your third knee replacement."

"I'll become bored after my third day of watching malaria kill blood."

"We'll have the best—"

"And just how does malaria kill blood?" Angelique put her breasts out a little farther, like two guns pointed at Peter. She made it a point to ignore Everett, though he was the one in her sights.

Both men froze. Peter fought valiantly not to look at Angelique's cleavage. She could feel Everett look her up and down. Then Peter smiled and asked, "Miss?"

"Angelique Carlson." She shifted her glass of cranberry juice to her left hand and put out her right. Peter took it.

"An angel, I am certain. I am Peter Luzick."

This older man was a charmer, or probably had been in his younger days. Angelique could see in his eyes he was married to his work, a crusader looking to make a mark on the world. He had wavy strawberry blond hair, graying at the temples, and he had a dark mole on his left cheek. Two oval indents on the bridge of his nose told he wore glasses that he undoubtedly kept in a pocket of the blue Dockers he wore. His light blue Oxford shirt had its sleeves neatly folded up to the elbows.

Peter let their hands touch a few seconds longer before he said, "And this stubborn young man is Everett Preston."

She shook Everett's hand briefly and asked Peter, "You were about to tell me about malaria and blood."

Peter's brows popped up. "Why would someone as lovely as you be the least interested in something as boring as that?"

Angelique shrugged. "I have an interest in blood."

Peter continued to look at her as if he wanted to ask her more, but he nodded at Everett and said to her, "This young man here is the one you need to talk with. What are you drinking?"

"Just cranberry juice, Peter."

She turned her full attention to her quarry. Everett was smiling. Angelique locked her eyes on his. "And what's so amusing?"

Everett broke her gaze, took the half-filled glass from Angelique, held it up, smiled a confirmation, and asked, "Cranberry juice? Blood? Rubies and red shoes?"

"Aren't you a little *under*dressed?" Angelique decided he would do.

He never got to tell her about malaria till the next morning.

That was back in June.

Now, Everett was addicted to her, and Angelique decided there in the dark of their bedroom she would make him even more addicted. She put both her hands around the cold glass of water for a minute before she placed it on the nightstand. She removed her nighty and panties and slipped under the warm covers. Everett moved to his back, still asleep. Angelique smiled and slid her hand under his pajamas.

Everett jumped. "Damn! Your hand is cold!"

Angelique gripped him with both. "Then you need to warm it up."

He squirmed, and she laughed.

42

"Jesus, John, ya sound like a paranoid freak."

Barry sat in John's small living room, eyeing his friend closely between sips of beer.

John had just told his friend about the Blue Man and the Green Woman. He sat on the arm of his living room chair and took a drink of his own. "Stalkers might be a sign it's time to leave the big city."

Barry rolled his eyes and sighed. "This again?"

"What?"

Barry took a pull from his beer. "When was the last time ya went out, had some fun?" Before John could reply, he said, "I betcha I could call your boss, and he'd tell me ya haven't had a day off since Labor Day."

"I worked on Labor Day."

"Exactly. And I betcha he'd say ya've worked every weekend since your vacay in July."

John smiled. He'd met a nice girl at the beach. Sophie. They'd had a great week.

Barry was short and a little overweight, what some might call thick. His wavy hair still had some summer highlights even though it was early-fall. He had to push up from the sofa to clink his bottle to John's. "I see that memory in your eyes. That's what I'm talking about." He took another swig. "All work and no play will getcha all coiled up. Even springs need to spring every once in a while." He used the sofa's arm rest to pull up to stand. "Let's go get the Smileys out of your head."

John grinned. *Smileys... good one.* He looked at his watch: 10:27.

Barry put a hand to his mouth like a megaphone. "Ladies and gentlemen, your attention please. John Wilkins is thinking about dancing with something cute and warm—"

John laughed. "Shut up, perv." He stood with his friend. "Fuck it. Let's go."

They clinked bottles and downed them.

Fanny's had been a disco back in the 70s, a rock bar in the 80s, a techno bar in the 90s, and now it was a meat market. Wednesday through Saturday nights it was packed shoulder to shoulder with a few illegal high schoolers, but mostly nubile college chicks and thirty-something MILFs. A few hot cougars prowled about too.

John and Barry went straight to the bar and ordered beers.

The music and the lights and the heat and the hum of people filled John's senses; the bitter freshness of the beer moved down his throat. He took another sip and said to Barry, "I don't know about this. A lot of youngsters."

Barry was about to reply when a woman on the other side of John laughed.

"You're not so mature yourself." The voice was a little deep, a little seasoned.

John felt the woman turn and lean her back against the bar. He copied it so that they were shoulder to shoulder facing the crowd. They didn't look at each other.

He took a drink of beer and responded, "That depends on your definition of mature."

Another fast song started, and the dancers danced, but John felt like another dance had just started here at the bar.

The woman was quiet.

John turned and faced her. She had shoulder-length straight brown hair pulled back on both sides and clasped on the back with something that glittered gold. She was a good ten years older, probably pushing forty, but she obviously paid good money to look younger so that she could fit into clubs like Fanny's. Her skin was tight with few wrinkles, and her brows were painted on, probably tattooed.

She was sculpted to look like a model for some anti-aging cream. Her thin muscled arms matched the tight body in the yellow and black dress. And the enhanced cleavage was perfect, not too large and in proportion to her size.

John made eye contact with the bartender and winked. The girl smiled and nodded.

The woman finished her drink just in time for John to take the new one that had already been made.

John handed her the drink. She raised her brows, impressed. "Maturity is a relative thing, *young* man." They looked now at each other, both making a point not to look anywhere else but the eyes.

John clinked his bottle against her glass. "Touché." He smiled and turned to move back to Barry.

She touched his hand and said, "My name is Barbara."

"John," he replied and faced her again. He nodded back at his friend. "And this is Barry."

She barely acknowledged Barry and said to John, "Yes."

Their hands continued to touch. "Yes, what?" John asked.

"Yes," Barbara smiled, "I do want to dance, and I have a friend here."

John chuckled. "Direct. I like that."

Now Barbara looked at Barry then back at John. She moved close to his ear. "If he can't handle himself, I'm not the sharing kind."

"I'm a one-woman man," he whispered back.

She moved back with a smile, took his bottle of beer, and put it and her drink on the bar. She gently grabbed John's wrist and led him to the dance floor.

By the second song, Barbara moved close, her hands finding his shoulders, and as they gyrated to the beat, one hand moved to his neck. Her hands felt warm even through his shirt, and he imagined he could absorb her warmth.

The lights and sound and smell of the dance floor swirled about, and he could feel the rhythm start to move through him. The dancers moved with the music—an orgy of purling, twirling arms, asses, and legs.

Before he allowed himself to get lost in it all, John looked for Barry. His friend stood with Barbara's friend. The two were chatting and smiling.

Another woman was smiling, too. She stood just behind Barry, watching John on the dance floor.

That smile.

Green shimmering dress.

That smile—

"Hey..." Barbara said, her hot hand now on his face trying to turn his attention to her.

John looked at her and realized he had stopped dancing, He looked back to the Green Woman. She was still there behind Barry. Smiling. Now gently waving a hand.

John walked over to his friend.

"Hey!" Barbara called, but John didn't hear her. In four steps, he reached out and grabbed Barry's arm and turned him around.

"Yo!" Barry said, stunned by his friend's move. He nearly dropped his beer. "What the f—"

John placed him in front of the Green Woman. "This is her!"

Barry looked at the woman. She looked as shocked as he— perhaps more so.

John only saw that stupid, happy-to-see-you smile.

She was African-American, perhaps fifty but pleasant looking enough. She had straightened her dark hair and parted it down the middle, curling into her clavicle. Wide almond-shaped green eyes, with a few crow's feet at the outer corners, matched her sequined dress. She was nothing like Barbara or her friend, who obviously worked their bodies every day. This woman worked hard but didn't work out.

Barry shrugged. "This is who?"

John growled in his friend's ear, "The *Green Woman.*"

Barry laughed. "Who? Smiley?"

The woman responded, "I beg your pardon?"

But what John heard was, "*Do you really want to do this now?*" and she kept on smiling.

John pointed a finger at her. "Fuckin' right, I want to do it!"

"Do what?" The question came from both Barry and Barbara, who had joined the little party. Sherry moved behind Barbara.

They looked expectantly at John, who realized he looked quite mad at the moment. Only Barry understood a little of what was happening.

"Do you mind telling me what is happening?" the Green Woman asked, her eyes fixed on John.

John heard: *"We need to talk."*

Now all stared at the Green Woman.

"Who is this?" Barbara demanded of John.

The Green Woman looked at Barbara (but John only saw the grin). "Who am *I?*" she responded. "This man accosted *me!*"

John heard: *"It is important you do not make a scene that makes you look like an idiot."*

"What?" both John and Barbara said.

Barbara's friend, who had been hovering behind them, guffawed. "Who talks like that?"

The Green Woman turned her eyes to John's. There were no pupils, no whites—just a solid, glowing green...

John Paul Wilkins!

The words of his name felt like three shoves inside his head, his mind. His eyes unfocused. He felt like falling backwards—and *back there* was a yawning abyss. He struggled to stay on the edge, stay standing. He reached out to grab anything to steady him.

Barry saw John's eyes go blank; he even saw the pupils go wide. He grabbed his friend's hand and arm. He smiled embarrassingly and said, "I guess he's not over the flu like he thought he was."

Barbara looked concerned.

The Green Woman declared, "Sick people should stay home."

John heard: *"See you soon..."*

People around them parted to let them through. John's legs felt heavy like he was walking through water.

Barry guided his friend to the door where another man grabbed the other arm and helped Barry take John outside to the cooler, fresher air.

"I'm a doctor," the man said. "I can call an ambulance."

They sat John on the sidewalk next to the entrance of the club, his back against the wall.

John felt like his head was filling with mud. A strange inertia forced him around. Was the Toilet Bowl of Life flushing him away?

"No, thanks," Barry replied. "He's been stressed out recently. He just needs a little rest." Barry got out his cell to call for a cab. He took a few steps away.

The doctor leaned over John and opened each eyelid to check the pupils. The streetlights and club marquee made John's eyes water. He shut them tight.

The doctor put a warm hand on John's forehead. "John?"

John Paul Wilkins.

"Can you hear me?"

Wake, John Paul.

"Have you taken any drugs tonight?"

Open thine eyes and see the wonders of the Light!

Like diving into a very warm pool, waves moved through his body, caressing his skin, his organs, seeping into his bones. John's mind calmed, and his balance returned. His world no longer revolved down.

He laughed.

Barry wondered for a moment if the doctor was laughing, but he saw John chuckling, and knew there was something wrong with his friend. Perhaps a trip to the ER wasn't a bad idea.

The doctor stood and said, "He's disoriented but doesn't seem to be in any danger. He may be dehydrated and drinking alcohol hasn't helped."

John took a deep breath. He opened his eyes.

The Blue Man smiled a familiar smile.

"Oh, shit."

John Wilkins remembered where he had seen the Blue Man before.

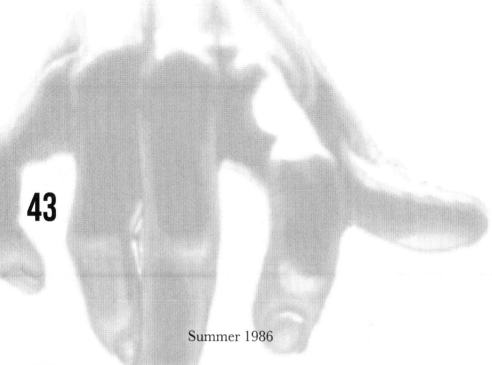

43

The penny shone brightly on the sidewalk. The morning sun caught it just right to glint in the boy's eye.

He looked up at his mommy. She was warbling (as his dad called it) with Jimmy's mom. They stood off from the entrance of the grocery store, as they did every Monday morning.

Other mothers would show up shortly, sometimes up to six total, and Johnny would be the only boy among them. He wondered why his mommy didn't get a sitter like the other mothers did. The one time he had asked, she had promised to give him five pennies for the gumball machines. Five gumballs for an eternity of warbling mothers and boring shopping.

Johnny looked back at the penny. Like a mirror, it flashed lying on the sidewalk at the corner of the building. Cars stopped at the intersection, taking their polite turns before moving on. The boy watched them for a moment, then looked at his mommy, then looked at the penny.

A car turned and shadowed the penny, making it flicker. He could swear he heard the penny say, *"I'm here for you, Johnny. I miss you. Come and get me!"*

He looked at his mommy. Still warbling.

Not taking his eyes from her, he took a small step at the penny. He didn't have to look back at it. It's call now was a physical thing.

Come and get me, Johnny!

Another small step. She took no notice.

Just for you, Johnny! No one else!

He had to be patient.

Johnny stood to the right of the main entrance. The cement was still wet from its morning cleaning. He didn't like the damp smell that rose from it.

One more step took him to the front doors, and they slid open. The store exhaled, and Johnny smiled.

Oh, the sweet smell of fresh bread. He loved that smell. That heavenly scent wrapped around him like a blanket. Any other Monday, he would have stood there until his mommy tired of the warbling, but the penny was insistent:

Johnny! I'm waiting, Johnny!

He gave it a quick half-look and watched his mommy. He was waiting for her hands to start. When her hands moved with her mouth, she would be focused on the conversation, giving Johnny the chance to get the penny.

But luck gave him a better chance: Stephanie's mom approached from the opposite direction.

Johnny took three big steps which took him to the other side of the entrance. His movement caused the doors to open again.

Ah, that smell. His mouth watered.

Then it happened. The hands started. Mommy must have something important to say. His dad was right: Only an act of God could stop the birds from warbling. Johnny turned. The penny was even brighter.

He ran to it.

Did he hear bells? A hundred—no!—a thousand bells sounded from the shiny penny!

And there it was between his feet. A brand-new penny.

Johnny squatted down. He remembered his kindergarten teacher saying that the man on it was important. Abe Lincoln. Was he the one calling to him?

He picked it up, warm and smooth between his fingers. He

stood, looked back at mommy, her wings flapping and still warbling, and put the penny in his pocket.

Another penny sat on the cement between his feet glowing like the first one. *Where did it come from?*

He squatted back down to get it, too, and two men's shoes, shiny black, appeared in front of him. Dark blue dress pants rose up to a black belt, a bright-white shirt, a light-blue tie, and a suit jacket that matched the pants, and, inside it all, a smiling man whose teeth were as bright as his shirt.

"Those your pennies, child?" The man's voice was musical, rising and falling like he was reading a poem, soft like a single bell.

Johnny quickly put the second one in his pocket with the other. "Uh-huh," he replied. He wasn't supposed to talk to strangers, but this man's smile was *good*. Yes, that wide smile and white teeth told him this was a good man. Mommy would talk to this man, maybe even his dad would, too. So he added, "I got two of them."

"Did you find them on the ground like that one?"

Johnny thought the man was talking about the first penny, but the man's blue eyes, as blue as the suit he wore, gazed down at the cement.

Another shiny penny lay where the other two had been.

"How—?" Johnny pinched his pants and was pleased to find the other two pennies still in his pocket. He picked up the third and stood to face the man.

"You losing your pennies, child?" the man asked, amused.

"No," Johnny drawled out in wonder. "That's the third one I've found in that spot." He was amazed.

"Really?" the man responded. "You know what they say about finding a shiny penny?"

"No, what?"

"Well," the man said, now serious and no longer smiling, "they say they are pennies from Heaven."

"Wow," Johnny said, "You mean God gave me these?" He put a hand on his pocket.

Now the man laughed. His head moved back with his hands clasped in front of him, just above Johnny's head. It was the first movement the man had made. Johnny thought he heard that single bell again.

"No, child," the man finally said. "God has given you more than mere pennies. No, they say if you find a shiny penny on the ground, that an angel put it there to let you know you are special."

Johnny considered this and said, "That means three angels gave me these." The tip of his middle finger moved over his pants. He could feel the flat solid roundness of each penny.

"Or one angel thinks you are *very* special," the man added. "But look, child, there are more pennies." He pointed behind Johnny. "You must have many angels thinking of you today."

A line of shiny pennies led back to his mommy.

Johnny jumped at the first and picked it up. He turned around to show the man, but he was gone.

Johnny shrugged and turned back to get the rest of the pennies.

"John Paul Wilkins, Junior!" Mommy yelled, then saw the boy picking up the last two pennies just behind her. Somewhat relieved he was nearby, she asked, "Did you find a couple pennies, dear?"

He dug into his pocket and pulled out at least a dozen bright pennies. "The man said angels gave them to me, that they are pennies from Heaven."

"Man? What man?" Mommy demanded.

Johnny shrugged. "He's gone. Can I get some gum?"

"What did I tell you about talking to strangers?"

"He didn't feel like a stranger," Johnny replied. In fact, he felt like he should know the man.

His mother looked about briefly, exchanged worried glances with the other ladies, and said, "C'mon, John Paul," dragging the boy into the store. The ladies followed in their wake.

An hour later, Johnny twisted the handle on the gumball machine to make sure it was in the correct position. The ten machines were lined up five over five, bright-red bottoms with their glass tops filled with a rainbow of colored candies or toys. Only one had gumballs.

He took one of his bright pennies and put it in the slot. He turned the knob and heard the beautiful sound of balls hitting the little metal door. He put his hand under the opening and lifted the silver door. Three blue balls. That made Johnny think of the man in the blue suit. He shrugged and popped them into his mouth.

He turned to his mother who watched him as she handed the cashier some money. Bags of groceries filled the cart at the end of the register area. He worked the hard balls between his teeth, knowing that in a few minutes they would reduce to nearly nothing.

He looked down to his bulging pocket and dug out another penny. He put it in the gumball machine. He turned the knob.

Stuck.

Back and forth.

Stuck. Broken!

Johnny panicked. He looked back at Mommy. She watched the young cashier finish bagging the groceries.

He tried the gumball machine knob again, slowly. Forward. Nothing. Backward. It slipped home!

The bright penny, it must've been Abe Lincoln, said, *Don't try it again, Johnny! Once is good enough!*

He believed it.

Johnny used his fingernail to lift the penny from the slot. "Please, Mr. Abe Lincoln, c'mon outta there!" he whispered to the penny. The face appeared, then the bottom of the coin. He used his other finger to trap it against the red metal bottom, and slid it off, secure between his fingers.

He looked at it and wanted to say thank you. He didn't want to be the one to have broken the machine.

The store doors yawned. Mommy stopped with the cart, half in the store, half out. He felt her looking at him. "Let's go home," she said. "You can help push the cart."

He put the rescued penny in the pocket with the others. He turned to join her.

She smiled and pointed at the floor behind him. "Looks like you dropped one."

He looked back, stunned.

There on the floor, beneath the machines, was a shiny new penny.

44

October 2007

A ngelique let the nightmares—and the shadow within—come.

... thick, clotting darkness, flowing into her nostrils and mouth...

... ice filling her lungs... filling her belly, becoming pregnant with darkness...

... his white hand... long thin fingers, emerging from the shadows...

Tinkerbell.

... fingers becoming teeth...

Remember.

She feels the vampire's porcelain fingers (teeth!) inside her belly; clawing up her esophagus; sharp, quivering tentacles in her throat; pushing out of her mouth.

Her scream becomes a font of blood, spewing out of her mouth—

No matter how prepared she was for the nightmare, for Anders, she still couldn't control her violent reaction.

She jumped out of bed, scrambled through Everett's apartment flicking on every overhead light, and darted to the bathroom to puke.

Everett comically tried to keep up with her and ended up sitting on the edge of the tub rubbing her back, and whispering, "It's okay, it's okay," as she knelt and left her offerings to the porcelain god, heaving away. When she was finally done, Everett gently cleaned her, carried her to their bed, and tenderly put her within it. He crawled in beside her, embracing and spooning her till she stopped shaking and fell back to sleep.

That morning, he made her oatmeal, added half a banana and a little milk, and stood quietly beside the bed until Angelique finished it all and fell back to sleep.

When he returned home from work, he didn't ask any questions, making small talk of his day's mundane events.

No queries during dinner. It was as if nothing had happened the night before.

And this pissed off Angelique, until...

She followed Everett into the kitchen. "When did she call?"

He hesitated as he scraped off his plate into the disposal. "She didn't."

Angelique was about to say bullshit when he added, "She came by the lab two days ago." He rinsed off the plate. "Felt I should know a few things." He put the plate into the sink before he turned to face her. "Knew you wouldn't know how to tell me about all this."

Angelique's knees began to shake. She had to sit, nearly falling into the chair at the small table there.

"She said the details are yours to tell, but she knew she had to warn me." He sat in the other chair across the table from her. "Actually, she said I was in for a shock. She said you're suffering from PTSD, and that you have violent nightmares this time of year."

His face was stone. Angelique was afraid of what he might say next, so she said, "I was attacked a few years ago."

He leaned forward. "I know. I looked it up. Your mother hinted at shadows in your past, a darkness within you, that comes up this time of year. And the connection with the Vampire Killer and the death of your father. When she said you've worked hard to put it all behind you, I figured there had been some serious therapy."

Angelique wanted to tell him... tell him everything, but it wouldn't come out.

"I take it your silence is confirmation. And given your avoidance of alcohol, I can guess you've been in rehab."

Her heart shrank. She felt like melting into a puddle and evaporating away.

He was silent for a few moments of eternity. "She told me what to expect and what I needed to do." He leaned forward and put out his hands. "I came home."

He didn't ask her for anything more—no explanations or revelations.

She put her hands into his. She decided to take a leap of faith.

Angelique told Everett everything about The Night and John Paul Wilkins, strategically leaving out certain details.

She stood and pulled him up. "We have somewhere to go."

In the car, she directed him to an older area of Baltimore, to a house that had been transformed into apartments. He silently followed her inside and down the steps to a basement apartment.

She stopped at the door and turned to face Everett. She was scared. Her eyes said, *I'm sorry*, but she couldn't bring herself to say the words. Instead, she said, "This is a part of my life no one else knows about."

It wasn't entirely true. Years ago, John Paul had discovered her, what he would have called, *delusion*. As far as her life today was concerned, she was being honest. She unlocked the three locks that secured the metal door and pushed it open.

Two humidifiers hummed in the background.

Angelique watched Everett step into the apartment. He scanned over the ugly green sofa and long coffee table both stacked with books and papers. He leaned over and lifted the screen on the laptop charging on the sofa. It glowed to life. Angelique watched him unzip his coat and step into the main room where six shelves of books stood.

She couldn't follow, stuck at the threshold; her knees wanted to move, but her feet were rooted in place. Part of her wanted to see his face as he got a look at the books, their titles. Her obsession.

She knew it was more than that. The Night had defined her in a fundamental way, and despite what everyone said, from mothers to lovers to shrinks, she knew the reality.

Vampires were real.

And there was only one thing that kept her from falling off a cliff into psychological obscurity.

She had to find Anders. She had to touch the creature. She had to know.

All this was what her brain wanted her to say to Everett: Step into the room and spew it out. Let him have it all; let him share it with her. She knew this was a heavy burden to hand over, this vampire that hung on her like an albatross. If only her feet would move, would step into the room, Angelique could let it all go, hand it to Everett and let him decide to join her. But these feet—they were grounded; they were the only part of her at this moment that didn't truly believe.

Normally, she had mastery over them, and could force them to go, to do. At the rehab, at her mother's, in her classes, with Everett. But now... now they—

Angelique had an epiphany, a clarity of thought not unlike one she had long ago when she had been given a card with a black and white drawing of a young woman. She only saw the young woman until her eyes shifted perspective, from white to black, and the picture became an old woman.

Her feet couldn't move now because of her perspective. She knew Everett needed her, but her feet believed she needed Everett— needed his expertise, his approval, his help. Her feet believed she needed him more than he needed her. It was fear of his rejection of her obsession, of the defining event of her life, that shackled her feet. She realized she cared what he thought, and she didn't want him to run.

This was fear, a much different fear than that on The Night, but fear, nonetheless.

He had been in there an eternity. What the hell was he doing?

She heard the soft thump of a book shutting, and that uprooted her feet. She took a hesitant step through the door.

Everett stood next to a bookshelf with his back to her. He turned, smiling. "This is the oldest book on hematology I have ever seen." He opened it and gently turned a couple pages. "Damn," he mused. "London, 1887." He shut it and put it back on the shelf. "Peter will want to see some of these." He stepped to another shelf and removed a book. "Of course, most of these he might laugh at." He held up Jenkins' *Vampire Forensics: Uncovering the Origins of an Enduring Legend*.

He put it back and scanned the shelves. "So, this is your little secret, Angelique?" He nodded and turned to her. "I get it. Vampires. Blood. You need me only for my mind."

He did his best to look serious, but his eyes betrayed him.

Angelique moved closer and said, "Oh, much more than that." She shut the door behind her and pulled him to the ugly green sofa.

A little later that night, they returned to Everett's apartment. They enjoyed a long, hot shower together, then they lay naked on the clean blue couch watching an old Hitchcock movie. The gray light of the T.V. drowned out the single weak light in the kitchen.

Angelique couldn't sleep, and she was glad for that. She didn't want any nightmares tonight. Perhaps if she stayed awake, she could avoid them. She wondered why she had never thought of that: to stay awake through the night and sleep during the day. She smiled at the irony of it.

"You awake?" asked Everett.

"Thinking."

"Me, too." He shifted beneath her. "I need the bathroom."

Angelique sat up and found a decorative blanket to pull around her. She was afraid to fall asleep, so she stood with him.

He padded his way to the bathroom, and she went to the kitchen.

She pulled the blanket tight around her, sipping a glass of water. She still didn't know what he thought about her and her obsession. His humorous comment at the library acknowledged he understood what the obsession was, but he had said nothing else—not on the ride back, not in the shower, and not on the sofa.

The kitchen clock read 3:52 A.M. She still had three hours till dawn.

Angelique heard his feet padding down the hall. "You want any clothes? It's chilly," he called out.

"Bring a heavier blanket," she returned.

She went back to the couch and absently watched the movie. She needed him to talk about how he felt about all this, but she was afraid to initiate it.

Angelique heard his feet returning, no slippers or socks. He was still naked, but he held the blanket she had requested.

They snuggled beneath it watching yet not watching the movie.

Everett reached for the remote and muted the T.V. "I've been thinking. Have you ever considered staying up during the night and sleeping during the day?"

Angelique chuckled. "Great minds think alike. I was just thinking I need to stay awake for another three hours."

He smiled, too. He looked at the T.V. then at her. "That gives us plenty of time to talk."

Here we go.

He shifted his body to face her, and she moved to face him. Angelique wondered if their being naked under a blanket had anything to do with the revelation about to come from Everett.

He said, "First of all, thank you for sharing all this with me. I know you're a proud woman. Telling me some of your past had to have been difficult for you."

Angelique felt a 'but' coming. She watched his mouth and knew the words, *All this is a little crazy, Angelique. Perhaps you still need more therapy. I'll help you through it.* She felt like puking, and it had nothing to do with nightmares and shadows.

Everett looked into her eyes. "I believe you believe in the supernatural." The corner of his mouth turned up. "In vampires." He ran a hand through his hair. It was a nervous reaction he had when he didn't really want to talk about what was on the plate before him. Perhaps he was nervous, too. Perhaps he was afraid of what she would say or do once he made his revelation. Angelique hoped so.

"I, ah, have been wanting to talk to you, for some time now, about something that has been..." Everett hesitated, and Angelique felt cold and more than naked under the blanket. The pre-vomit spit oozed into her mouth. "... working around in me. And showing me your library. It made this even more important."

Just say the fucking words! You want out. You can't join me in my search.

Then the other corner of his mouth turned up.

He's fucking with me!

"So," he continued, "what would you say to a larger place, one where we can keep your library and whatever else you need at your disposal?"

"You're a fucking asshole," she whispered, but she smiled. As the relief poured out of her, she wanted to hit him, hug him, kiss him.

Everett reached behind him, leaning out of the blanket, and lifted up a cushion. He pulled out a folder. He brought it around and set it between them, the blanket falling from her naked shoulders. His eyes lingered on her for a moment.

"I have begun looking at a few places," he said.

Angelique threw off the blanket with the folder.

"You're going to pay for this," she growled and pushed him down on the couch.

He laughed as she crawled atop him.

The next hours went by quickly, and the sun came up for a new day. Everett stayed home, and they slept off and on throughout the day.

There were no nightmares... no clawing hands inside her... no Anders laughing at her.

This was the first time in a long time Angelique felt she was in control.

45

The cab came to a jerking stop, waking John from the dream. Blue Man. Pennies from Heaven. *Smileys*.

There were other dreams, other memories swirling in the back of his mind, but they blew away as the car door opened and the cool October air rushed in. Barry helped him get out and practically carried him into the ER.

The receiving nurse was pleasant and helpful. After getting John situated in the waiting room, Barry took his friend's wallet to find his health insurance card and went to give as much information as he could to get John admitted and in line for an examination with a doctor.

John was exhausted. He sat in his seat, eyes closed, trying to block out the gurgle of voices and other noises that poked his mind. After the mind-fuck he had experienced, he didn't want to hear any voices at all.

A heavy weight plopped into the seat next to him. There was a familiar sigh.

John tried to be pissed at his friend, but it was too taxing. "What did you tell them?" he asked. "That I'm having a nervous break-down?" He kept his eyes closed. He was afraid his friend would have a look of piteous concern he didn't want to deal with at the moment.

"Whad ya expect?" Barry replied. "Ya sure seemed like it to me."

John let out a long breath.

A little over an hour later, a matronly nurse called out John's name. He and Barry slowly stood and walked over to her. Another younger nurse appeared with a folder. The older one explained that Ronda would take John to the examination; Barry had to stay in the waiting room.

Ronda smiled at John, but he was in no mood or condition to smile back.

Like a zombie, he followed the nurse to a room. She respected his need for quiet and silently took his vitals. She wrote notes in the file folder and placed it in a holder on the door. She even refrained from the fib all nurses told. They both knew the doctor wouldn't be coming anytime soon. She moved slowly out through the door and closed it.

John sat on the end of the examination bed. It was almost too bright in here for him.

The room was a little smaller than he expected. The bed sat along the light blue wall, the foot facing the door. The rest of the room was hospital white. A picture of a red and white lighthouse on a sandy promontory hung on the wall beside the door, and a matching blue cabinet hung above a gray counter at his right, within which was a stainless-steel sink.

John hopped down and took a small paper cup from a dispenser. He filled it with cool water; he could feel it through the thin, paper walls. He took a sip and realized his mouth was hot and dry. He crushed the cup and tossed it in a stainless-steel garbage can, one of those he had to step on the little lever to open the top. He hopped back onto the bed.

John had a little time to think about what had happened at Fanny's. But as he tried to recreate the scene in his mind, his brain became heavy and thick, a torridly humid day blooming in his brain. It was as if a part of him that was hidden deep inside (the Wolf?) didn't want to think about what had happened.

He was surprised when the doorknob turned, and the door opened. A doctor in a white coat stepped through, his back to John

222

to make certain the room's door was shut. Then he turned around—

The white coat opened to reveal a blue suit. The Blue Man smiled at him.

John jumped and crawled back on the bed into the corner, breathless.

The Blue Man said, "You are a strong man, John Paul Wilkins. Most people would've crumbled into a small coma after experiencing what my sister did to you. But we had to be certain. Even we can doubt the Will of God." He moved his hands to pray, mumbling something foreign. He put a hand over his heart then took the folder from the holder on the door.

He looked at it briefly and tossed it on the counter. "You're going to be okay in a day or two."

He sat on the end of the examination bed. John was still trying to push into the corner. "Call me... Aaron," the Blue Man said. "I'm here to help you—and to bring you a request."

Like the wind that announces a coming storm, something stirred in John's heart. A physical feeling swept through him. He opened his mouth but couldn't speak.

The Blue Man smiled even more. He laughed, a happy laugh that sounded like a thousand tinkling bells. John looked about.

Aaron looked about, too. "They are very happy to know you care about who seeks your help."

John closed his eyes and concentrated. "Who?" he croaked. His mouth had become hot and dry again. "What?"

Aaron laughed and the bells were even louder. "Two excellent questions, John Paul Wilkins." He moved closer. "Look at me, child. Look at me."

John forced his eyes open and saw that Aaron's eyes were glowing orbs of deep blue light. "The *who* is no other than the Christ." Aaron grabbed John's hand. A feeling of penetrating warmth and peace joined the wind in his heart. "And the *what* is quite simply this: Your Lord Christ asks you to save your world."

John woke to a memory of the ocean, a flowing, undulating blue that moved through him and around him. As he moved out of the waters, the ocean became blue eyes... then dark and shadows...

He sat up. He was in his own bed.

Barry must have arranged it. John had to have been at least partially conscious to leave the hospital, get into a taxi, and walk into his apartment building to the elevator, but it was like walking in a smoky corridor. He could barely remember anything, and he didn't remember much once he got home. It was as if Aaron the Blue Man had done something to him. Switched his brain to half-power. Allowed him to get to his own bed and sleep.

How long had he been in bed?

The apartment door lock screeched. Someone was using his key to enter.

Barry.

Then the last words of those blue eyes slammed into his consciousness: "My associate, call her Carrie, will be calling upon you very soon. Please do not be rude to her like you were before."

The thought of this Carrie—he figured it was the Green Woman—unlocking his door and coming into his apartment sprang him into action.

He swung his legs to the side of the bed. His head pounded. It felt like a superball bouncing about in his skull. He saw he was still in his jeans, but shirtless.

The refrigerator door shut, followed by a cupboard door shutting.

John braced himself for the Green Woman to open his bedroom door.

But it was Barry.

"Good," his friend said. "The doc was right, said ya'd be awake this afternoon." He carried a plate of cheese, grapes, and raspberries. "Don't ask about this." He lowered it to allow John to see it better. "The doc said it'd be good for ya, but don't eat it all at one sitting." He placed the plate on the nightstand. "Consider it a prescription for recovery."

"I'm not hungry."

Barry crossed his arms. "The doc said ya'd say that. Ya're to force down one piece of each. That's all. Easy."

The doc? That was no doctor. Actually, John wasn't certain what

224

exactly had occurred in the examination room. But that was certainly no doctor.

He rubbed his eyes then saw Barry was waiting.

Barry saw the stubborn clench in his friend's jaw and said, "Listen, I have to go to work, but I'm not going till ya eat something."

"You'll be late."

"And in trouble."

John didn't feel like arguing. He knew his friend could be equally stubborn. He was void, like what little emotion he had left had just been used up. "Whatever..." John grumbled and reached to the plate to get his three bites.

"Good!" Barry said and grabbed his friend's hand and placed a set of keys in it. "I called Drew to let him know ya've been in the hospital, and that the doc says to rest for a day. I'll check in on ya when I get home."

The bites made John feel better. He lifted the plate to his lap and took three more. "How did he seem?"

"I made it sound like he's been working ya too hard." Barry turned to go but stopped himself and said, "Try to get some rest."

Barry left, the apartment door shutting a few moments later.

John took a raspberry, put the plate on the stand, and lay back slowly. He put it into his mouth and smashed it with his tongue. The juice spread through his mouth, light and fresh.

The last thing he remembered was swallowing goodness.

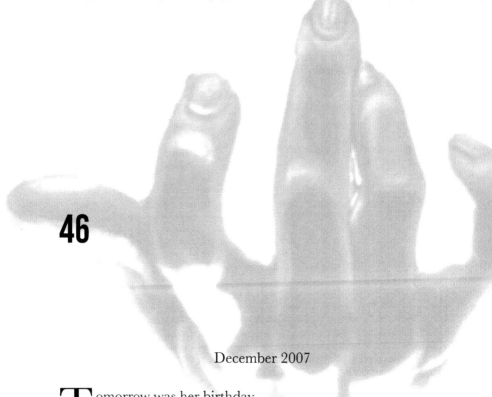

46

December 2007

Tomorrow was her birthday.

Angelique already knew they were going to dinner with their friends Dylan and his fiancée Tabitha. She already knew they were going to some posh restaurant. And she knew Everett had been planning a gift. Planning it a while now, replete with phone calls cut abruptly short when she entered the room, a few late nights at the lab, and—

It slapped her: *He'd better not be getting me a ring!*

She looked up. Everett stood at the door. He looked half-scared and half-elated. "You need to come down quick to see this."

An early birthday gift? *Please not a ring.*

Angelique sat in her library, the room promised by Everett when he suggested they move into a larger place. One side she dedicated to school, and it was clear of clutter with her laptop on a desk beside a bookshelf composed only of class texts, past and present. The other side she dedicated to her obsession: the hunt for the vampire Anders Saffenssen.

It was a total mess except for the desk with its desktop computer and large screen. Her collection of occult books had expanded with shelves covering all the wall space. A large flip board—one side a corkboard, the other a chalkboard—stood beside the desk. A number of newspaper clippings and printed pages dedicated to the Vampire Killer covered the cork side.

Angelique always took off her slippers when she entered the library. They sat in the middle of the doorway just inside the room, pointed out so that she could slip them on when leaving. She had finished some research on an anthropology paper and had crossed the room to sit and read from an old book, *Satan Is Alive and Well on Planet Earth*, when Everett's summons came.

She unfolded her legs from beneath her, clapped the book shut, went to the door, and put her left foot into a slipper.

"Better hurry!" came from down the hall.

As she put on the right, she prayed, *Please no ring.*

Angelique rushed down the stairs, turning left into the living room. She was pulling her hair back to tie it into a ponytail when she saw the words "BREAKING NEWS: Vampire Killer Returns" in the title line at the bottom of the T.V. picture.

A cold gripped her belly, contracting her groin and anus. Goose-flesh popped up like little pins beneath the skin of her arms and legs. Her throat became thick and narrow.

On the screen, a woman was talking, a half-dozen mics pointed up at her face. A press conference. Angelique thought the shock had affected her hearing until Everett pointed the remote:

"… cluded that this is not a copycat. As with all unsolved cases, there are details that were not disclosed to the media or to the public. The two murders in question…"

Angelique looked at Everett. "Two?"

"Just listen." He nodded at the T.V.

"… Tuesday night, and as some of the media has already reported, last night…" Today was Saturday. "… with a hole in the neck and exsanguinated." The speaker hesitated and concluded, "That is all we can report at this time."

The crowd of reporters erupted, but the sound and the image reduced to a small square next to a news anchor. "That was Carol Seidich, communications director of the Baltimore Area Police Department, confirming what WEZY reported this morning, that the notorious Baltimore Vampire Killer has returned, claiming two more victims whose names are being withheld pending notification of family."

Everett's arm came up again, and the sound muted. "You okay?" He knew what had happened five years ago, how this Vampire Killer had mutilated the children of five friends of the Carlson family, and how Angelique still maintained the killer was a real vampire who had attempted to attack her before going on its rampage through Baltimore.

Angelique seemed to be standing beside herself as she watched the press conference, but Everett's words pulled her back inside. Her hands still held her hair, ponytail half-tied.

Her cell phone buzzed in her pocket. She didn't have to look at it to know it said, "Diane." She didn't feel like talking to her.

Everett guided her to the couch.

Angelique felt raw and exposed. Memories of Anders' attack, his notes to her, the photos of the dead bodies. It all flooded into her and out of her.

She laughed.

"You okay?" he asked, a little concerned.

This was the best birthday present ever.

She hugged Everett and replied, "Happy birthday to me."

Later that night, her dreams confirmed it.

Angelique had learned in one of her psych classes that there was a dusk to dreaming, a place between consciousness and unconsciousness, that the dreamer could move into and stay cognizant and manipulate the dream. A lucid dream state.

The professor had explained that sometimes the sleeper is in dream REM but also conscious, moving out of the dream but not coming awake. In this lucid dream state, the sleeper could manipulate the narrative of the dream and see more of the imagery and symbolism emerging from the subconscious.

Angelique had always been afraid to try it, fearing her shadows would devour her in her dream. But she didn't see her shadows tonight.

Perhaps they gave Angelique a little birthday present of their own and stayed away. Or perhaps she just got lucky and they couldn't find her dream.

She had a feeling it was something else.

Anders was back, and he was busy—away from Angelique—out bringing some early Christmas *cheer* to the denizens of Baltimore.

Of course, none of this was consciously in Angelique's mind when she went to bed that night. But as she floated like an autumn leaf on a cold pond, she became *aware*, and she knew she was alone in her dream. She moved into the dark waters below her and found herself in a graveyard, a place she hadn't visited in... forever.

Her father leaned casually on his gravestone. When he saw her, he stood at attention and smiled, happy to see her.

Dark carrion birds fluttered and swooped around him.

He smiled as one stood on his head and plucked out his right eye, long wiry veins and arteries and nerves pulling taut then snapping with a pop. Blood dripped from the ball when the bird flapped its wings and flew away. It flowed from the hole in his head and down his cheek.

His laugh gurgled into choking when another flew into his mouth.

Others pecked at his now bloody hands and feet.

A large bird alighted on his chest and pecked at his shirt, ripping away the blue cloth and the flesh beneath, exposing the heart. It cawed before it feasted.

A final one, an ugly mix of gray and black, kept to the air. "Tinkerbell!" it tittered, swooping down at them.

Her father kept smiling, kept trying to laugh, and she knew if he could talk, he would have said, *Stay bright, Angel!*

She awoke, already sitting up in bed, Everett holding her.

She knew.

A short time later, they were in the kitchen waiting for the kettle to whistle.

Angelique couldn't sleep. She was shaking with excitement.

As she prepared her Earl Gray and his red rooibos, she told him the dream.

Everett was calm when he said, "That's one fucked up dream."

He sat quietly at the table watching her.

She placed his tea in front of him and sat opposite. They were silent for a few moments. She wondered if he'd make the connections.

"Happy birthday," he said.

Angelique looked at the clock on the wall: 11:52. She smiled. "For the next few minutes."

Everett took a small sip then said, "I get that you see this Vampire Killer is a good thing, but this dream…"

She said nothing. She wanted him to see it for himself.

"So, this Anders, the Vampire Killer, is announcing to you he's back?"

Angelique picked up her cup, but she had to hold it with both hands. She blew the top of the cup then took a sip. She swallowed and concluded, "More than that. He wants me to find him."

She wasn't certain how she'd made that logical leap. Perhaps it was just a wishful one. She didn't care. She knew it was true. Anders was announcing to her:

Time to play, Tinkerbell.

47

A rolled-up newspaper leaned against his apartment door.

It had to be for one of his neighbors. John didn't subscribe to a newspaper. It was after ten o'clock, he was tired, but he picked it up and went to his immediate neighbors. Each told him it wasn't theirs.

Whatever. He shrugged it off.

He unlocked his door, took off his coat, shut the door, and tossed the paper on the sofa.

He slipped off his shoes before he went to the fridge. Only one beer left. No salsa. He grabbed a bag of bar-b-que chips, and, with beer in hand, went to the sofa and reached for the T.V. remote.

All part of his routine.

Except a newspaper wasn't part of that routine. Neither was tossing it on the sofa and it unraveling. No part of his routine came close to the bold headline:

VAMPIRE KILLER RETURNS.

He felt like something had grabbed his balls and squeezed.

That foul pre-vomit spit filled his mouth.

He put the chips on the coffee table and took a swig of beer. That made his stomach feel worse.

He thought of Angelique.

It had been two months since the last time she had slipped into his mind.

With a shock, he realized it was her birthday.

He put the beer down before he could drop it.

Fucking headline...

VAMPIRE KILLER RETURNS.

A slow drumming started, and John realized it was his heartbeat.

The drumming became a pounding on his door.

Had to be Barry. John was going to ask his friend to get some more beer—a lot of it.

He staggered to the door, opened it, and—

Green Smiley stood there. Except, she wasn't smiling.

Unbidden, Aaron's words came to him: *My associate, call her Carrie, will be calling upon you very soon. Please do not be rude to her like you were before.*

John was about to say, "Soon?" but she put up one brown index finger to stop him.

Carrie wore more demure clothing than what she had worn at Fanny's, a light-green turtleneck over a dark-green knee-length skirt. Her green eyes seemed darker. It all contrasted with her brown skin and dark, straight hair.

When the elevator door dinged down the hall, she smiled, and it lit up the entrance to his apartment like a light bulb.

Blue Smiley, Aaron, as he had called himself, was in his blue suit, probably the same one John had seen him in at all the other encounters. His pale skin blended with his white shirt. He wore no tie.

He stood beside Carrie. Had they not been of different races, they would've looked like an older sister and her younger brother.

Carrie said, "John Paul—" but Aaron's hand grabbed hers. They looked at each other and seemed to exchange silent dialogue. She nodded.

Aaron said, "John Paul, may we come in?" He produced a paper bag with a familiar logo that said *Corazon*. "I brought you some soul food."

The ill feeling went away. John shrugged and said, "Why not?

I'm going to wake up in a few minutes and find I've been dreaming."

He knew he was lying to himself. He felt as if he were just now waking from a two-month dream. Since that night at Fanny's, life had gone on as if it hadn't happened. Work had been going well, despite some of the economic issues plaguing the country. He had even had a good visit with his parents at Thanksgiving.

And there was Hannah, who had come into town to visit family and had stayed at his hotel. They had a wonderful week together, and when Hannah had told John she was staying another week, he found he was glad. They'd exchanged a few emails and phone calls since she'd left. He liked her, and he believed Hannah liked him.

That had been the dream.

Reality was all Smileys and Vampire Killers.

A massive hurricane was back *there* in the past and in the back of his mind. It had always been back *there*, and he had kept ahead of it by keeping busy, by looking forward. He didn't want to turn around to look. He avoided anything that might remind him it was *there*.

He didn't want to acknowledge the past. It was messy, and it had brought out a part of him that was scary if not embarrassing. A dark, feral side that even now, just with this thought, chuckled and whispered, *I'm still here.*

Calm waters, sunny beach. A slight breeze at his back. That was the way he liked it.

All gone.

The hurricane (*her*-icane) had snuck up and had buffeted him awake.

The Smileys weren't smiling.

And just what were they anyway?

The Lord Christ asks you to save your world.

God, his head ached.

John looked at them. They looked at him.

John said to Aaron, "When you say soul food you better mean wings and beer." He waved them in.

Aaron went immediately to the kitchen as if he were familiar with the place. As Carrie passed by, she placed a hot hand on John's forehead, the heat moving through his skull into his brain and down his spine. His dizziness stabilized; the fatigue drained away. He felt better.

Stunned at how that touch had affected him, he followed her into the living room and saw the newspaper headline.

He looked at Carrie getting comfortable on the far end of the sofa.

He realized all this wasn't just the hurricane (*her*-icane). He pointed at the newspaper. "*You* did this."

Carrie exaggerated surprise. "I beg your pardon? Did what?" Her green eyes showed joy and concern.

Smileys.

Why were they here?

The Lord Christ asks you to save your world.

"John?" Aaron stood beside him, a plate of berries and cheese and nuts in hand. "If you were serious about the wings and beer, you're going to be disappointed," he declared with a smile. "Have a seat, please."

Carrie patted the sofa next to her.

He was going to be tag-teamed.

Aaron completed the John sandwich and set the plate on the young man's lap. "I assure you, some of this will make you feel fresh and strong." He picked up a raspberry and a cube of cheese and placed them into John's hand. "We are here because of you, child."

Child. That brought back a memory of shiny pennies. Pennies from Heaven.

John absently put the soul food in his mouth. Aaron was right: He did feel a little stronger.

Carrie placed a cashew and two blueberries in his empty hand. "We just want to have a little chat."

"About saving the world." He put Carrie's selection into his mouth.

Carrie's face lit up as if he had said magic words.

Aaron leaned out to say to his sister, "I do believe he's being facetious."

John shook his head. *What the hell,* he thought, *if I indulge them, the sooner they leave.*

He looked at the plate and the small pile of cashews. "I see you found my stash. I have to keep them hidden from Barry."

Carrie placed a couple in John's hand. Aaron placed a raspberry and blueberry next to them.

"You need to eat," Aaron said.

"Build up my strength to save the world."

Thousands of bells rang, like those he had heard at the hospital, but they were here in his apartment.

"I suppose we have an audience?"

Aaron replied, "Most certainly."

"Except for the other Protectors, of course," Carrie added.

"And the Choir," said Aaron. "They never stop singing about the Glory of God."

More bells.

"Actually," continued Carrie, "if the truth were told, only half of the Host or so are paying attention. There is always a lot of work to do." She took the plate from John's lap and placed it on the coffee table. "God's Will be done.

Aaron repeated, "God's Will be done."

Like a studio audience reacting to a show on stage, the bells sounded.

"Listen, John," Aaron said, taking one of the young man's hands, "think of the life of humanity as a grand, epic story where characters come and go, interacting with each other in a great dance of complexity. The Greatest Story Ever Written."

Carrie took John's other hand and lifted her free right hand just in front of his face.

Aaron's left hand rose with Carrie's, the two hands hovering a foot apart from each other. Blue light oozed from his fingers, green from hers. "This story," Aaron continued, "is called the Book of Life. Some characters are merely words, others are sentences, still others, paragraphs."

"Yours, child, is a whole chapter," finished Carrie.

The two lights merged between the hands, and from that point, as if a veil had been parted, a scene emerged. A large building stood to the left, windows reflecting the silvered shapes of nearby trees. Ahead in a gravel parking lot, a young man was getting into a car.

John recognized the side of the old apartment building where he had lived while he was in college. The perspective was on the right side, and it moved past the back corner, emerging from the building's shadow into the moonlight. The young man... he had just put on his headlights.

That's me! That's The Night!

Something caught in John's throat. He couldn't breathe. He was watching The Night from someone else's perspective.

"Hey! What's going on?" the other John yelled. There was a movement in the shadows across the street. "Angelique!" He rushed into the shadow between garages.

John saw himself step out of the shadows, pulling Angelique into the moonlight. He looked directly at the one looking at him. "Hey! I need help!" that younger John called out.

The view lingered on the scene a moment then shifted to the left. On the other side of the apartment building stood another man. He was bald and pale in the moonlight. He wore a dark suit with no tie, the shirt open two or three buttons. He held a wide-brimmed hat.

The bald man looked from the young John to the perspective, back to John, then back to the perspective once more. He growled and barked. His mouth opened, and two long eye teeth glistened in the moonlight.

The image stopped there, like hitting pause on a DVD player.

"His name is Reynald de Avallon," Carrie whispered. "He became what you see over 800 years ago."

John was glad she had whispered. He focused on those teeth and remembered Angelique lying on the stretcher, him leaning down to her, and her saying, "Teeth." He remembered the savage, fanged face of Angelique's attacker in that alley.

Another whisper, from Aaron: "And the thing that attacked your —" He hesitated, choosing his words. "—friend is his accomplice, his familiar. His name is Anders."

Angelique's voice came unbidden into his mind: *His name is Anders Saffenssen, and he is the Vampire Killer.*

The hurricane (*her*-icane) began to wail. It wasn't behind him. He was in its eye. There was no escaping it.

John had heard that name numerous times throughout his affair with Angelique. It often came up in discussions with the detective (what was her name?)—and sometimes Angelique moaned his name in her nightmares.

The teeth... the pale skin.

John gasped. He had been holding his breath.

The hands closed together, and the image disappeared.

Aaron squeezed John's hand and faint warmth spread up his arm to his body.

John closed his eyes. The warmth helped him to push down the panic that threatened to make him scream.

"Open your mouth," Carrie demanded, and John complied. She placed two sweet raspberries in it. "Mash them and let the juice linger."

He smashed them with his tongue. The sweet light taste, a taste of the earth, a taste of life, spread through his mouth then down his throat. It passed his heart, and it seemed that his blood captured that life and moved it through the rest of his body. Soul food.

"Vampires." It was all he could say.

Aaron and Carrie both smiled. The bells tinkled.

Their grips on his hands loosened, but John squeezed them, a plea not to let go. He took a long deep breath. He opened his eyes and said, "You want me to save the world from that?"

Carrie looked at Aaron, that look of silent conversation. She said, "We cannot lie to you, John. If these two creatures were all that mattered, we would not be sitting here."

"This is about Angelique."

Aaron corrected, "Your *relationship* with her." He looked down. "I was there that night to ensure you were not harmed."

Carrie squeezed his hand. "All that time you were with her, you were workin' them angels hard, child."

Workin' them angels.

John looked in disbelief at Carrie, and fell backwards... into a memory...

48

May 1999

C ar doors thumped shut. Trunks and hatchbacks raised open.
      The intro to Blink-182's "What's My Age Again" started,
and everyone sang along as charcoal grills and coolers of beer lifted
from the one truck in attendance and alighted upon the grass.

They all had agreed that today was too good to be spent in
boring classes.

John Paul Wilkins loved it here. It was one of his favorite places.

It didn't take long for the grills to fire up. The girls went off to
change into Daisy Dukes and swimsuits (and a couple bikinis, to all
the boys' pleasure). An air compressor rumbled and hissed, and
inner tubes began to inflate—the same tubes they used for winter
tubing parties.

Spring skipping parties, in John Paul's humble opinion, were the
best parties.

And Shady Falls was the best place to have them.

Shady Falls was the unofficial name of this little piece of heaven
on earth. No one knew who had found it, but kids had been coming
here for years—decades maybe. One of John Paul's close friends,
Charlie, believed it wasn't a part of Valley Run Park. They drove
through the park for a good twenty minutes to get here, going from

paved to dirt road, twisting through the dark forest, and emerging into this clearing perfect for playing badminton or soccer or laying out. Charlie figured it was a part of private land with this one access.

A pond, maybe a hundred yards across, spread out from the clearing, and off to the left rumbled the falls.

Normally, they pulled up to the shore so that if they stayed late, they could turn on their lights and continue to play and swim in the cool, dark waters.

Today, since they were skipping school, they knew they had to be home before their parents got home from work.

Last summer, the day after the last day of school, Charlie and John Paul came out here for the first of at least two dozen times since. Charlie wanted to see where the falls came from. With a couple other friends, they went up the trail that took them beyond the falls to the creek that fed it. They spent hours walking up through the creek and discovered another pond. Charlie declared that Shady Falls was man made, that their creek was a diversion from this pond. It was probably a watering hole for cattle long ago, which accounted for the clearing where they parked.

Now it was a not-so-secret party sanctuary for kids.

Everyone knew of Shady Falls, but only eleventh and twelfth graders (and the few *invited* underclassmen) were allowed there. It was like parents kept away out of respect for the place and its history. That is, until a certain Steven M. Clear, four years ago, failed to think clearly.

One of the attractions of this little piece of heaven on earth was the falls itself. Kids rolled big inner tubes up the path that ended a good thirty yards up the creek where the waters ran swiftly over a smooth sloped area that flowed over a ten-yard drop into the pond. One at a time, they climbed aboard a tube, floated to the falls, and went out into the deep part of the pond.

But then came Clear.

Crazy bastard went without an innertube. Inebriated and high, his machismo cost him his back, and to this day he still couldn't walk.

Parents became concerned. Police sometimes showed up.

Inner tubes had to be hidden.

As long as no one was tubing the falls, no adult said anything.

But every summer, at least one asshole had to do a "Clear" and ride the falls without a tube. And everyone thanked God afterwards no one got hurt.

Shady Falls was beautiful, secluded, and most considered the falls a thrill ride. Except for the few, like John Paul, who just couldn't bring themselves to brave the falls.

Nope. John Paul had never even pushed up a tube to chicken out at the last minute. He often climbed up to the edge of the falls to be a lookout to signal when the next tuber could go. He toasted all the tubers when they came out of the water.

But there was no way he was going to tube the falls.

Warm, thin arms wrapped around John Paul's chest. A chin rested on his shoulders. "Hey, big boy..."

Sheila.

John Paul had asked her out two weeks ago, and they had made out a few times. He liked her. A lot. She wore a one-piece swimsuit, and he could feel her breasts on his back. The heat from her body soaked into him.

He smiled. Before he could say something naughty, Jeannie appeared before him.

Sheila's arms hardened. He felt her smile.

Jeannie was just plain hot in her T-shirt tied in the front and her tight blue jean shorts that were no better than panties. She was a good foot taller and put her hands on John Paul's shoulders. "Just how big a boy ya gonna be, Johnny Paul?" She moved into him, Sheila pushed, John Paul's face went right into Jeannie's cleavage.

Sandwiched.

Everyone cheered.

Johnny Paul.

Fuckin' Charlie. He's the only one who knew about the old name his parents used to call him.

They released him enough that he could turn his face to breathe.

Charlie stood there with two beers in his hands. "We all took a pledge today..."

John Paul was released enough to see the group of partiers behind his supposed friend.

"...that we wouldn't party until you, you fuckin' coward, tube the falls."

"Wil-kins! Wil-kins!" all the partiers chanted.

Sheila and Jeannie joined along, jumping with the rhythm, forcing John Paul to jump with them.

"Okay! Okay!" Charlie called out. "I think the sandwich has had its effect." The girls laughed and let John Paul go. Charlie held out a beer to his friend. "Let's get him all partied up first. Remember! No party for us until he goes!"

John Paul took the beer and laughed. "You're all a bunch of assholes!"

"Wil-kins! Wil-kins!"

They kept chanting as he downed his second beer.

Charlie put another in his face when Sheila rolled up a tube.

Four beers gave John Paul a good buzz; six, he was drunk. He took number three from Charlie and saw another unopened beer in his friend's hand. There was no getting out of this.

John Paul looked around at the partiers, and he realized they all had tubed the falls at least once—except him. They wanted him to be a part of the group, to have that extra thing in common that cemented their friendship even more. Here were a dozen seniors, soon-to-be graduates, who were what many of the teachers at school claimed was one of the tightest graduating classes they had ever seen. Four years of good, smart, closely-knit kids.

Most of the trouble they had gotten into was the result of their rivalry with the high school across the county. Different cliques got along or at least avoided the friction that could arise.

But one thing they all liked to do was party.

So, John Paul *keeping* them from partying was unbearable.

He finished the third beer and took the fourth. "Okay, let's do this!"

Sheila announced, "Wilkins is gonna lose his virginity!" and they all cheered and whistled and turned him toward the trail.

Someone cranked up Tom Petty's "I Won't Back Down" from

one of the cars, and the group sang along as the procession pushed up the hill.

One of the guys broke off to stand as the signaler at the edge of the falls.

Charlie rolled the tube. John Paul, Sheila, Jeannie, and a few others—probably there to ensure he didn't chicken out—followed.

With each step, John Paul's buzz weakened, and his heart tightened. He drank more of the beer in his hand.

Sheila took his beer and swallowed a sip. She handed it back and reassured him, "It's easy. You'll be fine."

He walked along quietly.

From the trail, he could see where the path curved towards the creek, and he could hear its swift waters.

He wondered how he'd gotten here.

Fuckin' Charlie. Fuckin' master manipulator.

As they approached the creek, John Paul felt it didn't look that bad at all. It was perhaps twenty feet across with a canopy of trees, like a tunnel, keeping it cool and shady. The humidity of the tunnel made the thin shafts of light from above glow through the shadows. The water moved quickly. Off to the right, they could hear the waters of the falls rumble.

The tube made a strange echoing thud where Charlie laid it down at the edge of the water. "It rained two days ago, so the creek should push you out pretty far. Just sit your ass in there," he pointed at the center of the tube, "and hold on till you get to the falls. Let go when you're in the air."

John Paul had seen it done maybe a hundred times, but here, now, he was about to do it.

Sheila put a hand on one shoulder; Jeannie, the other.

John Paul felt he was in a courage sandwich.

"Easy-peasy," Jeannie whispered in one ear.

"I'll be waiting for you down there," Sheila whispered in the other. She turned to run back down to the pond.

Fuckin' Charlie did this. Fucker's been planning this for weeks probably. Hot chicks and peer pressure.

John Paul looked at his supposed friend and found him smiling proudly.

Fuck 'em all.

He looked around. His friends waited for him. The party waited for him. He saw the light at the end of the tree tunnel just before the falls. *That was what?—twenty, twenty-five seconds to the edge? A few seconds in the air? Splash. A minute or so to swim out? Not even three minutes.*

He downed the rest of his beer and handed the can to Jeannie. He took off his shirt and handed that to her, too. He stepped out into the water.

Shit, it was cold!

It pushed against his shins and calves. Here it was a little deeper than in the center where he would have to launch.

Charlie pushed the tube into the water.

John Paul took a step away. He looked into the eyes of his friend then turned and stepped out to the center.

"Dude! Don't be crazy!" Charlie actually sounded concerned.

"What's he doing?" Jeannie asked.

That was the last thing he remembered...

... before he woke up on a stretcher.

The rumbling of the wheels across the grass brought him up from the darkness. He gasped as the bright sunlight seared his eyes.

A warm voice said, "You're okay, child."

Pieces of his mind fit together. A woman spoke to him. His eyes caught up, and a shadow moved into his vision. Green eyes and a dark face, a brown face. A warm voice came out of its mouth: "Child, squeeze my hand if you can understand me."

He squeezed both hands. He wasn't certain he could feel anything in either one.

"He's responding," the voice said, "Let's get the monitors on him, just to be safe."

More pieces of his mind moved into place. His mouth tasted like mud.

The stretcher stopped and lifted and slid on metal. Shadow engulfed him. The face stayed right in his sight the entire time. She was an older African-American, perhaps in her early forties. Her dark wet hair was pulled back in a small bun. John Paul could see worried eyes. Flaring nostrils, an angry mouth. This woman... he felt he should know her. Her eyes... her bright green eyes... they reminded him of other eyes. He couldn't focus his thoughts on anything. He felt like he was chasing something at night, flashlight in hand, trying to catch a glimpse of it.

A truck engine started. John Paul looked around. He was in an ambulance.

A male voice: "Doctor Angelo, are you coming with him?"

She must have seen the question in John Paul's face. "I'm Doctor Carrie Angelo. You're going to be fine, child."

The other voice: "She pulled you out of that pond. Maybe saved you."

Dr. Angelo smiled. A bright smile... a familiar smile... as bright as her green eyes. She put a hand on his forehead, and he felt a calming warmth spread out from that touch down his neck, into his core. "You rest now, child." To the other person: "Let's not have any sirens, please."

Then this Carrie leaned close to him, their noses nearly touching. "You're workin' them angels a little early, child."

She squeezed his right hand hard, and she moved out of his sight. The ambulance doors slammed shut. He was alone with the paramedic.

It took all his strength, but he lifted his right hand.

Two shiny new pennies.

49

December 2007

W *orkin' them angels.*
    John opened his eyes.
Pennies from Heaven.

Stretched out on the sofa, he didn't see *them*. His mind wanted to tell him something, wanted to connect the dots between his dreams. He didn't want to follow that line between them. He felt it would lead to more dots that would make the *something* momentous, consequential.

Were *vampires* one of those dots?

John's stomach turned.

Aaron moved into his field of vision. "Sorry about that. We should've let go of your hands sooner."

He helped John to sit up.

The plate of soul food appeared in his lap.

Carrie sat down to let him lean on her.

Aaron moved the coffee table closer, standing beside it. He had a large manila envelope in his hand, one end cut open. He removed the papers within but held onto them.

Carrie grabbed John's hand, that warmth spread through him,

and his stomach settled. She said, "We have much to tell you, and you will have a choice to make."

"Two days ago," Aaron began, "our agents intercepted information from the Baltimore police department. It was kept quiet from the public until today. I take it you haven't seen the television?"

John never had time to watch T.V. anymore, and if he did it was reruns of his favorite shows. During the day, it was next to impossible, and he paid little attention to the staff and their gossiping. He paid half-attention to the patrons, unless it was a problem that needed a solution. He was just too busy.

Carrie squeezed his hand. "That's why I put the newspaper at your door." She looked at Aaron. "It has begun."

John looked from one to the other. "What do you mean?" he asked. "What choice? What's begun?"

Aaron laid a photograph on the coffee table. A dirty, naked woman with matted hair, her back and ass to the camera, lay in a fetal position behind a dumpster in what looked like an alley.

Dark alley—Angelique floating in the air—a man pressed against her.

Aaron lay another photo atop the first, a close up of the young woman, a pretty woman, perhaps in college. She had both hands under the left side of her head like a pillow, purposely positioned to look like a child sleeping.

The next photo showed a single breast and her left shoulder. Mud and garbage smeared her white skin. Her chin had been turned, pointing to her right side. John thought it was garbage on her neck—wanted it to be garbage—but it was clear she had been bitten by a wide mouth. The upper half circle had two larger holes (long white eye teeth!), and the lower half was a dashed curve, the teeth having bit deep into the skin. In the center was a hole, clean of blood or scabs, a puncture surrounded by curled, torn skin.

John sat back, bile rising in his throat. He breathed short gulps that pushed it back down. The nausea subsided.

He remembered years ago seeing similar—but not as graphic—photos of young people lying dead in alleys.

"John Paul," Carrie said, trying to soothe him. She patted his hand. "There is a man, too, in those photos. He was killed last week."

Aaron sat back down on the other side of John. He held the other photos and envelope in front of his face. "These are the same as a series of murders—"

"The Vampire Killer."

"Yes. Bitten and impaled in the neck, their blood gone. No physical evidence." Aaron left that hanging.

Carrie continued, "At least that's what the media was told. The killer left no physical evidence: no DNA, no saliva, no prints. What was not shared with the public then was that there were two killers."

"Anders and that Reynald." Two *vampires*.

Aaron shifted to see into John's face. "There are now *three* different sets of bites. The man a week ago was killed by an altogether different thing."

Three vampires!

Linked to Angelique.

And it wouldn't surprise John to find out his ex's obsession with the occult was connected to these new murders.

The *something* his mind had wanted him to see popped into his consciousness—

Workin' them angels...

They say if you find a shiny penny on the ground, that an angel put it there to let you know you are special.

These two had been with him all his life.

John was exhausted. The eyewall of the *her*-icane kept buffeting him.

Angelique.

Shadows.

Dead bodies.

Vampires.

He closed his eyes. He kept hearing *Workin' them angels... angels... angels...*

Smileys.

Angels.

John felt Aaron's hand on his forehead. "John Paul, I know this is a lot for—"

His eyes popped open. He sat up. "Are you serious? Jesus!"

Carrie grabbed his hand—hard—and said very calmly and

deliberately, "Please—do—not—use—the—Lord's—name—in —vain."

John had to grit his teeth. "Per—haps—I—was—rea—lly—call —ing—to—Jee—sus," he mocked, shaking their hands for emphasis.

She let go, exasperated.

Aaron shook his head and smiled.

John opened and closed his hand to get some feeling back into it and said to Aaron, "What? Am I supposed to save Angelique from these monsters?"

Aaron took a breath, exchanged a look with Carrie, and replied, "We are afraid she had made certain choices."

John remembered her growing library in the last days of their relationship. The occult and vampires. He wondered what it was like today. Perhaps her time in rehab had reset her psyche. Perhaps she had put The Night behind her. The look on Aaron's face said otherwise.

The Night.

"You were there that night."

Aaron looked down and replied, "Yes."

"I needed help."

Aaron shook his head and said, "You have to understand there are rules. There are things we can and cannot do. And those we can do are only when we are allowed. Carrie and I are charged with many duties, one of which is to keep you safe. It's why you have all the Pennies from Heaven. At your *friend's* time in your life, we knew there were dark forces surrounding her, and when she moved into your building, we had to stay a little closer."

"And like her, John Paul," Carrie added, "you're going to have to make a choice. If we are aware of Angelique Carlson, then the shadows of her life—those creatures and those who serve them— will undoubtedly discover you." She looked at her brother. "If the Darkness doesn't know already."

"What do you mean *discover* me? What's there to discover? I went to a community college and became a hotel manager. I'm an average man living a simple life. I'm nobody."

Carrie's green eyes flared. "Do you think the Christ just pulled your name out of a hat, child?" Her hand grabbed his. "He chose you an eternity ago. His Father wrote your life before your universe was created."

"Listen, John," Aaron said, "the Dark chose Angelique just as the Light chooses you."

John couldn't help but to say, "Two sides of the same coin. Light and Dark."

The bells returned. The angels smiled.

John looked about then at Carrie. "You can't snap your fingers and make a six-pack appear, can you?"

Carrie's eyes hardened.

"Didn't think so."

Aaron stood. John noticed no wrinkles in his suit. In fact, he couldn't recall at any time either of them appearing dirty or worn.

"Well," the angel said, "we must leave soon. Do you have any questions for us?"

Questions? I have a million.

John tried to grab a few swirling around him. "That light thing you did. You were talking about the Book of Life."

Before he could construct the question he wanted to ask, Carrie said, "We accessed it." She considered her words and added, "There are things we cannot speak about, but I can say that we can replay parts, so to speak, when we are given permission."

Aaron said, "Sometimes dreams and visions are glimpses into the Book."

"And memories." John had been having dreams of the myriad of times he'd gotten Pennies from Heaven. He'd just had one. He couldn't remember all of the Pennies he'd found over the years. There were so many of them. Twelve full tennis cans of them stood on a table in his parents' garage. A nearly-full thirteenth can sat on the dresser in his room. John had a suspicion these two Smileys had been nearby for each one of them.

They had said they had been near during his relationship with Angelique. "Why let me near her?" They knew whom he spoke about.

Carrie looked concerned. "Rules, child. And permission. We, the Protectors, are in your world to ensure the Book of Life unfolds as it is written. As much as we would want to do a thing, we must ensure our actions do not interfere with the Word. Since we work to preserve the Story of this world, we cannot destroy anything created in this world. The Dark, however, operates outside of the Story. We had thought she had been put into your life to lure you into her shadows. It became clear, however, the Dark knew nothing about you. Those Children of the Night had designs upon her alone.

"When you fell in love with her, we were worried—as were you, we could tell. Even in the midst of the heat of your love, you always knew there was a coldness in her—a darkness."

Aaron said, "Your storylines crossed out of seeming coincidence. But there are no coincidences in a story that is already written. There are only plots and subplots that are to be played out by the characters in the Book of Life."

Carrie stood beside her brother. They held hands. She said, "We have known about you and your story before you were born. You were," Carrie paused, "*Chosen*," she said the word like it was a title, "by the Great Narrator to play an important character."

John laughed. "And that's supposed to make me feel better about all this? Am I supposed to feel honored? Do I have a choice?

They both replied, "Of course you do."

"If the story is already written, how can there be choices?"

Aaron smiled, "Time for us to go."

"Convenient."

They turned to the door, and John stood. "Wait! I need to know your names—your real names."

Carrie looked to Aaron and said, "Let's indulge him in this."

"Are you getting soft for him?" returned Aaron.

She laughed and replied, "I always have been. Two things, John Paul, and we must leave. First, our names: I am called Karael; he is called Araquiel. The second and most important," the two angels placed a hand on John's head, "may the Holy Spirit guide your heart."

Like diving into a swimming pool, a wave of warmth and... love... moved down his body from their hands to his fingers and toes. His heart felt like it physically opened, and he started to cry.

He fell down onto the sofa, his body wracked by huge sobs.

"There, there," said Carrie. "You'll be okay. Rest for a little bit."

"We'll return soon," added Aaron.

They quickly went to the door and left.

And just as sudden, his sobbing stopped. John took a deep breath. He struggled up from the sofa and went to the window that faced the front of the building. He looked down. Two black SUVs sat at the entrance, doors open with a man waiting at each. Both men wore long black coats, gray pants beneath. The angels Karael and Araquiel emerged from the building; Karael entered the rear vehicle, Araquiel the front. The SUVs moved down the street and took a left turn.

Gone.

Someone knocked at his door.

On his way to the door, John wiped the tears from his eyes and face, rubbed his cheeks, then asked, "Who is it?"

From the other side: "Beware of neighbors bearing gifts."

Barry. John was glad to have a human to keep him company. He didn't want to have to think about the last few hours. At least not right now. He opened the door and thrust into his face was a six-pack of beer.

50

Two days after the *best birthday ever*, Angelique stood in the kitchen absently scrambling eggs. Her mind's eye saw the map and the locations of all the murders. She bent her will upon those pins in the map. There had to be a pattern. If Anders wanted her to find him, he would've made a puzzle of those sites only she could solve.

An arm encircled her.

She jumped and squeaked.

"Sorry." Everett reached around her and turned off the stove. "You're going to burn them."

"What the fuck, Ev?" Angelique put the spatula down and moved the pan with the eggs to a cold burner.

She turned around.

He smiled. His eyes sparkled. He was excited about something, and it wasn't her naked body under the short robe she was wearing.

This pissed off Angelique a little more.

"Before you blow like a boiling kettle," Ev said, pulling her close to him, "let me ask you a question." He moved his mouth to her ear. He smelled clean. His cologne filled her lungs. "How about a lab in the basement?"

Angelique found it difficult to be petulant, but she retorted, "With what? Another loan?"

Angelique was a little concerned about their finances since they had gotten this new house. Working for Peter at Johns Hops didn't earn big bucks. This house and all its associated expenses—and the fact that Angelique didn't work—was starting to seem like a bad idea.

And now he suggested a lab in the basement?

Angelique pushed him away—a little. "You can't do your research at home, Ev."

His grin made him look like an impish child. "For *your* research."

She hadn't expected this, so it took her a moment. It was a declaration of his belief in her, that she'd succeed.

She didn't think his grin could get any bigger, but it did.

He said, "I have a little secret to share with you." If this was going to be a confession, he didn't seem contrite. Angelique was intrigued

Everett Preston was a rich man.

He didn't flaunt it. No one, not even his aunt and uncle, knew it. Well, his tax accountant and attorney knew, he explained. Beyond that, not one friend, coworker, or family member.

He obtained a loan to buy the house they now lived in.

He used a loan to get the average sedan he now drove.

He lived frugally.

It was a condition of his inheritance.

It all washed over Angelique like a warm water—until the word *inheritance*.

"What inheritance?"

They sat at the kitchen table, and he told her about his mother's aunt, Carmilla, who had had no children of her own, and how she had kind of adopted Everett. He stayed with her often as a child. When his own parents had died in a car wreck during his high school years, Carmilla took care of him even though Aunt Nelly and Uncle Fran had gotten custody. He visited her when he could while in college.

Unbeknownst to everyone, Carmilla was rich, and she left it all to Everett.

And like Carmilla, Everett kept it to himself. Didn't spend it.

Carmilla told him in her will, "Only use it when you need it, when the time is right."

"And now," Everett declared to Angelique, "*we* need it."

And if being rich wasn't enough, Everett confessed he had made some questionable connections during his college years.

Within a week, Everett paid off all their debts—mortgage, car loan, student loans, everything—and had made a number of shadowy deals for some sophisticated lab equipment. As that was on its way, he had a construction team work on the basement to get it ready for the lab.

Over the next few weeks, large deliveries appeared in unmarked vans and trucks, their contents going straight into the house through the unused garage. Neighbors had no way to snoop to see what that young couple was doing to their basement.

While Everett kept up the appearance of working, Angelique supervised everything.

"The lab's the easy part," he said one evening. "Getting the blood, especially infected blood, will be more difficult."

But again, he had his connections.

Whole blood would come from a friend who was a big wig at a new company called Ecsed Sanguinibus. They dealt with blood research, blood sales, blood pharmaceuticals, and, most recently, cord blood for stem cell research. Given a few days' notice, he could have whole blood delivered easily. Malaria-infected blood would have to come from his lab. He could smuggle out small amounts occasionally, but eventually he'd get caught. If Angelique and Everett managed to catch this Anders, Everett told Angelique, they'd have three maybe four months before the FBI came knocking.

Angelique had seen an entire hidden side of Everett over these past few weeks. She realized she didn't really know him. It had been enough that he accepted her obsessions with the occult and vampires, explained to her about blood and malaria, bought a new home for them so that they could do as they wished. But now this talk of hidden riches and nefarious connections and stealing infected blood—it made Angelique a tad more enamored with him.

There was a quiet twist in Everett's psyche that had emerged since she had shared her library with him. Now, with the laboratory becoming a reality below them in the basement, Everett Preston demonstrated a devotion to her and a commitment that they would somehow find and capture Anders the vampire.

That quiet twist became another confession at dinner.

They had prepared a roasted chicken and some roasted vegetables. Everett had been unusually quiet. Angelique wanted to confront him about it, but something kept her silent.

As they ate, Angelique was musing aloud about how they could systematically search this large city for one vampire. "We'll need some kind of—"

"You know how I've always wanted to be a surgeon since I was a boy?"

Everett's comment was totally non sequitur. Head down, he looked at his plate, the piece of chicken breast all alone. There had been a small green salad and some French-cut green beans, both with a little balsamic.

Angelique remembered watching him do this for the first time they had dinner. He had ordered a gourmet burger, ate the fries and salad first, took the meat out of the bun, and ate the bun and condiments like a burger. Then he cut the round sides of the meat to make a square, ate the round sides, and looked at the remaining meat like he was studying it. He cut off a small cube, looked at it, then put it in his mouth.

She remembered thinking, *Peculiar eating habit: not a deal-breaker.*

He did this to all pieces of meat—like a surgeon in an operation. That was how she explained it to herself. Having put being an MD behind him, he got a little kick out of performing surgery on dinner.

Now, however, he looked like a child about to confess to breaking his mommy's favorite vase. He sat with his back straight and his head down. His hands rested on either side of the plate, eyes on the chicken breast. The room became tense.

Angelique only then noticed the T.V. was off. A rarity. When they could, they watched the news and speculated between bites about criminal motives (often driven by money) and intelligence (little to none). Recently, they had been watching for news on the Vampire Killer, particularly if he had taken another victim.

Angelique waited. Everett took in a breath and let it out slowly. He picked up his knife and fork and cut a square of meat, not from the side but from the center. He looked at his work. "I like to cut things up into little pieces."

Ohhh-kaaay? Angelique kept quiet.

Still holding the square of meat, he looked at Angelique. "Living things."

She almost laughed. He was going to smile then laugh and say, *Psych!*

He looked like a robot, completely still, arm bent up to his face. When Angelique didn't say anything, he added, "Like dogs... and especially cats." She knew he hated cats.

They sat there looking at each other.

Cartoons may exaggerate it, but there are times in one's life that a light bulb *feels* like it appears and blinks on, and it *feels* like it's right above one's head. Angelique smiled because that light bulb illuminated a vision of Anders on a table with half a right arm and half a left leg... an ear missing... the chest opened up. All manner of butchery had been done to the vampire. And there was Dr. Everett Preston hunched over his expensive microscope studying something taken from the beast.

It was a beautiful vision.

"Put that down, Ev."

His face fell like a child who was about to be punished. He slowly lowered the fork.

She held out her hands across the table. He looked at them and put his hands in hers. "Listen to me carefully," she began, enunciating each word clearly, "I am going to take you to our bed and fuck you into tomorrow." She remembered the date. "Consider it a Christmas Eve present."

His face twitched in a dozen places, a dozen emotions running through him. She pulled him up and all but dragged him to their room.

Christmas stopped being magical to Angelique the year her father died. Since then, it never mattered much. She received the obligatory gift from her mother—jewelry she never wore—and cards from the usual suspects. She sent out her required cards, never writing anything in them other than her name.

The emotionless nature of it all suited Angelique just fine.

This Christmas morning, she awoke before Everett for a change. She started the kettle for their teas. She was considering buttered toast or fruit when—

Her cell phone rang.

She hadn't realized she had turned it on and put it in her pajama pocket. She looked at it. "Diane." She never called this early in the morning.

Everett must have heard it upstairs. The ceiling creaked from his movement.

But the ringing phone and that name on it made her heart flutter. She turned on the T.V.

"BREAKING NEWS."

Words that made her grin.

The newscaster was saying, "… Killer left Baltimore police with a grizzly Christmas present early this morning."

"Damn," declared Everett. He stood just behind her.

"Whatever gift you have to give me this morning," Angelique said, spinning and throwing her arms around him, "Anders has outdone you."

Everett put his arms around her and whispered, "I doubt it." Before she could ask, he told her, "Get to your library, and you'll find out."

She was excited and intrigued and hurried to her library.

Angelique opened the door expecting to see something spectacular, though she didn't really think anything could be more awesome than another Anders antic.

Nothing.

She heard him grunting up the stairs.

"You stay in there!" he yelled. He was at the top of the stairs.

She heard something drag down the hall near her door.

Now her curiosity was piqued.

Everett appeared in the doorway. He held a long white cardboard cylinder.

A painting? And not even in a frame?

He tried to look calm, but Angelique could see he was excited. He pulled off the plastic end. "Close your eyes."

"Really?"

He started to put the end back on.

She closed them.

He slid out the contents and moved past her to a table. "Keep them closed," he warned. She heard him move things to the floor.

She became a little annoyed. "You better not be fuckin' up my research," she growled.

He chuckled.

"Open up and come over here."

She saw him looking at the large painting he had put on the table. He even nodded approvingly at his handiwork.

She was going to be patient and act surprised and mildly excited. Then rub his nose in Anders' shit.

Except that it wasn't a painting.

It was a large street map of Baltimore, perhaps five feet by five feet, organized by quadrants and grids, laminated. There were five red half-inch dots she recognized as the locations of the old murders related to the Vampire Killer.

Everett dug into his robe pocket and produced a box of blue pushpins. "For the new murders," he said and embraced her. "Merry Christmas." He jumped. "Oh, wait." Stepping into the hall, he pulled in a large cork board. "The map fits on this perfectly. I'll mount it today."

She went to him, placed the board against the wall, put her hands around his neck, and pulled him to her. She kissed him deeply, their tongues slowly dancing. She pulled away slightly, lips still touching. "You barely beat him for the best present."

He kissed her. His hands moved under her shirt and beneath the elastic of her panties.

She came up for air and whispered, "Two-thousand-eight is gonna be a great year."

51

March 2008

John's days went by fast. Despite the floundering economy, his hotel was doing very well. He was busy, often crazy busy.

There were two times each day when he felt the most anxious. Whenever he woke in the morning, he half-expected to see *them* grinning—Carrie holding a glass of some juice and Aaron holding a plate of nuts and berries—standing at the end of his bed. He hated the alarm and what it might announce; relieved it was just another day.

And all his days seemed to blend into one long work shift: employees needing this, patrons needing that. And when he got close to getting caught up with his paperwork, more would magically appear.

He loved all of it. He was good at it. And the hotel prospered because of it.

Then he would get off the elevator at his apartment building, and that second wave of anxiety would hit him. Would they be in the hall, waiting at the door? He'd open his apartment door and expect to see them on his sofa. Or after that crack and soft hiss of his beer, he expected a knock at his door.

For three months his days had been a rollercoaster ride of emotions.

And during those months, his nights were perplexing.

For the first week after the angelic encounter, he would lay in bed, alone with his Quandary (with a capital "Q"). That's what he called it.

They called it a *choice*, like being told by his mother to either take a punishment now from her or to wait for his father to get home.

The problem was that there was no difference.

He felt the angels had omitted or evaded important information —or perhaps, as they had said, there were rules they had to follow.

Regardless, he had the feeling this entire "chosen" thing was something beyond his control... or avoidance. Either he chose it now, or it was going to come to him.

For a week, he fell asleep each night considering his Quandary, and he woke up tired and anxious.

Expectant.

John didn't know what was coming, but at least he didn't have any angelic visitors.

Barry sensed his friend's unease, and he got John to go out. As before, clubbing seemed to take John's mind off whatever was troubling him, but the Quandary was always there between his eyes, knotted and wrinkled, like some distant headache he couldn't shake.

And there were his dreams.

They didn't come every night. Some nights were blank. But the first was so real that when he woke, he believed he was four again. He was in a strange room. "Mommy!" he called out, but that wasn't his voice. Then like a cup that had spilled its milk now filling in reverse, the present returned.

All those pennies on the sidewalk at the supermarket. And now he saw himself, as a child, picking up each one—

From the other perspective.

Aaron!

A few nights later, he was five and the blue-eyed carnival barker in the blue shirt and blue jeans told him the bag of a hundred coins —"gen-u-wine U.S. coins"—was so easy to win that even a little boy like him could get it. Four ping-pong balls into half-filled glasses of water. And he did it. A bag of coins.

Bright shiny pennies.

Aaron.

Carrie was in the dreams, too. She was the lady who had given him twenty-five pennies when he had lost his quarter down a storm drain at a store, except that there were no penny candy machines at this store. She was there when he was in line to buy a Gatorade, and the lady in front, who was wearing a long green coat, spilled out her purse at the end of the register to find her keys. She left all the change there for the boy behind her. Exact amount of silver coins to buy the drink... and fifty-three shiny pennies.

The dreams were exact re-runs of all the times he had ever received shiny pennies... or new visions of them, from the perspective of one of the Smileys.

John knew they weren't dreams at all. The Book of Life was showing him this Quandary was not a recent thing. The table in his parents' garage was a shrine to all the blessings from the angels in his life, two of them in particular. Twelve full tennis ball cans— 16,176 glittering pennies.

John looked hard at the thirteenth can sitting on his dresser across the room from his bed. It had been the last can, ten years old, containing one thousand two hundred twenty-seven pennies—with room for maybe a hundred more. In all, he had found 17,403 pennies.

He had received only a few shiny pennies since high school. Perhaps he hadn't needed that many new blessings. Perhaps something was happening. Perhaps this choice was drawing near.

Perhaps he needed to cash in his blessings for something.

The Quandary.

Pennies from Heaven.

What was the connection?

The next morning, the winds of March brought with it another victim of the Vampire Killer. Number five.

Number four had been back in early February, a high school cheerleader. She had been found still in uniform, her body arranged in a jumping jack pose with a pompom in each hand. Hole in the neck, exsanguinated.

For a time during the first two weeks of February, there had been something about the serial killer and their victims every day on the local news.

John had to remind himself that there were three killers—three vampires—and he wondered if the public was ever going to find out.

It was a small miracle (or perhaps not) that the national media hadn't jumped on the Vampire Killer story.

But the March winds had brought more than another murder. Three minutes after John had seen the "Breaking News" on T.V., he got a call from Andrew.

"You better get here fast," Andrew said. "NBC News just walked in."

By that evening, CNN, FOX, ABC, CBS—what seemed like every national and local news station—walked through the doors of the Heritage Hotel.

Correspondents and production teams replaced tourists.

John was busier than busy.

Reports were made from the police station, from every murder location, with the victims' families. The first wave of the Vampire Killer murders, five years ago, were reviewed. Experts reported on the similarities between then and now. Interviews had been done with worshippers of the church, the Carlson's old church, of which the first wave of victims had been members.

John still wondered how the Carlsons' names had been kept out of the reporting. Were the police still suppressing information? With all these reporters roaming the city, investigating the Vampire Killer, how did Angelique keep out of the limelight?

The front doors of the Highlight Hotel seemed to be open all the time, reporters and crews flowing in and out.

However, by the middle of March, with no new victims, no "news" to report, the city breathed more easily, the reporters went away, and a few tourists arrived.

John started to breathe a little easier, too. He was sleeping better. He felt better.

Then came his latest dream.

He is holding something heavy and transfers it to his left hand. He reaches out with his right to part the heavy tan curtain before him. He wants to be on the other side. He has to search for the split.

He finds the split and pushes through, stepping onto a wood deck. Warm salt wind caresses his face and chest. He looks down and sees in his hand the thirteenth tennis ball can of shiny pennies. His chest is bare; he's wearing swimming trunks.

He looks out at the beach, the darkening waters of the sea, white caps curling toward him. It always strikes him as vast... forever... "The edge of the world."

The expanse before him, the forever, reminds him of a book he had read in college. To escape the constraints of the world, the expectations she didn't share, the protagonist walks into the sea and dies. Death is the only true escape from the demands of the world. What's the name of that book?

He looks up. He sees it's dusk. What few clouds hovering above capture the fire of the setting sun behind him, a mix of blood and ashes.

He looks at the edge of the world, at the darkness of the coming night.

He steps toward it, moves to the stairs that lead down to the beach—

"You're soooo predictable," Angelique says, her icy hands and arms embracing him from behind. Her frigid naked body presses against his back.

The shock sends the heavy tennis can to the floor. One thousand three hundred twenty-seven shiny pennies splash out across the wood deck, some down the steps. A copper puddle at his feet.

"Noooo!" she screams, pushing him aside and falling to the floor.

Bile rises in his throat as he looks upon the thing that is moaning on its hands and knees. It—she—Angelique—is grayish white, like a grub, bald... Her skin is translucent, a clear pellicle covering... corpse skin.

And she is scooping the pennies into her mouth!

It is a horrid hole in her face, the lower jaw jutting out like a shelf.

"Go away!" she growls, her eyes dark, blank, deep, her mouth glowing, pennies dropping from the wormish lips like copper saliva.

He goes to the rail to throw up—

And sees within the coming night, a hurricane of shadows rushing at him. He feels warm rain hit his chest, his arms. A dark rain...

Blood!

John gasped, a single spasm shaking him awake. His skin burned from where it—she—had touched him. He sat up.

He was alone. His bedroom was dark. Faint street sounds filtered through the window.

But Angelique had been right there with him. He could still see her scrambling like a rat on the deck. The eyes... the mouth...

And off to the east, the approaching Darkness of eternal Night. Blood.

John felt his chest. No sticky moisture.

He noted the time: 11:56 P.M. He'd only been in bed a little over an hour.

He threw off the covers and stumbled to the kitchen, throwing open the fridge. He got a beer, twisted off the cap, and took a long pull from it. He could feel the bitter freshness of it go down his throat, his esophagus, to his belly.

He took a deep breath. He could still hear her growling, moaning.

He went to the sofa and turned on CNN. The anchor was reporting on the President's speech earlier in the day: "And the quandary we face is how to get small businesses hiring again..."

Quandary. *The* Quandary. *My* Quandary.

John felt like throwing the remote at the screen.

He took another sip from the beer, imagining he was swallowing down the dream to disappear into his belly.

She was gone.

The Quandary would have to wait until tomorrow. He had to be at work by nine. He downed the rest of the beer, turned off the TV, and as he went back to his room, he focused on what he would have to do when he got to the hotel: purchasing, schedules—

He was asleep before the sheets settled around his body.

He had no more dreams that night.

52

Angelique Carlson leaned against the old empty building that used to be a furniture store. One lonely window on the second floor remained, the rest boarded with gang tags scrawled on them.

The building smelled old—even in the light rain—like the ghosts of furniture.

And it joined the other empty buildings along this side of the cold street in this area of Baltimore. It was a neglected cemetery of dead buildings, with the occasional car or city bus that hurried through. Across the street, the dying buildings seemed to be waiting to join their brothers and sisters on Angelique's side.

Besides Angelique, the only other living thing within sight was the old dog across the street.

It burrowed into a black garbage bag, its white bobbed tail pointing like an accusatory finger at the leaden rain clouds. It pulled out then dug at the bag with its front paws. Garbage splayed out behind it. It dove back into the bag.

Angelique watched this for some time. Her hooded jacket offered little protection from the rain. A drop of water trickled down from the hair at her temple to her check then rushed to her chin. Cold wetness covered her shoulders and back. None of this concerned her.

The dog across the street did.

She wasn't so much interested in what the dog was doing as she was in what the dog evoked in her. Even now, as it dug for scraps in the pile of garbage bags between buildings, she felt a thrumming as if someone were pounding a timpani drum just behind her.

The first time she saw the dog was from the bus on her way home from classes two days ago. She had been talking to a young woman who had commented on the book she was reading, *Vampires in Their Own Words*, and the young woman had gone into a quiet but animated one-way discussion about the goth culture right here in Baltimore.

As if Angelique didn't already know.

The girl had been excited to find a stranger interested in such things.

Angelique was about to ask her how old she was when she saw the dog on the other side of the street. The bus went by fast. The thrumming was short and exciting, and Angelique wanted to stand and try to get a better look—but the girl wouldn't be denied.

A finger poked her knee. "Can you believe that?"

Angelique had no idea what the girl had asked. The thrumming stopped. She mumbled an acknowledgment, the girl resumed, and the dog was soon forgotten.

Then yesterday, at nearly the same place, there was the dog again, trotting along the street. Angelique jumped out at the next stop, about a block away from the dog, and ran to where she had seen it.

Gone.

She had gotten home an hour late, had to eat late, and had to explain to Everett about… What was it about this dog that caused such a reaction in her?

Everett listened quietly, shrugged, and cleaned up the kitchen. That night (the dog), Angelique's brain boiled (the dog)—she couldn't sleep. (The dog the dog—*the dog!*)

Today was different. She got off at the stop before where she had seen it and walked on the pitted and cracked sidewalk a while before she realized that this area of town was a little seedy, perhaps dangerous. A light and steady cold rain kept people off the street.

Then across the street the dog popped out from between two buildings, sniffing the wet sidewalk, moving quickly in the open, and stopping in alleys.

And here it was, digging away in a pile of garbage bags, evoking odd feelings in her.

It looked part Rottweiler and maybe Labrador, a mottled mix of blacks and browns, a few spots of tans—and the white bobbed tail. Its face and paws seemed faded (do dogs get gray hair?), but it moved, slinking away swiftly. It wasn't feral, but it was close.

It ripped into the garbage bag easily enough.

Angelique stood across the street absently watching this creature, digging into her own mind as to why it stirred her so.

It stopped and looked up, hunched, tail down.

"Git ut, ya feckin' cur!"

A small green bag of garbage shot out of the darkness between two buildings just behind the dog. It was already running down the street.

Cur...

"Gotdamn feckin' cur!" A large man followed the thrown bag. He surveyed the dog's handiwork. "Lookit dis shite!"

Cur...

Something swirled in Angelique's memory, but she had to put it down. The dog was now a speck down the street. She couldn't lose it. She ran to the next intersection then slanted across to the same side as the dog.

It was gone.

Shit.

She ran on, turning into an alley, sprinting down the narrow way to a parallel street. Left: nothing. Right... She saw the dog turning up into another alley. She followed, keeping pace with it. It emerged into the light of another street, crossed the road to the driveway of a house, and stopped. It sniffed the corner of the house, lifted a leg, made a little squirt, and proceeded to the back of the house.

Angelique stopped in the shadows of the alley, watching.

Her mobile phone rang. She saw it was Everett but quickly

turned it off. The time: 6:17. She had been following this dog for over two hours.

The thrumming started.

Cur...

She looked up. Dusk.

The dog stopped at the back of the house, crouched down, then laid on its back, submissive.

"Where have you been, you old mangy cur?"

The voice came from some distance away, but it was clear. To Angelique, it seemed to rattle in her head, an earthquake in the soil of her memories. Old ones buried deep beneath a lifetime of others came loose.

Memories never go away, someone had told her. *They get covered up with a multitude of others, but they're still there, still able to come up and haunt you.*

Who had said that? It seemed so long ago, but the logical side of her mind knew it was just a few years back. During her hiatus.

CUR!

"Fuck..." she breathed. It came up, clawed up, a memory that had been waiting, growing in the soil of her soul.

The cur is long gone by now.

That voice! *His* voice!

The memory pushed up through the soil like a twisted, gnarled vine, thickening, branching, red, bloody leaves sprouting and dripping. She felt it in her chest. It rose in her throat.

"My old friend."

The Night!

Anders Saffenssen, blond ponytail gone and replaced with a kufi cap, stepped out from the back of the house and kicked the dog.

It didn't make a sound.

The vampire picked it up by the scruff and tossed it. He pulled the door shut.

Angelique considered it a minor miracle that he didn't see her as he danced down the driveway, turned left, and kept on walking.

She didn't dare move. She stood as still as the buildings on either side of her, their shadows protecting her. She didn't move her eyes to follow him. She didn't breathe.

When she did take one, it was slow and long, and she exhaled it the same. She stepped out into the dusk, half-expecting to hear, *Hello, Tinkerbell.* She looked in the direction he had left and saw no sign of him.

It. Vampire. Vampire Killer.

Angelique took out her phone and turned it on. It read 6:57. *Time flies when you're scared shitless.*

It rang.

She pushed the talk button but said nothing.

"Babe? Hello? You there?"

"Everett," she whispered.

"What's wrong? What's going on?"

She looked across the street at the house. It was old, abandoned. Like most of the other houses and buildings in the neighborhood, it was faded and warped. Most of the windows were boarded up except two on the second floor and a small one at the point of a gable.

"We can stop searching."

Angelique could see no house number, and she didn't know the street. She turned right, away from the direction Anders had gone, toward an intersection.

"What are you talking about?" Everett's voice said he already knew.

"I found him." Before Everett could respond, she added, "More like I stumbled upon him."

"Where are you? It's night. It's dangerous."

He was correct. She could become the next victim of the Vampire Killer. Angelique came to the intersection. At least the street signs were there. "Come quick. Come and get me."

53

John awoke, his heart feeling measurably lighter. Only the faintest of light emanated from behind the curtains in his room. It was early. He turned to his back.

When he saw the two angels standing at the end of his bed, John wasn't surprised, and he *knew* his dream last night had been something more.

"That was you, wasn't it?" he demanded, sitting up.

Aaron—Araquiel, whatever his name was—replied, "Why, whatever do you mean?"

Carrie, bristled, her brown face hardened, and her green eyes flashed. "And *good morning* to you, too," she grumbled.

John looked at Carrie. "I've never had a dream *that* vivid."

She shrugged. "It wasn't me."

John noticed they both wore sweat suits, as if they were going out running this morning, Aaron in his typical blue, Carrie in her green.

"It was one of you..." John couldn't say the word. He had been thinking about it for a while now, but it couldn't come out of his mouth.

"One what?" Aaron smiled.

Carrie leaned close to him. She didn't smile. "Say it, child. If you believe what you think, then say what you believe."

He laid back into his pillow and put the heels of his hands into his eye sockets. A headache started behind them. Maybe he was dreaming. If he went back to sleep in this dream, he'd wake up alone.

Then say what you believe...

He removed his hands and looked up at the ceiling. He could see they were still there, on the periphery, like they had been all his life.

John took a breath. "One of you—*angels*—influenced my dream."

Carrie appeared beside him. He felt her warm hand on his shoulder. It patted him like he was a child. "There, that didn't hurt, did it?" she asked. "Don't let pride keep you from moving forward. And moving forward sometimes means you must change your thinking."

"As for your latest dream," added Aaron, "nothing of this world was involved. We," he pointed to himself and his sister angel, "had nothing to do with your sleep or dreams."

May the Holy Spirit guide your heart.

Their parting words two months ago. Since then, John knew the Book of Life had been showing him important events of his past, mostly of all the times he had found or been given Pennies from Heaven. But the awful dream last night had been something different. Was it this Holy Spirit?

John had grown up Catholic and had pretended to know what it all meant: the Trinity, Immaculate Conception, Confession, priests, sisters... He could go on. He had forgotten all of it—had never really known it.

"The Holy Spirit," he whispered.

"Yes."

The deep, melodious word came from the doorway. It commanded respect and power in that single syllable, love and danger.

The angels stood at attention then bowed and murmured something unintelligible. A severe heat pushed into the room, but it produced no pain or sweat. It was a different heat.

A holy heat? John wondered.

A tall man in a white robe and gold belt, his nose at the top of the door frame, bent to enter the bedroom. He motioned to the kitchen. "Leave us," he commanded.

The two angels hurried out, the apartment door closing behind them.

The man was beautiful, an athletic model who had stepped from the pages of a magazine. Long, straight blond hair framed an angular face. His thin, slightly upturned nose rose above red, full lips, capable of a great smile or a fearsome grimace. His ears protruded perfectly to either side of—those eyes. His eyes were *yellow* but flecked with something that sparkled. Gold?

John swallowed, feeling the heat radiating from this man, and something occurred to him. "Are you Jesus?"

The tall man froze a moment then laughed—too loudly. Some neighbor was bound to come knocking on the door, yelling for them to keep it down so early in the morning. Nothing moved on his body but his head; nothing was wasted; everything was still but the jaw that bobbled and a slight movement of the chest. A laughing mannequin. His eyes closed as if to keep in the tears.

"What is so humorous?" came a female voice of equal authority yet tinged with a mother's embrace and a grandmother's wisdom.

As tall as the man, she stepped into the room. His twin. Her blonde hair, pulled back into the longest braid John had ever seen, came over her left shoulder, down between her breasts to a loop at her waist. It wrapped around her like a belt and tied to itself, securing her white robe. Her eyes glowed an iridescent purple and faintly lit the room. The heat doubled in intensity. John hardly noticed.

The male pointed at John lying on the bed and said, "He thinks I am the Christ!"

The female smiled and shook her head. "You have to admit, Uriel, you have a way of entering that is, shall we agree, royal? What does he know of us or the Christ, for that matter?"

This calmed her twin—a wordless agreement.

They looked at John. He looked at them.

"Introductions?" she asked.

The man stepped forward and bowed slightly, grudgingly. "I am the archangel Uriel. I am the guardian of this Earth and commander of the Protectors."

His twin stood proudly, her left shoulder just behind his right. "I am the archeia Aurora, his divine complement, his twin flame. Each archangel is blessed with one." She put a hand on her brother's shoulder. "We archeiai have their backs when they're in trouble." In one step she sat on the bed at John's feet. As tall and as large as she was, there was no weight displacement, as if she hovered over the bed.

"Your question was humorous because Uriel was recently, mildly, chastised by the Christ to bow in honor to you." She leaned forward as if to tell John a secret. "The last human he bowed to was Noah—"

"And he had earned it," interrupted Uriel.

John understood what that comment implied.

"Child," Aurora said, "We have come to plead—"

Uriel appeared beside the bed next to his sister. There was no movement of the archangel, no steps. He blinked into the spot. "We do not have time. We are busy. We guard the Earth and protect it from the Darkness even as it is consolidating and building its power. We have your orders." He halted to correct himself, to use other words he had been told to use. "We have your choice. You must fly to Rome, to the Vatican, and enter Saint Paul's Basilica at the first light of the day on May fifteenth, which is the Day of Ascension. This is the next time when the veil between worlds is thin. As the light of the morning sun touches the Holy Altar," he hesitated again. "Something will appear: a gift for you and only you. If you take it, you will be bound by your soul to it, and it to you. In this choice, you will join us in this fight against the Darkness."

"If you are in the Holy City that morning," added Aurora, "you can enter the church alone and unhampered. We will make it happen."

Now it was John's turn to laugh. "I have no money for a trip to Rome, let alone for a stay there."

"This is no holiday for sightseeing, child," Uriel growled. "Christ has chosen you to pluck a worm from the Fruit of His Father's making. Sell everything, sacrifice all—but only if you choose to take His Hand and walk into the Darkness. If you choose to do His Will, then He will provide."

Aurora stood beside her twin. "If, however, you choose to stay here in your simple life, you will have status quo... for a time. The Dark stirs, John Paul Wilkins, and the Lylitu will rise up and eat your world from the inside out. You and all you hold dear will become slaves to Darkness. She will consume all Light, and there will be no joy. No love."

A grave concern crossed her face, yet no wrinkles or lines appeared on her countenance, but her fear made her purple eyes glow brighter. "This is not the Apocalypse, child. This is not written in the Book of Life. This is the Enemy's way of unwriting the Book, of thwarting the Creation." She extended her arm, her hand flat out and face down.

Uriel extended his over hers and bowed his head. After a moment, he said, "The time of the Antichrist is yet to come. It has been written, and it shall be done. But this Lylitu, this perversion, is a mistake—*my* mistake. And it is *my* responsibility. The Christ has intervened once again on behalf of humanity. He has chosen you, child, to do this task. You will not be alone in this. But it is your choice."

"The fate of humanity?" asked John.

"Yes," they both responded.

John was a little perturbed. "Oh, humanity. No biggie."

Uriel looked to Aurora as if to say, *See? What did I tell you?*

But Aurora smiled as they lowered their arms. She said, "We will leave you to think upon this. Remember: Saint Paul's Basilica on Ascension Day." Silently, they left.

John lay in bed, dumbfounded. Angels and archangels and— whatever she was. Darkness and an Enemy and now this Lylitu— whatever that was. And there was a point of no return.

To hell with work. He went back to sleep.

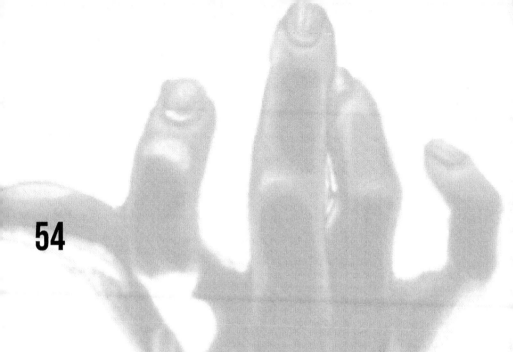

54

E verett had called in sick to work.

Angelique had skipped classes.

That morning, they had waited until 9:30 to be safe. They wanted the sun fully up for their endeavor.

They stood in the shadows of the alley across from Anders' house.

"You really didn't get the irony of it?" he asked again.

Angelique had told him "no" last night and again a few hours ago when they were eating breakfast—what little she could eat.

She was nervous. A piece of toast and two cups of coffee. This was one of those rare mornings where Earl Grey tea wasn't enough. She had bigger things on her mind than the name of the street where Anders lived, nested. Whatever vampires called it.

But standing here in the cool Baltimore morning, it made perfect sense. If the vampire did want her to find him, this was the perfect street.

Carfax Road. Carfax was the name of an abbey in the novel *Dracula*. Were this any other day, she would've indeed been enjoying the irony if she wasn't so nervous.

What if Anders wasn't here? What if he had other places he could stay?

What if he knew she was there and was waiting for them to come inside?

She stood across the street from Anders' house, filled with questions.

Calm and cool Everett. He was a scientist. He knew what was going through his lover's mind right now. And he had the perfect response.

"We've planned our work, so let's work our plan."

It wasn't a *fools rushing in* plan. He liked to study, to observe. He turned around and looked at the buildings. He pointed to the one on the left. "Let's see what we have in there."

They went back to their car and got a toolbox, a couple of different tire irons, and a couple flashlights. The large plastic tote container of camera equipment stayed put for now. They put all this down in the shadowy alley and spent two hours walking around the block and adjacent blocks.

There was no human activity anywhere nearby. No one to see them, to wonder, to question, or to call the authorities. There were no security cameras. No cars had driven by. It was a blighted area of the city. Anders had chosen well.

More likely, he had scared off any possibility of discovery. That suited Angelique and Everett's plans.

They got into the building and found it sound. It had been gutted to the point that Angelique couldn't tell what business had been done here in the past. However, there were a few signs that the homeless or drug users had occupied it. Still, it looked as if no one had been inside for quite a few months.

Since there were no major security measures on the building, there had to be someone who came by periodically. She hoped it was to check the locks and the outside of the building.

Everett believed they'd be safe within, as long as they were careful about how they entered and exited the building.

Everett replaced the padlock they had broken with a similar one. He even dirtied it so that it looked used from a short distance. He rigged it so that the door looked closed and locked when they were inside. Only the old key would betray it. He assured Angelique a number of times, he didn't think they would have to worry much about intruders.

A second-floor window, one of the few not boarded up, served as their observation point. Everett set up a digital camera with the lens in the lower left corner. It had a four-hour battery, and he had three other charged batteries in reserve. He could rotate and change them as needed.

Everett was "sick" for the next two days, staying with Angelique at their command center, watching and reviewing and watching some more on the laptop that was recording the house across the street. The dog came and went each day, always returning to the house. Anders had disappeared.

That changed on the third evening.

Everett had gone home to rotate batteries and grab some food. He'd be gone for a few hours.

Angelique sat absently watching the house on the computer screen. Then, on cue, the dog returned from its daily marauding only to flop to its back, begging not to be punished.

Anders.

Angelique got up and went to the window, staying in the shadows.

Anders stood in the driveway, hovering over the submissive dog. As with the other evening, he wore a kufi cap, this one red with gold-stitched designs. He looked odd, his face whiter than she remembered.

Angelique realized he couldn't have returned to Baltimore without a makeover. Along with the red kufi, he wore a blue sweater over a white shirt, khakis, and penny loafers. No dark rock star like years before. But he still wore the gloves.

Cold hand, long white fingers...

Angelique shuddered.

Anders grabbed the dog by the scruff, tossed it into the house, and jauntily walked down the street like he had three nights ago.

Three nights ago.

Had Anders been in the house all this time? Why? He must have returned while she and Everett were getting things together that first night. They didn't want to risk being seen—or worse, caught—by the vampire, so they stayed home till the next morning.

Had the dog not been leaving the house in the mornings and

returning at sundown, Angelique and Everett would have doubted Anders had been in the house.

Had Anders killed someone that night somewhere in the city? Had he brought a victim to the house to feed in seclusion? Had he come back alone?

What the hell was going on?

At least she knew her old friend had been in the house.

Angelique looked hard at the house. She wanted to run across the street to check it out while Anders was gone. There was the dog to consider, of course. Old that it was, she knew it would defend its territory... its master's lair. And there was Everett to consider, too. He was due back any moment. He would be thoroughly pissed off if she went rushing in where angels feared to tread—where anyone would fear to tread, for that matter.

Three nights. Was this some kind of pattern? She hoped so.

Did Anders go out hunting every three nights then hang out in his dilapidated house between feedings? She and Everett would have to stakeout for weeks to discover a method to the madness of the Vampire Killer. That was something Everett the researcher would agree to.

Angelique knew at some point—sooner than later—she'd *have* to go over and see.

The creaking wood of the stairs announced Everett had arrived. Angelique went back to her chair and tried her best to look bored. He had some soup, bread, and soda for dinner.

"Anything interesting?"

She needed time to think. This ball just got rolling, and she didn't need him to slow it down. "Just the dog."

"Well," he said, "it's been three nights and only a dog. We've been lucky so far, but the longer we stay, the greater the risk of a city worker or the police coming by. Even areas like this have occasional patrols."

She wanted him to shut up.

He continued, "That lock we broke had to have been put on the alley back door not long ago. Probably replaced an old, rusted one. Somebody doesn't want anyone in here."

Somebody doesn't want anyone in here.

278

Anders doesn't want anyone in here.

It was perfect. He was the one who had put the new lock on the building.

"Ev?" Angelique asked.

"Huh?" he replied with a mouthful of bread.

"Did you check the building next door? Does it have a lock on the alley door like this building?"

"Yeah," he replied, still chewing. He stopped and swallowed. He sat frozen for a moment, allowing Angelique's questions to lead him where she wanted him to go. He focused on her. "The same as this building. And it may have been put on about the same time as the one we broke." He took a sip of soda. "I see where you're going with this, but we can't be certain."

He looked at his watch. "I have to work tomorrow." He moved over and knelt beside her, grabbing her hand. "But this doesn't change anything. We have to be careful."

Oh, it changes everything.

Angelique waited exactly an hour before she hit the spacebar to wake the computer.

She minimized the video feed and opened the playback app.

She ran the most recent file in reverse.

While she absently watched it, she thought about why she'd lied to Everett, why she only told him about the dog.

Part of it was that she wanted Anders for herself. This entire ordeal was a personal thing—her thing. She could feel something building, and she didn't need Everett doing any kind of risk analysis. He was simply too cautious. This wasn't a controlled lab environment where he could start over if an error was made.

The city was looking for the Vampire Killer. How long before police showed up in the area—forcing Anders to move? This would be all over. She knew there'd be no second chances with finding Anders.

Angelique knew what she had to do.

Anders was a vampire, an undead creature that *slept* during the day.

She'd check the house tomorrow—

The dog appeared in reverse, and she hit play. There it came trotting up the street and turning into the driveway only to drop to its back, paws up, an omega in the presence of an alpha.

Except there was nothing else on the screen.

The dog lifted into the air and floated to the back of the house.

Angelique waited, knowing Anders had walked back down the driveway and off to whatever dark deed he had in mind tonight.

She reversed it again and clicked play:

Dog... dog down... no Anders.

She paused it. And there he was—or not was.

It was a fuzzy form, an almost invisible thing, as if light passed around it. Odd that her eyes could see it, but the camera detected only a distortion, as if something had erased the image.

She played the recording slowly.

The form moved slightly, the dog rose into the air, the dog floated out of sight to the back of the house—nothing but the house—the fuzzy form appeared, moved to the end of the driveway, turned down the street, and was gone.

That thrumming she had felt days ago when she had seen the dog for the first time was back.

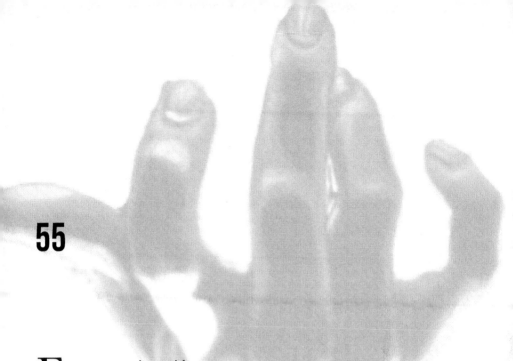

55

E verett wasn't stupid.

He was disappointed that Angelique had lied. He didn't know about what, but he could guess.

He saw the look in her eyes. She was going to do something rash, impulsive. He had to be ready.

He had intended to go into work tomorrow, but now he knew he had to be ready for whatever Angelique was to throw at him in the next hours.

No sleep for him tonight.

He spent his time in the basement lab and in the garage.

Either the lab would receive a certain occupant, or he would find the dead body of the woman he loved.

Perhaps he, too, would end up as another victim of the Vampire Killer.

56

A boy leaned against the arm of a chair in the hotel lobby and looked intently at an apple. He couldn't be but seven or eight years old. Odd that a boy ate an apple rather than a frosted Pop Tart.

He crunched on it and chewed.

John wondered if there was a worm in the apple.

"… do you?"

John Wilkins hadn't heard a word the bride-to-be had said. He had felt distracted since he had awoken this morning. Every few minutes or so, the words of the archeia Aurora swirled in his mind and heart: *You will have status quo… for a time. The Dark stirs, John Paul Wilkins, and the Lylitu will rise up and eat your world from the inside out.*

A worm in the apple.

But that was someone else's apple right now. John had to keep his life simple: going to work and going home. One day at a time. In fact, the hotel—his job—had become a sanctuary from the Quandary. He knew the angels couldn't accost him here. The hotel had become so busy that he didn't have time to think of much else.

When he had come to work today, he found his hotel had become the hub of a nuptial celebration, and that Andrew had promised his manager John Wilkins could easily pull off a spectacular event given the week he had to do it.

A week to do a wedding. Andrew was a vindictive asshole. He didn't like his manager taking unplanned days off.

… and eat your world from the inside out. Aurora's purple eyes held sadness and challenge.

A warm hand touched his. "You okay?

Sandy—John couldn't think of her last name at the moment—looked concerned. She wasn't even twenty-two, an associate at Wal-Mart, and she was getting married.

Cute and nearly as tall as he, Sandy had straight shoulder-length brown hair and the lean body of an athlete, probably from years of basketball. She was one of those few people who saw life as an adventure, a look of smiling innocent wonder on her face most of the time. But now was not one of them as she looked over the man who was supposed to plan the most important day of her life.

The Lylitu will rise up and eat your world from the inside out.

Sandy was about to say something more, but John said, "Don't worry, Sandy." He gave her a bright smile. "I have a world of problems on my shoulders." He knew exactly what would deflect her. "Here," he said and held out his hands. "Hold this bag."

Sandy's eyebrows knotted suspiciously, but she half-smiled and took the imaginary bag.

John took his problems, imaginary things from his shoulders, a dozen or so, and put them in the imaginary bag. By the tenth, Sandy giggled and acted like the bag was heavy. By the end, they both were laughing.

John took the filled bag and tied it up. "Wait a sec." He walked to his office, tossed it in, and shut the door.

Sandy beamed.

"Okay, my dear, you were saying?"

She got a little serious. "You're coming to the wedding?"

John had a feeling he knew where this was going. He smiled his ornery grin and replied, "Why, Sandy?" He winked.

Sandy hit him on the arm. "Ted beat you to it. No, silly. I need to know if you'll be bringing someone."

There it was. She was playing matchmaker. John was surprised she didn't just come out and ask about his social status. She must have a friend who was also single.

In the four hours working with Sandy this morning, he had read her like the headline on a newspaper. *Make me look good.*

So, he sat down with her and Ted (cursing Andrew, who occasionally strolled by with a grin on his face—such an asshole) and immediately set up a tux fitting for the groom and his men. The two of them were impressed that it could be done so quickly.

After Ted took off for the appointment, John had taken Sandy's warm hands in his and had told her he had quite a few favors to call in, that he would use them all up for her.

That wasn't necessarily true, but he wanted her to believe that everything was under control. He had promised her, right there in his office earlier this morning, that her wedding day would be a memorable one—one that wouldn't cost her half of what she imagined.

He had made one phone call after another, acting as Sandy's intermediary.

His first call, for the church, was with a pastor who owed him for freeing up rooms for a small conference a year ago. Check.

Reservations for the rehearsal dinner on Friday night? Check.

An appointment with a seamstress to check over the great-grandmother's wedding dress? Check. She had *really* owed him. She owed John for rooms he had gotten to keep her parents and in-laws from killing each other. Check.

An appointment that afternoon for Sandy's friends to try on gowns at a wedding consignment store? Check.

Sandy had been clapping with excitement. Then John had taken the bride-to-be by the hand and said, "You and I have one more thing to do," and he pulled her out into the lobby.

That was when he had seen the boy eating the apple.

A worm in the apple.

Now all the worms and apples and Quandaries were in the imaginary bag in his office.

He looked Sandy in the eyes and replied, "I don't have anyone, Sandy."

The bride-to-be purred, "We'll see about that."

John smiled back. "First, let's see about flowers. I'm certain I can get the hotel to take care of it for you."

Sandy gave him a big hug and squealed, "You're a miracle worker!"

John feigned a serious look and whispered, "Don't say that too loudly."

He didn't want the angels to hear it.

Later, John told his friend Barry about Andrew's asshole move.

"Jesus! You get all the luck!" Barry shook his head amazed. "Don't you remember *The Wedding Crashers?*"

John wasn't concerned about weddings and women. Despite Andrew's move, he really wanted the bride and groom and their families and friends to have a good time. Weddings should be memorable experiences. Being concerned about other people and solving their problems helped to keep his mind off all the things in that bag back at the hotel. But he couldn't say as much to Barry. "Sorry, Barry, I really don't want to go. I'm just going to show up and leave. No biggie. In and out. That's it."

"Yeah, in and out all right."

John ignored him.

They sat in Barry's kitchen, drinking beer and eating chips and salsa.

John avoided his apartment, if he could.

"Well," Barry added, taking a sip from his bottle, "I couldn't go with you anyway, ol' friend. I have a date."

John smiled big. It was great news to cap off a great day. He tipped his bottle to Barry's, and his friend tapped it, a clear tinking sound that reminded John of bells. Not wanting his mind to go *there,* he asked, "Anyone I know?"

"Ha!" Barry laughed nervously. "Nope, and it'll stay that way."

57

E verett thought of everything.

He had set up a large black blanket as a curtain across the farthest corner from the command center window. Their laptop and small lamp could stay on at night and not attract eyes from the street —especially from the house across the street.

The house of Anders the vampire.

Angelique, however, liked to sit in a lawn chair in the shadows of the window and watch the house, wondering what was over there.

Did Anders have a coffin filled with smelly earth?

Did he hang crosses upside down?

Did he burn candles made from the fat of his victims?

Angelique doubted most of the old legends she had read.

One thing she did believe: there was something about three nights.

She believed three nights ago Anders had killed someone and had hung out or slept—he did *something* for three nights—before he emerged this evening at sundown to do it all over again.

Angelique found she was thirsty, and she got up from the chair and went back behind the curtain, saw that the camera feed counted its time, and bent over to get a bottle of water from the cooler she and Everett kept stocked with water and other foods.

She heard the woman through the closed window before she

appeared on the laptop screen. She had that obnoxious squeal of a drunk bimbo. Perhaps she was a prostitute. More than likely, she was a bar fly who wouldn't be missed for days. Had there been people living in this neighborhood, she would have woken all of them.

Angelique noted the time, 12:14 A.M., and she maximized the live feed window on the computer and watched.

The woman appeared—alone—yet she looked as if she were talking with someone. As she approached the decrepit house, she pointed at it and called out, "Here?" She tried to pull away from something then halted. She bent over then seemed to hover above the ground, head down, arms dangling, feet dragging on the cracked asphalt of the driveway.

Angelique slipped around the curtain and went to the window to see Anders carrying the woman, one arm around her waist as if she were nothing but a bag of clothes. They disappeared behind the house. Immediately, the dog came out and sniffed the ground where the woman had said her last (final?) word. Anders came back out, and the dog crouched low.

"Where?" Angelique could barely hear him.

He bent over and picked up something. An earring?

"Go on!" Anders said to the dog, waving it away. It took off.

The fucking animal was an accomplice?

An ugly vine deep within her punched through the packed surface of her mind, a gnarly, twisted thing that evoked a grotesque memory. A dirty, cluttered alley, a dark green dumpster, the shadows, white teeth, white tail... the dog crouching, snarling, lunging... a yip and a scramble... it ran away... a gloved hand... Anders.

Anders! The dog!

A setup!

The vine sprouted more vines, each one another memory—the shadows, her childhood, her father's death, the Vampire Killer, John Paul Wilkins, the violent dreams, the drinking, rehab, Everett, the occult. Vampires. Vampires *in* shadows. The vines seemed to bore holes within her skull, pushing out and around her face and down her shoulders and breasts and back, boring into her belly.

She turned from the window and vomited. Her knees shook,

and she staggered back to the chair at the command center. "Fuck," she hissed, plopping into it.

An old, panicky feeling squeezed her throat. It was the old Angelique, the one she left back at that rehab with that mousy doctor. She had been helpless and empty then.

As she had healed, her obsession with Anders, vampires, and the occult had become a compulsion that consumed her. It possessed her—this need to find the vampire, somehow capture it, study it, and take its secrets. She wanted to torment it like it had done to her. She wanted to become its master. This fire in her belly compelled her every day. One day at a time. To this week. To this place. Right here, right now.

But this *now*, this revelation—Anders and the dog—unbalanced her. Instead of that fire in her belly, driving her like an engine, she felt more like she was on a high-wire, crossing a dark chasm, the light that had been on her, gone.

She felt unstable, precarious.

There had been nothing of chance in that alley on The Night.

Angelique had been a target.

She had never been in control of anything.

And now in total darkness, the high-wire wavering, she could slip and fall.

Angelique gasped from holding her breath. The nausea passed.

The ugly vines in her belly churned.

She looked across the room, through the window, at Anders' house.

What if I step off the wire, fall into the darkness below?

A new fire started in her belly, the vines becoming fuel for a new engine.

Falling would be her decision.

She realized with the clarity of a sudden breath that she hadn't made any decisions in her life. Like a paddle ball on an elastic band, a force would hit her, and she would bounce, only to come back and be hit by another force.

She wouldn't be pushed off the high-wire or lose her balance—she'd step off, a willful decision.

All she had to do was walk across the street.

She took a deep breath and opened the cooler for water. She took one, twisted off the cap, and took a swig, swishing it around in her mouth to get the taste of vomit out. She spat it out and drank half the bottle, using the rest of it to dilute the splash of puke near the window. She checked the camera feed on the computer, ensuring it was still recording. The time on the screen showed it had been almost an hour since Anders had come home. Her mobile phone showed fifty percent battery. She turned it off and put it back into her pocket and grabbed a thin pocket flashlight.

She stepped off the high-wire and fell into the yawning darkness below.

Filled with immense relief, she crossed the street. She walked up the driveway she had seen Anders walk an hour ago. The house loomed larger here. She imagined a kind of sentience, as if the windows were eyes that watched her walk to the rear of the house.

The back door had a large pet door. That explained how the accomplice-dog came and went. Angelique tried the doorknob. Unlocked.

It opened into the kitchen.

Angelique needed a bigger flashlight. This small one only made everything gray and black.

As she crossed the threshold, she wondered what the fuck she was doing. If she found Anders, was he going to surrender?

Of course, Tinkerbell, I am your prisoner.

She took a deep breath. She had jumped off the wire. There was no turning back.

Where would a vampire hide?

Directly across from her, a threshold opened into another room. A closed door stood in the corner to the left. She checked the door. It opened to stairs going down to a damp, musty basement. *How stupid would a vampire be to trap itself in a basement?* It needed seclusion, darkness. Anyone walking through the house could find and trap it in a basement. Seclusion and an exit. Where did few people go in a house?

Angelique smiled. She looked up.

At the top of the stairs to the second floor, she shined her light on the hallway ceiling. As she suspected, she found an attic door, the kind that pulled down with a folding ladder. There was no dangling rope which meant someone—something—had used it to pull the door up.

She opened the first door to the right, an empty bedroom, and found a chair in the closet.

To help with light, she opened doors to rooms with unboarded windows. The streetlight was minimal at best. She took her time, moving slowly, and positioned the chair below the attic door. She tested her weight on it then stood up to get the wooden ball that was a handle. She pulled gently, then the rope slipped down about eight inches and halted. She stepped down then shined her flashlight on the rope-handle.

Was she going to pull down that door? It had springs she knew would make obscene noises. If Anders didn't know she was in the house, that door would announce her.

She was at an impasse.

The absurdity of her situation made her smile. She almost laughed. She felt like she was on the edge of a moment when, if she allowed it, she could start laughing and not stop.

What am I doing?

"Fuck it," she breathed. This is what Anders wanted: for her to find him. She had jumped off the high-wire, and she welcomed the abyss below. *Ready or not, here I come.*

Angelique shut off the flashlight and put it in her pocket. She took a breath, reached up, and pulled down the door. The springs made one loud sound, like an unbalanced gong. She moved the chair out of the way and pulled down the attic steps.

Like a fog, the smell of shit and piss wafted down the opening. And something else.

She gagged, glad she had emptied her stomach earlier, but the water threatened to come up. She pulled up the collar of her sweatshirt over her nose and tried to take a breath to steady her stomach.

Angelique expected a roar and teeth and pain.

Nothing.

She took out the thin flashlight and put her left hand over the bulb end. She turned it on. Her hand glowed red. Was that from the blood inside her, blood that would be food for the beast up in that attic? She hoped he was already sated.

Angelique looked at that glowing hand. The light within. She could use that light to show the way out of the house and away from this.

Her future was up there, however much it stank.

She spread her middle and ring fingers. A thin shaft of white shot up to the ceiling. She directed that light to the first step and put the weight of her right foot on it, lifting her body.

I have to know.

She placed her left foot on the second step.

I have to know.

She had to see Anders. Even if it was for a moment before he killed her. Everything she had suffered—her shadows, The Night, PTSD, her abortive relationship with John Wilkins, her hiatus—it all formed a nexus to this next step.

I have to know.

As her head neared the opening, the stench, like some old latrine, threatened to knock her down. The sweatshirt was a poor filter, but she managed to take a deep, gagging breath and hold it, bringing the glowing hand to the right edge of the attic's opening.

She took another step.

The humid, rancid darkness pushed down on her. Her heart pounded in her chest, echoing in her ears. Her lungs screamed for air. She lifted the lighted hand higher and spread her fingers.

The triangular beam illuminated a bald, white head not ten feet away. Anders lay prone on the floor atop a large thick sheet of plastic that covered most of the attic floor.

Next to Anders lay the woman, still as a piece of driftwood. Her blouse had been ripped off, her neck and left shoulder covered in drying blood.

Angelique gasped finally, taking a deep breath.

Nothing moved.

She removed her hand from the end of the flashlight.

The darkness pushed back. She stepped up into the attic. The sweatshirt dropped from her nose, the stench now unimportant.

Anders the vampire looked like a corpse with pants, blood

covering most of his face and chest. His belly distended as if he were pregnant. Like a tick, he had gorged himself and rolled off his bitch.

The woman looked chalky, making her smeared lipstick seem bright like blood. Her eyes, like faded blue marbles, were fixed on the rafters above her. A small pool of blood, the size of a plate, cooled on the plastic beneath her neck and head. Her hand almost touched his ungloved hand, a dead bride for the undead vampire.

Angelique stepped onto the attic floor, closer to Anders, bending to avoid hitting her head on the angle of the rafters. The flashlight revealed the woman's tattered neck, chewed and ripped open. The light caught something in the far corner. She found a number of wigs, garment bags, stuffed gym bags, a dozen pairs of shoes, a radio, cleaning wipes, a garbage can, a number of gallon jugs of water.

He lived up here.

He killed up here.

Angelique squatted beside Anders. She grit her teeth and grabbed his gloved left hand, making certain not to touch his skin. It flopped down on the plastic.

He was as still as the corpse beside him. Angelique wondered if feeding caused a kind of napping for digestion.

She had so many questions. And she would have the opportunity now to find answers.

Angelique found the discarded glove. Dyed black, it had no soft inner lining, but the workmanship was exquisite. Her mother had owned expensive gloves, and Angelique had learned what to look for in a pair. The quirks and fourchettes of this glove were small and intricate. The leather felt strange. She reached down, grabbed the middle finger of the one on Anders' left hand but kept her eyes on the exposed right—

Cold hand, long white fingers.

—and gently yanked the glove off.

The vampire's head moved.

Still a corpse.

She put both gloves in her empty jacket pocket.

She reached into her jeans pocket and pulled out her phone. She called Everett.

"Something happen?"

She laughed then gagged again at the smell. "You can say that. Get the van and all the stuff we need to get our little vampire—"

"What? I'm not ready here!"

"Ev, dear." She stood and pushed Anders' head with her foot. She looked at the protruding belly. "I have a feeling we have plenty of time."

58

Andrew Peterson held up the florist bill for his manager to see. He didn't like to get unexpected bills, and he knew it was a counterstrike to what he had done to his friend with the wedding.

John smiled inwardly, took it, signed it, and handed it back. From behind the main desk, Kara stifled a smile and handed John a small stack of mail. Lauren came out from the back office to watch.

Andrew was only half-pissed. He had spent the last hour with Sandy helping with arranging a dozen rooms for the family attending the wedding. The hotel was booked solid. "What? No apology?"

John removed his coat and put it over his arm. "I'll never apologize for supporting true love. How many are booked?"

Andrew would've given his friend the finger but for the fact they were in the lobby. His face spoke volumes. John said, "I thought so."

The owner folded the bill and put it in the breast pocket of his sport coat. "And you're going to the wedding. You can take cards and brochures."

John laughed and looked at the ladies behind the counter. "He's such a romantic." They smiled and acted busy.

John turned to go to his office, thinking he might indeed have a little fun at the wedding when a young woman stood and stretched.

She had been hidden behind a newspaper, sitting in one of the plush chairs of the lobby.

Blonde hair woven into a tight rope behind her head, she was dressed to work out: black spandex bottoms, white and purple spaghetti strapped top, cut off at the midriff enough to show just how much she worked out—which was a lot. Damn, she was good-looking.

She caught his eye, smiled, bent over (John got the impression it was so he could see her cleavage) to fold the paper on the table, then proceeded straight out of the lobby.

"Nice..." It was Andrew. Like men do when there is piercing beauty nearby, he had to acknowledge the obvious. "See how she smiled at you?"

"Yeah, right," John replied. "Where did she come from?"

Andrew sighed. "Blottie checked in—alone—last night. Paid for three nights."

John looked at his friend. "Blottie?"

"Yeah. Blonde. Hottie. Blottie." Andrew frowned at another bill he had just been handed. "It's what all the guys are calling her."

John smiled. "Funny."

They lingered in the afterthought of her beauty then walked off in different directions.

John decided to hang out in his office for a while, catching up on some paperwork. He had the front desk security camera on his computer screen just in case the woman came back. And she did an hour later.

She walked up to Lauren at the front desk and did the strangest thing: She looked directly into the camera and smiled, as if directly at John. Whatever she had asked about, she had gotten her answer and walked off.

Later that morning, Marshall Ewan asked John to go to lunch. In charge of facility maintenance, Marshall was long overdue on his persistent appeal for a new sprinkler system in the hotel. Once a month for four months now, he took John to lunch to talk about facility issues which would lead into how the hotel needed an updated sprinkler system.

As long as it passed city inspections, both knew nothing would be done about it. Marshall knew that. But he had a sympathetic ear in the hotel manager, and he liked John and he liked having lunch with him.

Except this time, Marshall immediately brought up the beautiful patron.

"Yeah, I saw her," John replied.

Marshall took a sip of soda. "And that outfit this morning. Damn. She was sweaty in all the right places."

John laughed—and the laugh caught in his throat when she walked into the restaurant.

Marshall saw him hesitate and turned around.

Her hair was loosely curled, cascading down her black leather jacket. She had on a white and yellow dress with black boots. She removed the jacket to reveal her dress as a halter that covered everything firmly. The back of the dress angled down like an arrow pointing at her ass, punctuating what everyone should be looking at. And everyone was.

The dress contrasted with her bronze skin. Bare shoulders, bare arms—the skirt barely came down to her knees. She was like a flower in a bed of weeds.

John was going to say as much when she made eye contact with him... and smiled. Perfect white teeth.

"Jesus, she is perfect," Marshall breathed, echoing what John was thinking.

"She's beautiful, and she knows it." John tried his best to find something wrong with her.

Jacket over her arm, she turned and went to a table in a corner.

Marshall took a drink and said, "She's gotta be waiting for someone."

"She checked in alone, I was told."

Marshall turned back to John. "Then there's hope for me?"

"Go over and chat her up."

Marshall harrumphed. "Right."

They finished their lunch. There was no more discussion of old sprinkler systems.

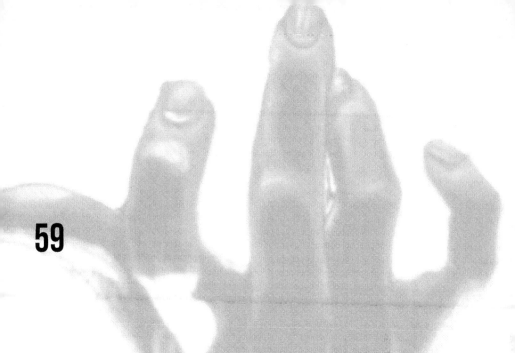

59

Today was Wednesday the 26th, and Angelique knew it would be the most important day of her life. Three days had passed since they had caught Anders, and she knew he would wake up this day.

By first light on Monday, they had secured the inanimate vampire to an "X" shaped half-inch thick stainless-steel table. The shape would limit muscular mobility. Chains held arms and hands tight in the upper half of the "X," legs in the lower. Chains went around his neck, his chest, and his hips. Everett wanted to remove any chance of leverage.

Using thick gloves to mitigate any coldness that might emanate from the creature, Everett performed an initial examination. Angelique sat on the basement steps and watched as he cleaned off the dried blood and makeup, wiped down the vampire's entire body, pointing out that the bulging belly was smaller. But there was no pulse, no blood pressure, no gastrointestinal activity; the electrocardiogram and electroencephalogram showed nothing.

Dead. Corpse.

He stood by the vampire a few more minutes, looking at the small penis and scrotum. He still had gloves on, and he moved the member. "Serious atrophy. My guess is that it's old."

He removed the gloves, washed his hands, and went to get ready for work.

Angelique sat there on the steps that Monday morning and wondered where Everett got the energy to do all this and still go to work. She slept most of the day, waking when he came home a little early. He inhaled some leftovers and went straight to bed.

Tuesday, with Everett at work, Angelique felt antsy, impatient. She checked the chains and the table, tried to watch the news, checked the chains and the table again, and went to her favorite coffee bar.

By noon she'd had enough. She stood beside the body, took one of Everett's scalpels, and cut Anders' leg. She hoped it would produce a scream, wake him, something. The slice spread dryly apart, a little darker within than the white skin without, three inches long, an inch deep, a quarter-inch wide.

Nothing.

As disappointment started to squeeze her heart, the incision knitted back together. Not even a mark.

Angelique smiled. "Not quite a corpse, my little vampire."

Everett knew she had done something. Angelique was still smiling. He was only mildly upset because she had neglected to record it. "Not that we'll get anything," he added. "We couldn't get anything at the house." He kissed her on the cheek. "But we have to be thorough. We have to record everything we do from here on out."

They hooked up all the equipment to the vampire, got everything up and running. Everett set up a video camera at the end of the table just beyond Anders' left leg.

Everett used his stethoscope to listen for internal sounds. He checked blood pressure. The ECG and EEG showed flatlines.

Still a corpse. But they knew differently.

He let Angelique repeat her experiment at the same place she had cut earlier—with everything recording. It closed.

They rewound the video and watched the replay. The vampire lay on the table like a corpse. No fuzzy distortion.

Thinking aloud, Angelique said, "Perhaps it's a consciousness thing."

Everett looked at the creature. He started recording. "Again," he said.

Angelique cut, but this time, Everett removed a small sliver of skin from along one of the flaps of the wound. It closed and filled.

In the petri dish, the sample lay for a few minutes as Everett looked at it under the microscope. "Damn," he whispered. He looked up and grinned. "There goes the curse theory."

Everett opened a laptop. It showed the feed from the microscope's camera. He hit a button on the keyboard and the image changed to what looked like a wall of rough limestone. The microscope showed the cells of the skin sample. Then something moved between cells. Everett increased the magnitude. Tiny black hairs poked out from between the cell walls. Some kind of cilia.

There was something inside Anders' body.

Angelique grinned, too.

When Everett suggested they shut down and try to get some sleep, she didn't argue.

The sooner she went to sleep, the sooner tomorrow would come.

Everett had gotten up early Wednesday to get into the office early so that he could come home early. He was torn between keeping up appearances and wanting to spend every moment he could with their prisoner.

Angelique was patient. She laid in bed listening to the faint sounds of Everett downstairs. When she heard the kettle whistle, she knew it was time to get up and see him off.

So that she could get some quality time with her little prize.

She plopped into a kitchen chair and ran a hand through her messy hair.

Everett poured water into a tea mug.

Angelique could smell the bergamot from the Earl Grey.

"You want the rest of this? I gotta run." He held up a plate with a half-eaten slice of toast and two wedges of apple.

"Sure, babe." She acted half-asleep, but she tingled with excitement.

He placed the plate in front of her. "You got a couple more minutes on the tea." He put a gentle hand beneath her chin and lifted her face to his. He kissed her. "Please be careful."

He was just too smart.

She smiled. "You know I will."

He kissed her again. "Uh-huh." He flung his satchel over his shoulder. "Pay attention to the notes."

"I love it when you leave me love notes."

He didn't smile. "I'm serious."

"Cross my heart and hope to die."

He looked at her strangely, then he said, "I wish I could be here when it comes out of its sleep." He sipped his cold coffee and added, "Maybe I'll get lucky and it won't happen till sundown."

"Maybe."

They looked at each other. "Love ya," they said in unison.

She quietly drank her tea and ate Everett's leftovers, waiting until she knew he was really gone.

The first note was a Post-it she found on the door to the basement just above the knob.

PLEASE DO NOT TOUCH ANYTHING

The second was a piece of cardboard he had suspended from the ceiling with thread just inside the steps. It looked like it floated at face-level.

IT IS VERY IMPORTANT YOU DO NOT TOUCH
ANYTHING

She pulled the sign down, bit on an apple wedge, and started down the steps.

"Ah, Tinkerbell! Good! I was just thinking about breakfast."

Her heart leapt into her throat. She choked on a piece of apple and coughed.

"You, too?" she heard. "I'm also choked up about our reunion."

That voice. All the things he had said to her in the alley behind her apartment building. The pressure of his body against hers. Those memories came up like the other ugly vines, twisting and growing and embedding into her belly. They threatened her resolve. But the new fire in her belly raged against them, consuming them.

300

Angelique forced the rest of the apple into her mouth and went down the rest of the stairs.

Anders tried to move, his chains shifting and rattling.

"Come around here, old friend, and let me see you." He chuckled. "I won't bite." When she didn't move, he added, "I can hear your heart beating like a scared little fairy child."

Angelique didn't doubt that. She had no idea what his abilities could be, how his senses had changed, what limitations he had. There was no reason to hide. If he could break free, he would do so, and all this would be over. But she had a feeling Anders was captive.

She stepped around the top of Anders' table.

"Ahhhh. There she is. Savior of the city. Tinkerbell the Terrible." His sardonic voice announced her like a princess entering a hall.

She saw what the notes were about.

On the table between his legs and on the floor, Anders had shit a thick black goo, probably a by-product of his feeding. Everett had left another note on the floor near it.

STAY AWAY. DO NOT TOUCH.
Luv ya! E

She put out her index finger and touched Anders' right bicep. Fish-like cold—not freezing. She moved her finger down to his inner elbow. She knew from helping Everett that the black cilia didn't protrude from the surface of the skin, but she could see a dark shadow beneath it where she touched him. Perhaps it sensed her heat and followed it.

So many questions.

She tapped the tip of his nose. "Oh, I *will* be terrible, my little vampire."

"I have no doubt."

His face was alive now. She saw that it was exactly as she remembered, minus the makeup, of course. His gray lips curved up in a smile. His skin felt dry and rough as she moved her hand over his pate, but it had no elastic, youthful quality.

She wondered if he appreciated the irony of his situation.

But something told her not to look into his eyes. "You're my little vampire now. You're exactly where I want you."

Anders tittered again, and his smile broadened, exposing his dangerous fangs. "Oh, no, my precious Tinkerbell. You are exactly where *you* need to be."

He raised his head as far as he could to see the mess he'd made. "Could you be a dear and pick me up some nappies?"

60

The last week of March had been unusually warm until Friday the 28th, as if nature played a joke on Sandy and Ted's nuptials. It had been in the upper fifties all week, but a cold nor'easter threatened the weekend; snow had been forecasted Saturday night.

The church was beautiful, and John noticed some of the flowers he had sent to the rehearsal dinner were set up at the entrance and in the narthex. He sat in a back row with older, underdressed people whom he figured were daily regulars. He wondered if they felt put out by these occasions, their routines interrupted. But he noticed one of the elderly women tearing up during the vows and figured they, too, enjoyed the hope a wedding brings.

Sandy and Ted were all smiles, making up for the lack of sunshine outside. Everyone smiled with them. Except...

Somehow, the service made John a little sad, and he tried to explore why that was. He certainly didn't feel left out; he had no notions of wanting to get married. He didn't feel it was an empty vow, like Barry and some others felt. He knew that when the right person came along, and he felt the pull or the need to join with that person, that he would have no qualms.

As he thought about it, he knew that being married was a good thing, that somewhere within him was the discipline and desire to be joined with someone. But right now, there was no pull to do so. So, why was he having this undertone of sadness at the moment?

The congregation stood and John followed. It was the end of the ceremony. The priest was announcing the couple. He had missed the kiss. Applause erupted. Some cheers. A whistle.

Why was he sad? It was bothering him now.

Organ music commenced and the newly married couple, smiles beaming to everyone, marched down the aisle, past the last row where he stood. Sandy and Ted both gave him broad smiles, and they turned right to go out of the church.

There was a futility growing in his heart. Not just for the couple, he realized, but for...

You will have status quo

... this church...

for a time,

... and the parents marching out...

and the Lylitu will rise up

... the friends and family in attendance...

and eat your world

... everyone he knew...

from the inside out.

... and himself.

He followed the people out into the cloudy day, joining the gauntlet that led to the surprise limo he had arranged for the couple. He should be excited to see their faces when they saw it. But he was starting to feel sick. He wanted to go home and curl up in bed.

There she was. On the other side of the gauntlet, just on the fringe of the crowd, a broad-brimmed black and yellow hat angled on her perfect head.

She was watching him. Their eyes locked. The woman smiled, a wide-open smile.

Oh, shit! Not another one!

Then Sandy's face was in his.

"Thank you—thank you—thank you!" she yelled then hugged him.

Ted joined in the hug and lifted them both off the ground. "Dude! This is awesome!"

The bride's hands were around his face. Such joy in her eyes. "You're coming to the reception?" It was less a question and more a demand.

"I, ah…"

Sandy hugged him again. "You have to! You won't regret it! Promise!"

John gave a half-smile. "Yes."

She squealed then joined her husband in the limo.

The blonde woman was walking away, a price tag dangling from the back of the hat.

61

E verett came through the door, and the first thing he asked was, "Is it awake?"

"Yes," replied Angelique. She was just as excited as he was. "And I didn't touch anything, like you asked."

He put a blue box on the floor and removed his jacket, hanging it on a peg on the wall. He grabbed the box's handle and held it up.

She took it and could feel cold coming from within. She saw it had no markings or writing. A cold, plain, blue metal box.

That contained blood.

"That was the most difficult thing I've ever done."

Had Angelique not known the dark side of her lover, she would have only guessed he referred to betraying his job and especially his friend Peter. But she knew he also referred to the pains he had to take to secure the infected bags of blood, then there was getting the box through security.

She didn't care what he had to do. She knew he'd get it done. This was too important.

He took the box back and said, "The healthy blood we already have will last a month or so in the fridge, but this infected blood only lasts two weeks."

She followed him to the kitchen.

Everett whispered, "I could only manage two bags." Like

Angelique had suspected, Everett, too, took no chances about the vampire's abilities, what enhanced powers or senses he had. He opened the box. They had cleared off the top row of the fridge for the blood. Four bags already lay upon it. He pulled out some surgical gloves from his pocket and put them on. Then he took out one bag and showed both sides of it to Angelique. A large "X" covered the labels on both sides. He placed it on the right side of the shelf. The other "X" bag he placed next to it. He shut the door.

Everett removed the gloves, found a heavy-duty garbage bag, and put them in. He turned to her, took her face in his hands and kissed her deeply. In her ear he said, "We just did an inventory, so I figure I have a couple weeks before the jig is up."

"I hope you have a guy who can get us to safety before that happens."

Everett kissed her again. "I've already taken care of it. You have a little time to play with your monster before the shit hits the fan."

She turned away and set the timer on the microwave. "You need to eat first, my love."

A little while later, Everett suited up in a kind of Hazmat suit and cleaned Anders' mess. He had already gathered samples that morning. Anders played opossum, though they knew he was awake. Everett bagged all materials and substances and kept them in a sealed container that he took to a friend who had access to an animal incinerator. He stayed until he was convinced it all turned to ash.

When he returned, a little past midnight, Angelique sat in the kitchen, waiting.

"What's happened?"

"He says he's hungry."

Everett considered this. "Good."

"There's more."

He followed her down and stopped on the last step.

Angelique stood next to the vampire. "You feel it, too?"

"Cold."

Anders continued to feign sleep.

"You can stop, my little vampire," Angelique said.

Anders opened one eye then smiled. "You're no fun, Tink."

When Everett came around to the other side of the table, Anders ignored him. "It just got noticeably colder down here, don't you think?"

"Funny," Angelique replied.

Everett checked the computer. "I installed some environmental sensors based on your report about the..." he halted, remembering to whom he was speaking. "Sorry."

Angelique smiled at him. "That was then," she turned her smile to Anders, "this is now."

Everett looked at the vampire then said, "There are no environmental changes."

Angelique put out a hand to touch Anders' bald head. She felt the cold field about an inch away and hesitated. "That cold had reached into my bones. I couldn't move, could barely breathe, like he had inserted the cold into me."

Anders put out his lower lip, mocking her. "I'd say that was nothing personal, but I'd be lying. Of course, I could be lying now." He became serious. "Lies light the way through the dark." He licked his lips. "But I can wax philosophical all night. You brought me here for a reason. I doubt it was to starve me."

"And look at his skin." Everett put on gloves.

"Please tell Mister Doctor not to touch me."

Everett ignored him like a veterinarian would a complaining lab animal. He pushed on the vampire's belly. "It's gotten darker. Perhaps the substance in it rises to the skin surface when it's hungry."

Angelique watched Everett probe Anders' stomach. "He's touched you plenty of times, my little vampire."

With both hands, Everett pushed down. The area curved as if a ball were in the abdomen.

He concluded, "It's the substance that needs feeding." He took the gloves off. "I wish I had a CT scanner, or even better, an MRI."

Angelique looked at Anders' flat belly. There was the key to everything. She put a hand over it. It was colder than the head. "After we make our revelation and publish our papers, I imagine you'll have your own lab with everything you want."

Everett frowned. "I wish you'd wear gloves."

Angelique removed her hand and rubbed it with the other.

She looked at Anders. "Tomorrow, my little vampire."

He rolled his eyes. "Whatever."

Thursday morning, Angelique purposefully avoided Anders. She went to her favorite café. She did a little shopping at the mall.

She returned close to two o'clock. She heated some soup and went down to see her vampire.

The basement was much colder.

Anders' skin looked slightly darker, especially on his abdomen and face.

She said nothing.

"Oh, that's rich," Anders complained, "eat in front of the starving prisoner. Please, Tink, I need a little sippy. I know you have it."

He could mean the blood upstairs or her own. She didn't care. She held out her bowl of soup.

He rolled his eyes.

She smiled and went back upstairs to wait.

Everett walked through the door at 5:42.

He put a finger to his lips and went to the fridge, grabbing one of the bags of infected blood. From his pocket, he pulled out a tube with a roller clamp. He waved it in the air as if to say, *I almost forgot these.* He put a number of others on the table. He also produced a number of blank blood bag labels. He put one on each side of the blood bag to cover the "X"; he didn't want Anders to become suspicious.

They put on surgical scrubs and protective gear then went down the stairs.

Anders barked a single laugh. "It's about time, Tink. You'll be left with nothing but a dried husk if you don't get me a big sippy."

At the bottom of the stairs, Angelique said, "Is that what happens if you don't feed regularly?"

Anders saw them and acted surprised. "And look, they got all dressed up for the occasion. Tinkerbell, you shouldn't have."

Everett placed the blood bag on the table behind him. He opened an app on the laptop and hit some keys. The red lights on the two video cameras blinked on. He turned to Anders and began to place EEG electrodes on his head.

Anders let out a sigh of disgust. "Please, Tink, how many times do I need to ask you to tell Mister Doctor to stop touching me?"

Everett held back a smile.

Angelique said, "It's a necessary evil, my little vampire. You know all about those, right?"

It took Everett a few more minutes to hook up the rest of the monitors.

With gloved hands, he pushed down on the vampire's belly. "The ball or whatever it is feels more solid than yesterday. The skin is darker." He looked at another screen. "It is noticeably colder than yesterday. No discernable changes in the environment."

Angelique asked Anders, "What about the effects of starvation?"

Everett grabbed the bag of bad blood. On the tubing, he checked that the roller clamp was closed. He inserted the tube into the bag.

Anders deigned to look at him a moment then turned to Angelique. "You do it, Tink. Feed me, and I'll answer three questions." He smiled and added, "As a show of good faith, I'll answer your question and it won't count."

Everett passed the bag to Angelique. Anders licked his lips; they remained dry like black worms. "I may have been exaggerating when I said a dry husk. But, yes, we do…" he considered his words, "… wither if we go without feeding for a significant time."

"We?" Everett asked.

Anders ignored him.

Angelique and Everett exchanged a look.

She put her thumb on the roller. Everett cut the tubing about a foot from it so that the blood could squirt out.

"Question one."

"What? No show of good faith?"

Angelique smiled. She worked hard to be calm, yet she knew she held danger in her hands, and danger laid on the table. "I'm not the one in chains. One: Will you fall asleep if you have all this?"

Anders looked intently at the blood. "No. Not enough."

She smiled. "Now open wide."

Anders closed his eyes and opened his dark mouth, his fangs now milky white glass daggers. Hunger definitely changed something in the creature.

Angelique put the end of the tube in his mouth, squeezed the bag, and rolled back the clamp. The dark red blood moved down the clear line and squirted into Anders' throat. She squeezed hard, careful to keep the flow into his mouth.

Anders didn't swallow. The blood somehow moved on its own down his throat.

"Shit!" hissed Everett, and he jumped back. Anders' belly fluttered and moved as if the ball in there were alive.

Angelique squeezed the bag as hard as she could then rolled the clamp shut and stepped back.

Anders' eyes popped open, his head angled back, chin straight up. He gurgled and blood vomited out toward the steps, covering his face and head. It dripped from the stair railing.

"What have you done?" he screamed. He made one painful wail.

His body convulsed.

He lay inert. A corpse once again.

62

The reception was just four blocks from the church. Outside, it was still overcast with a light, cool wind but no rain. Many walked to the party, a procession of brightly dressed celebrants who waved joyfully at passing cars who, in turn, honked in acknowledgment.

John joined them, and by the time he arrived at the hall, he felt a little better, caught up in the jovial mood of the walkers, some of whom were guests at his hotel, and they treated him as one of their own. All the while, however, he scanned the streets looking for the blonde woman. He knew she would be at the reception.

And he knew what she was.

He'd had his status quo, time to contemplate his Quandary, and she had appeared this day to remind him of his choice: allow the world to be consumed from the inside out or embrace this holy destiny and stand against the rising darkness. He knew his earlier feeling of dread was probably some kind of manipulation to hammer in the point that all of this was going to change—for the worse—and that he had a choice to help fix it... or to let the *worm* destroy it all.

Oh, well. He may as well enjoy this while it lasted. When he saw this angelic blondie, he was going to give her a piece of his mind.

As he entered the hall, a pretty young bridesmaid in a lilac gown locked her arm with his and pulled him towards the front near the head table. She said nothing, but John could see the huge conquering smile on her face as they hurried past the three other bridesmaids of the wedding party.

So, he was to be a piece of meat today. So be it. He smiled at the ladies, and the girl pulled him even more to assert her authority.

"Easy, Conan," he warned, smiling.

"What?" she returned.

"Conan?" he queried. When she didn't respond, he said, "Conan the Barbarian?"

She dragged him around the table to a chair at the end. "This is your seat," She pulled it out and pointed. He chuckled and sat. She bent down to his right ear and whispered, "I am next to you." Her breath hinted of alcohol and mints. "The others might try to get you to move, but you won't." When he didn't say anything, she asked, "Wanna know why?"

"Because you're my master and I'm your slave?"

She moved even closer to his ear. "Hmmm. Something like that."

What is it with women and weddings? he wondered as she strutted away. He watched as the other women flocked around her. *Could be interesting.*

To ensure he stayed put, she brought John three things: two beers and her name. Calista. She was cute and short and perhaps a little heavy, but mostly in the right places. She had a broad smile, and a glint in her eye that hinted she could be naughty and nice. Like the other maids, her brown highlighted hair was pulled up, exposing a slender neck.

Of the four maids, she would have been the prettiest were it not for a taller, black-haired vixen. This beauty was claimed by a beau who followed her like a security guard.

After twenty minutes of following orders and staying put, John started to get antsy. A quick scan revealed no Calista, so he stood, grabbed what was left of his second beer, and joined a couple at the wedding cake table, admiring the bride and groom figures at the top.

John moved around the table to keep the hall in his line of sight, for he knew Calista would come running when she saw he was out of his seat. He smiled at the thought.

"Here," a girl said and put a fresh beer on the table in front of him.

John didn't see her approach. She looked remarkably like Calista. A young man in a suit appeared on the other side of him. Her boyfriend, probably. John got the feeling he had been downgraded from slave to prisoner.

"Hope you know what you're getting yourself into with my sister," she said.

The boy patted John on the shoulder. "I'd introduce myself, but after she's devoured you, I'll never see you again."

The girl gave the boy a withering look, and he looked down.

Now John laughed. It was all a tad melodramatic. They didn't join in his mirth—which was a little disconcerting.

"Grendel's mother, huh?

"Who?" they both asked.

John looked at both and said, "Beowulf?" No response. "What are they teaching you all these days?" He took another drink.

The girl replied, "That's senior year. We're sophomores." She was pleased he had thought she was older.

"So, you two are my guards?"

"You got it," replied the boy. "Elliot," he introduced himself.

"Julie," added the girl. "And you're John."

"I'm the prisoner."

Now Elliot smiled. "At the very least."

Julie shot her boyfriend another look. John sensed she was afraid Elliot was on the edge of disclosing secrets that would scare John away. Neither wanted to suffer the wrath of Callista.

The music faded and the DJ said, "Okay, ladies and gentlemen, we're about to welcome the wedding party, so if you could get to your seats, please."

John looked at his watch: 5:00. Everything was moving along smoothly. Dinner was going to be at 5:30, they would cut the cake at 6:15, toasts and the first dance would be at 6:30, followed by party time. He and Sandy had ironed out all the details. John was a little proud of himself, this being the first full wedding he had planned.

Julie and Elliot followed John to his seat. They sat with him during the procession. The DJ introduced the bridesmaids and groomsmen, and Calista and her escort all but ran along the white runner that had been pulled out for the show.

She yanked the poor guy around the table and sat herself between him and John. Calista's hand found John's, putting it on her knee. John caught Elliot's eye, and the boy smiled knowingly. This Calista must have a wild reputation. What the hell had Sandy gotten him into?

"Please stand for the bride and groom."

You won't regret it! Promise!

Yeah... thanks, Sandy.

"Ladies and gentlemen, please welcome the new Mister and Missus Markey!"

Applause erupted, and the newlyweds marched down the center of the hall on the runner—

And behind them, as if she were just arriving, was blondie.

She removed her hat, price tag now gone, long blonde hair like molten gold, and stepped into the hall. A man in an expensive suit stepped beside her. She leaned to him and said something, he nodded, and they moved to the back of the hall to a table out of John's sight.

"What's the problem, *dear?*" Calista asked, her voice both sticky and edged. She had seen where John was looking. She squeezed his hand. A threat? This was getting a little bothersome.

John stood, peeling his hand from Calista's. He saw Julie make eye contact with her sister, and Julie elbowed Elliot, who in turn stood.

Julie cleared her throat. "Uh... the, ah... dinner line is going to start in a minute."

No, it's not.

John looked to Julie and then to Calista. "Well," he said directly to Calista, "then, my lady," he took her hand and kissed it, "you will have to save me a place in line. My bladder is talking to me." He leaned down to whisper, "If you need to start a plate for me, I like my meat red and rare."

Calista flushed and grinned like the Cheshire Cat.

John smiled then looked up to see the entire table looking at him, as if he were taking a huge risk only they knew about. He excused himself and made his way toward the bathroom at the back of the hall. With a little detour and a little luck, he might be able to have a little angelic confrontation without his mistress-warden having a fit. But first...

The entire table watched Calista's conquest stop in the middle of the dance floor, waiting. Elliot caught up to him. John asked Elliot something, and Elliot's head hung low. John proceeded to the back of the hall, and Elliot slowly returned to the head table.

Calista slammed her hands on the table, hissing, "What're you doing?"

Elliot shrugged, helpless. "He wanted to know if I was going to hold his *you know what* while he pissed."

Calista slammed her hands again on the table. "Well?" She waved him away in the direction of John. "Be certain to wash your hands."

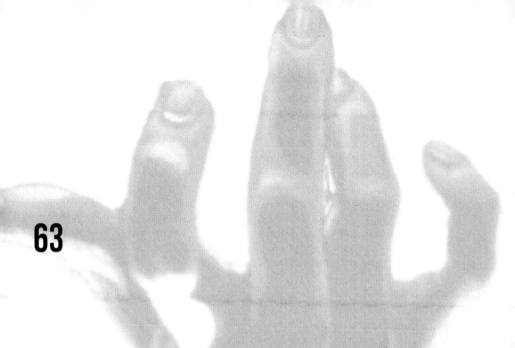

63

Everett finished cleaning the lab around three Friday morning. He took all the infected materials, and anything else he needed to burn, to his friend's animal crematorium to destroy it.

While he was gone, Angelique sat in the lab next to Anders. He was still passed out, asleep, shuddering every few minutes.

The infected blood did what she had hoped: incapacitated the vampire. She had given him most of the bag, and he had reacted violently, convulsed, then turned off. They had it all on video, and she watched it now, without sound so that she could focus on the image, for the third time:

She and Everett were in their white surgical scrubs and PPE. Anders was a fuzzy image on the X-table, like he was in the videos from the house. There was no definition or detail in the blurred shape, just a form that moved slightly on the table. Everett handed her a bag of blood. She chatted with the fuzz. Everett cut the tubing to make it shorter. She held the blood bag over the area of the vampire's face and squirted it into his mouth. Something black fluttered in the middle of the indistinct form. She and Everett jumped back. A small spout of red popped into the air, Anders gagging on the blood. Then the form shook. And something dark pushed up from the belly to the chest area. Dark blood spurted onto the steps and floor. The form stilled, and the fuzziness dropped from it. Anders laid naked and unconscious on the table.

In less than a week, Angelique believed she had discovered the secret to this creature. Something lived within it. A parasite? A symbiont? As soon as Everett returned, they were going to find out.

When he returned home a little after 5:00 A.M., he was worn out. She was exhausted, too, if she was being honest with herself. They agreed to get a little rest, but Angelique felt she was too wound up for any sleep. By the time she finished brushing her teeth, Everett was out cold.

She smiled at the thought.

She slipped into the bed and thought about the video, how when the vampire went inert, Anders' image appeared.

Neither had thought to set an alarm.

Angelique opened her eyes and saw it was full light outside. She sat up. She was still in her clothes from yesterday.

Everett stirred but didn't wake.

The clock said 3:57 P.M.

"Ev." She nudged him. "Ev, wake up."

His eyes blinked open. He popped up to a sitting position next to Angelique.

"Shit!" he exclaimed.

They hurried down to the lab.

Anders was still out. He looked like a corpse in the video feed.

They went back upstairs.

Angelique wordlessly started a quick breakfast of eggs and toast, coffee and tea.

Everett listened to three messages from his boss then called Peter and explained he and Angelique had food poisoning and had gone to bed without setting an alarm. He had just gotten up to call in and was going back to bed.

Angelique heard Everett's side of the conversation and smiled at how convincing the lie was.

Everett wolfed down his breakfast and went downstairs. He left the door open.

Angelique had a feeling she knew why.

He was down there a while, and when he returned to the

kitchen, he had a box under one arm. In the other hand, he held a laptop.

He looked like a doctor about to give bad news to a patient. "You can't be down there when I open it up."

"I know."

"It's too dangerous."

"I know." She really did. They had no idea what could pop out of the vampire. A vision of the movie *Alien*, the tiny creature bursting out of the astronaut's chest, didn't seem so unreal at the moment.

Everett realized she wasn't arguing. He barked a single laugh, set the box on the table, and opened the laptop. He placed it in front of her. "You can watch from up here."

Anders' motionless body appeared on the screen. He had stopped the occasional shuddering.

Watching him, Angelique wondered again if the video distortion had something to do with the vampire's consciousness—or whatever constituted consciousness with an undead creature. What might it have to do with the black substance moving within its skin? Was the substance connected to the spherical thing in its belly? There were so many questions.

Everett reached into the box and pulled out a new set of scrubs and PPE.

Angelique finished her tea.

Everett tried his best to take his time with the PPE, duct-taping all possible openings, and this time he wore a clear plastic mask that covered his face. He wrapped tape loosely around his neck.

He looked at her. He plugged in one end of a cord to his mask and the other into a transmitter on his belt. "I think I've lived my whole life for this moment." His shaky voice came from the computer.

Angelique smiled. "Go do what you do best."

Everett Preston, in white scrubs and PPE, went down the basement steps.

On the laptop screen, he appeared at the bottom of the steps and walked around the vampire chained on the X-table. He looked over the body. Everett looked at the camera and said, "If you can hear me, stomp."

She did, and he gave her a thumbs up. He was smiling, and Angelique realized this was his element. He would've made an awesome surgeon. He had given that up for her and her quest. And here he was about to slice open a thing—something more than a cat, something more than an old man's knee or a woman's elbow. She wondered if Everett the boy had ever dreamed of cutting open a living person, let alone a vampire.

Angelique held her breath.

Everett rolled a tray closer to him and took a scalpel. He looked at a laptop on a table behind him. "I am Doctor Everett Preston. It's 5:33 P.M., Friday, March 28th, 2008. The specimen is a creature, yet it was presumably human before transforming into its current state. It exhibits no measurable outputs, no data. It is essentially a corpse. My associate, Angelique Carlson, and I are naming this specimen, for lack of a better term, a vampire. I'm cutting from the bottom of the sternum to the pelvic bone." It was like a line he had drawn with a marker. No blood. "I'm cutting into the musculature of the abdomen." He angled his elbow up to cut deeper into the vampire. "Because of the vampire's ability to regenerate and knit its flesh, I must cut quickly. I am filling the incision with gauze to try to keep the flesh apart."

Angelique breathed. It was the oddest thing to watch, knowing that last night Anders had been moving and talking to them as if he were alive. She didn't know what he was. Undead? Reanimated? Something else? This thing in the belly of the beast might lead to answers—probably a shitload of more questions.

Everett stuffed gauze into the cut and resumed slicing the musculature deep into the top of the abdominal area. He jumped and yelled, "Fuck! Something shocked me!"

Angelique jumped, too.

Everett looked up to the camera. "It was like a cold shock."

Maybe this presence in the belly had something to do with the vampire's odd freezing ability. *Questions.*

"I hit something hard." Everett flexed his hand and arm. "It felt like," he paused for a moment, "ice on a sensitive tooth." He resumed cutting from the pelvis to the belly, stuffing gauze as he slowly approached the center where he had stopped.

Angelique noticed the time read 5:58.

He put the scalpel down, rubbed his elbow, and took something from the rolling tray. He placed part of it into the incision, and Angelique recognized it as half of a retractor. He secured the other half in the incision, connected some parts, then used it to open the abdominal cavity.

"Ha!" Everett uttered a single laugh of amazement. He delicately cut some more.

A round black *something*, a little larger than a softball, lay in the exposed abdomen.

Everett moved to get the camera—

Anders' body fluttered, a fuzzy wave covering him, enveloping him.

Angelique stood. "Everett!"

The blurred body moved, and as Angelique grabbed the door to the lab, she heard:

"You're in trouble now, Mister Doctor."

64

John figured he had two maybe three minutes before his guard returned. And fortune smiled on him when he saw blondie at the bar near the bathrooms.

She took a glass of wine from the bartender. Her red, luscious lips touched the edge of the glass for a sip, and she wrinkled her nose and mouth.

John grabbed her free arm and pulled her into a recess in the wall that led to the doors to both bathrooms. The wine sloshed around the rim of the glass but did not spill.

She was not surprised. She was smiling.

John put a finger in her face. "I know what you all are doing. Tell your *friends* to give me a little space."

She looked at the wine a moment then handed it to him. "Can you take this?" Her voice was nothing like he expected, squeaky like a young college cheerleader.

Stunned, he took the glass.

"What is the speed of dark, Mr. Wilkins?" she asked as if he was a teacher, and she honestly wanted the answer.

"What?"

Something shiny appeared in her hand, and she pressed it against his belly. John slowly looked down to see a four-inch blade indenting his shirt.

"That fast," she responded to her own question, still smiling.

She was about to say more when Elliot put a hand on John's shoulder and said, "You're going to—"

John felt the movement more than saw it, his eyes still focused on the woman's hand and the knife. He saw Elliot being taken into the ladies' room. There was no life in his eyes.

"That fast, too," the woman chirped matter-of-factly. She nodded in the direction of the closing door. "Shall we?"

The woman's companion had a dead Elliot face down on the floor. He had pulled up the boy's shirt and was stuffing a handkerchief into a slightly bloodied two-inch incision in the middle of the back just above the pants. As the woman locked the door, the man dragged the body into a stall. John could see the body lift up, hidden mostly by the stall wall, and the man put it on the toilet. He crawled under the wall then checked the stall door. Locked. He wiped his pants and sleeves.

Taller than John, he was Mediterranean, with short jet-black hair parted on the side. Where the woman looked to be in her early twenties, the man had a weathered, older look. Steely eyes examined himself in the mirror as he washed his hands. He said something in Italian.

The woman replied in Italian and rolled her eyes.

John looked at the floor where Elliot had laid. Not a drop of blood.

A finger touched John's lips. The woman was shushing him. He could still feel the blade at his belly. She whispered, "Well, Mr. Wilkins? Do you know the answer?"

His mind was very clear. He watched the older man work the lock on the opaque window of the bathroom. He felt the menace of the woman. And he knew the answer to the question: "Darkness has no speed. It's eternal."

She was impressed and nodded her approval. "Indeed it is, Mr. Wilkins." Her tweeny voice sounded ironic to the situation. John would've laughed if his life didn't hinge on the woman's whim. He knew she was just as deft with the knife as her partner.

John heard the window slide open. Cool air blew in from an alley somewhere to the side or behind the hall.

The bathroom door moved. They heard voices on the other side. Then came a thump as someone yelled through the door, "John? Elliot?"

Calista.

The knife pushed a little, cutting through John's shirt.

The woman whispered, "We're going to be leaving now." She smiled evilly. "Shame, though. That little hussy would've ground you into dust."

More thumping. "What are you doing in there?"

"Shall we?" the woman asked, motioning to the window. The man must have already left.

As he walked to the window, John realized this had to do with the Quandary, that these killers were from the other side. The Dark Side. It looked pretty dark at the moment, that was certain.

He imagined these two reporting to some Darth Vader, who breathed and growled they had done well.

At the window, he looked down and saw a fifteen-foot drop. He should be able to dangle down and manage the fall. He didn't see the man, but knew he was near. Running was probably out of the question. After seeing what they could do, he knew his chances of escape at the moment were slim. Best to comply and keep them happy.

A black sedan with dark tinted windows pulled into the alley, and the woman said, "Go on..."

He stepped over the sill as a more violent thump came from the door. Someone was trying to kick it in. Another kick.

"Hurry up!" The woman pushed him, and he almost slipped off.

John dangled from the ledge of the window, his nose against the cold brick. As he tried to look down, he heard a muffled crack, and he felt something large fall behind him and thud on the ground.

Hands gripped his feet and lowered him gently. He stood beside a dead blonde assassin, her left eye a bloody black hole.

"Tell Vader dark's not fast enough," he said to her.

"Get in the car, quick!"

Aaron. John wasn't surprised.

A man came around to collect the dead body and take it to the trunk. He wore the same gray pants and black polo shirt of the uniformed men he had seen with the angels.

As John jumped into the back seat of the sedan, a series of screams and yells came from the open window. Elliot had been discovered. Aaron climbed in beside him, and the uniformed man got into the front passenger seat. The driver, uniformed like his partner, hit the gas and the sedan peeled out and away.

65

"**O**h, this is perfect!"

Anders laughed and giggled, his naked body shaking.

Everett picked up the lab and camera equipment he had knocked down. When Angelique had screamed his name, he had jumped and scrambled about, looking for anything to act as a weapon. He had made a bit of a mess, but nothing was damaged, fortunately.

"Little monsters living in bellies!" He laughed some more.

Angelique stood near the center of the X-table and looked at the black ball. She hadn't seen it clearly in the video feed; the camera's angle had been too shallow. Then as Ander's had come awake, his form shimmered like a heat mirage and went fuzzy.

She had nearly leaped down the steps to find Everett jumping about, and for a moment she thought something had come out of Anders and attacked Everett. The laughing had calmed her enough to ask, "What trouble?"

Anders continued to laugh and say, "Perfect," until Everett came up beside her.

Angelique looked at him to ensure he was okay.

He was pissed off but kept his calm. "It's fucking with us."

Anders stopped laughing and made an "O" of surprise. "You're a Sherlock without the shit, Mister Doctor." He chuckled again. He was proud of his accomplishment.

Angelique was furious. She balled her fists and was about to pound the vampire when Anders said, "You can beat me till my bones crack, Tinkerbell, but you *know* I will heal as if nothing happened." One last laugh. "And I won't feel a thing." He sighed ironically. "I love being me." He lifted his head to try to look at his open belly. "As for the trouble," he nodded his bald, gray head, "doing *that* will have consequences."

Angelique and Everett exchanged a glance and looked at the black ball.

Anders put his head back on the table. "You two have called to the Darkness, and soon it will answer back."

Angelique's head started to pound, a slow drumming headache. She put a fist to her forehead and growled, "What the hell are you talking about?"

Anders smiled sadly, "Hell, indeed, will soon come a-knockin'." He tried to shrug. "Besides, I owed you both for that sludge you gave me."

"Malaria," Everett said, and Anders looked at him with contempt. Everett smiled. "The virus kills blood cells. You were drinking mostly dead blood."

Anders grimaced and looked at Angelique. "We are even. Can we go back to our deal? We can trust each other now, Tink."

Angelique continued to rub the heel of her hand into her head. Was it the adrenaline? Or was Anders somehow in there thumping around. *Fuck, this hurts.*

Everett embraced Angelique, pulling her to the steps. "C'mon, babe..."

She shook him off. "No. Something's happening."

"Yeah, it's fucking with us."

She took a deep breath and looked at the vampire. "Blood for answers."

A smile curled on Anders' lips.

"Ev, dear, please get me some *good* blood for our little vampire?" The headache started to recede.

Everett's face hardened. He opened his mouth, closed it, and went up the stairs.

"You have two questions, but I get a little sippy before I answer the next one." Anders frowned dramatically, jutting out a pouting lower lip for emphasis.

Angelique looked at his bald pate. She considered his hunger, the ball in his belly, and the threads of cilia throughout his body. She looked about the room. It didn't feel as cold. She put her left index finger on gray forehead—

"Ange, no!" Everett yelled.

The cold shocked her, but it was like a nine-volt battery, and she moved the fingertip down until it came to the tip of Anders' thin nose. "Ah, my little vampire, I thought we could trust each other."

Anders' face twisted. Was that fear? He tried to smile through it and said, "But *I'm* not stupid."

As if I am? She countered to herself. His words echoed in return: *…will soon come a-knockin'…*

Anders watched Angelique's face. The vampire smiled slyly.

Everett thumped down the steps, blood bag in gloved hand. Before he handed it to Angelique, he found some gloves.

She nearly forgot. They had agreed that wearing gloves when feeding the vampire would keep him guessing about the blood. She took a pair from Everett and pulled them on. He handed her the bag.

Angelique checked the roller clamp and held up the bag. Everett cut the line short.

As she tipped it at Ander's mouth, he kept his eyes open this time, and he smiled as she looked at his fangs. He opened wider, and she rolled the clamp back. The red blood squirted into his dark mouth. Anders moaned, and Angelique looked to Everett who now had the camera and was recording the feeding. Not that there was much to see; it would record as fuzzy.

Two questions.

She had a thousand. But one now pushed down the nine-hundred ninety-nine others.

She squeezed the bag. The blood didn't pool in the mouth. The vampire's throat didn't move to swallow. The blood traveled on its own down his throat and emptied into the hole that was the vampire's stomach.

Everett had the camera focused there. "I don't think I'm getting this," he said. "It's still fuzzy on the screen."

Angelique emptied half of the bag, and they watched the growing pool of blood encircle the black ball. It quivered, and the vampire moaned again. Anders' skin lightened. The ball stilled a moment then relaxed and spread out, a gelatinous mass mixing into the blood.

"Damn," Everett said, "it went from solid to liquid."

"Ahhhh." Anders whispered. His eyes closed; his face slackened as if he had fallen asleep. But his mouth said, "Do you hear it?"

"Careful, babe," warned Everett. He kept the camera on the abdomen.

She nodded. She knew the vampire had baited her to use one of her questions. She leaned close to his face and said, "Anders, you owe me."

"Yes, my little Tinkerbell," his voice a little clearer, stronger, "ask the right question."

She looked at the gloves on her hands.

Angelique handed Everett the blood bag and searched about the lab. She found Anders' black gloves. In the light, the leather looked odd, soft and pliable.

Everett's face showed he was curious about those, too.

"Your gloves," she said and held them to his face. His eyes remained closed, but he smiled. "Why do you wear *these* gloves?"

"That's a silly question, little Tink," he replied. "What you're really asking is what they're made of?" He moaned like a junkie. "That leather is the only thing that can completely block our power, so that we can shake a hand, squeeze a neck." He chuckled. "We have an interesting little Nazi who makes them for us."

The room seemed to stop between seconds. Nothing moved, no sound. Hearts stopped beating.

Then Everett gasped and said, "Are you saying they're made from human skin?"

The smile on Anders' face melted away. "He's not allowed to ask questions." He moved his face to Angelique but kept his eyes closed. "But you can."

"Nice try, my little vampire."

A slow smile curved on his face.

Angelique grimaced at the gloves and put them on a table to her left.

Anders opened his mouth for more blood, signaling she had one more question.

Everett squeezed more blood into his mouth.

The vampire moaned.

Angelique leaned close to its ear. She looked at Everett and whispered, "Who is *us*?"

A larger smile appeared on the creature's face. "That's better, my little Tinkerbell. A layered question. Good." He opened his eyes, and the smile faded. He faced Angelique. "You need to know what is coming, yes?"

She made no move. She barely breathed. Everett leaned a little closer.

Anders turned to Everett. "More than what is in my belly?"

Angelique felt Everett move.

She only had eyes for her vampire.

It looked back at her. "They're all the same question, Tink." He closed his eyes. Was that a little fear between his eyes, around his mouth? "My father is coming."

66

The sedan made three swift turns then slowed to a normal speed.

No one said a word.

Aaron, in his typical blue suit, finished a text on his phone.

John looked at him.

"Yes?" inquired the angel.

"I thought you said you can't destroy anything in this world. That there are rules you have to follow?"

Aaron lifted an eyebrow. "What did I do?"

John nodded his head sarcastically. "Oh, you just poked out her eye. Otherwise, she's okay."

"I killed her." The uniformed man in the front passenger seat held a large pistol with a suppressor. John had learned in movies that those in the know didn't call them silencers, and this fellow looked like he *knew*. "I killed the other one, too." He turned in his seat to face John. "I did it for you."

He didn't look like a killer, this man in the front seat. Put a suit on him and he would look like some Wall Street broker or bank vice president. He had sandy-blond hair parted on the side, blue eyes, and a sprinkle of freckles on his cheeks. If it weren't for the sulfurous smell of gunpowder and the weapon the man held, John would've said the man was a liar.

I did it for you.

John realized two—no, three—people were dead right now because of him.

Because of the Quandary.

Aaron grabbed John's hand and that angelic warmth spread through his body.

The angel said, "Don't beat yourself up about this. It would have happened eventually. We just figured we had a little more time to let you deal with this on your own."

The sedan turned into a parking garage, and in a few minutes, they were down a few floors and parking between two black SUVs. Five uniformed men holding tool boxes were waiting; so, too, was Carrie now dressed in a green business suit and light-green flats.

Aaron got out of the car. The driver, his short fiery red hair cut military style, got out and helped John.

"How is he?" asked Carrie nodding to John. The driver brought him to her. She put a brown hand on his forehead and looked closely into his eyes.

Aaron shrugged. "He may go into shock. He's realizing all this is a little dangerous."

John shrugged off the driver and stepped back from Carrie. "I'm okay." He was pissed. "And stop talking about me as if I'm unconscious."

Small hand-held vacuum cleaners came on as the five men got to work on the sedan, cleaning it of any evidence. One of them popped the trunk. John turned to see both dead bodies, which were lifted out and placed into the front of the car: the man at the wheel, the woman next to him. One of the cleaners removed a bloodied plastic sheet from the trunk.

Aaron stood beside John. "That sheet was already there. It was meant for you."

"And here I thought they were going to take me to Disney World."

"He's okay, all right," Carrie observed.

Aaron motioned to the others working on the car and said, "These men will ensure the knife used to kill the boy will be found so that you'll not be implicated for murder. But you will be sought after by the police."

Carrie interjected, "A person of interest."

"You'll have to account for what happened," Aaron continued, "kept in the police station for hours, probably overnight, undergoing their intense questioning."

Carrie shrugged. "Or you can come with us."

John put an arm around each of the angels and said sarcastically, "You two are my new best friends."

67

" A ngelique, we have to go. Now!"
She looked at Everett, a scared little boy who had just done something naughty and wanted to get away before the police arrived.

Or whatever was going to arrive.

She felt differently. This was an opportunity. A bird in the hand was one thing. Two in hand was a major profit. The logical side of her mind told her that they could do all they wanted to Anders and keep the "father" for more important things. The other side of her mind whispered other possibilities. She didn't want to go there.

All they had to do, logic said, was to get the father to drink some tainted blood.

Besides, one more bag was all they had. And it was viable for only days now.

This was going through her mind as Everett pleaded with her to leave.

"That's right, Tinkerbell," Anders mocked. "Run, run as fast as you can, but you can't outrun the Shadow Man." He laughed.

The vampire's words punched her in the gut. She gasped. A high-pitched hum sounded in her left ear.

Anders hadn't been the only shadow in her life.

This father figure had been with her all along.

Everett saw the change come down Angelique's face. She slumped. He pulled her up the steps and guided her to his car outside. He strapped her in the passenger seat.

He drove away from the house.

Another vampire. A "father." This implied age and power and danger. She felt Anders was even a tad afraid of daddy coming to visit. The two men in her life were scared.

She realized she wasn't.

She actually looked forward to it.

Wanted it.

She realized they had stopped.

Everett had parked in the lot of a hotel. He was speaking...

"... away from here as far as we can. I have enough money. We can disappear."

Something unthinkable was now clawing its way up through the dirt of her memories. Anders had been an important part of her life. But he hadn't been alone. Since she was a little girl, she had seen multiple shadows, but she had believed they had been a singular thing. And her realization that Anders the vampire had been behind them had confirmed that. But to know that his "father" had been with her, too. It had been a family affair all along.

Father... son...

Angelique smiled.

"What are you smiling about? This is fucking serious."

The smile left her mouth but stayed in her eyes. "We're staying, my love." She looked at the hotel. "We can stay here tonight, but we have to go back tomorrow." She reached for his pants and unzipped them. "We have to get ready for another guest."

68

C arrie and Aaron simultaneously hung up their phones. They sat for a moment, unusually quiet.

John sat in the back seat with them. He was directly behind the driver, Aaron in the middle, and Carrie next to her brother. John felt it was odd he thought of them as siblings, even though they were of different races. Yet, they shared similar physical characteristics in an odd, undefinable way. The primary one was their smile.

They weren't smiling right now.

They weren't talking.

John had a deep feeling they had just received bad news.

So, he looked absently out the window, the world rushing by, the hum of the SUV's engine and the droning vibration of the wheels doing their best to lull him to sleep. The shock and adrenaline of the past hour kept him animated. He didn't see the angels grab each other's hands.

They were on their way to Washington, D.C. to prepare to fly to Italy. With the death of Elliot and the two assassins, John knew his life as he knew it was over. He wasn't safe.

He imagined no one he knew was safe if he stayed here. It was the Quandary, and if he left, it would follow. But as they drove south down the Baltimore-Washington Parkway, passing Arundel Mills Boulevard exit, he felt a hole open in his heart, as if something had pushed a shovel into it and removed a huge chunk. He took a deep breath to fill the hole, but nothing could fill it—it was bottomless and dark and painful and personal. It began to rise up to him or he began to fall into it, a grave for his soul. He could lay in it and all this danger would go away.

Aaron laid a warm hand on his head.

Sleep.

He did.

John awoke as the SUV passed beneath a road bridge, signage on it announcing one way for arrivals and the other for departures. Streetlights raced by at regular intervals. As they made their way around a broad turn, he saw a huge airport terminal, its control tower poking up, lit by massive beams of light. It reminded him of an old aircraft carrier, a long, flat top with a single rectangular structure in the middle. But as they neared, a wide parking lot appeared, and a myriad of cars came and went from the terminal.

The SUV merged into the departures' lane, but instead of continuing to the airline entrances, it took a right. It approached a guard booth with a large sign: "Please have all diplomatic papers ready for inspection." Two armed guards stepped from the booth. The driver rolled all the windows down and held out papers to one of them. They exchanged no words. The guard took the papers to the booth.

The other guard looked within the SUV, waiting for his partner to validate the papers.

That guard returned, handed the papers back to the driver, and said, "Move along." He waved at the booth. A third guard must have been within.

The cross bar moved up, and the SUV proceeded to a hangar.

"I suppose I have a passport now?" John asked. No one answered.

Within the hangar awaited a group of uniformed men in grays and blacks, a priest, and another more richly dressed priest.

The driver pulled over to the far side and got out to open John's door. In addition to his short bright red hair, he had light-blue eyes. He was clean shaven, and he had an odd scar beneath his left ear from the lobe to the jawline and forward perhaps three inches. He stood silently. He slammed the door shut behind John.

John watched the redhead for a moment. The man walked briskly to the jet, which then whined alive as its engines fired up.

John came around the SUV, and he saw the opulent priest had been replaced by Aurora. John wondered if the others only saw the priest. Her bright blonde hair glowed, and she was a foot taller than all those around her. No one noticed her.

The angels approached her, bowed, and stepped aside. Aurora looked at John, her face hardening, then turned to the angels. "He doesn't know," she stated.

The angels hung their heads.

A wave of anger crossed her face, and she said to the angels, "I thought I was clear on the phone two hours ago." She turned back to John. Her face melted into concern and pity; it punched him in the gut. "We are safe, and we have to go."

"Wait," he said, and grabbed her arm. It was like grabbing hot iron without the pain. The heat shocked up his hand and into his arm and shoulder—

"He's waking," John heard from far away, beyond a rumbling.

The sound reminded him of a water park he had visited as a boy. He had made friends with another boy, dark-haired and dark-eyed with a hyena-like laugh that just made others laugh with him, and they had snuck under the massive water slide. The waterfall made a cave, and it rumbled and vibrated like he felt now.

The gentle rumble tried to pull him back to sleep, and he realized he was lying down. A part of him whispered he had been asleep for far too long. Time to wake.

He took a deep breath and smelled... food. Ham? Potatoes? His stomach leaped and growled. He opened his eyes and a smiling pleasant man hovered over him.

"Ah, Mr. Wilkins. May I call you John?" He helped John to sit up and continued to hold his hand. "I am Father Richard Napton of the Vatican Council on Special Projects." The priest shook the hand he held and laid it in John's lap.

Father Richard Napton was a thin man, perhaps in his mid-forties. His graying hair belied the strength of his countenance and particularly his hazel eyes that sparkled.

John imagined this man worked out in a gym as much as he prayed. In fact, the white priest collar looked quite out of place on him. He produced a bottle of water and said, "I'd offer you a beer, but all we have right now is this."

John nodded, afraid to open his mouth and let the growling out. God, he was hungry.

Napton reached behind him and found a plastic cup. He twisted off the cap of the bottle, poured some into the cup, downed it, then handed the bottle to his guest.

John took a small sip to wet his mouth. The cool water only awakened the hungry beast in his belly. It moved around, searching for food.

He saw he was already on a jet, and from the feel of it, already at cruising altitude. As he sipped the water, he looked around. Soft tan leather seats, white curved walls, oval windows. He sat upon a sofa-like seat along the left side, probably for sleeping as he had been doing. Across from him near the bulkhead, the redhead with the scar sat facing forward.

"I'm a special project, I take it?" John said, wiping the sleep from his eyes. He took another small sip of water.

Father Napton laughed and sat beside him. "Undoubtedly. You are the biggest special project of his Holiness, the Pope." He looked around for a waste container for his empty cup. He placed it on a seat tray across the way and turned his attention to John. "Well, I'm certain you have a thousand questions, so what I'm going to do for the next few hours, as you eat dinner, is to give you a little history lesson."

The jet jumped and rumbled. The plastic cup fell to the floor.

Father Napton smiled uneasily. He obviously didn't like flying. "As I was saying," he continued, "there is much you have to learn—quickly—and there is no time like the present." The jet jumped again, and Napton steadied himself on the sofa. "We had better get belted in." Napton motioned to the seats across from them.

As John stood, another man stepped into the cabin. The red-headed guard also stood and clicked something beneath two of the seats, and they swiveled to face the two behind them. The newcomer took a seat next to the window. John noticed it was dark outside.

Carrie and Aaron followed the newcomer. When John and Father Napton moved to the seats, the angels sat on the sofa.

"Ah," Napton said, motioning John to the other window seat. The priest sat next to the newcomer and clicked his belt locked. "Good. You all can help. John Wilkins, you know these two," he motioned to the angels.

"Wait," John interrupted. "You know what they are?"

Napton smiled. "Of course. The Protectors have aided our cause since our inception. These malakim come and go as they feel we need them. But all this you will learn over time." He patted the newcomer on the arm. "This is Bishop Stephen Angsterson. He deals with the financial aspects of our team."

John sat up. A bishop. They silently shook hands, the larger man sizing up the young one. John was about to ask the bishop a question, when a younger priest arrived with a steaming plate and a glass of iced tea.

John could smell the salty ham and potatoes and corn, and that ignited a rumble in his belly.

The bishop across from him heard it and twitched a little smile. The holy man watched Napton reach over John, open the armrest, and pull out and over the young man a seat tray. He took the plate, thanked the server, and put it before John. The glass of iced tea already had beads of condensation.

John's mouth watered. He realized he was gripped by an appetite no cliché could describe. He hadn't eaten since that morning, planning to have a big meal at the wedding reception. The assassins had interrupted everything, the assholes not even letting him have a decent meal.

John looked at his steaming plate. When was the last time he had had such a meal? At his parents' months ago? When would he have another?

He put his napkin in his lap, took the real silverware in hand, and proceeded slowly to savor each bite. A brief glance at the others showed them eating heartily, especially Angsterson, who wolfed down his food as if it were his last meal—and he knew it.

John let the others disappear from his focus, turning his attention to taking a bite of ham then potatoes then corn then a roll then a sip of iced tea. Around the plate. One bite at a time, swallowing each before taking the next.

Carrie watched this with interest as she nudged Aaron. They held hands, conjoining in the way angels do, discussing their charge sitting across the aisle from them, his odd behavior.

John hadn't had a better meal in a long while, and he looked at his empty plate and wondered if he could get another. He noticed the angels looking at him, Carrie in her green suit and Aaron in his blue suit. They weren't eating. He imagined that being heavenly beings, they didn't have to eat often, and it was berries and nuts when they did.

He gave a half-smile, an embarrassed look as if he could almost see himself being very anal in the way he had gone around the food on his plate. He also imagined his look of disappointment at the empty plate on the tray, the look of a starving, rescued refugee.

It struck John that he was. He was caught up in a war as old as the universe. God only knew (literally) why he was important, but both sides had forced him to flee his family and home. War had made for him a new life. He was heading to a new home... and he wondered how long he would be safe there.

...Then the Lylitu will rise up and eat your world from the inside out.

There was nothing safe in his life anymore.

An arm appeared and took his plate. The serving priest was clearing away the meal.

"John?" Father Napton held a large clasp envelope, and the young man slowly took it. Napton handed one to Bishop Angsterson. The priest offered one to the angels, and they politely refused.

"Very well," Napton continued. "If you would remove the packet from the envelope, please. As we know, this briefing is for John's benefit, but I ask you all to jump in if there is something pertinent to add." He paused to allow anyone to add anything. "So, John, what do you know about the Poor Fellow-Soldiers of Christ and the Temple of Solomon?"

Thus ends the first book of
The Dark Matter Series.

The Dark makes its move in book two:
The Dark Gambit
Coming 2023

GRATITUDES

A Love Letter for the Lights of My Life

Dear Friend,

May I call you friend? I feel since you've invested money and time into this book, we can at least call each other friends.

Let me begin with a warning: this is a little long. Typical end-matter pieces might be a page, two at the most, but no great endeavor is ever accomplished by a single soul. I have many to thank.

But first, allow me to explain why this is called "Gratitudes" and not "Acknowledgements."

Acknowledgements sounds like legalese. *Gratitudes*, to me, means something more. It's a deeper, warmer word for being thankful. I don't want to acknowledge the lights in my life, I want to express my profound and sincerest appreciation for them being a light in the darkness.

That includes you, my friend. So, thank you for supporting me, and I encourage you to continue. This book is the first of many. I promise the tale will get even crazier… and more epic. It will move from the realm of vampire thriller into dark fantasy and the fantastique as the story expands beyond the lives of Angelique and John. The second book is coming soon.

As I finished an edit of the first version of this book (*then* it was a different story), I began to send out query letters. I started to feel little twinges of impostor syndrome as the rejection letters accumulated. But I really wanted to *see* the book on a shelf, so I investigated self-publishing. I came across Ally Machete, the fearless leader of then Ambitious Enterprises and now The Writer's Ally. I attended one of her workshops, and we became friends. She hooked me up with Harrison Demchak, one of her editors. He gave that early draft (*then* entitled *The Dark Betwixt*) a thorough review—a twelve-page report that essentially said: too many flashbacks; start over in the past. Plus, he said the title just didn't work.

Start over?

New title?

I had spent nearly three years on that book!

He was right, of course. Those changes to and re"vision" of the story set me on a path that led to the book you just read—and much of the rest of the series.

So, thank you Ally and Harrison for your encouragement and direction.

I knew I was going to need a little help. I hired Anna Rasshivkina as an editor. She was a fantastic sounding board. After she read the first chapter—which began, "Angelique Carlson hated shadows. They moved."—she asked me an important question: "What if Angelique *loved* her shadows?" That question brought my dark protagonist into focus. She also suggested the alternating chapters. Thank you, Anna, for helping me to see the story more clearly.

I also need to mention the Pittsburgh writing group Write or Die (WorD). Some of the early drafts were shared with those fellow writers. They forced me to think more about how Dark Matter affects the biology of humans. One of them asked where the Dark Matter came from. I explored its origins… and I discovered something more menacing than the vampires in Angelique's life.

Many thanks goes to the many friends who agreed to read those early drafts. Of particular note is my hair stylist, Michele Stoeckle, an avid vampire fan. We had numerous chats about the story and characters as she snipped away at my locks. Aaron McKissick asked me some valuable questions that influenced some of the smaller thematic threads in the narrative, especially with respect to John Wilkins. A special thank you to Melissa Shurilla who listened to (or rather read, since a lot of it was my ramblings come to her via texting or emailing) my thoughts on the nature of evil and how it affects Angelique and John. I wonder how we got any work done—but we did.

Other friends who have helped and encouraged me on this journey: Kay Krueger, Christine Michaels, Debra and Joseph Pfeifer, Patricia Adams, and the Tea Lady, Danielle Spinola. More recently, for the current iteration of *The Dark Stirs*, thanks to Carl Clarabout and fellow author Danielle Wilson for their comments and encouragement.

When I had heard one of my wife's Irish cousins had written a book, I just had to ask her to read for me. Who better than a published author, right? She is also a helluva journalist. Being a true Irish woman, Angela Doyle Stuart is as blunt as an empty whiskey bottle over the head. I'm being sarcastic. She's a sweetheart. Angela has been a font of positivity. Thank you, Cuz.

And there's my aunt Ann Pauley. Even when I was a boy, she and my Uncle Mike (God bless his soul) always had faith in me. Perhaps they saw more in me than what I saw in myself. She has always been interested in what I was writing, and when it came time for readers, she volunteered. A big thank you to her.

Another early supporter—I'm talking fifth grade—was my cousin Nancy Cranwell. I had written a science-fiction story (with some horror elements) that was derivative of H.G. Wells' *War of the Worlds*. She had it printed into small booklets. That was the first time I had seen my name on something that looked like a book. I knew then I wanted a real book with my name on it. *Earth Invaded* was the beginning of the dream, and Nancy was the one who got that started.

When I saw on social media that a high school acquaintance had started a Hollywood talent agency, I took a literal shot in the dark and asked Toni Asterino if she would consider representing an author. Much to my surprise she said yes. I put together a pitch deck for presenting The Dark Matter Series to executives. Nothing has come of it (yet), but her faith in me at that time was a Godsend.

There's another Toni who has been not only a source of encouragement, but also a source of inspiration. She is a talented artist and graphic designer. She read an early draft of the book and developed for me a number of awesome drawings and pictures for what then was going to be a self-published book. You can see an early concept book cover she did for me on my website. Check her out on Instagram. Thank you, Toni Vingle, for your support and your art.

There's this thing called a platform. It's all the social media and website stuff an author needs to create a brand. On the social media side, I want to thank Bridgeway Capital for introducing me to Toya Wilson-Smith. She helped me with creating my Facebook and Instagram pages. And on the website side, my deepest appreciation goes to an old student of mine, Booker Walton, founder of the IT company MTC. He put me in the hands of Preston Smith and Lori Ridgen who worked their magic to bring my vision to reality. I need to give a very special thanks to Preston for putting up with some of my crazy notions for the website.

And to COURAGE AFTER DARK and its fearless leader Lexi Mohney: Thank you for taking a risk on me and believing in my story—particularly the concept of Dark Matter. Especially, thank you for guiding me through a third re-"vision" of the story—especially in helping me to see the series is four books instead of three. Your wisdom and gentle pushes have made my dream of becoming an author come true. The same can be said for Clementine Willow-ilde, whose advice has been a tremendous boon, and for Breanna Bartels, who joined the team late in the game but has contributed her art and wisdom to the marketing efforts.

To Cheyenne Sampson: When I read the draft after your edits, I didn't think you had done much more than the comments in the tracking. About halfway through the book, I pulled up the "R3" (third round) I had sent to you, and I compared the manuscripts. I was astonished. Lexi chose wisely. Thank you for caring about my style and voice—thank you for caring about me.

How do I thank my parents? I mean, *really* thank them. It's not like I'm thanking them for a birthday card or a gift. Their DNA is in me. I would not be here were it not for them. They instilled in me a love of reading that morphed into writing. They stayed out of my way as I pursued my weird, nerdy interests. I'm certain as they quietly watched me mature—perhaps shaking their heads with perplexity when I wasn't looking—they wondered why their first-born child has such odd interests. But this book in your hands right now wouldn't exist without them. I'm going to say thank you… but I really mean so much more.

And a grand thank you to my children and grandchildren. The girls helped me decide on a cover for this book. My sons have pushed me to lead and be better. All of my beloved family mean the world to me.

Each of these people—and there are so many more—have been lights in my life. Like a Christmas tree in a dark living room, collectively they have enriched my life and pushed back the doubt that occasionally darkened my mind.

However, atop this Christmas tree is the brightest light, my wife Deb. She is my bright star, more brilliant than all the other lights; my triple-star Polaris: partner, friend, lover. I sometimes refer to Deb as my cheerleader, but that puts her on the sidelines, so to speak. She's been at my side since the day I told her I was going to write a book. She was just as excited when I declared it would be longer than one book. As I received rejection letters, her light of encouragement pushed me to keep working. When Lexi offered me a contract, Deb whispered, "I told you so."

Her steadfast positivity has been and forever will be a beacon of light in the darkness. She was and is a compass to direct me out of the dark, macabre places I need to go to write the story. Deb is the matching bookend to my parents. These two forces have molded and nurtured me into the man I am today. Deb is just as much responsible for this book in your hands as my parents. Thank you, Deb, for being my partner, my wife. Thank you for being the brightest light. I love you.

ABOUT THE AUTHOR

John currently lives in Pittsburgh, Pennsylvania, with his brilliant English wife, Deb. She keeps his life fun and bright while he writes about the dark and macabre. He might be a Boomer, but he feels more like a Millennial.

John is the first son of Jack (John P., Sr.) and Willie (Dwillis) Wallman. He has a brother Mark, and a sister Mary Louise whom everyone calls Mimi. He enjoys visiting his twin sons, Lance and Drew, and their families—especially his grandchildren.

He's an avid tennis fan and a pretty good player. When he's not on the court, he's enjoying the fantastique in all its forms—from Star Trek to Stephen King to Middle Earth.

John has worn a few hats throughout his adult years—from secondary education to human capital management to the nuclear industry to corporate retail.

Most of his energies, however, are spent in the universes of The Dark Matter Series, writing about reluctant heroes and angels and monsters and other dangers. *The Dark Stirs*, the first book of the series, is his debut novel.

Check out his website:
johnpwallman.com

Made in the USA
Columbia, SC
10 July 2022